BRAND LOYALTY

Cally Phillips

First published by HoAm Presst Publishing 2010.
This edition published by YouWriteOn.com 2010
Copyright © Cally Phillips 2010
Cally Phillips asserts her moral right to be identified as the author of
this work in accordance with the Copyright, Designs and Patents Act
1988.

A CIP catalogue record for this title is available from the British
Library.

For George

who shares my meaning and memory

Name is the thief of identity.

And reality is what we choose to believe.

A. THE LAST TIGER

'Existence is useless!' Nike shouted gleefully as he threw the controls into hyperdrive, pushing the spaceship towards the black hole, risking all in an attempt to break the space-time continuum.....

'Pizza?'

'May as well... I've just crashed and burned YET again.' Nike turned from the console and grinned at Omo, the purveyor of the pizza. 'Where's Flora?'

'In front of the US™ as usual,' Omo replied.

A shriek from the direction of the ULTIMATE® US™ screen proved his hunch to be correct. The boys ran towards the common room to find Flora jumping up and down in an aggravated manner.

'What's up?' they asked in unison.

She pointed at the 90 inch screen which held pride of place on the feature wall. On it was a tiger, in a poor state, effectively breathing its last.

'Look,' she gasped. 'It's the last tiger. The very last. Dying.'

'Uh, huh.' The boys were unimpressed.

'Pizza?' offered Omo.

Flora threw him the dirtiest of glances. Nike realised he'd better try another approach. 'Where'd you get that programme from?'

'It's a live stream,' she replied.

Now Nike was interested. 'No. No way. They never.... it's got to be archived.'

'NO.' Flora was adamant. 'I'm telling you. This is a live stream. We are watching the last tiger in the world DYING right now, right here, in our living room.'

Omo squinted closer at the caption in the bottom righthand corner. 'No, Flora, it's in a zoo, in Berne.' Omo was good at missing the point.

'What's a zoo?' Nike asked. 'Where's Berne?'

The reply came as a spoken response simultaneously typed out on the lower left quadrant of the screen.

ZOO: Definition. Short form of zoological gardens. A public garden or park with a collection of animals for exhibition or study.

BERNE: Place name. Capital of Switzerland. Founded in 1191 – The period known as the medieval period in history. Toblerone chocolate bar and Emmental Cheese brands originated here. Albert Einstein worked here. THIS INFORMATION HAS COST YOU TEN KNOWLEDGE CREDITS. FOR MORE INFORMATION...

'Stop it,' Flora screamed. 'I can't see what's going on. Stop asking stupid questions. Just WATCH.'

The boys sat on the sofa either side of Flora who had sunk back into the luxurious faux leather, and munched on their pizza as the tiger breathed its last.

When finally it was dead, a commentary began, giving details on 'the once mighty tiger....'

Flora cried. Omo and Nike were shocked. They'd never seen Flora cry before. In fact, neither of them was sure they'd ever seen anyone actually cry before. Not live, in front of them. It was a day of firsts. And lasts, if you were the tiger.

Nike wasn't too bothered by the tiger. It wasn't the sort of thing he was interested in. And he couldn't afford to ask questions except on the things that DID interest him. Asking questions only got you into debt. Nike was running out of credit at the ULTIMATE® knowledge bank. He was always running low. He asked too many questions. And where knowledge is a currency, being overdrawn was always a danger for a guy who couldn't stop asking questions. Being overdrawn is no fun. It meant that instead of playing the usual games he would have to do some 'productive' consuming. Nike hated being 'productive'.

PRODUCTIVE: Definition. In History being productive of or engaged in the production of goods or producing commodities of exchangeable value. In current parlance being 'productive' is a component part of the ULTIMATE® way of life where to be 'productive' is to engage in activity directed by ULTIMATE® (usually the engagement or analysis of consumer behaviours) with the aim of gaining knowledge or memory credits which can then be exchanged via the ULTIMATE® knowledge and Memory Bank system.

Nike had developed quite sophisticated ways to cheat the system. Omo didn't like to ask questions. Wasn't interested. So Nike traded knowledge credits with his pal on a daily basis. But it had come to the point where he'd used up nearly all the credits on Omo's vault as well. And if Flora ever stopped crying about the tiger and went back to her own knowledge vault, she'd find that her password had been hacked and her bank account raided too. Nike wasn't proud of that, but it was like an addiction.

However much Flora tried to explain to him that it was pointless... because knowledge wasn't meaning and meaning was personal and so there was no point to any of it, other than the point you created yourself in your own vault... Nike just couldn't stop asking questions. So, now that he was in a barren desert, it was time for more drastic action.

'We should go and see my Nan.' Nike suggested.

'Why?' A question from Omo. That was unusual. But it was not a real question. Not a question with meaning. For Omo, 'why' was like grunting. No thought went into it, it was just a knee jerk reaction and he didn't care if he got an answer or not. Questions didn't interest Omo, and answers interested him even less. Omo was a model citizen in that respect.

'She's got lots of stories to tell. Her vault is amazing.

And (this was for Flora) she'll know about tigers. She knows all about animals and nature and that sort of historical thing.' Nike put his best case forward.

The deal was done. They would go and visit Nike's Nan.

'We should take her something. Something real.' Nike said.

'Something real? What?' Flora replied. Omo just sucked on an ULTIMATE® sweet and said nothing.

Nike answered, 'I don't know. What do old people like?'

The US™ screen replied.

GIFT GIVING: In History, a Scottish tradition. On visiting family members or acquaintances, one would take a gift of some sort. Acceptable gifts included a range of consumer items such as Flowers, chocolates, wine.. Live animals and expensive consumer items are not appropriate. YOU HAVE 10 ULTIMATE® CREDITS LEFT TODAY.

'Boy,' said Omo. 'You're really going to have to be careful on the questions now.

'It's not fair,' replied Nike, 'I didn't even want an answer to that one. I wasn't even asking a question. I was just thinking.'

Omo laughed. 'Don't think out loud, Nike. How many times has Pryce told you that?' He put on Pryce's accent, *'Thoughts are best kept in the head. Meaning is personal and thoughts are personal. There is no currency in thought or meaning so don't bring it into the public arena.'*

'All right, all right.... give me a break,' Nike replied, 'we'll get her some flowers. Where....?'

Flora cut him off short. 'I'll sort it Nike. I can buy things without losing question credits. I know how to shop.'

'Thanks Flora.'

'No problem. Now get me some pizza will you?'

The boys went off to provide Flora with pizza, happy that she was eating at last. And that finally they'd distracted her from that hideous tiger.

In the kitchen they waited for the 'ping' which would tell them the pizza was done. A whole four minutes. That's because they didn't have the newest microwave. You could get a pizza in 36 seconds if you had the latest model but who needed their pizza in 36 seconds? Who cared? While the Project Kids were supplied with all their requirements, if they wanted the very best of the best, they had to put in more 'productive' work. And it wasn't worth it for a microwave when there were so many other things you could do with your credits. So they waited the regulation four minutes. Normally not a problem, but today it seemed like a long time to stand in a kitchen waiting, so the boys resorted to conversation. Of a kind. Conversation was an art going the same way as the tiger, certainly amongst Project Kids such as Omo and Nike. They were better at doing, or avoiding, 'productive' work. Their lives were lived virtually and real interaction was neither encouraged nor considered normal. Of course they talked to counsellors when schedules had to be changed or the like, but most needs could be met by a virtual exchange.

'It wasn't pretty was it?' Omo said.

'The tiger? No. It was kind of ratty. I reckon it would be better off dead than living like that.'

'I meant Flora crying.'

'Oh.'

'Girls used to cry all the time' Omo observed. 'In History. I saw about it on the US™. Cry and cry and cry.'

'Why?' Nike mouthed... he was wise to this. If he asked this question out loud he'd break his credit limit and he'd have to spend the rest of the day in 'productive' work to regain his balance.

'Not clear,' Omo replied, 'Emotions. Hardship. Love. All kinds of silly things. NOT things you should be asking questions about. Not with your credit rating.'

PING. That was the pizza ready.

B. AN ULTIMATE VICTIM?

Helen was nearly seventy. If she was in the community you wouldn't say she was old but it was old for VCC people. That's people, like Helen, who lived in ULTIMATE® homes. VCC was a kind of shorthand slang for such places. Helen, who had an awkward sense of humour, said it was an acronym for Victims of Conspicuous Consumption or Victims of Caring Capitalism, but really it was shorthand for Victims of Credit Crunch. Such people were generally known as Victims and being a victim has never been a good thing to be.

VICTIM: Definition. A person injured or killed as a result of an event or circumstance, or destroyed in pursuit of an object of gratification. A dupe.

CREDIT CRUNCH: Definition. A term created by the media in 2008 to mark the beginning of the End of History, representing a sudden reduction in the availability of loans and other types of credit from banks and capital markets at given interest rates.

HISTORY: Definition. A time in the past when people worried about what had happened before their own time and tried to use their worries to predict what would happen in the future. A pointless exercise EXAMPLE: History is bunk.

Of course the people living through it didn't know that was what it was then. It was just another recession. A V shaped, or a W shaped or a bath shaped recession. Any shape you like wasn't going to save the financial institutions. Despite government bail outs time and again, the threat to economic theory led to a need to reinvent the world yet again, a reinvention that would take at least a generation, but by 2030 it was already just LIFE as we know it today.

Memories were short, if they existed in 2030. Without History there was no need for memory and ULTIMATE® had worked hard to undermine and diminish collective memory. Personal memory was stored, archived; a commodity to be viewed on a screen, not an emotion to be experienced. There was no longer any need for history and no longer any need for memory. Under ULTIMATE® you could split things into the periods: 'in History' and 'today.' No one paid much attention to 'in History' since it had long ago been shown that history was unimportant to the flourishing of the modern world. The world didn't even look forward any more. People just looked into the virtual world which was all that existed, all around them. Virtuality was all that was real in the ULTIMATE® world.

Omo, Nike and Flora stood in the reception of VCC Holyrood and didn't like what they saw. It was clean, it was bright, it was airy, but somehow it was..... not nice. Not the sort of place you'd want to end up. Which wasn't surprising, because the only people who ended up here were people who were VICTIMS. The disabled or those without families to support them, those who had fallen on hard times or for some reason or other had not prospered under the current economic system. People who had made no provision for their futures, or who had made provision for their futures but had invested unwisely and suffered as part of the Economic Crash. This was what the Credit Crunch which became the Downturn, which became the Global Recession to End History, afterwards referred to as GRsΩHist, became. Victims. Not a nice word. Not a nice thought. Not a nice thing. But an accurate description. And there were plenty of them. Too many. They were a drain on resources and it's lucky for everyone that they usually didn't live beyond 72. Statistically speaking. In that respect, Helen was old and living on borrowed time.

ECONOMIC CRASH: Definition. In History, a downturn in the economy. In current parlance the cut off before which our current system did not function. A time of uncertainty where people, governments and countries were living beyond their means, using now outmoded and illegal methods of economic and financial activity.

GLOBAL RECESSION: Definition. In History, a period of global economic slowdown where global economic growth is 3 percent or less is 'equivalent to a global recession'. Following the increasing regularity of global recessions in 1990-1993 , 2001-2002 and 2008-2010 the ULTIMATE® CORPORATION stepped in to reverse economic declines, introducing a new model and wiping away the last vestiges of the failed global economic system. This was finally achieved in 2020, leading to the stable economic system we now enjoy.

Helen didn't need the definitions, she'd lived the life. She still remembered. But interacting with the US™ was not something you could avoid and it passed the time. Unlike most people, however, Helen didn't believe all she was told.

Standing outside Helen's door, there was one embarrassing thing Nike had to get out of the way.

'Guys. My Nan. She's old. I mean, she looks okay. Not too wrinkly.. but she's weird and she has some strange.. well, you know... quirks.'

'Such as?' That was Omo. Omo didn't like the unexpected. The odd. The unusual. It made him feel uncomfortable. He didn't like feeling. And he particularly didn't like feeling uncomfortable.

'Uh... she tends to call me NICK.'

'Nick?'

'Yes.' A pause. Nike explained. 'It was a name in History.'

'Oh. Okay.' Omo accepted it. Life was easier if you just accepted odd things. Usually.

'Nick.' Flora repeated it, rolling it round in her mouth, 'sure she's not just hard of hearing? It sounds kind of like..'

'No. She calls me NICK okay. Don't question it. Just deal with it and don't laugh, or correct her or..'

'Nick.' Flora tried it out again. 'I like it. It sounds nice.'

Nike and Omo exchanged a glance. Girls. What could you do? Now, ready for anything, they knocked on the door. There was just a moment's delay then Helen's voice called out clearly, 'Come in.'

And in they went.

'Hello Nan.'

'Oh, Hello Nick. I thought it was them, bringing my lunch. Hang on a minute... I'm sorting through things on my memory vault....'

A black man became president. Economics became God and God became commercialised. The ULTIMATE® CORPORATION filled the gap, took over, and saved the planet. THIS MEMORY HAS BEEN MOVED AND STORED FOR YOU AT NO EXTRA CHARGE.

Nike, Omo and Flora stood obediently in the small square room, trying not to look too closely at the screen, but failing, since there was little else to look at in the sparsely furnished space. It was a pitiful 60 inch screen compared to the 90 inches they were used to, but it took up the whole of a wall. They did understand that really it was respectful to treat a Memory Bank as private unless you were invited to share the memories. And an old person's Memory Bank. Well.. that would have all sorts of things you probably shouldn't know about. Especially one who had lived in History. But how did you avoid looking? There was nothing else to do. Nowhere else to look. Omo began to feel uncomfortable. Again. Dammit. Why did that always happen?

Images and sounds flickered from place to place, like so

many Windows closing down and opening up and trying to fight each other for their proper file. Helen was a Windows Vista woman in a world which had forsaken Microsoft for ULTIMATE® technology.

'Sorry... sorry... I'm,' she was flustered.

A voice blared out.

Helen. The face that launched a thousand ships.

'What?' Nike couldn't help himself.

The US™ screen replied, as it was programmed to do. Within a nanosecond it *biolaser©* read the barcode tattooed on Nike's wrist and charged the question to his account.

HELEN OF TROY: Definition. In ancient mythology, known as 'the face that launched a thousand ships' referring to her incredible beauty which is credited as the cause of the Trojan war. THIS HAS COST YOU ONE KNOWLEDGE CREDIT. ADDITIONAL OR SUPPLEMENTARY INFORMATION IS AVAILABLE FOR ANOTHER TEN CREDITS. AFFIRM?

Nike was angry with himself. He'd come here to avoid asking questions and he was barely in the door. However, it proved his point and he grinned at Omo. 'Told you her vault was awesome.'

Finally Helen managed to sort herself out and power down her random memory folder. 'It's nice to see you. And your friends. What brings you all the way over here?'

Nike dutifully kissed his Nan and handed over the plastic flowers which Flora had obtained at a cost of only thirty minutes 'productive work.' Plus delivery.

Helen took them, held them up to her nose and smelled them. 'They smell just like real ones,' she observed.

Nike, Omo and Flora exchanged puzzled glances.

'They are real ones, Nan.' Nike said. She got confused.

She was old. What could you do? Nike slowed down and made himself very clear. 'Nan. This is Omo and Flora. He pointed at each of them, so she would be sure. O-M-O and F-L-O-R-A....'

'I'm not deaf Nick. Or glaikit.'

'What?' Oh, no. Another question.

GLAIKIT: Etymology. A Scottish word meaning stupid, foolish, thoughtless, lacking in...

Helen interrupted the US™'s flow by talking over it, though it was unclear whether her comments were primarily directed at the US™ screen or at Nike.

'Not deaf. Not stupid. Okay?'

'Sorry Nan.'

'That's okay Nick. You're a good boy to bother visiting me. It's been ages. What brings you here?'

Surely she'd just asked that?

'Nothing Nan. Just wanted to see you. And Flora has a question.'

'A question. Are you allowed to ask the kind of questions I can answer?' She laughed, in a half-mocking way. 'What's the world coming to?'

They exchanged surreptitious confused glances. But there was obviously nothing wrong with Helen's eyesight or mental faculties because she clearly saw their glances and accurately read them. She responded, 'That's a rhetorical question.' Laughing as she saw Nike's face drop, Helen waved at the US™ screen. 'Have this one on me.'

RHETORICAL QUESTION: Definition. A question not requiring an answer, used for literary effect.

Helen spoke to the screen. 'Example from my life?'

The US™ screen spoke back: *THAT WILL BE ONE MEMORY*

CREDIT. YOU HAVE 99 MEMORY CREDITS REMAINING FOR THIS MONTH. CHOOSE WISELY, ULTIMATE® MEMORY BANKS WORK FOR YOU TO ORDER AND PROTECT YOUR MEMORIES. FOR ALL ETERNITY. THIS WEEK WE HAVE A SPECIAL OFFER..

'Yes, yes...' Helen waved to fast forward. 'Answer the question.... Example from my life?' The screen replied:

EXAMPLE FROM LIFE: You were in high school. You were studying Plato's Republic

Nike couldn't help himself, 'Plato's Republic?'

YOU ARE NOT AUTHORISED TO ASK THIS QUESTION. YOUR CREDIT IS INSUFFICIENT.

Nike turned to Flora.... 'Go and ask for me?'
Helen cut in. 'Plato's Republic was an ancient Greek philosophical work which discussed the meaning of justice, introduced the theory of forms and considered the immortality of the soul. Oh, and poetry. He was a very influential political theorist.'
'Oh, okay.' Nike was glad he hadn't wasted credit on that one. Who cared?
Back to the US™ which had paused, waiting to complete its task.

MEMORY RECAP: You were in High School. You were studying Plato's Republic. Your teacher was the headmistress. She used to ask questions about the text and you all sat there, dumbstruck because none of you understood. She used to make you sweat and then after a long pause she used to say 'it's not a rhetorical question.' She thought this was funny. You thought it was mean. You thought she was mean.

Nike felt they'd gone down a blind alley. And he'd flagged up his credit rating for all to see. That was annoying. Why couldn't he control his desire to ask questions? It wasn't normal. He wasn't normal. He needed to do something about that. Perhaps he should flag it up at a counselling session with Pryce. Some modification was in order, clearly. And if the system wouldn't modify, he'd have to. It was getting irritating, and expensive.

Nike's problem extended beyond asking more questions than he could ever gain credit for. He wanted knowledge. To know things. They used to be called facts. Things. They interested him. He couldn't help it. It was like an addiction. And if he couldn't feed it one way, he'd feed it another.

Absently, without any real thought and certainly without reference to the retailer's recommendations, he pressed his sleeve and started recording as Helen spoke.

'When I was young.....'

Nike felt a wave of relief wash over him. Now all he had to do was sit back and listen. He'd get information by proxy and store it to make sense of later. That was the way to cheat the system. It wasn't something people did in general, so it wasn't protected against. Nike knew a lot of short cuts to the system. Had he worked as hard on 'productive' work as he did finding cheats for the system, he'd get in a lot less trouble. But, that's life. This way, when he got home, he could listen to it all again and he'd have lots to feed his thirst for knowledge. Without ever having to log in to the knowledge or Memory Banks. This would save him so many hours of 'productive' work, he could probably see it through till the end of the month, when his slate would be wiped clean and his credits restored for another month. Job done. In theory.

Of course, in practice, Helen's utterances would raise so many more questions than they answered and Nike had just committed himself to a life, if not of servitude to ULTIMATE® productivity, then at least to a great many hours doing things he'd rather not do. Answering meaningless questions instead of asking meaningful ones. Productive consumption it was called. He hated it. He was smart enough to keep that thought to himself.

'What's the problem, Nick?'

Nike came back from his reverie to find Helen asking him an unanswerable question.

'Nothing.'

'You were miles away.'

'Sorry.' He smiled. 'Uh, Nan. I was just wondering if there was a way you could bypass the US™ and just you know, talk to us?'

She smiled back. 'Yes, yes, of course. I'm fed up with it anyway. It's playing me up all over the place.' She waved her barcoded arm at the screen and gave it the instruction 'hibernate.' It flickered back at her in an alarming manner and then went to some kind of screensaver. It was something the Project Kids had never seen before. As close to magic as they could imagine – if they had had the concept of magic. They lived in a world where the US™ was a permanent feature of life. To even imagine it as other than central was a step further than Omo could have gone. He was baffled. He'd never heard the command 'hibernate' and he didn't know what it meant.

'Wow,' Nike opined. 'How..?'

Helen waved at him to stop. 'If you are going to ask how did I do that, I wouldn't. Ask a question and it'll come out of hibernation. It's programmed that way. Unfortunately. We have to find other ways of asking questions, if it's questions you want.'

'How?' Nike wasn't a natural. The screen flickered again and Helen once again suggested it 'hibernate' which once again, it consequently did.

'Don't put the sentence construction on it. Say the word you want me to talk about and I'll talk.'

'Hibernate.' Nike tried not to inflect the word.

'It's what some animals do in the winter. It's a way of staying in a dormant – that's like a sleeping state,' Helen replied.

'Not off then?'

'You can't turn the US™ screen off Nike,' Omo butted in. 'Everyone knows that.'

'Yes. Unfortunately.' Helen replied.

If Omo had been the inquisitive type he might have asked Helen why she would want to turn it off. But he didn't.

She turned to Omo...

'You have experience of fixing screens, Omo.' It was obviously a question but she managed to deliver it in an uninflected manner and the screen did not respond. Nike was impressed. So his Nan knew some cheats as well. Good for her.

Omo shook his head.

'That's okay. I'll get a technician. It's been playing up a bit recently. A lot of what you might call random activity.'

'Maybe you're not following instructions..' Omo began, trying to be helpful.

'Maybe.' Helen smiled.

'Nan, Why do you call me Nick?

The screen flickered.

ONOMATOLOGY:....

'Override and hibernate.' Helen spoke with authority. The screen obeyed. Nike found it amazing. Omo found it disturbing. Flora was still wondering if tigers slept through the winter and if so why. But she knew they weren't supposed to be asking questions so she kept that one for later. She had plenty of credits left for the month because she did plenty of 'productive' work.

Helen knew he wouldn't have been able to resist asking questions. Not her Nick. Despite the generation gap, despite the fact that his life was unrecognisable from the one she had lived or lived now or perhaps because of that; they had that in common. A thirst for knowledge. And it came in the form of questions. Luckily, she had some answers.

'Onomatology. It's the study of names. The study of the origin of names.' She turned to Omo. 'Do you even know why you are called Omo? Or Flora?'

'No.' They answered in chorus.

'Do you?' asked Flora.

None of them had ever thought to question their names.

'Names have meaning?' Nike was amazed.

'Yes' Helen prepared herself for a long afternoon. 'In the olden days people used to have books and books of names for babies. It took them weeks and months to decide and many arguments.'

'Of course in Scottish tradition your middle name was your maternal grandmother's surname. Which Nick, would make you Nicholas Blair Christie.'

'That's a mouthful,' Omo commented.

'My name's Nike.'

'It isn't. It's Nicholas. I was there. In those days, Nike was a training shoe. A logo. A brand. A sort of flash with a tag line JUST DO IT. That's Nike. It was ripped off from the Ancient Greeks. The Goddess Nike Athena...'

This was all so much Greek to Nike!

Helen paused for breath. 'But Nicholas. Of Greek origin meaning Victorious people. Often attributed in relation to the ancient Bishop reputedly considered to be Saint Nicholas. You'll have heard of Saint Nicholas?'

It was a question, but not a direct question so the screen remained dormant.

'No.' All three shook their heads

'Father Christmas. Santa Claus.'

'Uh yeah, sure, maybe.' Omo was beginning to feel stupid and he didn't like feeling stupid any more than he liked feeling uncomfortable, or for that matter feeling in general.

'Something to do with Coca Cola, before it became ULTIMATE® coke.' Omo wanted to show he knew something. He didn't like this game, if it was a game. And if it wasn't a game he liked it even less.

Nike was getting a bit frustrated too.

'Nan, I think we're getting off the point aren't we? You were telling us about names, not giving us a seminar in Brand Loyalty.'

Helen nodded. 'Patience, Nick. All in good time. Join me in a cup of tea. '

While it wasn't a question, all three shook their heads again. Tea. What kind of a drink was tea?

'Of course, tea is too old people for you,' Helen observed, 'I'll pour it out anyway. In case you want to try. Of course it's only ULTIMATE® not real tea, but what can you do? Okay, I'll get on with the story. Are you sitting comfortably?' And without waiting for their response, or the response of the screen to a potential question, she continued, 'Then I'll begin.' And laughed. They had no idea why. Helen gave up. *Watch With Mother* was long, long ago and the world had changed since the 1960's. Oh boy, had it changed.

'At the beginning of the 21st century, people got bored of calling their children by traditional names and celebrities started experimenting, using places and fashionable items as names. Then ordinary people jumped on the bandwagon, following celebrity fashion as they always did, and by the time the Credit Crunch had become the GRsΩHist people wanted to find new ways of identifying with the new economic order and so they began to use brand names for their children. Omo, for example. Your parents must have had a sense of humour.'

Omo looked blankly at her and before Nick could ask the inevitable 'why?' Helen continued.

'Omo was a washing powder. Omo washes whiter, Omo washes brighter. With a bright new powder for a bright new world.'

22

'Oh.' Omo didn't see the joke. None of them did. They couldn't contextualise and so couldn't hope to see the humour. Making racism a thing of the past was the legacy of the Black man in the White House. After this presidency, you couldn't judge someone on the colour of their skin any longer. Black men became white men out of political expediency, like women had became honorary men in times of war throughout history. It was a kind of social evolution. It might have been ULTIMATE® inspired.

Helen continued, 'Though the word's origin is Greek, for scapula, that's a shoulder blade. The Omo Brand prided itself on the notion that dirt is good, providing children with a way to explore their worlds and express their creativity. It espoused notions of freedom, enabling everyone to reach their potential. Its demographic was those people who wanted value for money as it was always a lot cheaper than its rival PERSIL. But they were both made by the same company. Some people said all washing powders were the same...and that caused a bit of a furore for a time but...' She paused for a moment to ask the US™ 'What is the Omo Brand? Detail please.' The screensaver flickered and came back to life.

Helen winked at Nike. 'It has its uses,' she observed, 'and saves me the boring bits. My memory isn't what it used to be.'

OMO BRAND: Detail: A Brand of the company UNILEVER,one of the early ULTIMATE® CORPORATION buy outs. Other Brands in the Unilever stable included Persil, PG Tips, Dove, Lynx and many other products in the food, personal and home care environment. THAT WILL BE ONE KNOWLEDGE CREDIT. YOU HAVE 406 KNOWLEDGE CREDITS LEFT FOR THIS TIME PERIOD. ANY UNUSED CREDITS CAN BE CARRIED OVER INTO YOUR NEXT TIME PERIOD. ADDITONAL BRAND INFORMATION IS AVAILABLE FROM ONLY FIVE CREDITS.

Then, as if exhausted by its work, the screen flickered and died again. But this time it went blank instead of to screensaver. It didn't look like 'hibernate' mode any more. Helen shrugged. A blank screen was a relief really. She remained convinced, like many of her generation, that US™'s were more trouble than they were worth.

'And me?' Flora asked, quite without realising she'd asked a question. The US™ didn't seem to notice either. At any rate, Helen got there first.

'You were named after margarine.'

'What's margarine?'

That was too obvious. The US™ hummed, and started on the word MARGARINE, but with a swift wave of her hand Helen cancelled the request and answered herself. Omo found himself focused on whether the screen had a hardware or software problem. It was certainly not functioning properly. He was not convinced the 'hibernate' setting was strictly legal. That bothered him. Like any good citizen.

'A fat based replacement for butter and hard fats.' Helen said.

And as the screen remained in sulk mode, that piece of knowledge cost no one anything.

Nike was impressed with how these facts just flowed off Helen's tongue. She was like a live knowledge bank. He supposed in History, before ULTIMATE® ran things, people would have to have this kind of knowledge stored in their own heads. It was primitive, but strangely compelling to him. He wondered if it was genetic. Was it something he'd inherited from Helen? He'd ask Pryce. No. Maybe he wouldn't. Maybe this wasn't something he wanted modified out of his DNA.

Helen was still explaining the origins of Flora's name.

'Flora was a Latin word for flower (Latin was a language that was dead long before even I was born) and the product was made with sunflower oil, which was supposed to be healthier than animal fat. And was also better than palm oil, which was the generic oil used in those times. Palm oil was a terrible thing because they cleared all the rainforests to grow it, to satisfy demands, and in doing so they destroyed fragile eco-systems and many wild animals became extinct because of it. Specifically orang-utans. I bet you don't even know what an orang-utan was?'

Flora shook her head. 'No. But I wanted to ask you. About tigers.'

'What about tigers?' There was no response from the screen in relation to Helen's question this time.

'I..' Flora faltered. She was still clearly moved by her experience and didn't want to cry in front of Nike's Nan, 'I saw a live stream the other day. Of the last tiger. We saw it dying. Live. It was horrible.'

'And your question?'

'Well. I wanted to know why?'

'Why what?' (The US™ would not demean itself to come back to life for such an impoverished construction.)

'Why did it have to die? Why did it live in a zoo? What is a zoo like and what were tigers like?' The questions kept flowing out, like the tears had flowed before. 'Where did they live when they weren't in zoos? What is a wild animal? Why can't we have them now?' Flora finished, exhausted.

And now the US™ didn't know where to start. It made the most confused, grinding noises; unearthly and primitively mechanical. Helen used the override command again. Omo might have observed that the screen didn't look happy if he could have imagined the emotion of happiness applying to an inanimate object, which of course he couldn't. He just noted that it was not behaving in the standard way. He was glad he wasn't a technician. He'd never thought it possible to play about with the screen the way Helen was doing.

Meanwhile Helen was dealing with Flora. Offering her the verbal equivalent of a tissue, to mop up the question tears.

'That's a lot of questions. No wonder you came to me.

You couldn't possibly have enough ULTIMATE® credits to get all those questions answered. Not without hours of 'productive' work.' Helen smiled. That wry, mocking smile which made you feel that she didn't really take the whole ULTIMATE® thing seriously. Which was dangerous. And which was probably why she was here, living in a Victim Home instead of out in the community living a happy and productive life.

'So I'll tell you.' Helen continued. 'But I'm mercenary in my old age. Like ULTIMATE® there's a price for my knowledge.'

Flora's face fell.

'Don't worry. I don't think it's too high a price to pay. I just wanted to invite you to my birthday party.'

A birthday party? Nike had never been to a birthday party. Not since he was about six anyway. He had a hazy memory of it. But not one he could find in his Memory Bank. There was nothing on his Memory Bank before he was 10. Nothing from before he started at The PROJECT⌂. He'd never considered that before. It was strange. But there was so much else for Project Kids to focus on, Memory Banks tended to get overlooked. They were for people who didn't 'have it all.' And as Pryce kept reminding him, as a Project Kid he *did* 'have it all.'

Whatever it all was, Nike wasn't sure it was enough. He realised no-one had responded to Helen's request. She sat there, hopeful. He took an absentminded sip of tea. It wasn't that bad actually. He refocused. A birthday party. For an old woman? Boy, these old people were really strange.

Helen was speaking again. 'I'm seventy next week. And I was hoping we could have a little celebration. Will you come? Will you all come?'

'Of course.' They replied in chorus.

'We'll have tea, and cake and candles and it'll be like the old days.' Helen smiled. Then frowned. 'Do you mind? Would you mind indulging me?'

Omo couldn't figure out whether the US™ was faulty, or huffing, or didn't deal with personal questions of the construction 'do you mind?' But it stayed silent. Unlike Nike.

'No, Nan. We'd love it,' he said. And almost meant it.

C. A BAD DAY AT THE OFFICE

Pryce was having a bad day at the office. Pryce invariably had a bad day at the office these days. It made him wonder but not question (he was beyond questioning) why it was that his job was so aspirational. On the face of it Pryce had everything one could wish from the ULTIMATE® lifestyle he'd bought into some twenty years ago. But somehow, something didn't fit. Perhaps it was because he was prone to question his own place in the order of things. Personal reflection was not part of the ULTIMATE® deal. Life was for living not for thinking about. But somehow Pryce couldn't break the habit. And it made him depressed.

Depression of course didn't exist in the ULTIMATE® world but that didn't stop the feeling of pointlessness Pryce experienced on a daily basis. He was forty years old and felt his life had passed him by. He was going nowhere, his wife couldn't stand the sight of him and his job took up all his time. Twenty years ago he'd wedded himself to Angela and to ULTIMATE® and the honeymoon was definitely over in both respects.

With nothing to look forward to, he allowed his mind to wander back to the twenty one year old man he had been nearly twenty years ago in 2011, when he'd made the life-changing decisions he now felt depressed by. In 2011 the ULTIMATE® Corporation had been cutting edge. Secret. Aspirational. A job with ULTIMATE® was a job for life in a world where nothing was certain. It had the mystique of the secret service with the security of the civil service and the pay packet of investment banking. Pryce shared the aspirations of his generation and had wanted some certainty in his life. Yes, it was a career he'd aspired to. Then. Not now. Now he knew better. Pryce wondered if he was the only person who questioned the ULTIMATE® world. Everyone else around him seemed happy, got on with their lives. No one else seemed to face each morning with a gloom in the pit of their stomach like he did. It made Pryce question where the problem lay. Was it with ULTIMATE® or was it with him? Either way, Pryce didn't want to get up in the morning. He sometimes wondered whether he was that unusual. Whether everyone else felt the same as him but in the ULTIMATE® world everyone kept their emotions close to their chests, because ULTIMATE® had written emotion out of life. That had been part of the deal. And Pryce had signed the contract.

Pryce mused that maybe he was more representative of his generation than anyone would like to admit. He wondered if his peers felt, like he did, that they'd sold themselves to the ULTIMATE® way of life not realising the long term consequences of their actions. As people always did. They bought the pretty package and didn't think of the payback terms. But how would he ever know? The beauty (if such you could call it) of the ULTIMATE® system was that no one ever expressed such feelings to one another even if they had them. Of course, Pryce might be the only one who felt like this. An individual in a world which had negated the value of individuality. That could explain his depression. He knew that if he presented his thoughts to his boss (as of course he should) he would be sent for re-training. Which would be even more tedious than the life he currently lived and would also probably result in a lack of privileges. And he couldn't imagine that would make him feel any less depressed. Any change was likely to be a change for the worse, so he kept his thoughts to himself. He sighed. Perhaps life had been and was always like that. Perhaps reality never lived up to the dream.

It was 10pm. He was still in the office. Something was wrong. Angela, his wife, would be mad when he got home late again. She was always mad these days. Whatever time he got home. At least if it was 11pm he could just fall into bed and sleep and not spend three hours in pointless arguments, designed to disturb his sleep. Pryce often wondered whether Angela was at the root of his problems. Nothing unusual there for a married man. He couldn't work out whether he had a problem with Angela or she had a problem with him or whether no one was temperamentally suited to be with the same person over twenty years. After all, people changed over twenty years. He wasn't the same person he had been in 2010. Was it so surprising that Angela was also unrecognisable from that time? Was this the problem? ULTIMATE® reckoned so. It was, after all, the ideological basis of the social counselling section, where he'd worked for the last five years.

Pryce had become involved with work for The PROJECT⌂ at its inception in 2016, contemporary with the first "intake" and had stayed there ever since. He'd enjoyed it at first. It had been a change from the pure theory work he'd been involved with before that. It offered him a chance to work "with people" and more specifically with "kids". Looking back, by the age of twenty five his relationship with Angela had already become rocky. He wanted children. She didn't. Angela's solution,

'Get a job working with them. Just don't bring them home.'

He'd bought it. Angela could be very persuasive. And now, the way things were, Project Kids wouldn't have to worry about marital relationships because ULTIMATE® had made marriage a thing of the past. The demise of the nuclear family (a concept that was bound to end in a cataclysmic explosion) was completed by 2020. In actuality, Brand had long since become the new family. And when globalisation took over, tribal branding became outmoded and all allegiance was transferred to the ULTIMATE® brand. You had to move with the times and the transition was seamless to most of the population. They just wanted the good times to go on indefinitely. ULTIMATE® delivered. Sign up and don't worry about the small print. It was ever thus.

Pryce would have gone home right then, even back to another argument. At least it would be human interaction. And maybe, if he played it right, Angela would act like the lover she'd once been not the wife she had then become. Despite all the evidence, Pryce hadn't completely lost hope. If he just did or said the right thing…. However, his boss Graham had been most insistent that Pryce did not leave for the night before they'd spoken. That was three hours ago. And Pryce was still waiting for the interface. So here he was, with time to kill, twiddling his thought-thumbs and trying not to get more depressed. His job as Project Counsellor was to manage other people's emotions not to have problems of his own, so his depression or mid-life crisis or whatever it was, had to stay bottled up inside.

Pryce decided to vent his maudlin mood by logging into his Memory Bank. Hang the cost, he had plenty of overtime due anyway. He knew it was pointless, he knew it was irrational. He knew it wouldn't change anything, but hey. The present was garbage, so maybe he could find some solace in his past.

'MEMORY BANK RECALL: 2010.' Pryce spoke to his US™ and up came the options.
GRADUATION
REDUNDANCY
JOB OPPORTUNITY

Oh well, why not go back to the beginning? He chose GRADUATION. And in the blink of an eye, there it was playing out for him on the US™. He didn't pick the option of *JOIN IN*. He was above that after all. It was just for analysis. Just to make sense of the past, not to vicariously relive it.

There was Angela. As she'd been at his graduation. Attractive. Funny. In love with him. She was raven haired. He hadn't known then that it had come out of a bottle and that her natural colour was mousy. He didn't know then that Angela didn't "do" natural. He bought it. Who wouldn't? Angela was still the kind of woman who always got a response. Even fully

32

clothed, she oozed a kind of sexuality that made a man feel somehow he was acting improperly. She always wore her blouse with just one button too many undone, a challenge NOT to look which made you look all the more. And made you feel dirty about doing so. It wasn't that she had the best body in the world, but she certainly knew how to use it to the best advantage. Angela had caught on quickly to the Lara Croft Avatar style of plasticity. And rendered it human. You might well say her "graphics" were amazing. Yet she was real. In the days before ULTIMATE® shifted the reality goalposts, Angela was well on the way to becoming a mistress of the art of ULTIMATE® reality.

'What're you looking at?' Angela had challenged Pryce on their first meeting. It was his twenty first birthday party. Somehow he'd managed to avoid her through three years of university and now, just before graduation, there she was. It was the first of many mysteries. He still didn't know who'd invited her, and the US™ didn't have that perspective on offer. Retrospectively he could see himself squirm. Yet at the time he remembered he'd thought he was so cool. How come if these were his memories, he looked totally different to how he had felt then? Just whose side was the US™ on?

'I… sorry… I wasn't looking,' was hardly the response of a cool guy now was it?

That was followed by the laugh. Angela had a dirty, dirty laugh which haunted you for days. At least she had in those days. These days she didn't laugh. All that came from her mouth these days, at least as far as Pryce was concerned, was cutting criticism.

Pryce sighed. He was using up credits here and it wasn't making him feel any better. He *backtracked* the memory. It was more than he could bear to watch Angela like that. And himself. It had been a time that had promised so much. How had life got in the way and changed the story? What had he lost in this ULTIMATE® life which told him he was a winner?

Pryce took his Memory Bank back to before Angela. Before graduation. He had been a clever scholar. Gone to a good university. Studied psychology with information technology. He was mature for his age and determined to get a good job, not just loll around like a stereotypical student for three or four years. He'd had more motivation. More self-respect. He liked a good time, sure, but he was driven. Or so he'd thought. Pryce, like so many of this cusp generation, was able to remember that life had been uncertain, with the possibility for things to go very, very wrong. It was a perspective most people never visited in their Memory Banks, but Pryce couldn't help himself. Call it nostalgia, call it what you like; from time to time Pryce went in search of meaning in the vaults of his Memory Bank. And his position as social counsellor allowed him access at levels which would have been questioned among people of lesser standing. Because he was supposed to be above the kind of wallowing that he was currently indulging in. Pryce was expected to be a fully signed up member of the ULTIMATE® reality, not a middle aged man putting rose tinted spectacles on a world which had collapsed. ULTIMATE® didn't deal with dreamers. Not unless it was an ULTIMATE® bought dream. Pryce was putting himself in a compromised position. Of course he thought no one knew. But with ULTIMATE®, someone always knew.

Pryce *fastforwarded* the memory. This was the kind of time travel people would have wet themselves over in 2000. Now it was just so many taps of a keypad or touch screen and there you were, surfing through your life, back and forward at will. By 2030 most people didn't bother with their memories because the everyday life experience contained more than enough to keep their unquestioning minds occupied. They favoured instant gratification which was paid for unwittingly through the very tasks which gave the gratification. This was the power of ULTIMATE® as it presented itself to the general population. You had to be pretty asynchronous in the pecking order to feel like you were being exploited by ULTIMATE®. And even if you did, a quick trip to your Memory Bank would remind you that things could and indeed had been a whole lot worse BEFORE.

Pryce went back to his graduation memory. He had been a young man full of hope, in a time of ridiculous uncertainty. It was the summer of 2010. Europe was in turmoil. Britain was in meltdown despite all calls for a "stable" government. Stability was far away from the reality of everyday life. Like everyone else in 2010, Pryce found himself smack bang in the middle of the GRsΩHist, known then simply as the recession. When he'd started at University the Credit Crunch hadn't even been a reality but by the time he graduated in July 2010, jobs were scarce and beggars couldn't be choosers.

And Pryce, like everyone else, was up to his eyes in debt. His dreams of a stable, serious career were being hijacked by global economics so he took the first job the milk round offered him. He was lucky. A blue chip company with a decent reputation was prepared to take him on as a graduate trainee. He didn't feel lucky though because it was in Industrial Psychology. It sounded tedious as hell. It was tedious as hell. But it was a job. For a while. About six months.

Then things really began to bite. Despite the promise of the 'new politics', companies went down and businesses went bust and everyone was very, very scared. And Pryce was made redundant. At least that's what he'd been told at the time.

Now, looking back at it, something didn't quite add up. He played with the perspectives on the US™ and came to the conclusion that actually he'd been headhunted. He'd had his mind on other things at the time of course. He *zoomed in* on the conversation with Angela.

'Of course you should take it.' She was adamant.

'I'm not so sure,' he voiced his indecision.

'That's so typical you,' she shifted her body so that he could do nothing else but look down her cleavage as she spoke.

'You can never see an opportunity staring you in the face. You never make the right move.'

Had he misinterpreted her comments? Had they been deliberately provocative? Obtuse? Pryce watched the ensuing scene like watching a car crash, though it hadn't seemed like that at the time. Life certainly changes ones perspective in memory as well as everything else, he reasoned.

He'd reached out for Angela. His "move" was obvious. She'd pulled back from his initial kiss. He was confused as to the signs. He was always confused as to Angela's signs, but this time he thought he knew what she wanted from him.

'Will you marry me?' he asked, down on one knee, his face level with that bottom button, his mind more on the immediate possibilities of the next twenty minutes rather than the next twenty years.

She pulled him off his knees. Rolled him onto the couch. Got him into a position he couldn't get out of and gave him what he thought was his reply through a physical rather than a linguistic response. Only once that was over did she speak.

'If you take the job at ULTIMATE®, I'll marry you.'

Twenty years on, *re-viewing* the memory, Pryce had to admit that it had been that way, but he really, really couldn't remember things happening in quite that sequence. He'd been sure the seduction was Angela trying to give him confidence. Now it sounded like an ultimatum and accorded with his present feeling that he'd been sucked into the ULTIMATE® Corporation without ever knowing it. Three months later, Angela and he were married and Angela was working alongside him at ULTIMATE®. A year later, Angela was outstripping him workwise and he was no longer looking forward to undressing her at the end of a long day. Work came first. Work always came first. And from this memory, it seemed like work had always come first with Angela.

Pryce felt used. By Graham, the boss he was sitting here waiting for at 10.35pm, by ULTIMATE® who had bought his life and given him a virtual package in return and most of all by Angela, who seemed to have been manipulating him all along the line. Pryce realised he no longer loved Angela. His feelings for ULTIMATE® were more complex.

In 2011 he had been like everyone else. Aspirational. Earning money was aspirational in those days. And economic fear created a whole new set of aspirations. You couldn't say no to a career in the ULTIMATE® Corporation even in 2011. Even though you didn't really know what you were buying into; if you got so far as to hear about them, to get offered a job, you knew you were going to be in on the start of not just the next best thing but the ULTIMATE® best thing. It was going to be bigger than Microsoft. Bigger than McDonald's. Bigger than Unilever and Levi's, GlaxoSmithKlineBeecham, and Monsanto and Coca-Cola and Mars and Tesco and Google and all those companies, brands and corporations ULTIMATE® inevitably swallowed up over the next, incredible decade when the world was re-inventing itself out of the GRsΩHist. Had history not been eliminated, the period 2010-2020 might have referred to as the age of recessions, mergers and buyouts. It was the journey from corporate imperialism to the new world. In the new world there was just one Brand Loyalty and it was to ULTIMATE®. Totalitarianism rebranded as consumerism. Wrapped in a pretty package and desired by all. Total global domination. Achieved through acquiescence.

Pryce had always thought himself lucky to be there or thereabouts at the right time. Just luck. Now he wasn't so sure. One way or another, his memory had cheated him. As he *replayed* the scene with Angela from twenty years ago again (telling himself he was doing so not because he wanted to remember their first sexual union but to make sense of his life – and not quite convincing himself on that point) he found there was an air of predictability about it all. An air of design. In the same way as it seemed unlikely that ULTIMATE® had got so big by chance, it seemed unlikely that he was just taken up in the

Economic Tsunami that went with it.

One thing Pryce knew about ULTIMATE® was that nothing was left to chance. So why, then, had he foolishly held onto the belief that his part in the whole thing was down to luck. ULTIMATE® didn't do luck. ULTIMATE® did complete world domination. You only had to look at their slogan: *'scientific advance and social development go hand in hand'* to realise that this was an all encompassing ideology. You could almost hear the *'Have a nice day with that, sir.'*

Back in 2011 when the phone rang and ULTIMATE® offered Pryce the job he'd been sceptical about, he was delighted. The first day sold him on the idea that a man with his qualifications would fit right in. His thesis on question theory impressed them – or so they said. And he had a wedding to plan. Of course he understood that he'd be a small cog in a big wheel and he didn't mind that. It would be better than Industrial Psychology. He felt for the first time that he had a future, a niche, that he was a stakeholder in life. He had no idea how big that wheel would get of course. No one did. Or did they? He was still wondering this when the US™ switched to INTERFACE mode. His relief was shortlived. It wasn't Graham. It was Nike, one of his protégés from The PROJECT△.

Pryce sighed. Nike was an all right kid, but he did tend to call at inopportune moments and with inappropriate questions. Particularly when he'd run out of his own question credits. You had to be on your toes with Nike, because before you knew it, he'd have stripped your account bare. It was nearly the end of the month and Pryce had been planning to carry over his credits. This evening had already given them a hammering, and no Project Kid was going to hijack what he had left.

'Nike. You know my office hours end at 8pm. What is it?'

'Uh... yeah...' Nike was obviously thrown by Pryce's hostile reaction.

'It's okay. I'm waiting for my boss to interface anyway.

But I haven't got all night. Shoot.'

'Uh. Well.. .it's... I'm not sure if it's all right, but I wanted to ask you..'

Pryce bridled.'If you've run out of knowledge credits Nike, you know what to do. Do some 'productive' work.'

'No. No. It's not that sort of a question.'

Was there ever any other kind of question from Nike? Pryce doubted it.

'Well?'

'It's kind of a protocol sort of thing.'

'What?'

The kid was talking in riddles. Even though Pryce had graduated top of his class, he knew that twenty years on just about any snot nosed Project Kid could wind him round their finger. That was the way knowledge had changed. They had it all on a plate. They didn't have to learn it or work at it they could just flip it up any time they wanted. They knew how to manipulate systems he barely understood. He'd need to be very careful here; he sensed Nike was about to take advantage. And he didn't want to be robbed blind and then have to file a report about it too. That was too much.

'Come on Nike. Just tell me what's on your mind.'

'No. It's not my mind. It's just... well, Omo said I should ask, but I think I don't need to. But Flora said yes, maybe and so... I wanted to know if it's all right to go to my Nan's birthday party?'

Pryce nearly fell off his chair laughing. 'Your Nan's having a birthday party?'

'Yeah. She's seventy. Next week. She lives in an ULTIMATE® Home and she doesn't have any other family, so I was thinking....'

'A birthday party? You want to go to a birthday party?'

'Yeah. Well.. is it cool?'

Perhaps it was because it was late at night. Perhaps it was because he'd earlier been viewing his own 21st celebrations.

Perhaps he was still ruminating on the confusion of meeting Angela for the first time. Perhaps it was because he was distracted, wanting Nike off the US™ before Graham came on. Whatever the reason, Pryce dropped the ball. Missed the point.

'Yeah. Sure. I don't see why not.'

'Cool. Thanks mate. That's all.' And Nike was gone, leaving Pryce to pick up the pieces.

Which of course he didn't have time to do. That's the way mistakes happen though, isn't it? You're doing one thing, thinking about another, something else comes in from left field and before you know it the thing you were going to check on files itself away and you don't revisit it again till it rears its ugly little monster head as the problem it is. But Pryce didn't have time to process Nike's request because immediately, Graham came on the US™.

Graham was three rungs higher up the ULTIMATE® ladder than Pryce and ten years younger. He was smarter, he was ruthless and he certainly didn't have depression. Graham would have been one of life's winners in any society but he was lucky enough to be an ULTIMATE® winner and he intended to stay that way. He would do anything to climb the ladder. And did. Pryce knew this about Graham and was reasonably wary of him. What Pryce didn't know was that Graham was currently having an affair with Angela, Pryce's wife. It was not the kind of question you'd think to ask the knowledge bank really is it? Or exactly the kind of question Pryce would have liked to ask, but not one he wanted the answer to. Like so many men before him, he shut his eyes to the signs and looked elsewhere for the root of his problems.

'Hey. Caught up on things?' Graham was cool and chatty and over-friendly in exactly the way that men are when they are having an affair with their colleague's wife.

''Bout ready to call it a day anyway,' Pryce replied, hoping Graham might pick up on his tone. It just came across as weak. He realised he shouldn't have bothered trying to sound cool, he was just giving Graham more leverage. Pryce never seemed to win where Graham was concerned. It irked him. But what could he do?

'Is there a problem?' Graham was digging for something. Graham was always digging for something. You'd have thought he had a PhD in undermining, as well as a Masters in thought control, if only Graham, at his tender 32 years had ever been to University.

It used to be that people went to University, or college or failing that the University of Life. ULTIMATE® changed all that. Using the McDonald's University paradigm before them, ULTIMATE® created their own, specific educational opportunities, and Graham had walked right in and sailed right through. Graham was an ULTIMATE® success. Ugly little bugger, but his liason with Angela proved that success means more than good looks to a certain kind of woman. To most kind of women, probably. Graham was lucky enough to have been born in a generation where how clever you were at coding your avatar to look and act cool was more important than your own physical attraction. And power always sells product.

'No problems Graham. No. I'm just tired. It's been a long day.'

Silence. A classic Graham tactic. Pryce had said all he wanted to, but couldn't bear the silence and had to give more.

'I'm not sleeping too well at the moment,' he admitted. Bang. Too much information.

'Oh. Sorry to hear that. Problems with Angela? D'you want to book in a session?' Graham did not sound sincere. He sounded smug.

'No. It's fine. Just a lot on my mind.' Pryce hated the likes of Graham to be aware he had any kind of problem. Far less talk about it, or see it. And he certainly didn't want a counselling session. With Graham or anyone else. Talking with Graham never made things any better and Pryce was usually left with the uncomfortable feeling that all he'd done was release information cheaply which could be used against him in the future.

'I'm fine. Really.'

'Oh, all right. If you're sure,' the weasel Graham replied. The tone told Graham all he needed to know. He'd got to Pryce. Needled him. Job done. He knew fine what Pryce's problems were. He was most of them, after all!

'But hey, let's book in some time to check on your workload. Some time next week, eh? Fix it up with the secretary. Night.'

And that was it. Graham gone, Pryce in bits and Nike's request forgotten. Which was why it didn't get written down in the casenotes.

D. ULTIMATE VIRTUAL REALITY

Helen had given up noticing that her room was small. What did it matter? A bed, a US™, a chest of drawers and a wardrobe. A chair to sit in. All standard issue ULTIMATE® Home products. She still didn't like but had grown used to the institutionally insipid magnolia walls. She never thought that would happen. It was a daily reminder that Victims had no choice in the matter. They were lucky ULTIMATE® took care of them. In History people had had to rely on the state, and by 2020 *Care in the community* was as much a myth as Helen of Troy. Ideals died with the GRsΩHist. Everything was re-invented by ULTIMATE® one little piece at a time, without anyone really noticing it, until there was nothing but ULTIMATE® everywhere.

Sure, Helen could remember a time when you still ate Mars Bars and Big Mac's, bought Persil, wore Levi's, shopped at Tesco or Walmart, and when people raved about these things. And then, later, when people became cynical and raged about these things. And then when the products became ULTIMATE® Mars Bars, ULTIMATE® Coca-Cola, ULTIMATE® credit. And after that, when caring capitalism went into its cocoon, to emerge as the new, improved, ULTIMATE® world where brands were all subservient to the ULTIMATE® brand. Where Brand Loyalty became a one party state. Everyone was branded and everyone was part of the Brand. And they loved it.

In Helen's eyes everything had become corrupted. Even memory. Memory was now mediated through ULTIMATE® and you were supposed to consume it through the US™ screen. But Helen could not bring herself to do this. The alternative was to use her own memory. She hoped that by keeping it active she could retain it, but it was a difficult task. Increasingly things only came back as little more than soundbites and the temptation was to go to the Memory Bank where you could get a full colour real-time recreation of events from your life. Helen still felt this was cheating. And avoided it as far as possible. Total avoidance was impossible.

She looked at the magnolia walls. And was back ten years.

'Magnolia, how insensitive,' she'd said as she entered her room for the first time.

The attendant hadn't picked up on her displeasure.

'It's a most practical colour,' she replied.

'It's institutional,' Helen pointed out.

'This is an institutional home,' the attendant replied without a hint of irony before showing Helen how she could close and open the blinds and giving her basic instructions in the US™, a thing Helen hadn't ever seen, never mind interacted with before.

'And this is your Memory Bank....' the attendant was running through the regular routine for new victims (sorry, residents), 'You can place any memories in here and replay them when you like. You can link it from your...' she tailed off, realising that Helen had not come with the requisite software to enable her to link her memories – Helen was a rural victim and had not kept up to date with technology. 'Oh well... you'll have a lot of time here,' the attendant carried on, undaunted, 'I suggest you put aside some time each day to add to the Memory Bank and before you know it the hard work will be done and you can just sit back and enjoy.'

Helen had felt there was a hidden threat even in this. Log your memories before your brain atrophies and all you can do is consume memory, not create it. And she was right. The whole thrust of the flagship ULTIMATE® ADAS® (Advanced Dementia Adaptive System) was to allow people to consume memories which they would in no way know were their own or not. Did it matter? As long as the memories kept them quiet and happy in the moment?

Helen had tried to go along with the system. Okay, even

at first it had been half-heartedly, but she had tried. The first thing that popped into her mind was magnolia. So magnolia it was. Left alone, she felt somewhat embarrassed, talking to herself out loud, not realising that the Memory Bank could tap right into your thoughts if you so instructed your laser embedded *brandloyalty* barcode chip. The one she'd just had 'linked up' to the central database. It itched just slightly for the first few days but you quickly forgot. No worse than the microchips people had put into their pets in the days when people had real pets with real desires to wander. Pets you could talk to so it didn't seem you were talking to yourself.

'Magnolia. Who could come up with such a travesty?' she observed, 'how could you take something as beautiful as magnolia blossom and pervert it into the most insipid paint colour known to man?' She sighed. But that wasn't memory. The statement led to the memory. The memory now came flashing back...

It was 1990. Helen was in the garden with Catriona, then aged nearly four. The magnolia blossom was at its finest which meant it must have been early May. It was hot. They were drinking home made lemonade.

'Me like the bubble tree,' Catriona said.

'I like..' Helen corrected her instinctively, the way parents do when they are in the middle of teaching the vagaries of English to their offspring. Then she actually listened to her daughter.

'The bubble tree?' she asked.

Catriona had pointed at the magnolia tree. 'Bubble tree,' she repeated, smiling.

On closer inspection she was right, the magnolia blossoms did resemble bubbles. Even as she was correcting her daughter, 'It's called a magnolia tree, darling,' Helen appreciated the wonder of a world where you could make up your own words, creating meaning for the first time. The wonder of childhood. And how quickly it passed. Catriona had once been wide eyed and innocent. How different from the wasted, thin, scared woman she had been the last time Helen had seen her alive.

The memory broke. Helen stopped thinking. But the US™ had stored it. The summer afternoon with the lemonade, the sun and the bubble tree was there for ever. Immortalised. And available to others for a price? Helen did not believe stored memories were personal. And that both annoyed and sickened her. But what could she do about it?

For a couple of years Helen had pursued a love/hate relationship with the Memory Bank. It was like itching a scab. She didn't want to put things there but she didn't want to forget. Well, sometimes all she wanted to do was forget, but she didn't want to forget permanently. So she went through phases of storing vast amounts of personal memories on her bank and phases of cold turkey where she refused to think about the past. Except during those times there was really nothing else to do in the VCC except review those memories you'd already stored.

It was several years into her ULTIMATE® life before Helen worked out a way to co-exist with the system. Once she discovered that you didn't have to talk out loud to get your memories transferred, she had always been suspicious that her private thoughts would transfer themselves to the Memory Bank. Eventually, through trial and error, she found that by sitting in her chair, eyes shut as if asleep, she could think her own thoughts, relive her own memories and if she had no credits left in her Memory Bank and didn't activate any connection via her barcode they didn't get stored in her Memory Bank. It only worked when she was out of credits though. So she tried to stay out of credits. Which was difficult because ULTIMATE® provided all their residents, even those in VCC Homes, with a basic level of memory credits per month. It was the ULTIMATE® pension. Helen tried to use them up on trivial memories so that she could save the really personal and private stuff for herself. She wanted to think for herself in her private world, not interact with the ULTIMATE® social environment. Lately, she'd taken to using Nick's offer to 'trade' them. She didn't know how he diverted the credits and she didn't care. He wanted them, she didn't. It was a good deal. And there was so little else she could give him.

Thinking for yourself was neither necessary nor encouraged in the ULTIMATE® world because the US™ could do it for you, or at least hold a repository of information that made personal thought unnecessary. And the past was an outmoded concept. History had been consigned to the trash bin, not even the recycle bin, and people who spent too many credits chasing historical detail could find themselves in hot water. Old people were given enhanced access to their Memory Banks as a means of keeping them quiet, but their interactions were also part of ADAS® system. There was a requirement for data. The likes of Helen could provide the data which would then be used to help them should they require the service.

The ULTIMATE® world came at a price. Re-inventing the present and paying for a future was only really possible where people remained ignorant of the past. The real past. Reality. That wasn't an ULTIMATE® concept. It was an ULTIMATE® product of course and could be bought with credits via the US™ like everything else. Like real plastic flowers.

Helen shook her head. Those kids thought that plastic flowers *were* real. Reality to them meant something you could hold in your hand, nothing more. Reality was the opposite of virtual. Virtual was the world they lived in, the world they embraced and reality was an outmoded concept, reserved for the likes of Helen. Nick's generation didn't have any idea of what a REAL flower was like because they'd never held a real flower. No one grew them any more. Why would you? When all life's interactions were via the virtual world who needed flowers shedding petals all over the place? In fact, it must have been quite extreme for them to actually spend credits buying her these 'real' plastic flowers.

REALITY: Definition. What is existent, or underlies appearances. Resemblance to an original. In common parlance, in reality means in fact.

And fact means whatever ULTIMATE® says it means, Helen thought. You didn't even have to get into the existentialist or post-modernist concepts of reality. ULTIMATE® had blown them out of the water. It just didn't matter any more what you the individual thought, or how you felt you stood in relation to the outside world. ULTIMATE® had rebranded reality the way it had rebranded everything else.

The real plastic flowers sat still on her shelf. Perfectly fresh, perfectly real, perfectly plastic. Mocking her. Proving that ULTIMATE® owned reality as well as everything else in 2030. Everything except what was in your head. And they tried to relieve you of that too, via the Memory Bank.

How had the world come to this Helen wondered? She remembered when Google and MySpace, Facebook and Twitter were the all singing, all dancing, must have lifestyle toys for a generation. How excited her son Torquil had been when he came back from a trip to his sister at college and started pouring out the incredible wonders of the world wide web circa 2004. How he'd begged to be allowed to use the computer for 'social networking.' To have a laptop in his bedroom.

'Get real mum,' he'd said. 'It's the future. You can't run away from the future,' with all the certainty of a fifteen year old.

'And when will you ever have time to use this stuff?' His dad had pointed out as they sat round the family dinner table. 'You've school, then I need you round the farm...'

'I'll do it instead of TV,' Torquil pleaded.

'If you've time for TV you've time for study,' Randall had pointed out. ' You've as much of a brain as your sister. You could go to college.'

'I want to be a farmer,' Torquil asserted, 'like you, dad.'

'Then you've no need for computers,' Randall pointed out. Conversation over.

Helen was glad techno worship had been a fad Torquil had grown out of. He had enough concept of a real life to avoid the virtual temptations of MySpace, Bebo and Facebook in his impressionable early teens. And by the time he was seventeen and they were moving he had grown out of it. Or so they'd thought. Yet it had got him in the end.

'Should we buy the lad a computer?' she'd asked Randall back in 2004.

'He can use the farm computer,' was Randall's response. 'A computer is a tool remember, not an object of desire.' He had smiled at her, sharing the memory of how they'd met, when computers were indeed objects of desire, which was lucky because they were pretty pitiful tools at that point in history.

Another memory stored in the Memory Bank. Another memory Helen often wished she could wipe away because the urge to look was too powerful and the viewing was too painful.

ULTIMATE® technology led the world towards a sparkling transformation. From their start point as a toy for adolescents in 2005, by 2020 social networks and personal vaults had become the intellectual equivalent of the progression from the riverbank through the twin tub to the fully automatic washing machine that washed at 15 degrees and never shrunk your clothes. How happy everyone was to embrace them. How everyone migrated their hard drives onto 'clouds' and let loose all their stored personal information.

Then it was not just information, it was their entire lives

which moved into the virtual world. People's facts and fictions all made it into cyberspace and the Memory Bank was born, ready for ULTIMATE® to register it and exploit it like everything else. Yet Helen still remembered when clouds were a feature of the weather, not a personal storage system.

Still, you couldn't do anything about it, you couldn't change it and you definitely couldn't fight it. Helen remembered being Torquil's age and having a similar conversation with her dad.

It was 1975. She wanted heated tongs. She wanted to impress a boy and he was busy swooning over the girl with the curliest hair in class. It was war.

'But dad, everyone has them,' she employed the familiar teenage mantra.

'What does your mum say?' He employed the standard response.

'She says no, but...' Helen still hoped she had enough girlish charm to wind her father round her fingers. She'd always been a daddy's girl.

'Well, you can't fight city hall,' came the response.

'I don't want to fight anyone. I just want to get some hair tongs so I can curl my hair...' Helen grumped.

'And why is curled hair so important all of a sudden?' her dad asked

'Everyone has it... well, it's cheaper than a perm..' she tried. He wasn't buying that one.

'You have beautiful hair, Helen. You are beautiful as you are. Why try to change yourself?'

'It's for boys.' Her mum came into the room, spoiling things as she always did.

'It's not for boys,' Helen threw back, 'it's for me. For my self-confidence.'

'I hope you aren't the kind of person who has to style themselves with the herd in order to have self-esteem,' her dad said in his best not angry but disappointed voice. 'I thought we'd brought you up better than that.'

'It doesn't matter.' Helen just avoided slamming the door as she stamped up to her room to indulge in some teenage moping before getting sidetracked into a good book. She never had curly hair. Nor did she believe her dad's often repeated 'city hall' claim. Not then. She'd only bought that when she moved into the VCC home as a sixty year old, broken woman. By 2020 her own life experience had taught her that with ULTIMATE® you could try but you couldn't win. She had lived with that fact every day for the last ten years.

Today was her 70th birthday and Helen, with the face that in her youth may have launched a thousand ships, or at least turned a few youthful heads found herself crying for a world that no longer existed. A life that no longer existed, not just a life she could no longer have. It JUST DIDN'T EXIST. Memory was powerful but treacherous. And memory was not reality. Helen acknowledged that reality had been reinvented into ULTIMATE® reality, and knowledge and memories were the intellectual property of ULTIMATE®. Of course she had easy access to them at a reasonable price. And she was supposed to be grateful for that. Her only weak act of resistance was to keep her personal memories in her head, away from scrutiny. But this in itself made them worthless. She had nothing to share and no one to share them with and her private memories would die with her. What kind of reality was that? What meaning?

Helen had often measured herself up against nature and felt herself small. She remembered a sense of insignificance when, as a young woman, and then as a not so young woman, she'd stood on a deserted beach, or looked up at a night sky, or stood in the middle of a field or a forest, marvelling at the acres and acres of blue sky above her. Nature had been in charge then and even though only a fool would consider Nature benign, it gave you a sense of yourself in the world. Yes you were small, you were insignificant, but you were a part of something wonderful.

Yet ULTIMATE® had killed nature. Like history, it just didn't exist any more in any meaningful way. It was ULTIMATE® who had constructed and owned the lives of Nick's generation and all generations since. ULTIMATE® was the only wonder of the post-postmodern world.

Which left Helen as part of what was a dying generation with all the punch knocked out of them. It was proof that capitalism would get there in the end. Although ULTIMATE® had seen to it that concepts like capitalism and socialism no longer existed any more. In reality or in virtuality. 'You can't fight city hall, dad.'

Helen brushed her straight hair and decided she was just going to try and enjoy the company of the kids. Be sociable for once. What did they call it now? Live social networking?

It was worlds away from the last 70th birthday she'd attended. 1966. The family had made the trip to the Edinburgh New Town apartment of her Uncle Bert and Auntie Alice. It had been quite a trip for the family, across the newly opened Tay and Forth Road Bridges.

'Daddy, how do they stay up?' she'd asked. 'Is it magic?'

'No, Helen. Engineering,' had come his response.

'More cleverer than magic,' she'd opined.

'More clever,' her mum had corrected.

And at Uncle Bert's she'd been running up the flagstone pathway in her haste to greet them and tell them about the bridges. She tripped and fell and when she picked herself up, she saw them all laughing at her.

'It's not funny,' she said. And they laughed all the more.

'It's not fair,' she cried.

'Innate sense of justice that one,' said Uncle Bert. 'She'll make a great lawyer.'

Helen didn't know what a lawyer was but she was certain she didn't want to be one.

'I want to be an engineer,' she retorted and they all laughed even more.

'You'll have your hands full with that one,' Bert told her dad.

And she remembered the musty old-people smell and the wing backed chairs and floral patterned china and textiles and the cake on doilies and how Auntie Alice had pressed a threepenny bit into her hand as they were leaving and whispered, 'Buy yourself a sweetie.'

It was a long, long time ago. Helen wished she'd managed to get something better to offer the kids to eat than ULTIMATE® coke and ULTIMATE® cup cakes. But she'd left it too late and had to beg stuff from the kitchens. Somehow she'd forgotten you couldn't just pop out down to the supermarket any more. She had always hated the fussiness of floral pattern suites but she would have given anything for a room like Uncle Bert and Auntie Alice's in which to celebrate her 70th birthday.

Since she'd entered the ULTIMATE® Home, Helen had kept to herself. She mostly stayed in her room and avoided the shared spaces. Most people did, if they knew what was good for them. The lounge rooms were frequented only by those who had run out of memory credits and wanted to play ULTIMATE® BINGO to win some back, or who couldn't be bothered with the work that involved and just wanted to witter or rant an incessantly pointless steam of consciousness. There was no meaningful social interaction, she'd quickly learned that.

The residents of Victim Homes were little more than guinea pigs for the latest 'advances' in ULTIMATE® technology. Like everyone else in the system their data was the only precious thing about them. But their data was 'end of life' data, with only two ways out, madness or death. Helen preferred to keep herself to herself. And her memories private. While she still had them.

But today would be different. Today she'd share her

time and her life, for an hour or two, with her grandson and his friends. And they would have a nice time. It would be an experience which she could store in her own head, irrespective of what might make it into the Memory Bank.

In preparation for the party, Helen had moved the furniture around to try and gain most space, but whatever she did, even borrowing a utilitarian chair from Archie next door, didn't make the space seem big enough for four people. Not once the table she'd managed to acquire to put the food on was in place. Auntie Alice would be birling in her grave. Genteel Edinburgh New Town it was not, even though it had once been a five star hotel in a prime location.

Helen wished she could have got 'real' food. She still couldn't get used to the idea that ULTIMATE® food was in any way real. Oh yes, it was on the plate in front of you. It looked good, it tasted good (well, it tasted...) it even smelled good after a fashion – one gets used to anything after ten years but Helen's memory told her that it wasn't like the birthday food she had at her 10th birthday or her 21st birthday or even her 40th birthday. And on her 50th birthday, Nick had been born. Cakes and candles were for him from then on, though he didn't even remember that now. He didn't even know when his own birthday was. The Project Kids had no value for the personal. They were socially constructed beings in the ULTIMATE® world. Birthdays were part of a life before ULTIMATE® and the memories were not stored. She knew it wasn't possible, but she had hoped the date just might stir something in him. It hadn't.

'Come on mum, blow out the candles,' Torquil had shouted excitedly.

'Yes, quick, before the fire brigade come thinking the house is on fire,' Randall had added, jokingly as the bright glow from the forty candles the kids had painstakingly stuck on the birthday cake they'd made themselves stood on the table.

'Before the wax burns the cake,' Catriona added,

54

concerned that her first great culinary effort would be spoiled.

It had been a simple birthday cake, a bit lumpy and heavy, but it had been made and shared with love.

Helen laughed. A cake with seventy candles. What kind of fire risk would that be? She sighed at the memory of thirty years ago. The family she had loved and lost. The ULTIMATE® world had certainly changed her reality. In the past she'd had hope for the future. Now she had none. Not for herself and more importantly, not for Nick, her sole living relative. She understood that this was Nick's world but she felt it was as hopeless for him as for her. That didn't seem right. She didn't know him well, of course, but there did seem some form of connection. Maybe he was just flattering her, but she thought she saw something of the curiosity of her own youth reflected in him. It was that curiosity which got him overdrawn on his knowledge credits every month and that was what kept him coming back to her. She filled a gap. She knew he was using her, but she was happy because if you turned it another way, it meant she still had something to offer. Something to give. Something real. So maybe there was hope for Nick. Everyone else she cared for was dead.

Back in 2000 she'd blown out the 40 candles and made a wish. In 2030 she couldn't remember that wish. Even without a candle, surely at seventy years old she owed herself a birthday wish. Randall would have done something special if he'd been there. But he wasn't. And because he wasn't, nothing could ever be special in a world which had become less like living and more like existing and now seemed more like a living death than a life, virtual or real. She blew out an imaginary candle. Made a wish.

Her wish was, for one day, to live like she wasn't afraid, wasn't without hope, wasn't just an inconsequential statistic in the ULTIMATE® system. To be real. Just for a day.

E. HAPPY BIRTHDAY - RIP

Helen answered the knock on the door. Archie from next door stood outside, holding a square cardboard box.

'It's for you. Came to the wrong room.'

Archie was a man of few words. For one moment, just a short moment, Helen wondered if this was Archie's inept way of giving her a present but looking at him more closely she realized he was simply annoyed that he'd been disrupted from his Memory Bank. Helen and her birthday were nothing to him.

'Oh. Thanks. Sorry for the trouble.'

He shrugged.

'And I'll have your chair back by seven.'

Archie peered round the door, 'Not here yet?'

Helen shook her head.

'Young people.' Archie snorted and headed off back to his room, leaving Helen looking at the large, square cardboard box he had delivered. There was no sign of posting, no indication to where it had come from or what it was. She put it down on her table and was about to open it when there was another knock on the door.

'Happy birthday, Nan.'

It was Nick, along with Omo and Flora. Fulfilling their promise.

'It's so good to see you.' Helen found herself embracing all three of them. They all took it, though it was unclear which one of them was most embarrassed by the show of affection. It was clear, however, that Nick had primed his friends to indulge his Nan on this, her 70th birthday. He was still young enough to believe that seventy was quite an age, especially for someone in an ULTIMATE® Home who could not be expected to live much beyond seventy two. Statistically speaking. This was a significant event for all of them.

Nick cleared his throat. 'We didn't know what to get you, Nan.'

'That's okay. You didn't need to get me anything. You being here is enough.'

'Yeah, but a present. It's traditional, isn't it?'

'Tradition. I hope you haven't been wasting your credits finding out about tradition? No time for the past, eh?'

Nike shuffled awkwardly...

'Anyway. There is one thing you could give me. Well, do for me, if you know how.'

'What?'

Helen pointed at the US™. 'It's still playing up. I wondered...'

Omo butted in. 'I'm sorry, we really don't know how to fix this.. you need to get a technician.'

Helen laughed. 'Oh no. I wasn't wanting you to fix it. I was wondering if you knew how to..' she whispered, 'switch it off.'

There was a silence. Switch it off. Who switched off their US™? Could you do it? Why would you want to? It would be like turning off a part of yourself. Losing a fundamental part of your identity. Omo shuddered at the thought.

Nick laughed. 'Well... we could try.' He went up to the US™ screen... waved his hands around in front of it, fiddled around the side and touched a few things, seemingly at random. Nothing as exciting as a flash or bang happened, but the screen's images scrambled, pixelated and, well, you might say died. At any rate it went blank.

Omo and Flora stared, amazed.

'Is it off?' Helen mouthed.

'Why did you want it off?' Nick asked loudly, smiling. He waved his barcoded arm at the screen, but no response.

'Well, I'd say it's off.' Nick responded affably. 'If it's not robbing me of credits, that's good enough for me.'

'Thank you.' Helen beamed at her grandson. 'I was hoping it could be a day like the old days. A day without interference from ULTIMATE®. A real day. Just for once.'

Omo and Flora looked uncomfortable.

'Fair enough.' Nick was unfazed by her request. It was a small enough gift for his Nan. And after all, it hadn't cost him anything. At least nothing he knew about.

'It means, I hope it means, we can talk more… freely. And whatever questions,' she looked at Nick, 'you feel compelled to ask, I can answer without the inconvenience of you losing knowledge credits.'

Nike smiled at Helen. She was pretty cool, this old woman. He was glad he'd come. It might be fun after all. Certainly it was going to be different from the usual day spent doing 'productive' work as part of The PROJECT⌂. He knew that being a Project Kid was a privilege, but it didn't feel like it most of the time. Then again, he didn't have anything to compare it against. Not that he could remember.

'Thanks, Nan.'

They sat down. Awkwardly at first, the generations with nothing in common. And it was to break the ice that Nike asked the question, 'What's in the box, Nan?'

'Oh, I don't know. I'd forgotten about it.' Helen turned her attention to the box resplendent on the table.

'Is it a present?' Nick asked.

'I don't know. I suppose I should open it.' Helen gingerly did so.

The kids sat there, in awe. A real live birthday present. What could it be? They all gasped, even Helen, when she opened the package and saw what was inside. It was a birthday cake. A big, round birthday cake, with icing and writing on it.

'Oh my.' Helen was speechless.

'What is it?' Flora asked.

'It's a cake. A birthday cake. Traditional, isn't it, Nan?' Nike was proud he knew more than Flora. And he was impressed by the size of the cake.

'Is it an ULTIMATE® birthday cake?' Omo asked. He thought perhaps this was something ULTIMATE® did for their old folks. Young people didn't care about cakes, or birthdays or presents; they got all they needed and wanted in the normal course of interactions and 'productive' labour, but old people, they lived in a different time, it might be a nice gesture to do something to remind them of the old days...

'No.' Helen was stunned. 'It's real.'

'Real?' Nike rolled his eyes. What was it with his Nan and her bizarre understanding of the word real. Of course it was real. There is was, sitting in front of her. He looked more closely at it.

'Hey, Nan, there's writing on it.' He read it out, ' Helen. 70 R.I.P.' He paused, then couldn't help himself, 'what does it mean?'

'R.I.P?' Helen had tears in her eyes. 'It's a message Nick. A message from the past.'

'How can that be? Where did it come from, Nan?' Nike was confused. More confused than he usually was.

Nike was confused and Omo was feeling uncomfortable. Flora took charge of the situation. 'Tell us about it,' she said, 'we'd love to hear.'

Helen took a deep breath and began to tell. 'I don't know where it's come from. How could I? But the message makes me think it could be from your grandfather.'

'But he's dead, Nan.'

'I know he is. But R.I.P... I don't know who else..' Helen couldn't allow herself to believe that Randall might be alive, but she couldn't come up with any other rational explanation. She dismissed the thought. She was just being emotional. It was silly. She was a silly old woman, confusing the past and the present.

'What does R.I.P mean?' Nike asked, thankful that he'd managed to disable the US™ screen. Otherwise he'd have lost half his month's credits by now. This was too strange a situation not to ask questions.

'It used to mean Rest In Peace,' Helen laughed, 'Yes. It

would be something you put on a wreath when someone died.'

Omo squirmed. 'That's a bit sick. Sending you a cake telling you you've died.' Omo was unsettled and really puzzled. What could it be if it wasn't an ULTIMATE® cake? And if it was? There was a dark side to ULTIMATE® he knew that, even if people didn't like to talk about it.

'No, Omo. It's better than that. R.I.P is also the initials of... are you sure that screen's off Nick?'

Nike nodded.

'Would you check?'

Nike asked loudly, 'What does R.I.P stand for?' and waved his barcoded arm at the US™ screen. Nothing. Not even a flicker. He smiled at Helen.

'It stands for the Rural Interests Party,' she said.

The kids looked blank.

'What's that?' Nike of course. He couldn't help himself.

Helen didn't know where to begin. 'Let's cut the cake first, have a drink and I'll tell you.'

That sounded like a good idea. They cut the cake. Each took a large slice. It was incredible. They had never tasted anything like it before.

'That's what I mean by a real cake,' Helen said.

'How can it taste like that?' Flora was amazed.

'It's a type of cake called a Victoria sponge.' Helen replied. 'It's made with eggs, real eggs and butter, real butter and flour and I'm guessing sugar beet, cause I don't know how they would get cane sugar, and raspberries, real raspberries....'

'It certainly doesn't taste like any cake I've ever had,' Omo said, licking his lips.

'No. This is real food, made with real ingredients, not the synthetic stuff we usually eat,' Helen smiled, 'It's a real taste of the past for you all.'

They polished off the cake between them. And even the tea they politely drank to wash it down with tasted better. Helen looked at the empty plate, as Nike licked the last of the raspberry off the knife.

'No evidence left, that's handy,' Helen said. 'Now, I'll tell you about the R.I.P.'

They sat back, ready to listen. But not ready for what they were about to hear.

'Before ULTIMATE® came to power, during the economic collapse, there was a last ditch attempt to find another way, to hold onto the old ways. Rural people, who didn't want to lose their way of life, banded together. It started before that, with fuel protests and moved onto trade protests and...'

Helen noticed that the kids were looking blank. 'You have no idea what I'm talking about do you?'

They shook their heads.

'Doesn't matter, Nan. Just keep telling us.'

'Okay. Well, it used to be the case that people split into rural folk and urban people. And the urban people made money and consumed products and the rural people farmed animals and grew crops and lived with nature not with commerce. And even though agriculture became an industry and then was destroyed as an industry though BSE and Foot and Mouth and quotas and GM crops and finally ULTIMATE® creating the alternative to real food, by synthesizing everything, there were people who still wanted to live this real life. And they formed the Rural Interests Party, to try and protect their way of life.'

'It started off peacefully enough. We lived on farms or smallholdings, and just didn't buy into the consumer capitalist model. We tried to be self-sufficient and mind our own business and keep to ourselves, and for a while ULTIMATE® left us alone. But not for ever. I don't know what changed things. Maybe all the urban people couldn't let go of their dreams for a rural idyll and ULTIMATE® deemed that RIP made them uncomfortable and less compliant to the ULTIMATE® way of life. Maybe they just wanted the space we took up. It's possible ULTIMATE® never saw us as a threat but just wanted everyone to be their consumers. Whatever the reason, things changed about 2014 and the ULTIMATE® way became hard to resist. Before then we were kind of left alone. They might call us names, like hippies, or gypo's or something, but they didn't really bother us and we didn't bother them. Certainly by 2018 things turned ugly and people in RIP began to challenge the ULTIMATE® way of life.'

'How?' Nike couldn't imagine how you challenged ULTIMATE®.

'First it was just an outright rejection of citizenship. Peaceful marches, organised activities. But pretty quickly it turned to violence. I was never for that. I believed that if we just left them alone, they'd leave us alone and we'd get forgotten and things would be all right. Well, things would be pretty tough, because we had to take a big drop in our standard of living what with the new regime, but it was preferable to becoming part of the whole ULTIMATE® world. But that was when we thought there was a choice, an alternative. In 2016 RIP had split into two main factions, one which just dropped off the radar you might say, keeping their heads down and losing their rights, identities and profiles within the system and the other of which decided to confront ULTIMATE® head on, using their technology, tactics, and marketing. It was in danger of becoming a brand in its own right. But a brand that wasn't ULTIMATE® which by that time was more or less unheard of.'

'Your grandfather, Randall, didn't like the idea that RIP might get sucked into ULTIMATE® the way everything else seemed to. He'd got involved before your mum (she looked at Nike) left and took you to The PROJECT△. He'd tried to steer a middle path, but after…. well, between 2016 and 2018 he got involved in what they called terrorist activities, him and a few others, but really he was just trying to protect what was his. Protect me, and your parents and you and keep us safe, away from ULTIMATE®. But the problem is, when you challenge a system like that overtly, they come looking for you. And they did.'

'What did they do?' Nike asked.

'Well, they burned our farm and took away your grandfather and…' Helen paused, still unable to say it, 'and killed him. They sent back his watch with a message telling me that he was dead.

'And my dad?'

'Do you remember your dad?'

'I'm not sure. I think I might. I haven't thought about it in years.' Nothing in Nike's PROJECT△ life encouraged him to think about this past. He had no memories of it in his Memory Bank and his few questions were always blocked. But he had a sort of shadowy feeling, somewhere in his brain, that told him he might remember something, if he tried hard enough.

'There's time for that. Not now. I can tell you things about him Nick. But I don't want to get you in trouble. We'll have to be careful. For now, you need to know that your dad did not want you to go to The PROJECT△. He and your mum split up over it.'

She took a deep breath, trying to keep the raw emotion sparked off by the memories under control.

'Your dad went off looking for your grandad, but when he came back, he assured me that grandad was dead.'

'Killed by ULTIMATE®?' Omo couldn't believe it. ULTIMATE® had saved the world, not killed innocent people who just happened to disagree with them. If Nick's grandad was killed by ULTIMATE® he must have done something pretty wrong. But Omo realized that now was not the time to voice this opinion. Best keep his mouth shut and see what happened next.

Helen continued, 'Yes, by ULTIMATE®. I know it's hard for you to understand now, even more than ten years on, because they don't broadcast it around any more but the ULTIMATE® death squads were real and very, very efficient. And they still exist.'

That was scary. And probably not true. Omo couldn't

believe it. Helen was old, probably going senile and certainly telling him things he didn't want to hear. Without any sort of proof. Now he understood why she'd wanted the US™ screen off. The US™ screen wouldn't corroborate anything she was saying. He was sure about that. He might even ask some questions later, on his own, just to be sure.

'And what happened to my dad?' Nike wouldn't let it go.

Chip off the old block there. No wonder he was always in trouble, Omo thought. He looked at his flatmate with new eyes. He didn't want the trouble to spread his way, and he was beginning to think this was inevitable. How did you go about changing your living accommodation? Pryce would know, if he ever dared to ask him.

'Well, after your mum left, taking you to The PROJECT⌂ he was gone for months looking for your grandad, and when he came back he tried to get the farm working again, but it was hard and his heart was no longer in it. I helped where I could, and we struggled on for a couple of years but then in 2020 he disappeared too. They told me he'd drowned himself. That's when I checked myself into an ULTIMATE® home. My life was over. There was no hope. I'd lost my husband, my children, my grandson… what was there to fight for any more? I'm not proud of it, but I was ill and frightened and… I couldn't see a way to carry on. I gave in. I know it.'

'I think you did the sensible thing.' Flora hadn't spoken in a while, but she had that girl's knack of trying to make sure that everyone felt comfortable. Omo was relieved. He knew someone should speak but he didn't know what to say.   Nike looked stunned. He was still trying to compute the information.

'Well, I did what I did, and I've been rotting here for the last ten years. And then, today…' Helen pointed at the empty cake box. 'This. A sign.'

'But what's it a sign of?' Nike was bursting to know.

'I don't know. Maybe you will help me find out?'

'How? How can I find out?'

'I really think we should be going,' Omo finally spoke. He knew this was getting out of hand. He knew Pryce wouldn't like this. Come to think of it, he didn't know if Pryce had even sanctioned this visit. They could be in big trouble already and they were certainly going to be in bigger trouble if they hung around here any longer. He just knew that. And however much he liked Nike, this was out of his league. Omo just wanted a quiet life.

'Yes, yes of course you must go. You don't want to waste your time here with an old lady's memories,' Helen smiled. 'It was good of you to come. It's certainly been a... memorable birthday.'

The kids got ready to go. It felt like a balloon had been deflated. Not that they knew what balloons were. No one needed balloons these days. No parties, no balloons. But they had a sick feeling in their stomachs that couldn't be explained by the rich, real cake. A feeling like something good had turned very sour, and a lack of understanding why it had happened. The feeling might be described as fear. It was an emotion that ULTIMATE® was trying to breed out of the Project Kids. Like all emotions. What did they need emotion for? Emotion wouldn't make them more 'productive' after all.

Omo made sure that he avoided a repeat of that embarrassing embrace by scooting out the door as quickly as he could. Flora submitted to a peck on the cheek from Helen but followed him as fast as was polite. Nike hung back.

Helen held onto him. Kissed him. And somehow, he wasn't embarrassed. She also put something into his pocket as she whispered to him,

'Come back. On your own. I want to talk to you about this. I think this could mean your grandfather is alive. I need your help. Please.'

Looking back on it, as they sat in their common room later, Nike couldn't believe what had happened that afternoon.

None of it seemed plausible or real by any definition of the word he could comprehend. But he put his hand in his pocket and felt the watch Helen had put in there. His grandfather's watch. He didn't dare take it out while Omo and Flora were in the room but he was going to look at it as soon as he was on his own. And he was going to go back to his Nan to find out the truth. That brought him up short. The truth. What was truth? What was real? What was his Nan about to get him into?

TRUTH: Definition. The quality of or state of being true. What is accepted as true is what is in accordance with fact or reality.

Nike realized that these definitions were all just part of ULTIMATE®'s way of getting more 'productive' work out of you. Using up more of your credits going round and round in circles. Defining and re-defining things in terms of each other ad infinitum. Pointless. Meaningless, as Flora kept telling him.

Helen sat alone after the kids had gone trying to make sense of what had happened too. Things hadn't turned out the way she'd expected, anticipated or planned. The cake had brought a random element into proceedings. With ULTIMATE®, life was predictable, and today had certainly not been predictable. She thought about the cake itself. It was surely a sign. A message proving that somewhere, somehow, someone from RIP was still active and still remembered her. Wanted her to know that. Wanted something from her? But what? She didn't dare to hope that Randall could be alive, but someone, somewhere had something to tell her. And this was the first contact. She'd have to be very careful though. She had no idea what she was getting into. Or what she was about to get Nick into. But the boy had a right to know. Surely. About his family. About the other life. The world that ULTIMATE® had tried to kill. The world his mother had sold him out of. You might say she was giving her child a chance of a better future, but the way Helen saw it, her daughter in law had sold her grandson, to a live experiment. And that was wrong. Helen didn't know how she would give Nick the information that far from giving him up to The PROJECT△ to ensure he lived a better more privileged life, Lauren had sold him for a fix of drugs. But she knew one day she would have to. The memory was every bit as shocking as the original event.

They were at home one day late in 2016. Torquil was desperate but not as desperate as the gaunt Lauren who needed her next fix.

'You can't take him,' Torquil pleaded, knowing that Lauren could and would do whatever she wanted. She always had. 'Dad, stop her.'

'I've got legal rights,' Lauren spat. 'He's my son. He deserves to live a proper life, not the weirdo alternative life you people are subjecting him to.'

There was a standoff in the sitting room. The young Nick became more and more distressed as he was tugged between his parents, his grandparents shocked but unable to intervene.

Lauren held her son fiercely. 'I've got ULTIMATE® on my side,' she said, showing Randall the contract she'd signed.

'It should have been signed by us both,' Torquil said.

His father showed him the contract. With his name on it.

'I never signed it.' Torquil was blazing. 'I would never…'

'If you don't let me take him, I'll make sure that ULTIMATE® know all about you and….' The threat was unspecific but it was enough. There was nothing reasonable people could do in this unbelievably unreasonable situation. Clearly Lauren would stop at nothing.

'Help me, dad,' Torquil begged.

'We have to let him go,' Randall replied, stern and

shocked.

And within minutes Lauren, and a confused Nick, were gone.

That was when the cracks really began to show. The first time Randall couldn't save his family from ULTIMATE®. The first time a son realised his father wasn't invincible. The first time Helen thought her father might be right that you can't fight city hall.

Helen was woken by a knocking on her door. It was a somewhat irate Archie, looking for his chair. It was seven thirty and she'd promised he'd have it back by seven. Not that he needed it for anything, but it was his property and she should have returned it.

All evidence of the cake was gone. Archie noticed the blank screen, however.

'I'll report that to the wardens,' he said.' You don't want to be without a functioning screen.'

Little did he know how much Helen wanted, no craved, being without a functioning US™ screen. How much she wished she was back at the farm, away from the ULTIMATE® prison they called a home. Free. In reality. Not just as a concept. Day by day, to see the sun, feel the wind and rain against your skin free. Not as a memory. As today. Every day. The cake proved that somewhere, somehow, there were people experiencing this. Who ever made the cake must have chickens, cows, a plough for the wheat field. Seeds and fertilizer, and maybe a dog…. It wasn't just a dream. Someone was still living this life. And they knew where Helen was. And they cared that she knew.

F. PRODUCTIVE WORK

It was back to normality. Omo, Flora and Nike sat in their rooms doing 'productive' work. Some more 'productive' than others of course. Omo was good at 'productive' work. He didn't like questions and didn't really care about answers so he was great at the daily tasks required by 'productive' work. His credit score rolled upwards. In contrast for Nike it was a constant battle to stop himself losing all the credits he'd just worked for by asking yet another expensive question.

Whereas Omo accepted he was part of The PROJECT△ and never queried either his own place in the system or The PROJECT△ itself, Nike would find himself in the middle of a batch of 'productive' work, thinking out loud, 'So what is The PROJECT△ anyway?'

Which would start the knowledge bank credits rolling on the US™ screen

THE PROJECT△: Definition. A social and scientific experiment with a generation.

And he'd just wasted another 10 credits for no real information. Nike just knew it was a deliberate ULTIMATE® policy, designed to get as much 'productive' work out of everyone as possible. Whereas in a similar situation Omo would just accept and Flora would shrug her shoulders and look for another way of regaining credits, Nike preferred to look for a way to shortcut the system. Omo and Flora didn't think, as Nike did, that questions could have a meaning. To them, the meaning was part of the system. You just played your part, did your 'productive' work and enjoyed the process. Because the more 'productive' work you did, the more ULTIMATE® would tailor the kind of work you did to your interests. That was your reward. Soon enough you didn't feel like you were doing work at all. It was one long round of virtual consumption, offering more than enough to keep you happy for hour after hour.

But the rationale didn't work for Nike because he refused to fit into the patterns. He was marked down as a system anomaly. Project Kids were essentially the guinea pigs of the ULTIMATE® consumer testing system. It was the biggest ethnographic study ever. The most comprehensive social engineering experiment since The Final Solution. Twentieth century consumer based computer survey systems were as nothing to this new ULTIMATE® way of achieving disclosure from citizens. And The PROJECT△ was the experimental forefront, the shop window for a whole new kind of citizen. It was creating people who lived only to produce and consume virtual knowledge, virtual memories, virtual relationships. They had become cost effective slaves who happily consumed their slavery and thought it the cutting edge in post democratic freedom. The promise was of everything tailored to the individual. Meanwhile the individual was tailored to the ULTIMATE® template of citizenship. Result? Perfect. All-embracing. Terrifying. And unnoticed.

For the participants, it seemed to be a really simple, really good deal. Project Kids were given a home and everything they needed to maintain a high living standard in the ULTIMATE® world. In exchange, their 'productive' work in the ULTIMATE® economy was open to constant analysis and scrutiny. The price they paid meant they got the best of everything, were first in the queue for new virtual experiences and were generally shielded and protected from the outside world.

In the outside world it could be a lot harder to spend your life in the pursuit of virtual consumption – you had to do a lot more work for a lot less reward. Most ordinary people still had to pay their way at least partially through some practical, real-time work. And in a world where the best was perceived as ULTIMATE® virtuality, people didn't want to be condemned to a daily diet of reality. As ever, people wanted the latest, the best, the ULTIMATE®. The PROJECT△ was this desire made manifest. And currently only for the privileged few. Project Kids were told *Just do your tailored 'productive' work and everything will be well.* Okay to be in The PROJECT△ you had to give up your past and your family but you were getting the ULTIMATE® present and were a significant part of the ULTIMATE® future. Life didn't get better than that, surely?

It was enough and more than enough for most Project Kids but not for Nike. He still felt unsettled by something he couldn't quite put his finger on. And so he asked questions. About things he shouldn't. In a world where History no longer had a meaning, Nike couldn't help himself asking 'historical' based questions. And while ULTIMATE® prided itself on tailoring 'productive' work schedules to specific interests, you couldn't stay focussed on history all the time.   History was an ULTIMATE® no go area.

While Nike was coded a high-risk participant, in fact he was of great value to the ULTIMATE® system because his data tested the system algorithms to their capacity. Inevitably he was on a high priority counselling list which meant that his social counsellors were meant to monitor him much more closely than your average Kid. Which they did. So in point of fact Nike was more controlled than most Project Kids. Of course he didn't know that. He thought he was playing the system and the system knew it was playing him. It was not a long term sustainable situation. It was like a very complex game of chess. For example Nike would artlessly ask questions such as, 'When did The PROJECT△ start?' and elicit the standard ULTIMATE® response,

THE PROJECT: History. The PROJECT△ started in 2016 though the seeds of its existence were developed in History through the many consumer based surveys and networks of the early new millennium. In 2016 ULTIMATE® technology through the 3 generation development of the US™ screen system

brought about the possibility of setting up the virtual environment of THE PROJECT△ in a physical form for a selected number of the chosen generation.

What the standard ULTIMATE® response didn't say about The PROJECT△ was that the selection process was rigorous in some very unusual ways. Ways which involved economic transaction. Project Kids thought they were special, chosen, but with no idea how they had been chosen.

ULTIMATE® took a pro-active stance as well, seeking out the 'right' kind of kids and buying them from parents who were struggling in a post recession era. The same parents were often using the newly legalized ULTIMATE® drug HABIT∞ to excess. It was the designer drug to end all highs and in the mid 20's it put parents into the kind of debt that made refusal no option.

The early 21st century obsession with celebrity soon spiralled out of control as a generation who wanted to be 'celebrities' were offered the virtual opportunity through their offspring just by signing them up to The PROJECT△. Usually Project Kids were either the product of parental obsession with the celebrity culture or they were sold to feed their parents drugs habit. They were victims of the twin desires for money and fame. Not so unusual. Not so special.

Nike could keep asking questions till he was blue in the face, or ran out of credits on this 'productive' credit line, and he would never find the little nuggets of information that really gave the meaning to the subject. He could find out that,

THE PROJECT prides itself on the quality of its accommodation.

As an explanation of the Project House he lived in. Project Houses were modelled on the best student accommodation possible in the Universities they had replaced. Nike's own accommodation had indeed been student accommodation at the now defunct University of Edinburgh. The information he'd worked to receive did not explain why this method of living was adopted. There was no explanation of why University had become a virtual consumer camp. It was the sort of question no-one, not even Nike, thought to ask. Everyone was kept so busy with all the meaningless questions they lost the will or the skill to ask questions with meaning. This represented one of ULTIMATE®'s better tactical advances. The whole relationship between questions and answers had changed since Einstein said 'the important thing is never to stop questioning' and Levi-Strauss proposed that 'the wise man doesn't give the right answers, he poses the right questions.' (That's Levi-Strauss the French anthropologist not the manufacturer of the branded jeans.) ULTIMATE® had invested a lot of time and money in question and answer theory. And Project Kids were the testing ground for making sure that the population would only ask the right kind of questions to receive the ULTIMATE® answers. For example: ULTIMATE® had a vested interest that the question 'Why do we have barcodes?' would be rendered into a meaningless definition and 'historical' explanation suitable to the 'productive' work schedule appropriate to Nike's developmental plan and, for the cost of some 30 credits, give the answer

BARCODES: Definition. Primitive versions were developed in history as a machine-readable code in the form of a pattern of stripes printed on and identifying a commodity. ULTIMATE® developed this technology and utilized a form of tattooing to implant the coding into the body, thus making the interactive process between consumer and computer one-step and constantly available. ULTIMATE® barcodes are a fundamental tool in the US™ system, allowing what used to be a primitive wi-fi capacity dependent on hardware, to become fully personally integrated.

Nike got answers from his questions, but no substance. Although he might have thought he knew the 'history' of the ßß™ (body barcode), he didn't know the meaning. And he certainly didn't understand that it was the meaning that mattered. He lived with the practicality, accepting it as normal. In the ULTIMATE® world Project Kids were amongst the first to have the barcodes technology embedded into their wrists. In 2020 ßß™'s were generally considered a progression of the body art tattoo fashion which in 2014 had seen all the best Brands find ways to encode themselves onto your body in a physical manifestation of personal consumer choice. By 2015, going into a shop such as Marks and Spencer was easy when you waved your M&S barcoded arm at the security guard, who smiled and offered you a discount. You didn't need money because the M&S symbol was scanned and immediately withdrew the money from your bank account. The days of real money were numbered. The days of reality were numbered.

ULTIMATE® changed the shopping experience too. Real shops were highly inefficient. Real products were expensive. A transition period saw all shops become more like Argos warehouses and pretty quickly the requirement to actually go into a shop and buy a real product became redundant as people could do all their virtual shopping for virtual product online. The basics were still produced of course, but when food became ULTIMATE® food and clothing became ULTIMATE® clothing and all brands became ULTIMATE® brands, retail 'therapy' changed in a fundamental way. Virtual retail therapy was born and flourished.

The ULTIMATE® ßß™, worn by the likes of Nike, while effectively a sophisticated interface device, also acted as a tracker. So as long as there was a US™ somewhere in the vicinity, you could tell where the Project Kid was. By 2030 the system had not been rolled out universally, but it was coming. And there was a time when people worried about carrying identity cards!

Project Kids had what might have been considered in the twentieth century the life of a permanent teenager. They spent all day every day playing online games or engaging in chat rooms, forums, online surveys and the like. Day in, day out they lived their virtual lives under ULTIMATE® scrutiny effectively functioning as guinea pigs for all the best and newest technology that ULTIMATE® had to offer. It was part of ULTIMATE®'s motivational algorithm. They were the geese who would lay the golden egg. But they were battery farmed geese, kept in a gilded cage, creations of a system it was no longer possible to question or challenge in a meaningful way. To ask, 'why did The PROJECT⌂ come into being?' would elicit the answer, at a price of 20 credits that:

The PROJECT⌂ is ULTIMATE®'s way of changing the world for the better.

After spending 20 credits of your hard earned 'productive' work on that, is it any surprise that Nike didn't pursue with the question 'Better for whom?' It would be better for ULTIMATE® that's for sure. Nike was resiliently inquisitive, though lacking direction and focus. On a whim, when he tried to find out what ULTIMATE® actually was, he would lose credits for a whole hour's 'productive' work for the answer:

ULTIMATE®'s mission statement is that social advance and scientific development go hand in hand.

When foolish enough to ask 'What is a corporation?' he got the standard response:

CORPORATION, OR COMPANY: DEFINITION. A group of people authorized to act as an individual and recognized in law as an entity, especially in business.

The question that should have been asked might be: 'Correction. What is the point of a corporation?' This was the kind of question the US™ avoided answering. Fortunately, before arriving at that potential scenario, Nike normally gave up on his questioning and went playing *Intergalactic enemy warfare* to raise more credits. The system won again.

Questioning a system has rarely ever been considered appropriate behaviour for members of that system. ULTIMATE® was no different and when Nike did it his actions were flagged up for Pryce to take special notice of. Which he did, usually. But just sometimes, Pryce didn't take the kind of action he was supposed to in these circumstances. Because however much Pryce found Nike a pain in the ass, he also had a sneaking respect for his questions. Sometimes he even thought about using his higher level access to get answers with more depth. Not necessarily more meaning, but more depth. His rationale was that maybe he could impress Nike if he did so. He imagined the day when he might see a flicker of admiration come at him out of Nike's eyes, instead of what he thought he saw. It seemed like pity or disdain but might just have been adolescent apathy.

Somewhat inevitably, the questions Nike started asking after his trip to his Nan's wirelessly transferred themselves to Pryce's system and flagged up 'a referral'. The consequence was that Pryce had a situation to sort out. Again. Sometimes Pryce thought Nike just asked these questions to get him to come running. It felt like Nike was pulling his strings. He didn't like the feeling. He thought about not going. But with Graham on his back, he thought it best to avoid any further potential problems. He didn't need another dressing down this week. So Pryce trudged to The PROJECT⌂ House where Nike, Omo and Flora lived. On the short walk, he tried to develop an optimistic viewpoint, reflecting that at least he now had a purpose to his day's work. The optimism didn't last the distance of the walk however and Pryce returned to his prior conviction that it was just Nike jerking him around again after all. He had to stop deluding himself that Nike was giving out a cry for help, or call for comradeship. It was not a request for guidance, it was just Nike being Nike.

Pryce's relationship with Nike was complex. He didn't see himself as a father figure, after all families had been abolished but he nonetheless felt a special bond. Pryce often looked at Nike and wondered how similar he had been at the same age. Pryce had been obsessed with the twists and turns of the psychological "thriller" genre whereas Nike played ULTIMATE® versions of such games obsessively on the US™.

Yet Nike took psychological gaming to a whole new level. Sometimes it seemed to Pryce as if the boundaries were blurred. Pryce wondered whether life was all a game to Nike and his generation? And then he questioned whether he'd had any more of a grip on the distinction between fantasy and reality at that age. Or any age. Despite all the differences, in more subtle ways their concerns were quite similar. If Pryce and Nike had realised how much they had in common they would have been surprised.

Pryce had his own set of keys to The Project House. It was part of the deal that he could come and go as he liked. Privacy was not an ULTIMATE® concept. The kids were all in their rooms, as they should be, engaged in 'productive' work. Their existence was essentially virtual, contained in their own ULTIMATE® space. They didn't have a scheduled meeting with Pryce due so they were not expecting an interruption. Not wanting to disturb Omo and Flora, Pryce went straight to Nike's room. He did pause to knock on the door first. Even though it wasn't in the handbook, Pryce was old fashioned enough to think you should have some respect for personal space.

'Damn.' Nike's response to Pryce's entry.

'Sorry?'

Nike turned round. 'Oh, it's just that I was about at level 24 and you put me off...' Nike grinned.

'No hard feelings?'

'No, but you could bump me twenty credits for the inconvenience.'

Silence.

'This isn't a scheduled meeting is it?' Nike asked, finally wondering why Pryce was there.

'No. But we need to reassess your 'productive' schedule in the light of the topic areas you're asking about, because, as you say, you're running low on credits. Again.'

Nike just grinned some more. 'Can't help asking questions,' he said. 'Is there a problem with that? I thought that's what the task was. Ask questions?'

As ever, Pryce intended to follow the standard question format when he started his 'productive' interview with Nike. But as ever, it didn't work out that way. Within seconds he had the uncomfortably familiar feeling that Nike was bending the interview his way. And it was taking Pryce all his energy to keep on track. Pryce took a deep breath, determined to stay in control.

'So what is this line of questioning you're following, about?'

'What do you mean?'

'The questions about The PROJECT△ and ULTIMATE®? Why are you asking these questions?'

'Because I want to know.'

'But what do you want to know. And why? '

'Why not?'

Pryce paused. Nike was just playing with him now. Probably just bored because he was low on credits and couldn't interface with the US™ properly any more without doing some 'productive' work. And it seemed Nike was allergic to 'productive' work. He was a pain in the butt. Pryce shrugged away the small feeling of regret which suggested that if he had more knowledge himself, if he could have given Nike an impressive answer, he would raise himself in status and Nike would start to see him as someone to respect. As ever, he was confused by his feelings when he tried to analyse them. Maybe it wasn't regret. Maybe he didn't want to form a meaningful relationship with Nike, maybe he just wanted, for once, to beat him at the game.

'Ah, it's just because you think you shouldn't? Just to be awkward. Do you have to be awkward? You are in a privileged position here, isn't that enough for you?'

Like so many adults before him who wanted but didn't know how to gain respect from young people, Pryce resorted to a tactic that came across as patronising. And was not going to work.

'How do I know it's privileged?' Nike grunted.

Pryce wasn't falling into that trap. He readjusted his position. He tried friendly, but again it came across as patronising. He really wasn't good at this. He wished he was.

'Look Nike, I'm here to help you. But we need to understand what your interests are in order to tailor your 'productive' work schedule into something fun for you and useful for us.'

Nike rolled his eyes. Same old same old. Except, for an instant he caught sight of an off guard Pryce. What he read in Pryce's face at that moment was a man desperately trying to connect. Nike didn't know how to interpret this and for a fleeting instant he thought that maybe Pryce found it all as much rubbish as he did. Was it possible Pryce might not be the enemy? Could they actually have something in common? But Nike didn't have enough experience or understanding of empathy to create his own answers for these silent questions. He reverted to type. It's a game. He's the enemy. I have to win.

'But Pryce, the problem is, I don't know what I really want to know till I start asking questions, and then I never seem to get far enough along the questioning before I run out of credits....'

He saw a flicker of something beneath the counsellor

calm. It could have been understanding. It could have been fear.

'I think I get you,' Pryce responded. It was just playing for time.

'So what can we do about it?' Nike demanded. Never one to sit back once he had the slightest advantage. And he read the situation as one where he could take the advantage if he was smart enough. So he did.

'Uh...' Pryce had lost his way.

'Maybe if we went through a session together,' Nike suggested, 'so you can see my problem.'

Pryce thought about this. Sounded harmless enough. He was still trying to work out how Nike had changed the situation on him. He was supposed to be in control. He was the one who should make the suggestions. He gave up.

'Okay. Shoot. Pick a topic.'

Nike hummed and haah'ed over the options on his US™ screen.

'See, I might ask... what's the point of a corporation?'

Pryce intervened before the question was logged.

'No, you need to be more specific. What is the point isn't a good question type.'

'Why not?'

'Uh... because it's a few levels in and you need to start general and work towards specific.'

'Oh. Okay. Can you show me?'

'Yes. You are in the Functional section of your 'productive' schedule so you need to be asking about the existence and working of things, not their point or purpose. And you need to remember that you are asking Historical questions. Which you should avoid.'

'Why?' Nike smiled. He knew full well why.

Pryce was not going to be drawn on that one. He carried on, 'For example, if you want to know what a corporation does, you might ask, 'Give me the definition of a corporation.'

Nike's US™ obliged.

CORPORATION, OR COMPANY: Definition.   A group of people authorized to act as an individual and recognized in law as an entity, especially in business.

'I hope that's on your credits,' Nike observed. Because I've already asked that question and I don't know where to go with the answer.

'Yes, these are all on my credits, for training purposes,' Pryce reassured him.

'Okay, then can I ask why?'

'Why what?'

'Why would you make a group of people able to act like an individual?'

'I think that's too deep.. you won't have the credits to get there in one step and you'll have to go through a lot of steps to get to the answer. It would be better to ask – what was the historic function of a corporation?' Pryce forgot until it was too late he'd just told Nike to avoid questions on History.

CORPORATION: Historic Function. To act in the best interests of its shareholders. Specifically in maximizing profit.

'You see,' Pryce pointed out, keen to steer away from History again. 'Now you can get more specific. You can find out about shareholders or about profit.'

Pryce thought he'd delivered a clear, simple explanation of how to use questioning theory to achieve a result. Without any real purposive aspect to the question. As it stood, Pryce had forgotten and Nike had never known what more or less every late twentieth century person took for granted; that the point of a corporation or limited company is simply to get bigger, richer, more all-encompassing. To make a mint for its shareholders. It was one of those 'factoids' of life that had become obsolete in the ULTIMATE® era. If either Pryce or Nike had thought it important they might have asked who the shareholders of ULTIMATE® actually are. After all, there's got to be someone behind the company. Someone living exceptionally well off the profits. But it wasn't a question either of them thought interesting enough to ask. And that showed the success with which ULTIMATE® operated.

Pryce had been well trained in the structure of question formation and he was passing on that knowledge to the wayward Nike. But the meaning behind the questions was of no benefit to ULTIMATE® and therefore training would not be offered in asking questions to obtain personal meaning. And Pryce's next question was really asked in order to reaffirm his role as mentor, an attempt to gain some respect from the young man who could usually run rings round him. It wasn't a question calculated to derive meaning.

'What is profit?' Pryce asked. The US™ screen obliged once more.

PROFIT: Definition. An advantage or benefit. In History financial gain: an excess of returns over outlay. The bedrock of the failed capitalist society.

'Uh, so what?' Nike asked. He was bored. Pryce didn't know when to quit.

Oblivious to Nike's boredom, Pryce was absorbed in the questions as much as in the session. Despite himself he found the analytic forms of questioning fascinating. Pitting himself against a system to gain information gave him a kick. ULTIMATE® had seen that in him all along. Maybe he was better suited to pure theory after all. But surely, surely he could get Nike interested in this too? He just had to get the boy enthused about the way you questioned. Adopt a meta-level approach. Nike had the intelligence after all, he just lacked the application. And a good mentor…. Pryce broke from the reverie and asked the next question, carried away on his own inner thoughts.

'What does the phrase profit motive mean?' Pryce continued.

Nike didn't have enough time to frown, realizing that his session was being hijacked, before the answer came.

IN HISTORY the profit motive became seriously compromised from the year 2010 and over the following ten years ULTIMATE® social research and development put a lot of work into finding a way to rebrand the concept. Economists were tasked with finding alternatives to the money economy. A whole new version of monetary policy developed and after the Global Recession, following the collapse of not just capitalism but history, profit was down-graded to the definition of an historical concept. Effectively, in the ULTIMATE® system, profit no longer has any valid meaning.

This was a nice, smart answer. And Pryce didn't believe it for a moment. Nike, well, he wasn't really interested. But he had to look for a way back into the game. A way to divert Pryce. Put him back in second place. So he asked, 'What is monetary policy?'

Pryce cancelled the question. 'Now that,' he said, 'is another example of the way you just ask questions without really thinking through what information you want to receive.'

Nike shrugged. 'It's a functional question isn't it?'

Pryce ignored this. It was just Nike being cute.

'Just what do you want to get a definition of monetary policy for?' Pryce asked.

'Because I don't know what it is,' Nike answered.

'It's nothing,' Pryce responded. 'Nothing any more, because it was part of the failed historical economic system and it won't give you any more useful knowledge to know the definition. Believe me.'

For one moment, Pryce understood the gulf between

his generation and Nike's. What had been his life was now History and History didn't exist. So a huge part of his identity had been lost. What was all a game to Nike had once been a huge part of Pryce's reality; the part he'd made his life's decisions on. All the definitions in the ULTIMATE® world couldn't show Nike the truth that Pryce had witnessed first hand regarding the shift in monetary policy.

Following the collapse of the banks and the bankrupting of many of the western economies, people became wise to the fact that governments had supported the discredited financial institutions with their hard earned money. People became angry that public debt had spiralled and that they were forced to pay time and again for the greed and mismanagement of the banking system. Even if Pryce told Nike this, it would be a story, a fiction, not something of value or relevance to his life. It was an irrelevance in the ULTIMATE® world of 2030. The greatest reality for a previous generation had become obsolete in the face of ULTIMATE®'s social transformation.

Pryce still remembered it. In 2010, people were just glad to be heading out of a recession. They could just about accept that 'austerity' measures would have to be put in place. That we would all have to suffer in the new style of government. The myth held for a while. But by 2015 when ordinary people realised just how much and what they were being expected to pay back for a party that only the banks seemed to have been invited to, they got very, very angry and this anger threatened democracy and freedom and rule of law. Of course Pryce remembered. It had been his life. However, in 2030, if people knew what was good for them, they had long stopped thinking about these failed systems and instead they worked within the ULTIMATE® system, towards a brighter future. Ruminating on a lost past was not the way to happiness. Pryce was tasked with teaching Nike that the past did not provide answers which would give him a 'productive' life as part of The PROJECT△. Pryce checked himself and proceeded with caution.

'I think it would be better if we could find another kind of topic for you to work on, Nike, and get you away from history for a while. I'm sure part of your frustration with it is that it's essentially just pointless... let's find something you are really interested in and work from there.'

Pryce realised he'd overstepped the mark in his futile attempt to gain Nike's respect. And that he was possibly projecting his own desires onto Nike. Poor psychology. Poor counselling skills. He needed to accept that their worlds were fundamentally different because their generations were worlds apart. In the battle for reality, Pryce's "real" world had lost out to ULTIMATE®S "virtual" alternative. And that was Nike's world. Pryce had to work with Nike in the ULTIMATE® world, not try and impress him with knowledge of a world that no longer existed. He reflected as to whether maybe it was his fault that Nike had become obsessed with History. It was certainly up to him to rectify the fault.

Nike shrugged and grunted in affirmation.

'Whatever.'

'Okay. We'll sort it out at the next scheduled meeting,' Pryce agreed. 'Till then, why don't you try and get to level 30 of your gaming. INTERGALACTIC ENEMY WARFARE isn't it?'

Nike pulled a face.

'Credits?'

'Oh of course... I'll put a hundred gaming credits on your account. That should see you through till our meeting.'

'Thanks'

'And Nike'

'Yeah?'

'Use it for gaming NOT for asking questions.... '

'Sure thing.'

G. WHAT DON'T YOU KNOW?

Pryce returned to his office thinking he'd done a good job. But his satisfaction was short-lived. No sooner did he sit down with his ULTIMATE® cappuccino than Graham was on the US™, larger than life and twice as ugly, demanding a personal interface. In other words, get up and come over to my bigger, plusher office and get a dressing down. Pryce sighed, picked up his drink, and went.

The theme of the meeting was IRREGULARITIES. Pryce could really live without this. Remember the party Pryce said the kids could go to? No problem? Well, seems there was a problem. Graham found one. Graham was excellent at finding problems where seemingly none exist. And Pryce was hauled over the coals. The conversation went something like this.

'Where were your Project Kids yesterday afternoon?'

'Doing 'productive' work, I expect.' Pryce attempted an offish tone. It was a mistake.

'You expect?' Graham had a definite sneer to his voice, 'you expect but you don't know?'

'I don't keep track on them every minute of every day.'

There was a prolonged silence. It was a classic Graham tactic. Pryce held on as long as he could. Clearly Graham wasn't going to break the silence and clearly the silence had to be broken. Eventually Pryce cracked. As usual.

'I could check back over the logs.'

A sigh. A look. A terse response.

'You do that.'

Back in his own office Pryce hated the way Graham made him feel. And he felt even worse when he went back through the records and found a gap. Damn. Why did this always happen? He was doing his best. Why was everyone so damned difficult to work with?

He had limited time for recriminations because he had to work out what the error was and correct it if he wasn't to have Graham at him for the rest of the week. The gap was while the kids were in Helen's room and had managed to disable the US™ screen, so there was no wireless access, and effectively no accounting for a period of about an hour. Pryce of course, didn't know about the US™. And had forgotten all about the party. They'd never followed it up after all with a travel voucher request. So with nothing else to go on and with Graham peering over his virtual shoulder he made a wild guess and reported back.

'There must have been a malfunction.'

Graham smiled. A sneering smile.

'But you didn't pick it up.'

Pryce was smart enough to know when Graham was going in for the kill. Nothing to do but take the hit.

'My office. Now.'

On his way there, Pryce reflected that Graham could easily have dealt with this over the US™. Another personal interface was unnecessary. Graham just wanted to intimidate him and this was better done face to face. He needed to come up with some better answer but he had only moments to wrack his brains as how it could have happened, and he wasn't ready for Graham to side-swipe him the moment he stepped into the room.

'Does a birthday party ring any bells?'

All too loudly. Pryce remembered he'd forgotten either to log this or clear this or do whatever he should have done with this. But did it really matter? An old woman's birthday party. For goodness sake. Hardly a crime, albeit an unusual event.

'Yes. They asked to visit Nike's grandmother. She's in a VCC home. I didn't see what would be the harm.' Confession seemed to be the only option. Pryce tried to underplay it, though he knew he'd just handed Graham a free hit.

And harm there was aplenty. Graham had a weapon to add to his armoury. Not only had Pryce neglected to fill in the requisite forms but now the kids had been off system and no one knew what they were doing. Graham would enjoy this for a long time to come.

So, before his ULTIMATE® coffee was cold, Pryce was back to The Project House to fill in the missing pieces. Interrogation was never his preferred method of communication, but he had to get answers which would get Graham off his back. However he did it. Method was less important than result at this point. He realized of course, that having allowed the kids to go, he was not in a strong position. He sighed as he entered the Project House. He was annoyed with the kids, mostly with Nike. All he had done was to try to help him and it turned out, again, that Nike made him look a fool. He couldn't face Nike first so he knocked quietly on Omo's door and on getting no response, opened the door. Omo was lost in his US™ screen. He jumped when Pryce tapped him on the shoulder. Good old Omo, a 'productive' worker. A model of ULTIMATE® technological dreams.

'Can you come to the common room please?' Pryce asked.

Omo nodded, gesturing to his screen, 'Just let me finish this question and I'll be right with you,' he beamed. A young man happy in his work. Good to see.

Pryce next went to Flora's room. She was also busy, online debating the relative merits of some product or other. Her fingers flew across the virtual keyboard.

'Hi Pryce.' She greeted him with a smile in her voice.

'Common room, when you get a minute please.'

'Sure. Be right with you. I'll be finished this review in a couple of minutes.' She flashed him a real smile. It almost brightened his day. Almost.

Nike was last. Pryce pulled himself together and re-focussed. He had to retain control. Not lose his temper. He was a counsellor, not a father. Still, he knew Nike was behind this. And he knew Nike would resent being pulled up twice in one day. He'd have to play it carefully.

'Hey, Nike?'

Nike spun round, closing down screens right left and centre. Never a good sign.

'Yeah. Pryce. What's up?'

'How's your game going?'

'Uh, yeah. It's... well.. you know... '

'Keeping in credit?'

Nike shrugged his shoulders. 'So..so. Uh.. surely it's not time for a scheduled meeting yet?'

'We need an extra meeting, Nike. I've called the others into the common room.'

Nike jumped up. 'Sure, I'm right with you, man.' He answered, with the attitude of a look-out who was attempting a casual whistle.

Pryce tried to keep his temper. Nike's smile annoyed him as much as Flora's pleased him. He knew he was too emotionally involved with both of them. He should ask for a transfer. He wouldn't give Graham the satisfaction. However annoying Nike was, Pryce wouldn't give in. Not yet and not without a fight.

The kids sat on the sofa and Pryce sat opposite. It was clear a telling off was coming and there was no way to cover it up. Not even with ULTIMATE® coffee and cookies on offer. No way was this just a casual call.

'So.' Pryce began, feeling out of his depth. He needed to regain equilibrium. Emotion didn't work with this generation. They just didn't "get it". It had been effectively programmed out of them. But it hadn't been programmed out of him. His tone was terse, whether they picked up on it or not.

'Where were you yesterday afternoon?'

The kids looked at each other. Omo to Nike, Flora to Nike, Nike to.... Pryce. The looks clearly said: 'You tell him, Nike, you got us into this.'

'At my Nan's, remember, you said we could,' Nike

replied.

Omo looked carefully at Pryce's response. He was increasingly sure that Nike hadn't even asked Pryce and he was expecting a lot of trouble.

'Yes, I remember.'

Omo breathed a sigh of relief. So what was the tension about then?

'Is there a problem?' Nike gave Pryce his most winning smile, hoping it would work, though he didn't know why he needed it.

'I just wanted to know how it went.'

Pryce wasn't giving much away. The boys knew that wasn't a good sign. Flora was still thinking about her product review, wondering if she could do one on this cookie. It was light and tasty and the chocolately bits were... but it wasn't a patch on that cake from yesterday. Nike decided to play Pryce at his own game. Test the water. Give nothing away.

'Nothing really. Just some talking and...'

'We had a cake,' Flora added.

That wasn't good. Too much information in the current climate. Nike and Omo looked at each other again and then shot Flora a combined look that told her to keep it buttoned. Flora didn't get it. Pryce did.

'A cake?'

There was no way out.

'Yeah. Someone sent her a birthday cake. As a present. You know old people.' Nike tried to underplay it.

'And how was it?' Pryce wasn't interested in the cake, except that they seemed not to want to talk to him about it and that made it interesting.

'The cake?' Nike effected surprise, 'or the party?'

'Both. Either. I did tell you I would want a full report on the visit.' Pryce banked on Nike not having been paying any more attention than he himself had been to the initial conversation.

He was right. Of course Nike hadn't listened to anything other than being told he could go to his Nan's. So he couldn't call Pryce on that one. But he did feel something, maybe the slightest sense of suspicion. Nike wasn't good at working out what his emotions were. He had them, and he knew he shouldn't, but he certainly couldn't make sense of them. Maybe he should try a line of questioning that would explain emotions to him. Maybe he should get out of this trouble before he plunged himself into more. Pryce would hit the roof if he suggested EMOTIONS as a 'productive' topic. It might be worth it just to see the response. Nike realised he wasn't paying attention.

'I'm waiting.' Pryce was really working hard to hold it together now. He was fed up offering carrots to Nike. It was time for a dose of a big stick. But what sanctions did he really have? He was still trying to work this out when Omo couldn't take the silent stand-off any more. It wasn't an emotional response. It was pragmatism. He had nothing to hide. Pryce wanted information. Give him information. Then he would go away and leave them to get back to 'productive' work. Which was much more interesting than this current situation. After all, he'd only gone along to Nike's Nan's to be polite. A quick resolution would be in everyone's best interests and if Nike wasn't going to offer a report, he might as well.

'I think she's probably losing her mental faculties,' Omo ventured. 'She was seventy and I think she won't last that much longer, really. She was old, rambling. It wasn't a lot of fun.'

He hoped this might be enough. He was being as helpful as he could. But Nike couldn't stop himself. He couldn't have Omo saying things about his Nan that were patently untrue.

'She is not losing her mind. She's totally with it. She knows more interesting things than you, or you (he waved at Pryce) or that thing (the US™).'

That would be the proverbial cat right amongst the pigeons now, Omo thought. Nike really couldn't just leave well alone could he?

'What sort of things?' Pryce was digging.

'I don't know. Just things. About the past.'

'We've talked about the context in which you study the past Nike.'

'You've told me it's all a waste of time.'

'Not exactly. I just suggested that where the knowledge bank doesn't answer all your questions, you need to reappraise the question value and type.' Normally Pryce would have thought about how such a criticism sounded, but today, right now, he just didn't care. Nike was due a telling off and if it was in front of his peers, maybe that would be enough to get the message through.

'Of course the knowledge bank can't answer all my questions. I want to know about my past. My Nan was there. She knows. She was in History.' Nike wasn't going to back down.

'You know that personal past is not a topic we can consider valid. As a PROJECT△ participant ULTIMATE® requires that you focus on the future and on purposeful questioning,' was Pryce's inevitable reply.

This was as far as Pryce was prepared to go. He had shown his displeasure. Nike should take a telling. There was a brief but awkward silence. He thought he'd got the message through.

'But what is purposeful?' Nike challenged him. The boy just didn't know when to give up. Pryce was not getting led down that blind alley.

'We've already agreed that you are finding History too frustrating as a subject topic. As a priority we need to adapt your production schedule for the next month. If you won't take responsibility for choosing a topic, I am authorized to do it for you, but I'd like you to have some say in the matter. It's your 'productive' time after all.' Pryce was being accommodating. Nike didn't see it that way. There was always a catch.

Flora didn't like conflict and she could see it brewing, so

she diverted the conversation and saved the day.

'I'm interested in animals, Pryce. In species extinction. Can we find something for me to do on that? Something to do with product testing. That would be a 'productive' topic wouldn't it?'

'Yes, I think it would. What's sparked your interest in that?' Pryce was back on familiar ground. This was the way he was used to interacting as a social counsellor. He continued, 'I'll check the change with my boss and make sure it's okay. If so, we'll upgrade in two hours. Have a lunch break till then.'

'I'd rather finish off the work I'm on just now. It'll only take an hour or so.' She flashed him a smile.

That was what Pryce liked to see. A kid so keen on her 'productive work' that she'd choose it over the option of free time. That was the way things were meant to be. He turned to Omo.

'Do you want to change your 'productive' task for the next month?'

'No thanks, Pryce. I'm fine with what I've got.'

There was a pause. Omo didn't like pauses. They were another thing that made him feel uncomfortable.

'So, just you Nike. Pick a topic.'

Nike didn't want to pick a topic. He wanted to be able to ask whatever questions he liked and to get proper answers. Like his Nan gave him. But he knew when to pull his horns in. He wasn't going to win on this one. Not right now.

'Uh, social trends in gaming techniques? Is that the sort of thing…?' Nike said the first thing that came into his head. It wasn't the time to suggest EMOTION as a topic. He'd save that for later when Pryce was less pumped up.

'That'll do nicely.' Pryce felt he was making progress at last. Nike was coming back in line.

'So is that it? Can we go back to work?' Omo was keen to get back to his 'productive' work. He hated all this social interaction stuff. He was happier with virtual interaction, like a good ULTIMATE® citizen should be.

But it was not that easy. Pryce couldn't afford to be half-hearted in this investigation. He picked up the loose thread, 'Well, I'd like to hear a bit more about the party.'

'Have you ever been to a party?' Nike tried to turn the tables. You could usually divert Pryce that way.

'Not for years. And depends how you define party.'

Pryce waved his arm at the screen. He had won. He could afford to be beneficent. Maybe all Nike had needed were some boundaries. To know that Pryce had a limit beyond which he wouldn't be pushed. Flora's smile and Omo's compliance gave Pryce the confidence that he could win over Nike too. He just had to play him right. It was time to give, to be a role model, to re-establish friendship.

'Have this one on me,' he said to Nike.

'What's a party?' Nike asked.

PARTY: DEFINITION. In History, a social gathering of invited guests. A group of people united in a cause – for example a political party.

'Why does it always do that?' Nike asked Pryce.

'Do what?'

'Give you nothing. Only give you enough that you have to ask other questions.'

Pryce thought.. ahh, that's the beauty of the system. But realized it was not a beauty to Nike and so replied, 'To keep you interested.'

'To keep you working.' Nike snorted.

Omo could see the way this was going. He just wanted to get back to his own work. He didn't want to be in the middle of something between Pryce and Nike that he didn't understand and didn't find interesting.

'What else do you want to know? We went to Nike's Nan's. It was a social gathering. We were invited. We were guests. We had that horrible tea and that weird cake and..' Omo was filling in gaps as fast as he could. If he'd known the party was going to cause this much aggravation he wouldn't have gone. Trust Nike to get them all into trouble.

'Ah yes,' Pryce picked back up on that, 'the cake. Tell me about the cake.'

'You're worse than the US™,' Nike grumbled. 'It was a cake. A birthday cake.'

'And what made it a birthday cake?' Pryce asked.

'It was a cake. And it was for her birthday.' Come on, Nike thought. This is stupid.

'Did it have candles?'

What did Pryce know about the cake? What did Pryce know about birthday cakes in general? What did Pryce know?

'I don't know what you mean.' Nike asked the US™. 'What's a birthday cake?'

BIRTHDAY CAKE: Definition. In History people used to celebrate the day of their birth by having a cake decorated with greetings and with candles on top. One candle for each year of their birth. They used to light the candles and sing a song (for the song cross reference Happy Birthday) If they blew them all out at the same time, they could make a wish. They believed that the wish would come true. FOR MORE INFORMATION ON WISHES YOU NEED TO SPEND ANOTHER 5 CREDITS. TO HEAR THE SONG 'HAPPY BIRTHDAY' WILL COST YOU 10 CREDITS. TO SEARCH YOUR MEMORY BANK FOR BIRTHDAY WILL COST 30 CREDITS.'

'No thanks.' Nike replied.

Omo was now determined to get this over and done with. To give Pryce what he wanted to know. If only he could work that out. 'There weren't any candles on it,' he stated.

'How would you fit seventy candles on a cake?' Nike laughed.

'There was just writing on it.' Before he knew it, Omo had gone too far. Given away too much. Made it interesting.

'What did it say?' Pryce felt he was onto something.

'Uh, happy birthday Helen.' Nike looked at Omo, willing him to agree.' That was it, wasn't it?'

Omo nodded. He didn't know why, he had nothing to hide, but he did feel that mentioning the RIP inscription would get them into some very sticky waters and he had really had enough of all this to last a lifetime. Best let it go.

'Where did the cake come from?'

Nike was able to be totally honest on this one. 'No idea. A friend I suppose. If we'd have thought, we could have taken her an ULTIMATE® cake for a present.'

'But we didn't think,' Flora said.

'It wasn't an ULTIMATE® cake?'

Flora had blown the gaff.

'No way. It was a real cake. It was delicious. Made with real ingredients.'

There was another very long, very uncomfortable pause.

'That's what she said,' Nike added, 'But I think maybe Omo's right, her mind was wandering on that one a bit. I mean, how could it not be an ULTIMATE® cake?'

He turned to Pryce. 'We played along with her. She's old. And a bit lonely I think. She was thinking about the old days and we thought it was best just to humour her. Isn't that what you should do with old people?'

Pryce knew there was more to this than met the eye. But he also realized he was beginning to lose ground. Or maybe they were using the cake as a diversionary tactic. He needed to get back to the main issue. The fact that they'd been out of contact. That wasn't acceptable. No one lower than Graham's level could really justify being out of contact. The Project Kids didn't have a privacy option on their ßß™ implants. So how had it happened?

'We lost contact with you while you were there. How did that happen?'

The kids looked at each other. They knew this was potentially serious. They had had the importance of total access drummed into them since they first entered The PROJECT⌂. It was one of the central tenets on their contract. It was a non-negotiable. This was a problem.

Omo decided to deal with it. 'Her US™ screen just died. That's all. I told her to get a technician. We didn't think it would matter because you knew where we were and we weren't doing anything, and we were only there for an hour at the most...'

Omo's nervousness almost convinced Pryce that this was the reason for their shifty behaviour regarding the whole event. Almost. But he was learning to question everything these days. Otherwise he'd be answering to Graham without all the information to back him up.

'How did that happen?'

'I don't know. It was just playing up. Flickering on and off...' Omo ventured.

'I don't think she likes it very much.' Flora added her penny's worth.

'What do you mean?' Pryce probed.

'No, she's just confused by it. She was sorting out memories and I think she overloaded it.' Nike came to the rescue. And added quickly, 'What was it like before US™?'

He was priding himself on his diversion when, inevitably, the US™ kicked into action.

BEFORE THE INVENTION OF THE US™: You have a range of options.

FOR 10 CREDITS THE HISTORY OF THE US™. FOR 20 CREDITS INFORMATION ABOUT THE DECADES LEADING TO THE INVENTION OF THE US™. 10 CREDITS PER DECADE AND SPECIAL HISTORICAL CREDIT CLEARANCE AUTHORISATION. FOR 40 CREDITS INFORMATION ABOUT THE ALTERNATIVES TO THE US™

Nike couldn't stop himself. 'What is the US™?'

The others shook their heads. No wonder Nike was always out of credits. Asking stupid questions when he already knew the answer. The reply came immediately, stripping him of credits.

The US™ was first marketed in 2020 and has reached its 3rd effective generation. It is ULTIMATE®'s most successful lifestyle product to date, bringing a whole new dimension to social interaction and truly fulfilling the original marketing slogan 'There is no more Us and Them, only US™.

'Nike. That can wait,' Pryce interjected. 'This is a group meeting. It's inappropriate to ask 'productive' questions in such a context.'

'So what can YOU tell us, Pryce?'

'You want me to tell you about the US™?'

'It'll save me a good sixty credits, which I don't have. And since we are talking about the malfunction of one, I thought it would be contextually appropriate to know something more about them.'

That was Game On as far as Nike was concerned. It was Pryce's job to help them hone their questioning skills and general knowledge.

'What I do know is that they are very reliable,' Pryce said tetchily, 'and so I can't understand how it is that the one at your Nan's conveniently broke down just when we needed to...'

'What did you need us for anyway?' Nike wasn't stupid enough to use the word 'spy.' It's a word he wasn't supposed to know the meaning of but he'd checked that one out quite some time ago on the knowledge bank (in the context of the History of gaming... so he thought he was covered... but not enough to just throw it into conversation.) Nike found it exhausting trying to remember the things he knew and wasn't supposed to, or didn't know and was supposed to. It just got worse and worse. No wonder Omo was always happy. His life was simple. He played by the rules. ULTIMATE® rules.

Even though memory was not considered necessary or skilful, Nike could remember the definition as given. It had struck him as important somehow.

SPY: DEFINITION. In History, a person who secretly collects and reports information on the activities, movements etc of an enemy, competitor etc. This word has fallen into disuse in our contemporary world, because the arrival of ULTIMATE® and the new economic order means there has been total transparency in dealings and therefore no need to use this concept.

Funny, thought Nike, because if you thought about Pryce's relationship to them, despite being called a counsellor, it seemed a lot like the definition of a spy. Apart from the enemy/competitor element. He wondered if you could spy on a friend. Not that he would consider Pryce a friend.

FRIEND: Definition. A person with whom one enjoys mutual affection and regard (exclusive of sexual or family bonds) A sympathiser, helper or patron.

Nike broke from his musing and as he came back to the present, he realised that Pryce was talking and he wasn't listening. Pryce just thought it was Nike being Nike. Dumb. Adolescent. His tone hardened.

'Did you report the malfunction of the US™?'

'No, we told her to. She wanted me to fix it.' Omo bent the truth just a little bit. He had a preservation instinct if nothing else.

'And has she done so?' Pryce had given up on Nike and

this question was clearly directed at Omo.

'How would we know?' Nike butted in.

'Poor old woman,' Flora added, 'her memories are all stored in the Memory Bank and it's not working properly. No wonder she's confused. How can she access her memories? It must be awful for her.' She smiled at Pryce. He liked it when she smiled. She had a nice smile.

'Can you make sure she gets it fixed as soon as possible?' she continued.

'Yes,' Pryce replied. 'I intend to.'

'And what did you want us for anyway?' Nike asked. He was getting more and more suspicious by the minute.

'Oh, just to arrange this feedback meeting,' Pryce replied. He saw Nike's subtle double-take on that one. That's one up on you sunshine, he thought. At last. He pressed home his advantage.

'Okay. Thanks guys. That's all for now. We just needed to understand why we couldn't get in touch with you. Make sure you don't go off access again eh? Just gives me a headache I don't need.'

'Sure. Sorry Pryce.' Nike felt like he'd won, so he could afford the smile.

'Yes. Sorry. It won't happen again.' Omo was a bit more conciliatory.

'It was nice to see you, anyway,' Flora said. Was she flirting with him? Pryce couldn't handle that. And couldn't get the idea out of his head. No, she couldn't be. Young people didn't do that these days. He'd ignore it. He ignored it. Almost.

He left. Rather too swiftly, and with rather too much of a flush on his face. Flora was twenty years younger than him after all, and very pretty. Too pretty. He'd need to watch that. Either she was flirting with him, which was dangerous; or he was projecting an action on her, which was equally dangerous. And distracting at a time he needed no more distractions.

As Pryce left The Project House he wondered what he

would be able to write in his report. What of this did Graham actually want to know? Certainly the facts. The kids had been at Nike's Nan's for an hour. The US™ screen had been playing up and broken down. They'd had tea to drink and cake to eat and been confused by the ramblings of an old woman who was trying to remember things without the help of her Memory Bank. That would do surely? That would be enough for Graham.

Right at that moment Pryce was more interested in what was going down with Flora. She shouldn't be flirting. She couldn't have had access to the kind of information which would have taught her the etiquette, the skills or even the existence of flirting as a method of social interaction. He'd need to go back into her logs. Was she inappropriately interested in him – or was he inappropriately interested in her? He shouldn't be thinking about this at all, he reasoned. And if he had any kind of a wife…. maybe he'd better leave it for now. He had enough trouble brewing with Nike.

Turning his thoughts to Nike, Pryce mused on whether the interaction with his Nan might explain why Nike was getting so interested in History. And whether the relationship should be stopped? It seemed harsh. He needed to think about it before he made a judgment call or alerted Graham. Not many Project Kids had any kind of contact with relatives. It wasn't encouraged. But maybe he could put a case in for Nike to be used statistically and analytically to see what effect such a relationship could have.

Pryce decided that the basis of his report would be that Nike had a predilection for trouble and his inbuilt solution would be that if they monitored the 'troublesome' relationship, it might give them some clues as to how best to handle him. Give them an insight into how to change things for the future. He also thought that if he could give Nike some positive feedback for a change, Nike might respect him more, even thank him. It might turn a troublesome kid into a worthy participant. And winning Nike round as a 'productive'

ULTIMATE® citizen would be a feather in his cap.

Pryce found himself thinking about his own grandparents. How he'd loved them and how he missed them now they were both dead. He tried once again to ignore the clear signs that he was getting too emotionally involved in the current situation, something he should report to his line manager. It only hardened his resolve not to be too hasty in severing Nike's ties from his only living relative whatever The PROJECT△ dictates said. For now, he'd wrap things up and get back to the office. Set up new production schedules for the kids and lodge his report. Get back on track.

Pryce was smart enough to realise he needed to get back on the ball. What he didn't realize was how many balls he was juggling at any one time. He had no idea how Graham was playing him. Because Graham didn't really care about the missing hour. He was more interested in diverting Pryce, in knowing where Pryce was at any one time. Graham and Angela met while Pryce was out chasing wild geese. They liked it that way. And they saw no reason for things to change.

H. ULTIMATE BIG BROTHER

Helen was enjoying her US™ screen being broken. She had never bought into the *'There's no us and them, only US™'* hype. Helen's relationship with the ULTIMATE® world was strictly us and them. The silent interface allowed her space and time to think without intrusion. A chance to let her mind wander and her memories run free for once. She understood that she would be considered odd by most people for even thinking that the US™ screen was an intrusion. After all, it was generally considered essential to modern life. It was the best thing since... well, the best thing ever. And yet Helen couldn't think so. It's not that she was against technology per se. Once upon a time Helen had relished every new technological advance. In her day she had also been right in 'the mix.' It felt like a lifetime ago. Another person, another life. Another story in another world. It was 1984.

You couldn't get away from it, 1984 was a seminal year. Not just for Helen, but perhaps especially for Helen. It was the year she'd read Orwell's novel for the first time. The book changed her life. It was still the time before Big Brother moved beyond cliché, into reality game show and then became part of History itself. Over the years one might say Big Brother became synonymous with visual rather than literate culture. One might say synonymous with an illiterate culture. The dumbing down of the message before it faded into obscurity with the onset of ULTIMATE® who had no need or desire for the population to ponder the meaning of Orwell's classic creation.

Back in 1984 itself, unsurprisingly, there was great interest as to how accurate Orwell's predictions had been. There was a lot of debate but few sensible conclusions. It was hard to avoid the debate. Helen, who had read very little since she'd graduated two years previously, was reading the novel on a tube journey on her way to a job interview. The London Underground was normally an intensely private public space, but this day..

'What do you think of it?'

She looked up to see a slender young man, standing over her, strap-hanging and pointing at the cover of her second hand Penguin classic copy of *Nineteen-Eighty Four*. She didn't know what to reply.

'Uh..I'm.. I've only...'

'It's very relevant, don't you think?'

'Yes.' It seemed the easiest way to get him to go away. But he wouldn't. He was determined to talk literature. Or politics. Or something. Although Helen was out of her comfort zone, he was difficult to ignore. He was handsome, with piercing blue eyes and a soft Scottish accent. He had a guitar slung over his back. He was clearly not your average commuter. She decided to take a chance and continue the conversation. She didn't really have much choice. He was determined to converse with her.

'Of course 1984 is an arbitrary date Eric Blair created by altering figures. It was finished in 1948 you know,' he added.

'No. I didn't,' she replied, hoping she didn't sound stupid. As the train pulled out of Leicester Square station she stood up, 'Uh, the next stop's mine,' she said, hoping she didn't sound rude.

He wasn't to be shaken off that easily.

'Me too,' he replied and smiled. What a smile.

They went up the escalator together and out into the hazy sunshine and urban clatter. He was talking all the way.

'I think its universality is part of its appeal. I mean, you can read almost anything into it.'

'Yes. I suppose so.' Helen replied, wondering what she should read into this man.

'It's been appropriate in every decade since it was written. In different ways... sorry..' he shepherded her to the inside as she was jostled on the overcrowded pavement. 'London,' he grimaced, 'the rat race.'

108

'Yes.' She realised she was not really contributing to this conversation but she didn't know what to do or say.

'I mean, some people say it's a diatribe against communism and others fascism, but if you think about it they're pretty much the same thing. The opposite ends of the spectrum come together to form a vicious circle. D'you think?' he was looking for something.

Helen was looking for the address for her interview. He noticed she was a bit pre-occupied and tried another tack.

'Are you lost?'

'No. Yes. I'm on my way to an interview. It's a hundred and something but.. the numbers...'

'Ah yes, even numbers are the other side,' he smiled. 'You take your life in your hands if you cross this street away from the lights,' he said.

They were quite far away from the last set of lights. He looked at the interview letter she clutched in her hand. She'd been using it as a bookmark.

'It's right over there. And you're a bit tight on time. Come on, let's risk it.' Without giving her time to argue he grabbed her by the arm and helped her skip through the heavy, hooting traffic until they stood, breathless at the other side.

'Here you are. Safely delivered to the jaws of the capitalist monster.' That smile again. She didn't know what to make of him. He was unlike anyone she'd ever met before but in a good way, she thought.

'Thanks.' She could only hope she was more articulate than this in the ensuing interview or she'd be stuck in Bracknell for ever and a day.

'Can I take you for a coffee... after?' He was persistent.

'I don't know how long I'll be,' she stated, hoping she didn't sound like she was putting him off. 'You must have other things to do...' better things to do, she thought, wondering if she did want to go for a coffee with him.

'I'll wait,' he replied.

At seventy, Helen wasn't sure if she was suffering from memory lapses due to age, or if it became inevitable over that much of a life that one's personal narrative became rewritten; like films that you swore had one storyline and then when you watched them again you found out that things happened in a different pattern. But while she barely remembered the interview which was to change her working life, she remembered clearly the excitement welling up inside her as she left the building and looked out on the street for the mystery man. And the disappointment when he wasn't there. That was a memory which had stuck with her for over forty years. It was a part of her life.

The Memory Bank had done away with the inconvenience of memory lapses. All you had to do was pay your credits and put your trust in the US™ system, that it would record and store your memories accurately, and you could revisit them at will. But Helen didn't have that faith. Never had. She had been tutored in the many meanings of *Nineteen Eighty-Four* until she knew the original Big Brother well enough to believe it could exist in infinite variations. It changed as the world changed. Yet it stayed terrifyingly the same. In the early 21st century people purported that it was really global capitalism Orwell was predicting and railing against. Helen knew that more than that, in its text you could see every scientific and technological advance debunked and described in a negative sense. You could read it as a prediction of the rise of the post-capitalist world of ULTIMATE® (though you'd have to be stupid to air that view out loud.) And every way you read it you would be right. That was the beauty of the work. That was the danger of the work. No one read *Nineteen Eighty-Four* in the ULTIMATE® world. They couldn't. It didn't exist in the system any more. Not in an accessible form.

The world had been different in 1984. And Helen had been a different person. She'd given up being a lab rat of the

M4 corridor, living in suburbia in Newbury and working in Bracknell for HP, exchanging it for a regular stint on the Northern Line from Balham to Tottenham Court Road. Every day for the first month she wondered if she would meet that guy with the blue eyes and guitar again on the train. She didn't. London was dirty and busy and in her desperation for something different she thought it was exciting. But it was worlds away from home.

1982. A sunny morning in July, in suburban Dundee. Helen was waiting for the post. Sitting at the bottom of the stairs, knowing her future would be determined by the marks on the paper in the envelope that would drop through it sometime before 8.30am. It dropped.

'Mum, dad, it's here,' she called out.

'Bring it into the kitchen,' dad replied. He'd stayed off work for this special day. The day his only daughter got her degree results. He'd done the same the day she got her Highers. Exams were important.

Helen had grown up in Dundee, an only child in a comfortable middle class family. Her mother was a teacher and her father a lecturer. The one thing Helen knew from an early age was that she didn't want to work in education. Not even with the long holidays taken into consideration. But as she was growing up, in her comfortable world, she had no idea what she did want to do or be. She did well at school – not surprisingly. She passed all her exams with A's and played hockey and netball for the school teams. She played the violin and did Scottish country dancing. She was quite the product The High School of Dundee wanted to turn out at the end of the day. She just missed out on being dux, but made up for it by getting into St Andrews to study Classics. She was academic but an all-rounder and unremarkable in every way. She was expected to get a 1st class degree.

The envelope remained unopened. They all looked at it.

'I'll open it if you can't,' her mother offered. Typical. Everything was always about her.

Helen took the envelope and ripped it open. This was her life, her future. She was not going to allow her mother to hijack this. She read it and burst into tears.

'It's okay,' dad said. 'Whatever it is…. It's okay…'

'It's a first, dad,' she said through the tears.

'Why are you crying?' her mother asked, unable to understand that tears could be for anything other than failure.

Her dad understood. She was on her journey. Of course a first class degree in a subject that had no obvious practical application didn't necessarily mean anything. But it was an external validation Helen had never taken for granted. Now there were other envelopes to open. From prospective employers. The one that arrived the same day as the exam results was from IBM. Helen had taken advice from the careers centre that a degree in classics would represent skills transferable to the computer industry. She'd never seen it herself, but in 1982 even graduate jobs weren't that easy to come by. Thatcher was on the rise and people had to get on their bikes. Helen thought the interview had gone well with IBM. She had convinced them, and almost herself, that she wanted a career there. She was even prepared to move to the West of Scotland for it. And here was their response. She opened it.

'Well?' Mum was desperate to know.

Helen scanned the letter down to the words… sorry to inform you…. Unsuccessful on this occasion… high quality of applicants……

'No.' She stated baldly with a shake of her head. She didn't cry again.

'Their loss,' dad said as he bit into his toast.

'How could they? Are you sure…?' her mum wrested the piece of paper from her, incensed that her daughter should have been rejected.

112

Helen winked at her dad, 'Can't fight City Hall, eh dad?'

He nodded sagely. 'Plenty more jobs in the fishpond Helen,' he replied 'and with a first you could still apply for a doctorate…'

That, Helen knew was her dad's preferred choice of career for her. But she did not want to end up a classics professor in any university, good or bad. Classics was a long dead world and she wanted to live.

A week later, she turned down the job offer from Mars. Her mum wasn't pleased.

'I don't want to go schlepping Mars Bars round places, mum,' Helen pointed out.

'It's a graduate trainee programme,' her mum replied tersely. 'You might not get a better offer.'

'I'm not selling chocolate for a living,' Helen replied and that was that. However much her mum tried to persuade her that management trainee experience was all the same no matter the industry, Helen failed to buckle. What did her mum know? She was a teacher for goodness sake. She had no experience of the real world. Dad was on her side. Mainly because he thought in a year's time she'd be happily ensconced in an academic career. They were both wrong. In August another brown envelope dropped through the door. From Hewlett Packard. The nemesis of IBM. Helen took only a second to think about it. She was off to Bracknell.

Bracknell had been quite an eye opener. Not in a good way. In Thatcher's Britain you went where the work was and the work was in Bracknell, Britain's rather second class version of silicon valley. It was a long bike ride to the Graduate trainee programme. Despite the story her careers advisors came up with, which she had churned out at interviews, about how Classics gave one a good grounding in pure language which would be useful for programming computers, Helen was not recruited for computer programming. The job was in marketing.

It was boring. From day one. Not as boring as programming though. She stuck it out for two years. Till 1984. The young man with the blue eyes and guitar must have been a good omen, she thought as she opened the envelope which told her she'd got the job and was going to work for Apple Computers in Tottenham Court Road. She wished she could tell him she got the job. She wondered why he hadn't waited.

Looking back, the 1980's were interesting times. Beneath the boredom. A revolution in computing was taking place in the form of the advent of the personal computer. Helen laughed as she remembered the limitations of the early computers and of how the advent of the Macintosh in 1984 had seemed like a truly revolutionary experience. She had bought into it bigstyle. And yet, what did these computers do? It was pitiful really. Graphics? Basic. Colour screens – you're joking. Music? No way. Networking? You're dreaming. If you looked back to computing in 1984 it was amazing to imagine that in less than fifty years the ULTIMATE® US™ would actually control virtually (and virtually control) all aspects of human existence. Incredible. Yet that was the harnessed power of exponential growth.

Helen had immediately handed in her notice at HP (her parents thought she was crazy giving up a good job, a good pay packet and a company car) to pursue a new venture in computer retailing (her parents called it becoming a sales assistant!) It was the first really not sensible thing that Helen had ever done in her life. The first risk she had taken. Apart from crossing the road with a strange man and hoping he'd be there to go for a coffee with her after the interview.

So, in 1984 Helen moved from the ticky tacky box world of the suburbs of Newbury to a room in a shared flat in South London without a backward glance. And travelled every day on the Northern Line. The job was selling Apple Macintosh product. More specifically, the Macintosh personal computer which

114

launched on January 24th 1984 and sold over 50,000 units in less than 100 days. It was a success story. Helen was employed to demonstrate its tremendous potential to prospective customers, of whom there were many. She was selling Steve Jobs baby. And Apple was going to change the world. Apple was going to set people free. Apple was going to unleash the creativity of the individual. Apple was going to kick IBM's ass.

Helen had to admit, even all these years on, that she could still clearly remember the sense of joy she got from buying into IBM's competitor. It had really rankled, being turned down by IBM. It was her first rejection and the first time she realized she was capable of holding a grudge. Selling Macintoshes seemed like exacting a personal revenge. But it didn't make her as much money as working at Hewlett Packard. Helen hadn't quite come to terms with the idea that money wasn't the only real measure of success in life. The euphoria of revenge quickly palled against the pay cut and the day to day reality of life as a commuter in London was far from exciting. But there were other compensations.

A slow afternoon a couple of months later and Helen was playing with the Apple in the showroom.

'Still on for that coffee?'

She looked up to see a familiar pair of blue eyes. He was still toting his guitar bag over his shoulder. She knew she should play it cool, pretend she couldn't remember him... but her heart was already racing, her face already flushing.

'I'm working,' she whispered.

'You got the job then?' he replied.

'Yes.'

'Despite me nearly killing you on the way over the road?' he laughed.

'Yes.' She smiled back at him. It was as if they were old friends. And yet, they'd spent what, ten minutes together two months ago. What was wrong with her? She wanted to ask him why he hadn't waited but before she got the chance,

'What time do you get off?' he asked.

'Five thirty,' she replied.

Her manager was honing down on her. Personal interactions during work hours were not encouraged.

'Can I help?' her manager asked.

The man smiled back at him. 'This young lady is being most helpful,' he replied. 'I saw the TV ad, you know, the one, *'showing you why 1984 won't be like 1984'* and I thought I'd come and see what all the fuss was about.' That shut the manager up. He hadn't seen the controversial commercial yet. It had only been shown during the Superbowl. These were the days before YouTube. He assumed the young man must have come from America. A casual manner and a guitar. He might be a pop star. With money. There were enough of them around these days. They were about the only people with money these days.

'Well, if there's anything I can do….' The manager replied... 'We are authorised to offer discounts for special circumstances.'

The young man nodded, as if he was considering the offer. The manager took his cue to leave but remained hovering behind the till, just out of earshot.

'If I buy one, will you come and install it for me?' The man with the blue eyes asked Helen.

'It's not part of the service,' she replied, missing the point.

'What's this?' he asked and she demonstrated the mouse. It was Jobs' radical new interface device.

'And can you record music on it?' he asked.

She laughed. 'You're joking. It's a computer, not….'

'Just asking,' he replied. 'Just trying to keep talking till you say you'll go out with me.'

The manager was hovering. Helen needed to close the deal.

'Yes,' she whispered. 'I will..'

116

'I'll be outside when you finish,' he said.

She gave him a look.

'I'll be there this time. Promise.' He nodded to the manager. 'I'm really looking for something I can record music onto,' he said, heading for the door.

The manager was left perplexed. After 'the customer' had gone he opined, 'The man's an idiot. Recording music on a personal computer. It's a personal computer for Chrissakes... not a recording studio. What world does he live in?'

Helen smiled. 'It might be possible one day,' she said and went back to making the mouse dance.

The young man was outside the shop at five twenty and spent ten minutes trying to distract Helen by pulling faces at her and tapping his watch when her boss wasn't looking. She was sure she was going to get into trouble but instead managed to head out of the door as soon as the clock hit five thirty with only a sarcastic comment,

'Watching the clock won't help you hit your target.'

She didn't care. He was out there. Waiting. Someone more exciting than the Apple Mac would ever be. He took her by the arm and they danced through the busy traffic, across the road to a café. It was hooching with people. Everywhere was hooching with people. London rush hour. It wasn't a place to be alone together.

'We could go to McDonald's?' she suggested. 'At the top of the road, it's not usually as busy this time of day.'

He gave her a withering smile. 'Do I look like I eat at Mickey D's?'

'I thought everyone ate at McDonald's,' she replied.

He laughed. 'Ah, so young. So beautiful. And so much to learn. And I've not even introduced myself.' He stuck his hand out, in what seemed a ridiculously inappropriately formal gesture. 'I'm Randall.'

'Helen,' she replied, aware of his flesh as she touched it for the first time. No Memory Bank could store that for you. The

117

aching sensuality of the first time touch.

They kept walking up the street. He was chattering on,

'When the universal experience has a profound impact on personal experience, that's when significant change happens.' He paused to let her catch up with him. 'Don't you think?'

Helen didn't know what to think. But she was prepared to let Randall turn her into a risk taker and accepted his offer of dinner.

'Obviously I don't mean McDonald's,' he teased her.

'Obviously,' she replied, trying to sound unfazed.

'I'll take you to the best place to eat in North London,' he stated. And they fought their way back onto the Northern Line.

She hadn't expected he was taking her back to his flat.

'I know. It's a long way from home.' It was his soft Scottish brogue that had really convinced her he was a risk worth taking. If he'd been one of the many slick southerners who had tried to get off with her since she'd been in London she probably wouldn't have given him a second glance. She couldn't be wooed in Estuary English. But his accent put her at ease.

'You can always stay the night.'

Helen opened her eyes. No, that had come later. The memory was getting confused. And it was such an important memory. How come it still came back to her as the kind of fuzzy blur it was at the time? He'd cooked her a meal. She couldn't remember what it was. It was good though. His food was always good. He'd shown her a VHS copy of the Apple Mac 'Big Brother' advert. It had blown her mind. The whole experience had blown her away. And she'd stayed over. And they'd made love. Helen had never done that on a first date before. None of this was anything like anything she'd ever done before.

She remembered going into work the next day in the same clothes. Unprecedented, unheard of and it didn't go unnoticed. It was a Friday. She sailed through it. She had a date that evening. All she had to do was get home get changed and get back to a gig in Finsbury Park for 8pm. It would be a tight call, but the whole world was in a whirl round Helen that day. She made it with minutes to spare.

The display posters proclaimed: Billy Bragg. Supported by Randall and the Reivers. And before she had time to work out how to get a ticket, Randall was there, ushering her in,

'She's with me. Backstage pass, pal.'

He kissed her and left her in the fast filling auditorium.

'Gotta go and get ready. See you after,' he said.

The music Lord Randall and the Reivers played was a kind of anti-folk music, punk influenced, somewhere between Billy Bragg and Runrig. As Helen stood there, alone in a crowd, two steps away from the man who had stolen her heart, the music melted into her and made her think of home, though Dundee was hardly the fantasy Scotland the Reivers or Runrig celebrated. The music was poignant, yearning and yet fresh and new. Until that moment Helen had never known what she wanted to do or be in life. She'd just gone with the flow, got on with it, unquestioningly; imagining that one day it would all be made clear.

In the darkness of an overcrowded room in North London, heady with an aromatic mixture of smoke, drink and sweat, she knew all she wanted was to be with Randall. For the rest of her life. The set ended with an Orwellian inspired song titled 1984, a heady, rocking number which encapsulated the angry young man she hadn't yet seen Randall as. She was lost. Her heart was bound to his forever. Backstage with him afterwards she held onto him tightly as he hummed his encore song, just for her. It was the song that had given the band their name, an upbeat, updated version of the ballad of Lord Randall. He hummed it now at a slower pace, lyrically, just for her. She literally felt her heart skip a beat. Randall was an enigma. There was so much depth to him. That night she had made her date with destiny, and determined not to let go. Ever….

…Helen opened her eyes and looked around her room. The blank US™ screen. The magnolia paint. The impersonal institutional feel. She missed Randall so much. She couldn't bear the present reality. She shut her eyes again and hummed the Reivers tune softly to herself. She could almost hear him singing it. She paused. She listened. She could hear his voice, inside her head. He was there, in memory, yet more real than the magnolia walls around her.

'Name is the thief of identity.'
'What?'
It had been his explanation when she had found out his name was not Randall but Callum Christie.
His voice came back to her, from the past, 'Our name isn't what people call us by. It's who we are. Remember that.'
And he kissed her. As he had so often kissed her over the years. She sighed. And opened her eyes. The pain of a memory that intense was too great for her to bear.

Helen had lived with Randall for nearly forty years with barely a night spent apart. And now, ten years on, she still missed him every minute of every day. It was a physical loss as much as a mental one. However hard she tried to block him out of her thoughts, somehow he was still always there, part of her. Part of her present experience. She couldn't live without him. But she had to keep his memory closed up, inside her. She didn't use the Memory Bank to see him on the US™ screen. She knew that he existed in just one place, her heart. And she would keep him safe there. Safe from ULTIMATE® at last. But today, right now, in the aftermath of yesterday, the cake and the moment of hope that someone was getting a message to her, she decided she would allow herself the pleasure of the pain of seeing him.

The knock on the door reminded her that the US™ was dead as well. She couldn't indulge her pain by seeing Randall virtually.

'Come in,' she called out, expecting to let in the repair men. She glared at the US™ screen. How could it have been that people used to go into ecstasies over a 42 inch plasma screen back thirty years ago? It was the bane of her life....

'Hello Nan.' Nike entered the room.

Helen beamed. 'I thought you were the repair men,' she said. 'Come on in. Sit down.'

Nike looked a bit uncomfortable.

'What's wrong?'

'Your screen's still not working?'

'Yes, thank goodness,' she looked at his worried face. 'Is that a problem?'

'Uh, yes, no.. uh..' He might be twenty now, but he was an inarticulate teenager to the last. 'It's just that I'm not supposed to go off access.'

'Oh, did I get you into trouble yesterday?'

'A bit.' He shrugged 'Ah, who cares. What can they do about it?'

Neither of them wanted to think about, never mind answer that question. Best divert.

'So what are you doing back here so soon?'

He held up the watch she had pressed into his hand the previous day.

'I thought I'd better bring this back.'

She took it from him. 'Thanks. But it was for you to keep. Your grandad would have wanted you to have it.'

He shook his head. 'I don't think that's such a good idea. I've already upset Pryce enough this week, and I don't want to ask him if it's okay.'

She held the watch close to her. 'Well, that's okay. I'll keep it here for you. But it's yours. It belongs to you. It's part of your history.'

'I don't have a history, Nan. I'm part of The PROJECT△.'

Another pause. Now they were getting closer to the crux of the matter.

'You said you wanted me to come back, on my own. I thought you might be lonely, here, on your own, without your Memory Bank working.'

Lonely. Now there was a concept not generally understood in the post-capitalist ULTIMATE® world.

LONELY: DEFINITION. In History; solitary, companionless, isolated or sad because without friends or company.

In the ULTIMATE® world no one was ever isolated. Each person was too important a commodity to be isolated. Everyone was part of the whole. A consumer in the ULTIMATE® lifestyle event. A cog in the ULTIMATE® wheel. How could you be solitary with a US™ screen interacting with your every movement? *There is no 'us and them' now,* remember. Only US™. Helen had often silently baulked at the significance of the trademark. Life itself seemed to have been copyrighted, trademarked and registered by ULTIMATE®. And no one seemed to notice or care. The definition of loneliness was one of many examples of ULTIMATE®'s complete mastery. How could you be sad when emotion was not considered a valid experience? It was logically impossible and became practically impossible. If it couldn't be commodified, it was of no use to ULTIMATE® and if it was no use, it was phased out.

In Helen's youth, emotion had been commodified like everything else. The prime example was music. Music spoke to people and you bought the music to enhance the emotion. Then the music industry collapsed. It wasn't a question of 'keeping music live' it became a question of keeping it real. Of letting people actually experience music other than as a commodified exchange.

Technological advance eventually killed music as it killed

all creativity. The battle over downloads was essentially an economic battle and when it became impossible to police the system or for the corporations to make money from the transactions, there was a moment when the ordinary people thought they'd won. But the corporations fought back. YouTube and the like flooded the market with 'free' creativity until the stock in trade became so devalued that no one bothered any more. If people wanted stuff 'free' then the proto- ULTIMATE® corporations would give them enough to stuff themselves like pigs at a trough. And quality turned to slops. It became impossible to find the good stuff amongst the rubbish and then it became impossible for most people to tell the difference. What need was there to create music when there was no way to sell it, and what point in writing novels when no one else was interested in what you had to say? The logical conclusion of everyone being able to be as creative as they liked was that no one could be bothered any more because as any demand and supply economist could explain to you; the stage after diminishing returns was that the bottom dropped out of the market.

So, sadness was no longer an emotion that could be commodified. Nike's generation couldn't feel the yearning brought about by songs such as those played by Lord Randall and the Reivers. Although in the ULTIMATE® world emotions were not banned, they were deemed unnecessary unless they were being pulled up from Memory Banks for five credits a time. And for the younger generation, it generally wasn't worth it. Emotion was irrelevant. Who needed it?

EMOTION: DEFINITION. In History, a strong mental or instinctive feeling such as love or fear. In contemporary life emotion is unnecessary because feelings are modulated by the knowledge and Memory Banks and are not useful commodities due to their lack of application in anything other than a personal arena. We are lucky to be free from strong emotions as it allows more 'productive' work to take place and society to generally be a more stable, balanced and comfortable place. In History emotions gave rise to wars and social unrest, both of which were destabilising economically and therefore phased out in the post-capitalist economic structure which was made global law in the 2016 ULTIMATE® United Nations declaration.

'What do you know of being lonely?' Helen asked Nike.

'Nothing really. I was on a 'productive' work cycle, looking at History. I thought it would be interesting but it's pretty nads really. I thought you'd probably have something more interesting to tell me. Because you were there.'

Helen laughed. She'd been there. In History. She may not have made history but she had certainly been part of it. And now she had a rare opportunity to share that with her grandson.

'What does nads mean?' Helen asked.

Nike was stunned. He'd come to ask questions, not to answer them. Especially when he didn't know the answer. He shrugged.

'No idea, Nan. Just a word.' His face told her everything.

'And you want to ask me questions, not to answer them?'

He smiled. 'How'd you know that?'

'Oh come on Nick. I'm your grandmother. I've known you since before you were born. I know everything there is to know about you... well... all the important things.'

Nike couldn't imagine that there were any important things to know about himself. Apart from that his name was NOT Nick. But she was old. He'd let it go.

'Come on then, tell me all the things you want to know.'

Helen didn't mind what Nick's questions were, it was just nice to have someone to share things with. Someone to stop her being lonely. And Nick did bear an uncomfortable physical resemblance to his grandfather when he furrowed his

124

brows and hunched his shoulders in that particular way.

'I want to know about the past.'

'That's a pretty big subject Nick, and not one I think The PROJECT⌂ would want you to spend too much time on. I thought that the future was all we thought about now. That and economic prosperity?'

'My past,' he paused, 'I mean our family. I want to know about our family. The truth.'

That was another unusual word from the mouth of a Project Kid. Truth. Haven't we already had that definition?

'You know this could get you into big trouble at The PROJECT⌂?'

He nodded. Then grinned. His grandfather's grin.

'Only if they find out.'

Helen sighed. He was not his grandfather. How could he be? He had no concept of the central message of 1984. We've all been found out already. So, what did it matter then? You can't fight but you can survive as long as possible. You have to take what you can get. And right now her grandson was here, and he was asking questions. He wouldn't be allowed to do that for much longer and so she'd better tell him all she could before ULTIMATE® stopped them once and for all.

'I don't really know where to begin,' she said. Before she could start, there was another knock on the door and this time it was the US™ technicians come to repair the screen.

The technicians suggested that maybe Helen and Nike would like to go to a public area while they fiddled with the screen. The room being the size it was. So Helen and Nike headed off for the dining area, but then Nike suggested they go outside. Outside. Helen couldn't remember the last time she'd been outside. There was never any point. But yes, the thought of outside suddenly was appealing. It kept Nike in ßß™ range of the US™ but meant that no one could really tell what they were talking about. It seemed like the perfect solution. Except where could they go outside? People didn't just sit around outside any more, even on lovely sunny days like today. It wasn't 'productive' and so it wasn't encouraged. She looked around and saw the imposing crags above. Once she would have yearned to climb up there. Not now. Now she was happy to stay on the grass below.

'Shall we walk?' Helen suggested.

Nike looked at her, bemused. Walk? Just for the sake of walking. Why?

She offered him her arm and he took it. 'I'm not that used to walking any more,' she said. 'Perhaps you can steady me.'

'Happy to Nan,' he smiled.

'Can you believe,' she said, 'twenty years ago I probably walked about five miles a day. Every day. Come rain or shine.'

'Why?'

'Walking the dogs.'

'You had dogs?'

'Don't you remember? We still had dogs when you were little. You used to come with me, just like now. Except it was you who was wobbly on your feet and me who supported you.'

Nike crinkled up his brow. Thought really hard. Tried to remember. Not easy for someone who had been trained not to store memories for the last twelve years. He thought maybe he could, but he couldn't guarantee if it really was a memory or if he was responding to the picture his Nan was painting.

'Maybe.' They kept walking. 'Was there one called Buchan?'

Helen clapped her hands together with joy. 'Yes. Yes. You do remember. He was a pointer. A crazy dog. Lived to run and obsessed with chasing birds. Any bird.'

Nike thought he had a memory. 'Did he used to sit and look at birds on the high wires?'

'The telephone lines. Yes.'

Nike had had a memory. And now he felt an emotion. Excitement, mixed with nervousness that this was something he really shouldn't be doing. Yet Helen acted like it was the most normal thing in the world. If they asked him, if Pryce questioned him, he'd just say he was playing along with her, helping her while her Memory Bank was being fixed. Surely they'd buy that.

'You were an early walker,' Helen said, 'you didn't bother with crawling, you were too inquisitive. Needed to be on your feet, exploring.'

Nike found he liked this talking about the past, his past, a person he didn't even know he had been.

'I wish you could tell me everything about back then,' he said, 'but...'

'But they wouldn't allow it, would they?' Helen finished his sentence. 'No, I don't suppose they would. And it would take far too long. We'd never be allowed to spend all that time together without someone getting suspicious. It would keep you away from your 'productive' work after all.'

'I hate 'productive' work.' Nike never thought he'd ever actually voice that thought, but here, outside, holding onto his Nan, he felt free in a way he'd never experienced before. It wasn't just the wind blowing off the crags, he felt like Helen blew a wind through his... mind... soul... he didn't know the right word. But it was a way that was new and it made him feel brave. He realized once he'd said it, why feelings were so dangerous.

Helen smiled. 'I'll cut you a deal. I'll put all my memories onto my Memory Bank, in a special vault and I'll give you the password.'

'You can't do that.'

'Why not?'

'It's against the privacy code. If we were found out...'

'All right, Nick. You've a point there. But, you're a bright boy. You can hack anything I hear. You run rings round Pryce I bet. If we work it out together I'm sure there's a way you can get access to my Memory Bank and then you can find out everything you want to know. Even after....'

He shook his head at her... he didn't want her to say it.

She carried on anyway, 'Even after I'm dead.'

I. THE IMMORTAL HORSES

The technicians in Helen's room were struggling with the US™. Clearly it was a software malfunction and they were hardware technicians. They'd had the thing off the wall, checked every circuit and run every diagnostic test possible on the biological components, and were one step off giving it a hefty kick as a last resort when the screen crackled, flickered and gave out a loud screaming stream of what might once have been called music but was now just a horrible noise (perhaps had always been horrible noise) and amidst a light show of flashing images came up the words

THE IMMORTAL HORSES

The technicians looked at each other. Bugger. Not another one of these. It was getting more prevalent and it was scary. It undermined everything they worked for. It was a hacking job par excellence from the cyber terrorists who threatened to destroy the ULTIMATE® way of life. Not that that was possible of course, but it did mean there was a big problem here. The system was compromised and many, many hours of form filling would be required before this US™ system could be off quarantine. They'd have to check the whole VCC building. It would send the old people off the edge. Old people were so uncompromising. And could complain so much. Even though they were here at the goodwill of ULTIMATE® and not paying for the experience like they should do, they would still complain. This could be weeks of work. Bugger.

The screen kept churning out the music till they managed to silence it, but the flashing messages kept on coming.

You've been hacked by
THE IMMORTAL HORSES

The technicians were just glad they'd been on their own

when this happened. If the 'client' had been present there would have been even more admin to complete. And like everyone else, they just wanted to complete their days work so they could go back to the virtual lives they lived outside of the daily grind. The only option now was to pull the plug. Metaphorically speaking. Reluctantly, they quarantined the system for the whole building. And the US™ screen went blank again. One of them went off to find a supervisor to explain themselves to. The other waited for the return of the 'client.'

When Helen and Nike returned to her room some half hour later (Nike wasn't sure about his ßß™ access outside and didn't want to incur Pryce's wrath again by being off access two days in a row) they discovered that she was still without a US™. The technician apologized. Profusely. Which Helen found funny since she didn't want the damned screen anyway, but nothing in the technician's mindset could imagine the imposed quarantine was in fact doing Helen a favour. He explained, very slowly (because she was old of course) that it was a software malfunction and so they couldn't simply replace the unit, they would have to shut down the whole zone and work on the software. The fault was receiving priority status and ULTIMATE® would get the smartest software technicians on it as soon as they could, who would work without break until the problem was resolved. But for now he stressed that it was vitally important that Helen must not, NOT, he repeated very carefully, try to switch on the US™. Helen assured him she would not.

The technicians left the building, cursing the VCC home who probably hadn't updated their virus software and would doubtless blame budget cut-backs or overworked staff or some such. Someone's head would roll but more importantly someone must fix it. The technicians were pleased that once they'd completed the admin, it wouldn't be their problem any more. They'd done their job. Or tried to.

Of course the first thing Nike did when the technicians had left was try the screen on again. Why wouldn't he? No one would know and the only way you found out how things worked was to find out how they broke. As he waved his barcoded arm at it saying

'What's wrong with you?'

The screen burst into life again with the words

You've been hacked by
THE IMMORTAL HORSES

Helen and Nike looked at each other. In silence. For a long time.

'So who are The Immortal Horses?' Nike asked. More in hope than in expectation.

'Have you not been warned about them?' Helen was surprised. She thought that The PROJECT⌂ would have warned the Kids about them, then on reflection, maybe not. Giving them an alternative world view would not benefit ULTIMATE® aims and so wrapped in cotton wool they would stay. Sometimes the level of ignorance ULTIMATE® required of their premiere generation amazed her. After all The PROJECT⌂ represented the vanguard, developing a template for what all people would be like in another twenty years. God help the world. Oh, no. Of course God couldn't do anything, because he'd been appropriated by ULTIMATE® as well.

She wondered if she should tell Nick what she knew about The Immortal Horses. Without time to weigh up the possible consequences, she took a snap decision. She didn't like

The PROJECT⌂, never had and this might be her only chance to try and reclaim him, if only that could be done, for reality. Whatever that was now. If The PROJECT⌂ rejected him (she wasn't sure that was even a possibility) maybe he could have a real life again. As real as ULTIMATE® would allow. She decided to take the chance, even though a small voice inside her head told her it wasn't her chance to take.

'They are terrorists, seeking to destroy ULTIMATE®.' She

paused, wondering what response this would get.

'What's a terrorist?' Nike asked, cursing that the US™ screen was broken just when he had some interesting questions to ask. He didn't seem phased. He didn't have Helen's concept of reality and danger.

'Well. They used to say, one man's terrorist is another man's freedom fighter...' Helen weighed up whether it was worth pursuing this further.

'Nan, don't, you're sounding like the knowledge bank. Just tell me, in straightforward terms.'

'Terrorists are people who use violence as a method to try and overthrow a government.'

Violence? Government? Just so many more meaningless phrases for a Project Kid.

'In this case, they are an underground organization, no one knows where they are based, and their aim is to get rid of the ULTIMATE® way of life.'

'But that's impossible,' Nike sneered, 'You can't....'

'Maybe so. But people with ideals don't care about whether something is possible or not, they care about trying to change things. About doing something and if necessary, dying in the attempt.'

Nike was amazed. 'Who are they?'

'No one knows. If ULTIMATE® knew then they certainly wouldn't still be around. They are a guerrilla operation and they must have found a way to hack into the US™ software. It'll be interesting to see what they do from here.'

Interesting? Had his Nan lost her mind? Interesting? The overthrow of ULTIMATE®. No way. Nike realized he was sweating at the very thought of it. He felt guilty. Felt like he shouldn't be here. This emotion thing wasn't good. And he couldn't stop it. He started to worry what would happen if Pryce got wind of this. What if Pryce had tried to interface with his ßß™? Then he thought of something far worse. What if The Immortal Horses had logged his ßß™ barcode? What if he was infected already? What if he was about to take that infection back to The PROJECT⌂? This was bad. Very bad. He needed to get out of there.

'Nan. I have to go. Pryce will be wondering where I am.'

Helen wasn't surprised by his response. He was a PROJECT⌂ product after all. She had had influence on him till he was seven, but despite the adage 'give me a child till he is seven and I'll show you the man,' ULTIMATE® had done a masterful job in the last thirteen years of rebuilding her young Nick, creating him anew as a compliant if sometimes wayward ULTIMATE® citizen. Branded Nike. He must have been a challenge but then if they could crack it with the likes of Nick, they must be well on their way to complete success.

'Okay, Nick. Don't worry about it. You know where I am, when you have more questions. And after this is sorted, I'll start work on the Memory Bank and the truth will be there, stored away, waiting for you to access.'

Nike had forgotten all about that; the Memory Bank, the past, the truth. He was now just thinking of how to save himself in the present. He didn't know what to fear, he just knew that something very, very bad could happen very, very soon and he didn't know how to avoid it. So he left.

And of course he was tracked all the way back to The Project House by The Immortal Horses.

Meanwhile, alone again, Helen turned her thoughts to her memories. Real, personal, private memories. After all, she had no excuse now. There was no US™ screen to reformulate or revision her reality. How odd it had felt being outside. Feeling the breeze on her face after so long. Breathing the air. It was nothing like the old days of course. She remembered when she had come to the VCC Home she had craved a room with a view over the park. She couldn't afford it. She couldn't afford any of it. She had to take what she was given. Her view, if she squinted, was towards the concrete monstrosity that had been the Scottish Parliament. Pretty soon she'd closed the blinds and left them closed. Forgotten that the outside world even existed. Because for her it no longer did.

And now, after ten years inside, she had almost forgotten that for nearly forty years she lived most of her life outside. How could you forget? How could it be that humans adapted to just about anything simply because they had to, not because they wanted to. She realised it was because she had given up on life. It had seemed the only thing to do. Because ten years ago, life had finally given up on her.

She didn't want to remember the dull horror with which she faced her first night in the VCC home, knowing that things would never be good again. Knowing that now she was paying the price for the life she'd led. The price she had known would have to be paid one way or another, but which she'd hoped to put off... well.. indefinitely. But no, like all bad things, it finally happened. She had been numb to pain at that point, having lost Randall, lost Torquil, lost Nick.. lost everyone and everything that was important to her. She mused that in one respect, living was about losing. A constant journey of facing losses. Existence, she could not call it life, in the VCC home, was the final stage. The stage after loss. When there was nothing left to lose. But life just kept on going. Survival in an ULTIMATE® version of the Big Brother world.

And yet, once, it had all been so different. Really so very different. Once, she could never have predicted this end. She found it hard to focus. Hard to think in any order as thoughts swirled round in her mind, jumbling together like so many jigsaw pieces. She wasn't even sure if all the pieces were from the same picture. The one thought, forcing all the others out, was the cake. A real birthday cake.

'Happy Birthday mum,' Torquil kissed her and entreated, 'close your eyes.'

She closed her eyes, enchanted by his excitement.

'You can open them now,' Catriona said as she came in bearing a birthday cake groaning under the lighted flame of forty candles.

'Put it down, put it down,' Helen laughed.

Torquil had turned out the lights and Helen was amazed how much glare there was from the candles.

'Come on mum, blow them out,' Catriona could barely contain her excitement.

'Make a wish, mum,' Torquil added.

She paused for merely a moment. What more could she wish for? And blew... and blew.... And they were out.

'Don't sing happy birthday,' she begged, 'you know how I hate that.'

So they didn't. Just in case that was her wish.

'Try the cake, mum,' Torquil said, 'I helped Catriona make it.'

'I can see that,' Helen laughed at the slightly wonky dimensions of the cake. She cut into it. Cut everyone big chunks and they ate it with relish. It was a bit uneven in density, but it tasted wonderful. It was made with the love of her children. At the time Helen thought it was a moment she would cherish forever.

Now she thought of the cake she had shared with Nick, Omo and Flora and marvelled at how good it had tasted. She used to grow and cook all her own food but realised she hadn't tasted anything but ULTIMATE® food for ten years.

Like seventy, forty was a milestone birthday. Randall was determined they do something special. Helen resisted. She had everything she wanted. She didn't need a fuss.

'Get your coat on.' Randall instructed her on the cold February afternoon in 2000.

'Where are we going?' she asked.

'It's a surprise woman,' he said. 'Do what you're told

without questioning for once in your life will you?'

'I don't like surprises,' she pleaded.

'You'll like this one,' he said.

He took the afternoon off work and they went to Cairnholy, an ancient burial ground which was one of their 'special' places. The views were spectacular and you could virtually guarantee you'd be the only people there. Certainly in February! The kids stayed at home and made the cake. Catriona baked and Torquil decorated. It was lucky Helen wasn't there to see the mess they made of the kitchen. They obeyed their father's instructions to clear it up, so she was none the wiser.

Helen enjoyed riding in the beaten up Landrover which was their main form of transport now. Fuel was becoming expensive and they tried to restrict their other car to trips to the supermarket once a week. Helen still shopped for the things she couldn't grow herself. Supporting a family of four on the rocky, infertile land was an impossibility given the time she had spare after washing and cooking and cleaning. Even if she'd dedicated herself to it forty hours a week, in real terms it would still have been cheaper to go for the BOGOF offers at the supermarket. In 2000 the food price increases hadn't yet kicked in. That would change.

Helen gave herself up to the warm, farmy smell of a vehicle more used to transporting hay and sheepdogs than people and stole a glance at Randall. It was sixteen years since she'd first seen him, strap-hanging on the tube but even now, especially now in this more familiar context, her heart skipped a beat when she saw those piercing blue eyes and that unaffected smile.

'We are happy, aren't we?' she said.

He turned and looked at her, 'Of course we are,' he replied. 'And we still will be forty years from now.'

Little did he know. Little did either of them know.

They got out of the Landrover at Cairnholy. They were alone, in nature. It was cold but bright and they stood together, marvelling at the link between past and present.

'I don't know how the kids did it,' she mused.

'Did what?' he asked, afraid that she'd got wind of the cake making that was going on at home. She was a terrible woman to keep a secret from.

'Camped out over the millennium.'

He laughed. Some six weeks ago the world had celebrated the onset of the year 2000 and Catriona and Torquil had demanded to be allowed to camp out in the ruined castle which sat in the home farm field, despite the cold weather. They spent the day building a bonfire and slept in their wellies. They crawled home frozen at five thirty, reckoning they'd given it a good go. Helen and Randall had gone and seen the New Year in with them and then headed back for home for a stiff drink and a warm bed. Helen was keener to see the sunrise on the first day of the year than spend her time drinking out the old year.

'Wouldn't you have been up for that at their age?' he asked.

'Probably,' she said. 'Would you?'

The conversation was cut short as the rain came down and they ran, laughing, back to the Landrover. Not before they were soaked of course. It had been bright when they set off and they weren't wearing hats. Randall had taken his off deliberately because it was a holiday and a hat was one of the essentials of his daily working life on the farm. Helen hadn't brought a hat, because she'd been surprised and hadn't known where she was going.

It was nothing that a hot shower wouldn't put right. Helen stood in the shower and let the hot water trickle over her and thought how easy it was for things to be put right. What did rain matter as long as you could get warm and dry? She towelled her hair and went downstairs. For cake. They were happy days. Helen wasn't so foolish to think that all the old times were the good times, they'd faced their fair share of problems over the years, but today, just today, she wanted to remember the good times.

The year 2000 represented new hope for everyone, even farmers. Helen and Randall were tenant farmers in rural Galloway and like all farmers, struggling to make a living. They'd been there fifteen years and felt part of the landscape. Life in 1980's London was a thing of the past. A story of a life that now seemed as if it had belonged to other people. Helen could barely remember it. She couldn't completely disown London though, since that was where she met Randall, so there would always be one good, warm feeling to come out of it. But the best decision they ever made was to leave.

1985. They'd been seeing each other for about nine months. It was clear that things were going to go a step further. Helen thought Randall was going to ask her to move in with him. She was going to say yes. They were in bed, after another fabulous meal cooked by Randall. He leant up on one elbow and said.

'I don't want to do this any more.'

She was shocked. What did he mean? He caught her look of horror.

'No..' he said... 'I don't mean us.. I mean... this... London.'

'Oh.' She didn't know how to respond. 'But you have to be in London. For your music.'

'That's going nowhere,' he replied.

'I'm sure you'll get another tour soon,' she said, realising that a big part of her hoped he wouldn't. She didn't like it when he was away, touring. Not because she didn't trust him. Because she loved him and wanted to be with him and they never seemed to have enough time together.'

'I don't want to tour. I don't want to be living out of suitcases any more than I want to stay here. Do you have a dream, Helen? A vision of the future?'

138

'I suppose so,' she said, realising she'd never thought beyond being with Randall, wherever, however, forever.

'And what is it?' he asked. That was putting her on the spot.

'Just to be with you,' she said weakly, hoping that was enough.

'Really?' he sounded amazed.

'Yes, really,' she kissed him to prove it. 'What's your dream Randall?'

He told her a story.* The story he felt defined what he wanted out of life. The story he hoped she would understand. The story which would change both of their lives for ever. And then he launched into the plan. And within a year they were living it. A farm or smallholding, somewhere away from the rat race. A real life, together far away from London.

'But I only want it on one condition,' Randall had added.

'What?' she'd asked.

'That you marry me,' he said.

She was amazed. They'd never brought the subject up but she'd thought he was the kind of man who thought marriage an unnecessary restriction. A piece of paper. Meaningless.

'Nothing I do with you will ever be meaningless,' he replied when she told him what she'd thought, 'but can we avoid the meringue dress stuff?'

She laughed. She had never been one of those girls who craved a wedding with a party and a dress and all the trimmings. Too much fuss. And nonsense.

So they married quietly and cheaply and both sets of parents, though they didn't like it, respected their choices.

Both sets of parents gave them what they would have contributed to the wedding in the form of cash which along with the small amount of savings they had, was enough to secure them the farm tenancy.

* for full story see appendix

Randall, ever the dark horse, had studied agriculture at college before becoming a musician, so he managed to convince the landlord that he had enough experience to make it worth a go. And there weren't that many people foolish enough to want to go into farming in the mid 1980's. It was always going to be a struggle. It was a struggle. But they faced it together.

The first challenge was Chernobyl. Soon after taking on the tenancy, and just before Catriona was born, the farm went under restrictions because of the danger of air pollution. That was just the beginning of it. Then BSE hit. The farm was mixed sheep and beef so they were as Randall so eloquently put it, 'Screwed both ways.'

They struggled their way back from that crisis, never quite believing the Blair government message in 1997 that 'things can only get better.' Randall and Helen lived in a world of reality where thing could always get worse. They did. Foot and Mouth in 2001. But they faced it, as they faced everything, together. As a family.

When Helen turned forty in 2000, Catriona, their daughter was fourteen and Torquil their son was eleven. Both were now old enough to be some use on the farm. It was a pretty relentless life however much they loved it. Had it been a good way for kids to grow up, Helen wondered? Memories started to flood back.

Catriona aged three experienced her first lambing with all the excitement children usually saved up for Christmas. She was shocked that all the lambs didn't have names.

'We can't name them all, there are hundreds.' Helen coaxed her daughter.

Randall observed the wavering lip and pulled Catriona up on his lap, beside a little lamb he was trying to bottle feed.

'But you can name this one,' he said.

Helen was amazed. Randall was not a sentimental man.

He didn't go in for pet names, knowing the practicalities of the farming life cycle far too well. He didn't do baby talk or hiding of ugly facts… but he loved Catriona 'Are you sure?' she asked him. The lamb in her own lap squiggled and squirmed. Catriona was just learning the toddlers divide and rule tactic and felt she had some room for negotiation.

'And that one? She pointed at the lamb in Helen's lap.

'Okay. That one too.' Randall capitulated. 'But that's all.'

Catriona beamed. She pointed at Randall's lamb.

'Lucy,' she said firmly. And then pointed at Helen's lamb. 'Eric.' She was adamant.

'Okay. Lucy and Eric,' Randall confirmed, 'but Catriona, it has to be the other way round. This (he held up 'Lucy') is a boy lamb and this (holding up 'Eric') is a girl lamb.

'Lucy and Eric.' She was not negotiating any further. Gender meant nothing to her. So Lucy and Eric they became. And Randall taught Catriona how to feed them.

Helen remembered that Eric went on to become a good breeding ewe while Lucy went off for roast lamb. Every year after that, Catriona proudly named the orphans. Every year when the sheds by the house filled with odd calves; those whose mothers had died or who needed special attention, or who needed to be twinned; Catriona, and latterly Torquil, would stand by the gate for hours, debating names. Randall allowed it, as long as they fed the calves they named. There was Teeny, who was a runt and Tiny, who was even smaller, and Infinitely Small, who Helen swore was no bigger than Crogo, the biggest of the dogs at the time. Another year a calf was born blind and he became named Egor. He followed his foster mother around everywhere and seemed to get on quite fine without the gift of sight. Then there was Amber, her name reflecting her colour. They all went to the same fate eventually, but they were singled out, given special attention and special love for as long as they needed it, before heading out into the fields to become just another calf with a tag in its ear and a destination of the table.

As long as people would still buy beef. Or until they faced death in the Foot and Mouth year. That was when the kids finally stopped naming cows.

Foot and Mouth changed everything. Even Helen found it hard to be happy amongst the stench of death and the fear of more death round the corner. The financial implications palled into insignificance compared to the visceral horror of it every day, all around. The world had changed. The millennial hope had gone. Big Brother had become a reality game show. The kids had watched it, more shocked than entranced that first season but pretty quickly became bored. Who wanted to watch a bunch of 'losers' sitting around talking about nothing all day and night when you could be out driving tractors or training dogs? This was the time before virtual living was more appealing than real life for young people.

Foot and Mouth was heartbreaking for Randall, but it proved the final straw for Catriona. As a fifteen year old, being surrounded by the stench of the senseless slaughter was too much for her. At sixteen she left home and went to college in Glasgow. Anything to get away from the memories of a beautiful life turned sour. Helen realized now, all these years on, that she'd never really thought about what it was that turned Catriona's life around. But on reflection she supposed it was Foot and Mouth. Catriona, and all of them, were victims as much as the slaughtered cows and sheep, and it was a human cost that didn't get counted. Without Foot and Mouth Catriona might have married a farmer, stayed in Galloway, been alive today. Randall would never have lost the daughter he loved so dearly.

At the time, Helen had accepted the sadness as she accepted all sadness. As the price she had to pay for having a perfect life. She understood that perfect didn't mean everything always the way you wanted it. There had to be some lee-way. The external world could never be expected to bend totally to the individual will. She was happy with her lot. Randall had

142

bemoaned the fact he couldn't take them all on holiday that summer after the Foot and Mouth restrictions were finally lifted.

'We never go on holiday,' Helen said,

'Maybe we need to, this year,' he replied. 'To get away from this… to get some perspective back.'

She knew as she looked at his careworn face, it was not about holidays. It was about losing faith in the dream. About not believing the story any more. About wanting something different, or something more.

'Why go anywhere?' she caressed him. 'There's nowhere I would rather be than here, with you and the kids. This is my life and I love it. We can get through it.'

'What can you possibly love about this?' he asked, a moment of depression engulfing him.

'It's enough,' she replied. 'We didn't expect it to be easy, did we?'

'Not easy,' he agreed, 'but not like this…'

'Don't do that,' she said.

'What?' he asked.

'It's my dream too,' she replied. 'And my dream is that I'm married to a man I love beyond life itself. We have two healthy children and we live in countryside which never fails to take my breath away. Every time I go out with the dogs on a cold spring morning, even a wet wintry morning, I thank my lucky stars I'm not still fighting for my place on an underground train, living a pointless life chasing meaningless things.'

He laughed at her passionate outburst. He couldn't help but laugh at her.

'You're an easy woman to please, Mrs Christie,' he said.

'Yes. I just need my husband to smile,' she replied.

He smiled. It was enough. It was perfect. Even in the face of the future. The moment was perfect.

Randall was right, in many ways Helen was an easy

woman to please. She didn't want things, she didn't even want experiences, in terms of trips or happenings; she just wanted to be able to live, to really live every day, being part of the nature around her, responding to the daily joys and emergencies that made up farming life. Chasing a cow down the lane. Fixing a gate when two bulls had faced up to each other across fields and when frustration got the better of them, simply charged through the barrier separating them, ignoring the fact that the barrier was two five bar gates which were reduced to matchsticks in moments. Staying up late and getting up early to help with the lambing. Struggling to get the ancient AGA to work so that the men had a decent hot meal every lunch time. This was enough for Helen. And if she could get a bit of time to hang on a gate herself, chatting with Randall while he tagged cows or dosed sheep, or to walk in the forest with the dogs, or gaze at the stars on a bright, crisp, clear, dark night round the back of the cowshed, then life was as near perfect as it could ever be in reality.

Helen opened her eyes and faced the magnolia walls once more. That was the thing with memories – real memories not the ones mediated by the US™ Memory Bank – you couldn't control them. And sometimes they took you places you'd rather not go. You couldn't just stick with the good ones because your mind wandered, trying to make meaning, make connections and the darker places stuck out just as vividly as the good ones. Perhaps that was how ULTIMATE® had become so successful. They presented a way of only keeping happy memories. Pre-washed and pre-packaged and in pretty shapes and colours. They offered virtual happiness but Helen preferred reality, however grim. That was why she would never fit in. Not here at the VCC Home, not anywhere in the ULTIMATE® system. She couldn't fight city hall. But she didn't have to take their handouts. In general ULTIMATE® were right in their belief that you could make people however you wanted them to be. What

144

was perhaps more shocking was that they had more or less achieved their goal wholesale in a mere twenty years. Now, life was as ULTIMATE® said it was for nearly everyone. But Helen could not capitulate. And her birthday cake proved she was not the only one. The existence of The Immortal Horses proved that there were a few, a very few, who were still managing to buck the system. But for how long? And how could she find them?

J. WHO'S WATCHING WHO?

As Nike walked from Helen's to The Project House, a walk of some ten minutes, he was entirely unaware that his every move was being monitored. He had grown up, after all, in a world where everything you did was subject to US™ technology. It was a combination of CCTV and wireless access monitoring of the ßß™ barcode embedded in his arm which held all his individual (we might say personal if such a thing didn't appear so totally impersonal) information. He didn't look up at the cameras or the hoardings which, while boasting of various ULTIMATE® products and triumphs, could interface with him constantly. He was more concerned with the walking aspect.

Walking the streets was alien to Nike. Project Kids tended to stay in the compound. Why wouldn't you? Within the compound, there was everything you could virtually need in the perfect world that ULTIMATE® had virtually created. Or created virtually. Or both. Project Kids were specially chosen and specially protected. The street was where the ordinary people hung out. The streets were dangerous. And in 2030 they tended to be pretty vacant most of the time. People didn't go out that much any more, unless they had to. Most people worked (or consumed) from home and there was no real community transport system. That had died after nationalisation turned to privatisation turned back to nationalisation and then became redundant as a consequence of OIL PRESERVATION measures along with a restructuring of the workplace in the late 2016's. Some people had seen it coming, but no one expected it to hit as quickly as it did. In 2010 people enjoyed complaining about the trials of travelling. In 2020 no one really travelled any more, except virtually.

If Nike had bothered to ask Pryce, he could have expected to be transported to the VCC home in a licensed fuel efficient pod (a type of electric car dreamed about since the 1960's) But he couldn't be bothered with the interaction. It might raise issues. Of course, Nike didn't need permission to leave the compound. The PROJECT⌂ wasn't a prison. It was just that he wasn't really expected to need to leave and for that matter to want to leave. ULTIMATE® expected he had been better trained than that. If he had thought about it, Nike would have realised there was no freedom of choice in the matter. Even if he did leave the compound, they could still keep tabs on whatever he was doing, so it didn't really matter. But Nike didn't think like that. He just did it. His brand suggested his nature. As far as ULTIMATE® systems were concerned his unusual action merely substituted one set of statistical information for another set and gave psychological profilers something different to do. It would all be logged and passed on to Pryce one way or the other.

Nike had his excuse all ready should Pryce pull him up. He'd run out of gaming credits. He hadn't got his new 'productive' work schedule so he thought it didn't matter what he did. Throw it back at Pryce. Attack is the best form of defence. It's all a game. He pretended to himself that he was free, in control, but deep down he knew that as a Project Kid he was never free to do what he liked, if what he liked wasn't authorized by ULTIMATE®. They owned him body and soul. Nike was beginning to resent that but didn't know what to do about it. So he did what he could – tested the system. He appreciated that there might be consequences to his current actions but right now he thought the consequences might at least be more interesting than the usual routine. At least it wasn't 'productive' work.

Nike remained oblivious to the fact that it wasn't ULTIMATE® who were watching him right now. It was The Immortal Horses. Both Nike and ULTIMATE® were unaware that there was a serious crack in the system. As Nike walked past the big glass fronted building on the corner of the main road, he didn't give it a second glance. Yet inside that building was a room which looked like an early 21st century trading room in a major banking corporation (because that was what it had formerly been) with bank upon bank of computers. The terminals were worked mostly by dishevelled teenagers who looked out of place and certainly nothing like the high powered traders they'd replaced. Their heads were down, their eyes totally focused on the screens as they collected data; although to them it was like playing the mother of all games. It was a game to them. But it was Nike's life. He was the character of their game right now. He was the protagonist they were pursuing through the streets. It was actually the game of all of their lives, if only they knew it.

The 'floor' of this unusual Trading House was being run by a man who didn't quite fit in with the rest of them. Known as Troy, he looked like a throwback to the twentieth century. Nike might have called him a hippy if he'd known what hippies looked like. But his attitude was all clued up. He hadn't been around in the "tune in turn on and drop out" 1960's and he was more guerrilla than beatnik. More Che Guevara than John Lennon. But he came from a later generation entirely. He was a child of the millennium. His childhood has straddled centuries. He had given up looking backwards for looking forwards. He was targets oriented and goal driven. The immediate target was Nike, the current goal was surveillance. The prize was a live link right inside The PROJECT△ Compound. The 'gaming' team had been trying to achieve this goal for months, if not years, and Nike was the latest in a long line of prospects. This time however, Troy was determined nothing was going to screw up the opportunity. This time it was different. As he watched his 'gamers' in action he realised he needed to take the mission away from the HABIT∞ kids who made up most of the 'workforce' in the building and give it to the few really trustworthy members who, like him, were motivated by ideology not by where their next fix was coming from.

HABIT∞: Definition. *In History, a settled or regular*

practice that is hard to give up. ULTIMATE® introduced HABIT∞
in 2013 in its attempts to deal with the out of control drug and
alcohol dependence issues.

Pryce had explained the HABIT∞ to the Project Kids in
one of their sessions when Nike had queried the definition. It
was the parental 'drugs' talk ULTIMATE® style. Pryce was
determined to be up to the 'facts of life' section of his contract.
'There used to be drugs. Heroin that made you sleep,
Speed that made you live life in the fast lane, Cocaine that made
you confident. Cannabis that made you laugh. Ecstasy that
made you dance all night with a feeling of love in your heart for
the whole human race. In History most drugs were illegal. There
were legal drugs too. Alcohol being the most prevalent. They
had similar effects; to mask pain, to make you feel better, to
make you feel happier, to stop you feeling at all. They cost a lot
of money, they caused untold pain and suffering, they
unstabilised the people who used them and destabilised the
economy they lived in. ULTIMATE® has done away with all that.
Saving countless lives and making them so much better lived. So
much more productive. In 2013 ULTIMATE® legalised and
regulated what might be called the drug to end all drugs. We
know it as the HABIT∞. It's administered by counsellors to
those in the population who need it, freely available and
doesn't stop them from undertaking 'productive' work.'
Nike had wondered if they could try it. Pryce shook his
head. Had he oversold it?
'No. You kids don't need the HABIT∞. It's for people
who aren't as lucky as you. It's one of the differences between
you and ordinary people. ULTIMATE® have constructed your
lives so that you will be able to live without needing the
HABIT∞. It's what they want for all people in the end. You are
the vanguard. ULTIMATE® aspire towards true freedom for all
the citizens. And you will be the first to achieve it. That's why
it's so important for you to be 'productive'. Your productivity

has so much more depth to it than that of an ordinary teenager on the HABIT∞. The assessments made from your actions, from your lives, will shape generations to come.'

Thus ended the 'drugs' talk. Like generations of parents before him, Pryce felt he'd done a good job. Omo bought it. Flora bought it. Only Nike felt like he might be missing out on something. He determined that one day he'd get out on the street and find someone to give him a practical demonstration.

The thought came back to him as he walked the empty street back to the compound. If only he could meet someone out here, he might find out something more about ordinary life and be able to compare it with the so called privilege which felt like a prison to him. It was frightening, but it was also strangely compelling.

PRISON: Definition. In history, a place where criminals were kept in confinement. In contemporary society there is no need for prisons. ULTIMATE® has done away with crime and with it the need for prisons.

Nike had only recently spent his credits on the definition, but he still had a nagging doubt in the back of his mind that somehow the compound *was* a kind of prison. The VCC home seemed like a prison too, and he was beginning to wonder if the whole world had become some kind of large prison. Were The Immortal Horses fighters for freedom as Helen had suggested?

At the precise moment Nike had this thought, Troy achieved the direct connection to his ßß™ barcode. Chance or fate? Neither of these were ULTIMATE® concepts of course. The Immortal Horses technology was sophisticated, but it could not read thoughts. Troy was hopeful that Nike was going to provide him with a real insight into The PROJECT⌂. If Nike was valuable to The PROJECT⌂, he'd just become even more so to The

Immortal Horses. Troy knew that Nike was an investment. The trading floor analogy was a pretty good one. Nike had just become not just an ULTIMATE® commodity but the ULTIMATE commodity.

Troy let go of the controls, returning the surveillance of Nike to a man in his early thirties who looked like he'd never seen the light of day.

'Keep the good work up, Griff.'

Griff smiled. He was enjoying himself and he was doing something which might be considered 'productive' if he wasn't part of a counter culture. Therefore, by definition he was doing something counter-productive. He'd only been on the surveillance an hour and look what he'd achieved. He was one of Troy's ideological converts, much more useful than the Habit∞ riddled adolescents who made up the bulk of The Immortal Horses workforce. As Troy left the room, the music went back up to full blast and the room rocked to the beat of a long forgotten music. Before the mind-numbing ULTIMATE® digitised mantra music, there had been live music. Music with melody and meaning. And it played constantly in the Trading House. Everything from Elvis to the Manic Street Preachers. From Ska to Heavy Metal. The Immortal Horses embraced music as revolution. It was a world away from the ULTIMATE® created mono-pap which was now considered music and had evolved out of a combination of dance music, elevator music and Nintendo style gaming tunes. While from an outside perspective it might be hard to spot the difference between the ULTIMATE® and The Immortal Horses lifestyles, to those who lived them there was all the difference in the world.

Back at the compound, Nike let himself into The Project House. He breathed a sigh of relief. He couldn't help it but feel, if not safe, then relieved that nothing had happened. He'd got away with it. Again. However, he realized that he should keep his head down now, do some 'productive' work and take Pryce's spotlight off him for a bit. Because if anyone found out about the trouble at his Nan's with the infected US™ screen, he was sure to be implicated. And that could bring nothing but trouble.

He sighed. He waved his arm at his screen to log in and looked at his options. His 'productive' work schedule still hadn't been changed yet. But somehow he'd got another 100 credits. Pryce must have put them on. Nike reasoned that he'd better start spending them. Act normal. Look like he'd been here all the time. That would mean asking a lot of questions to get his production tally up on his daily log. The best way to do that would be to ask quick questions, not putting any real thought into either the question or the answer. Questions he'd asked before. Boring. But necessary.

Nike was like a gambler who really thought he had a system on the fruit machine. ULTIMATE® let him think that, because that way their psychological profiling was all the more effective. They got right into his motivation. Nike had no idea how many games he was a pawn in, but like all gamblers he mistakenly thought he retained some level of control.

So he settled down, and started asking questions. Not expecting any real answers. Of course before long he had lost the will to be 'productive' and asked the most dangerous question he felt he could get away with at that moment. After all, it was all a game, wasn't it?

'What is emotion?' he asked.

He'd already had this definition at Helen's, so he wasn't expecting there to be any interest in the answer. But it would give him time to think how he could ask the question he really wanted an answer to: 'Who are the Immortal Horses?'

K. INFECTION

While Nike was thinking and asking unproductive questions, Pryce was keeping a close eye on his log. He saw Nike was pursuing EMOTION as a topic line. He knew he should have acted on this immediately but something stopped him. If he gave Nike some rope, if he could get into the kid's mind, work out what made him tick... Pryce had a myriad of justifications ready. Really however, his own emotion was ruling his judgement. Along with Nike he viewed the definition on the US™ screen.

*DEFINTION: EMOTION - **1.** A mental state that arises spontaneously rather than through conscious effort and is often accompanied by physiological changes; a feeling: the emotions of joy, sorrow, hate, and love. **2.** A state of mental agitation or disturbance.*

Pryce pondered on the combination of conscious mental effort and physiological change and what this meant. Nike was more interested in the immediacy of the words: *joy, sorrow, hate and love.* These were words which were foreign to a Project Kid's working vocabulary. There was no profit in emotion for ULTIMATE®. They, after all, had worked very hard to stop their citizens experiencing mental agitation or disturbance of any kind. Virtuality might seem individualistic but actually there was nothing individual, nothing private about it. Thought and feeling were risky concepts and as such, very appealing to the likes of Nike. Confusing, but appealing. But mostly Nike wondered why the definition he'd got here had been so different to the one he'd got at Helen's. That didn't seem right. Surely a definition was by definition a definition....

As for Pryce, he just wanted to work out why his emotions were so close to the surface all the time. It was something that could seriously compromise his promotion prospects, although he was beginning to feel he had no prospects, no future, no real life. Pryce remembered when lack of emotion was imposed on depressives through prescription drugs. So surely, what he was experiencing was not depression. He had too many emotions, not too few. Did he need a dose of Habit∞? No, that would be an admission of failure.

Far from ridding the world of depression, it seemed to Pryce that ULTIMATE® had effectively visited the state on the whole population through a virtuality more powerful than any medication. Yet in their emotional apathy, everyone else seemed content. Only he seemed depressed. How could that be? And more importantly, what could he do about it? How could he prevent people from seeing the weakness in his soul? The soul after all was no longer a viable entity in the ULTIMATE® world. Even ULTIMATE® couldn't commodify the elusive soul. Pryce laughed, remembering his early Catholic upbringing and the notion of 'wrong thoughts.' It was so, so long ago. Like a story that had happened to another person. A life that was not his. His present worry was that if he knew his own shortcomings, so did someone else. Someone or something more powerful than God.

His musings were interrupted by the ringing alarms and flashing word INFECTION on his US™ screen. In the remarkably predictable world of The PROJECT△, something remarkably unexpected was happening. It took literally seconds before Graham was on the US™ and there was a level of concern in his voice Pryce hadn't heard before.

'What the hell's happening in your Project House?' Graham yelled.

'I don't know. Why? I've just got red alarms going off all over... we've got an infection.'

'Shut them down.'

'What?'

'Shut down the systems feeding into your kids. NOW.'

Pryce couldn't believe what he was hearing. There was

no protocol for this. He vaguely remembered in his induction training programme something about major infection control, but like CPR, he'd never had to use it and he'd paid little attention. Infections were unheard of. Even minor glitches were not common but when they happened you just contacted technical services and they were sorted. The ULTIMATE® system was remarkably stable. And The PROJECT⌂ had up to the minute hardware supporting it. It was not like at the VCC Homes where they struggled with out of date equipment and people who didn't know how to use it. The PROJECT⌂ was different. Such problems didn't occur. Until now. Pryce would have to find instructions and quick.

'Shut the systems down and get round to your kids to make sure they're safe.' Graham was seriously panicking.

'Okay. I'm on my way,' Pryce replied, no time to enjoy Graham's uncharacteristic lack of control.

However, he didn't know how to 'shut the systems down' comprehensively, so he interfaced with a techie and left him to do the work. Thus buying The Immortal Horses valuable time. It was another mistake. Pryce was getting a reputation for making mistakes and Graham would make sure he paid dearly when the time came.

It couldn't have been more than five minutes later that Pryce entered The Project House. He went to Nike's room first. Even though he had been watching Nike's screen live.. well maybe he'd taken his eye off it for a moment while he was thinking... It was natural to assume that Nike would be the root of the problem. Entering the room, without knocking, he found Nike was staring at a blank screen.

'What happened?' he asked Pryce with a butter wouldn't melt tone.

'I thought maybe you'd be telling me that,' Pryce replied.

Nike shrugged. 'No idea. But how can I get on with 'productive' work when.....'

Cute. But Pryce wasn't in the mood for cute. There would be time to discuss the 'productivity' of emotion later. For now he moved on to Omo's room, just as Flora came out of her own.

'My screen's gone blank,' she said, surprised.

'There's an infection,' Pryce retorted, not giving himself time to reflect on the combination of mental and physiological effects seeing Flora had on him, as they piled into Omo's room just in time to see his screen reading

YOU HAVE BEEN HACKED
BY
THE IMMORTAL HORSES

Nike didn't react. Outwardly. He'd sort of expected this, but he wasn't going to own up to anything.

Omo turned round to Pryce as his screen went blank. 'What does it mean?' he asked.

'We have to shut the system down,' Pryce replied matter of factly, 'there's a system malfunction.'

'You said infection.' Flora was puzzled. 'What infection? How?'

'I didn't do anything,' Omo said, 'I was in the middle of my work and it just came up.'

'And you?' Pryce quizzed Flora and Nike, 'Did either of you get any message?'

'No,' Flora replied. 'My screen just went blank.'

Nike shook his head. 'Mine too,' he lied.

The evidence suggested that the infection had most likely come in through Omo's screen, and this was where Pryce would have to start investigations. Without all the facts. Because no one else knew that Nike had seen the infection message before, and not just in Helen's room.

'I didn't do anything.' Omo was getting worried. He was going to be the centre of attention and he didn't like that.

'When can we go back to work?' Flora asked. Ever the

optimist. Or pragmatist.

'My 'productive' schedule hasn't been updated,' Nike grumbled. 'What's wrong with the system these days?'

Pryce called them all into the common room. Time to sit down and calm down and try to work out what to do. The techie guy had obviously got the screens shut down, which itself was enough to disturb kids for whom constant online access was as vital as breathing. He sent Flora off to make them all an ULTIMATE® coffee, and buy himself some time to think how best to approach this. He had started off certain that Nike was behind this, but Omo seemed to be reacting badly and Nike surely wasn't that good an actor. Well, vactor. Actors had been done away with some twenty years before when ULTIMATE®'s virtual system of VACTOR'S came into their own. They made the 3d Avatar animations of the early 21st century look pitiful. They were more convincing and a lot cheaper and less temperamental than the 20th century Real Thing, and they were all these kids had ever known. But Pryce was digressing. No time for that. He needed to focus on the task in hand. Ask the questions. Answer the questions. Resolve the situation. But how?

'Okay. Let's look at this logically,' Pryce began.

The facts, such as they were known, were as follows. Nike, Omo and Flora had been going about their usual 'productive' work schedule. Pryce had got infection alarms and five minutes later the first thing the kids knew about it was that their screens stopped working. Apart from Omo's, which was obviously the last to be shut down. He'd got that HACKING warning from The Immortal Horses. Pryce meticulously checked what each of them was doing leading up to the infection. Flora was completing an interactive survey on the relative merits of ULTIMATE® clothing brands. Omo was contributing to the ULTIMATE® discussion on how best to improve theories of choice. Nike claimed to be gaming, though Pryce of course knew he was seeking definitions for emotion. He let that pass for now though. He didn't want Nike to think he was spying on him after all. He'd logged that question too. And Pryce could see no way in which Nike's activity would be relevant to an infection. Irritating, off topic, but not an infection threat. And after all, Omo's was the computer which carried the infection message.

Pryce had no idea how anyone would hack into the system, but he'd have thought it would be through games. He wracked his mind for the dim distant past of his youth when viruses could be downloaded in software or through opened e-mails. There would be no point him mentioning any of this to the fresh faced, puzzled kids in front of him, because they had no idea what viruses, emails or even software downloading meant. All were terms 'in History' which you didn't have to bother about, because the ULTIMATE® system was so transparent, immediate and ubiquitous that you didn't need to have any idea what you were actually doing in computing terms. This was part of the problem with the older generation. Those who had grown up with computers had expectations of an interaction with them where computers were tools which went wrong and they, as humans had to fix them. This was no longer the perception. The US™ just WAS. Remember, *there is no Us and Them, only US™*. It wasn't just catchy marketing speak. It was as fundamental a truth as could exist in the ULTIMATE® world. You didn't question it. You didn't ask yourself if you believed it. You just accepted it. ULTIMATE® would keep you safe. Except now, they hadn't.

'So, it looks like the infection came in through your terminal, Omo,' Pryce stated. He looked at them all to gauge reaction. If it had been Nike, surely he wouldn't let Omo take the rap? The kids all knew that Pryce would have to report that back to Graham. Omo would have to be assessed at a high level to see where he might have compromised the system. Pryce found three blank faces staring back at him.

'Any ideas?' Pryce threw that one out. From reaction, Flora and Nike obviously knew nothing about the whole thing.

Omo looked uncomfortable.

'Could it be connected with Nike's Nan's screen? That was playing up too,' Omo offered. He, like Pryce wanted a solution but he wanted one that let him off the hook.

'Any reason why it should?' Pryce asked.

There was a long silence. Then Omo admitted,

'She asked me to look at it.'

'And did you?'

'Well, I touched it, but I didn't do anything to it.' Omo felt like he was about to be caught up in something he knew nothing about.

It seemed unlikely that touching the hardware would bring about an infection but Pryce had nothing else to go on. This would have to go in the report too.

'And you, Nike?'

'I never touched it.'

'No. But you've been back there since...'

'The techies were there all the time. We weren't even in the room with it,' Nike replied. Cast iron alibi eh?

'Okay. Well, there's nothing we can do about it now.' Pryce stated the obvious. 'I'll get back to my boss with my report and we'll get things up and running again as soon as possible. We'll need to run diagnostics, and probably change all your schedules and the like... in the meantime, you're on holiday.'

'What's a holiday?' Flora asked. People didn't take holidays now. Not real holidays. If you wanted a break you took a virtual break, via the US™. And clearly they couldn't do that, not with the screens off and the systems down. It was one of the key social transformations brought about by ULTIMATE®.

Omo had at least a partial answer to Flora's question.

'Don't you remember the tenets of social transformation?' he asked her.

Flora shook her head. Her mind was full of the immediate present, not with how we'd got there. Omo explained.

'In History, people used to travel. It used up precious resources. It took time away from 'productive' work and they used to save up MONEY to do it. They used to go abroad...

'What's abroad?' Nike asked. Even though he knew.

'The world was split into countries, not regions and people would travel from one to the other to experience different ways of life.'

'How primitive,' Flora noted.

'Yes.'Omo agreed. 'But it's what they did. In History. Then things changed. They were changing before ULTIMATE® transformed the world actually. Travel became hard work. People had to queue at airports, there were terrorist threats at every step of the process of travel. There were ash clouds and freak storms and it was really dangerous. Anyway, everywhere became like everywhere else and the sun tan you got would most likely give you skin cancer.'

Omo reported all this like a story he'd learned, with no sense of meaning, feeling or irony. It was just something he'd learned along the way. Not something very interesting. Just another reason to be grateful that he lived in the ULTIMATE® world.

'Then ULTIMATE® developed the virtual experience which means that you can travel anywhere you like through the US™ system. It cost credits instead of money. It happened in real time with no wastage so you could have virtual mini-breaks anywhere you wanted without leaving your room. It was so much better that pretty soon people stopped going on real holidays. ULTIMATE® resolved the problems of carbon offsetting, time off work, the need for cars and caravans as personal possessions and ULTIMATE® even developed a way of giving you a healthy tan without ever having to expose yourself to the harmful rays of the sun.'

'How?' Nike asked.

'How what?' Pryce responded.

162

'How did they do it?'

Pryce sighed. Nike could never let well enough alone. What did it matter how it had been done? Any of it. It had been done.

Omo was on a roll now though. 'The information was gathered by ULTIMATE® through the sites people loved to interact with, and as the virtual holiday experience was developed, within twenty years the complete economic and social human genome was mapped, trademarked and owned by ULTIMATE®. Everyone played their part. Every time anyone interacted with technology they were part of it. ULTIMATE® made good on their statement. *There is no Us and Them, only US™.* Am I right?' Omo asked, bright eyed, looking to Pryce for confirmation. He was, after all, just reciting information he'd learned. But he was trying to prove to Pryce that he was a conscientious citizen, not the sort of person who would get involved with infections. Omo did not want to lose his place on The PROJECT⌂. He had nothing else after all. No family, nothing. This was everything to him.

'Yes.' Pryce couldn't decide whether to be proud of Omo or worried by him. He'd never thought Omo capable of such feats of memory or recitation. He'd have to report this as well. It probably wouldn't go in his favour. The pertinent question would be: Why did Omo need to remember such things when he could find the answers afresh on the US™? A retentive memory was not a plus in the ULTIMATE® world.

Omo had given a decent appraisal of the social transformation of holidays, but realising that Pryce had a real life perspective, with Omo spent, Flora picked up the baton.

'Did you ever go on holiday?' Flora asked Pryce. It was unusual of her to ask such questions, but then it was an unusual day. She caught him off guard.

'Yes.'

'Tell us about it,' Nike pressed him. 'After all, there's nothing else to do.'

Pryce tried to think what he could tell them. Tried to remember a holiday he'd enjoyed since the childhood trips to the country with his grandparents. Sliding down haystacks and fly fishing in rivers wouldn't cut it with these kids. He had to think of something else. He thought back to 2016. The last time they'd been on holiday, him and Angela.

'It was 2016,' he said.

'Before we came to The PROJECT△,' Nike observed.

'Yes.'

'How did you travel?'

'We flew.'

'You flew?' Nike was interested. No one flew these days. Not in reality. There was no need.

'Wasn't it very dangerous?' Flora asked.

'And environmentally unsound,' Omo added.

They all knew about plane travel in theory. The ULTIMATE® version. Pryce thought back to the reality of plane travel.

'Mainly it was just boring,' he said, 'a lot of waiting around and hours crammed into uncomfortable seats.'

'But how was the holiday?' Flora asked.

Pryce looked at her young, smiling face and remembered that last holiday. It had been marked by arguments. Over children. He'd always assumed they'd have them. And on holiday, he discovered that Angela had signed them up for the 3△G project. Where you gave up your right to children in exchange for privileges. One of which was the holiday. He'd felt cheated.

'That's a decision for both of us,' he'd raged. The Caribbean sunset didn't look so beautiful when you stood next to a woman who'd betrayed you.

'What about the woman's right to choose?' Angela retorted, bringing out of retirement a well out of date twentieth century argument. Typical Angela. She'd use anything to support her position. Smart, but not exactly principled.

She'd talked him round by promising that now she had taken the decision, now there was no chance of her falling pregnant, maybe they should start having sex again, something that hadn't happened more than a handful of times since they were married. Pryce had given up wondering why she didn't want to have sex with him, tired of all the excuses, and unable to truly believe that a fear of pregnancy had been the real fear behind the excuses. He was the one with the hangover Catholicism after all. But that night Angela had relented, almost convincing him that things would be different. They had made love constantly during the two week holiday and he'd begun to think that life would be better in future. That some hoodoo had been resolved. Then, on the last day, just before they headed off for the hell of the airport and the long flight home, she'd pulled the rabbit out of the hat.

'Take the job at genetics counselling. Work with kids. Just don't bring them home.'

With the enthusiasm of a man who thought life was about to get better, Pryce took the transfer. You couldn't always get what you wanted in life after all, and this might well be more practical. Did he really want the burden of being a parent? Wouldn't their relationship be stronger if they could devote all their spare time to each other without the pressures of bringing up children? But hardly was the contract signed when sexually, things went back to normal. Angela was too busy, too tired. She was insistent he should focus on his work. It had been a step down after all, working with children rather than pure theory.

'Work comes first, remember,' she chided him as she turned out the light and rolled away.

When he pursued her over the holiday activity, she dismissed it.

'It was just a holiday thing. It's over. Can you not find some virtual alternative. We've got all the privileges after all. It's the 21st century for goodness sake.'

She was suggesting that if work wasn't enough, he

should find a hobby. Virtual sex would be fine with her. Any sex would be fine with her as long as she didn't have to take part. Pryce took the rejection hard. They never had another holiday. The magic was well and truly over in that respect. But then, after 2016, no one took holidays any more. As Omo had explained, there was no need and a much better alternative was provided by ULTIMATE®.

Pryce came out of his reverie to see three sets of eyes watching him, waiting for something. What could he tell them?

'It's my private memories,' he said, 'not something to share with you. Best kept between me and my wife. There's no meaning in the personal.'

'Are you married?' Flora asked, amazed. She'd never thought of Pryce being married. She'd never thought that much about him at all really, but certainly not about him having a wife.

'Yes.' Pryce didn't want to pursue that line either. 'Look, why don't you three just relax and chat together while I get back to the office and find out what to do next.' Pryce suggested. 'We'll find a way round it.'

He had to get away from Flora and her questioning. Retain a professional difference. The days of 'my wife doesn't understand me' as a wooing tactic for a beautiful young woman were long gone. And precisely because of the way Flora showing an interest made him feel, he had to get some distance between them.

'Will we get our credits re-instated for the time we can't work?' Nike asked.

Cute again Nike. Always cute.

'I expect so. That's not the priority at the moment,' Pryce noted. 'First we've got to work out what went wrong and then we've got to get things up and running again. And in the meantime…. Keep away from the US™.'

That was a command none of them had ever expected to hear.

166

'One more thing,' Nike ventured, as Pryce was standing up to leave. He could see that they had Pryce on the run. Weakened. Now might be just the time.

'What?'

'Who are the Immortal Horses?'

You could have heard a virtual brick drop. Nike knew how to ask them didn't he? The most awkward question at the most awkward time.

'Uh, we'll talk about that when I get back,' Pryce stalled, 'I'll be as quick as I can. Have lunch. Don't worry.'

It wasn't elegant. It wasn't an answer. But it was all Pryce was giving out. He had to work out what he was authorised to tell them. He couldn't afford any more mistakes.

L. AWKWARD QUESTIONS

Pryce filed his report with Graham. Technical support were running every diagnostic and corrective test known to man on the system. It would take a couple of days. Which left Pryce with a problem. What could he do with the kids for a couple of days? They couldn't remember a life without US™ at the centre of it. It would be disorienting and disturbing for them. Pryce's job was to keep them on an even keel. Keep them out of trouble. Graham didn't exactly use the outmoded word 'babysit' but this was what Pryce was detailed to do. He would become less a surrogate father and more a surrogate US™ until the system was fixed and foolproof again.

'You wanted kids,' Graham smarmed, 'now's your chance to try it out.' His tone clearly said, 'Good luck with that!'

Pryce wondered for just an instant how Graham knew he had wanted kids. He didn't remember ever telling anyone but Angela that. How could it be on his files? He hadn't used it as a reason in his interview. Angela had suggested it might make him look too desperate. It might threaten their place on the 3ΔG programme. So how did Graham know?

But he had many more pressing issues to deal with, so he filed that query away in what was left of his memory and turned to the present crisis. Pryce knew his new role would mean answering a lot of questions he was not prepared for. His heart sank as he returned to The Project House where Nike, Omo and Flora were neatly sat on the sofa, waiting for something to happen. Waiting for an interaction.

'So who are The Immortal Horses?' Nike asked.

Nothing like hitting a man when he's down.

'A terrorist organisation.' Pryce responded. Hoping it'd sound boring enough to leave it there, but knowing it wouldn't.

'What's a terrorist?' Nike pressed his advantage.

'Okay, Nike, now remember I'm no match for a knowledge bank. I can't give you a definition, only my opinion.'

'Sure. Whatever.' Nike could see Pryce was uncomfortable.

'It's just... well, what else are we going to do?'

'Play charades?' That was Flora. Where did they come up with this stuff from?

'Charades?' Pryce echoed, astonished.

'Yes.' A pause. 'Pryce. What is charades and how do you play it?' Flora asked.

'What is the definition of play?' Omo added.

This was all getting out of control. Pryce felt his head spinning already. He'd never survive this.

'Okay. Hold it right there. We'll have to have some kind of structure here,' Pryce pointed out, 'I can't deal with all these questions at once, I'm only human. And we've got plenty of time, so let's just take our time and talk about things one at a time.'

The art of conversation had somewhat died after the introduction of US™. It wasn't something that people did, sit and chat together. All the questions and answers and interactions were virtual, via the screen. Pryce didn't remember just sitting talking being so hard, but then he'd not done it to any degree in years. Maybe that was the problem with him and Angela. They didn't talk. No one talked any more. Not really talked. What was there to talk about in the ULTIMATE® world?

And here he was, trying to interact with a generation he knew nothing about, despite having worked with them for the last fifteen years. He'd been bogged down in logging and admin and constructing suitable 'productive' programmes all that time. He realised he knew nothing practical about adolescents. Certainly not ULTIMATE® adolescents. Where did he begin? Pryce decided to try and recreate the sort of seminar feel he vaguely remembered from University. Not a father figure exactly, not a role model exactly, but a sort of mentor. Someone they could trust and rely on. Someone who occasioned respect. He had to try something. And it was the only thing he could think of.

'Okay. Playing was something that children mainly did in History, to pass the time, to entertain themselves. Several theories of play developed which suggested that children learned through play and what kind of adult you would become depended on your play engagement as a child. In fact ULTIMATE® used some of these theories in the early days to develop our own systems. In the late 20th and early 21st centuries game playing became big business and this brought about the development of many of the 'games' you engage with today.'

'History, history,' Omo yawned.

Pryce pushed on, regardless. 'Charades was known as a parlour game…. a game people played in their homes, in rooms like this.'

'But what was it?' Flora was getting impatient, trained as she was to the superfast US™ system.

'It's pretty hard to explain. It was a sort of guessing game where for example I would think of a word and you'd have to guess what it was.'

'What's the point of that?' Nike asked.

'How could we guess?' Flora asked

'I had to mime…. To pretend to do the word without speaking…. And you'd guess from that.'

'Sounds hard,' Omo observed.

'Sounds stupid,' Nike responded.

'Can we play it?' Flora asked.

Pryce shook his head. 'Not now. Maybe later.'

'Okay.' She smiled an accepting smile.

'So who are the Immortal Horses?' Nike hadn't forgotten.

'I told you, terrorists.'

'You didn't give us a definition of terrorist,' Nike pointed out.

'History, history,' Omo observed again.

'Not history if they've hacked into our system and shut it down,' Nike replied.

'I guess terrorist isn't really a good word,' Pryce agreed. 'It is a concept from History, not really applicable to our situation now.'

'But who are they?' Nike knew he was getting to Pryce and he'd push home the advantage.

'I don't really know,' Pryce admitted, 'a group of people, well, I thought they didn't really exist to be honest. And maybe they don't. Maybe it's a virtual virus simulation...'

'So why would ULTIMATE® create and use such a simulation, infect us and shut us down?' Nike asked 'It doesn't make sense.'

'You're right. It doesn't make sense,' Pryce acknowledged. 'Maybe it's a way of testing the system, to see how robust it is.'

'Maybe it IS real people. People out to destroy ULTIMATE®,' Nike challenged.

Omo and Flora looked at each other. They both remembered the birthday cake. The RIP inscribed on it. But no one wanted to say anything now. It was too frightening.

'I don't think so,' Pryce replied, sensing their unease.

'But there are people outside ULTIMATE® aren't there? Ordinary people. In the street?' Nike was giving it his best shot.

'I think you're getting confused.' Pryce replied, trying to calm the situation. 'Just because people aren't part of The PROJECT△ doesn't mean that they aren't part of the ULTIMATE® system. It is an all embracing system, not something you choose any more than you choose to be a human being rather than... a... a....'

'A tiger?' Flora was starting to wake up.

'A tiger?' Pryce was surprised.

'Yes. We saw the death of the last tiger. It was sad.' Flora replied, reliving the experience. 'Why did it have to die?'

'What's the point of tigers?' Omo wasn't asking a

question so much as offering a response to Flora's question. 'ULTIMATE® doesn't need tigers in the system any more than we need to play charades or ride on trains. We have to get rid of the pointless things from history to preserve the ULTIMATE® way of life.' Omo was pleased with his answer.

'But what if The Immortal Horses are real people? What if they do really exist? And live outside ULTIMATE®. What then?' Nike relentlessly brought things back to the central point. If only his skills could be harnessed properly, he could have a bright future.

'No one can challenge ULTIMATE®. Don't worry about it,' Pryce replied, less than convinced. For some reason the phrase 'for your comfort, but primarily for your safety.' resonated through his mind. It was the thoughtless mantra given out by air-stewardesses. Meaningless but potentially vitally important information. ULTIMATE®'s stock in trade. Was he just acting the part of an air steward here? Was the plane about to crash? He didn't know the procedure. He was shaken. And he realised he had to keep the kids from asking difficult questions. He had to divert them. And not by playing charades. He succumbed to an earlier line of questioning and called for back up.

'Would you like to meet my wife?' he asked.

A quick interface on his personal mobile US™ (a perk of the job) and twenty minutes later, Angela appeared at The Project House. Pryce hoped the diversionary tactic would work. He was amazed she'd said yes actually. He didn't expect her to help him in his hour of need. Especially not with her previously expressed views on children. But she'd been quite animated about the possibility. It certainly was a strange day all round.

Omo and Nike weren't in the slightest bit interested in marriage. But when Angela walked in the room, she proved she still had that something. She managed to exude that avatar-like sexuality which appealed to them in virtuality and stunned them when it was standing there in front of them. A lesson in the difference between reality and virtuality they wouldn't forget. Most people of course had no reason to make themselves look stunning in real-time. Most people didn't do that much interfacing. But Angela, even though she worked in pure theory, had hung onto the hair and makeup virtual plasticity of her generation. It was part of her reality. Part of who she was. Pryce couldn't remember if he'd ever seen the 'natural' Angela, so he didn't question it any more. He might, had he been unkind, have reasoned that the 'real' Angela was so well hidden because she was so ugly, inside and out. He wasn't unkind though, he'd just given up noticing. Seeing the looks on Omo and Nike's faces, made him look at her again though. Trying to see what they saw. What he'd seen himself. Because Angela had barely changed in looks over the last twenty years. 'Age shall not wither her' was her motto.

'You're married,' Omo observed, trying to sound disinterested. He was disinterested, in marriage. But Angela was like nothing he'd ever seen. If this was a wife…. Life certainly took on a different dimension without the US™ around to keep you occupied.

Flora found Angela another revelation in an extraordinary day. And she was interested in the concept of marriage. She knew about it in theory of course but ULTIMATE® didn't really need weddings or nuclear families, and the Project Kids had all signed, or their parents had signed on their behalf, a contract which waived their rights to engaging in marriage or parenthood. It was part of the 3ΔG scheme. The same scheme Angela had signed herself and Pryce up to.

Like Pryce, Angela was not used to dealing face to face with young people. But unlike Pryce, she was used to taking charge. She took charge.

'Any questions?' she asked.

Omo and Nike wracked their brains to think of any questions they dared to ask.

Flora just asked. 'Do you have children?'

Angela smiled and began to talk.

'No. We are part of the 3 Δ generation scheme. I'll tell you about it if you like.' And while Pryce went off to make them all a cup of ULTIMATE® coffee, Angela began:

'The 3ΔG scheme was set up as a response to world overcrowding. Following extensive research into chaos theory and various other things too complex for explanation to the general populace, ULTIMATE® revealed a scheme in 2013 which at first was voluntary, then became the norm; to instigate a moratorium on parenthood for 3 generations. There were benefits for people who chose not to have children. The population for 30 years was to re-balance with a 1% allowance for specially chosen breeding couples, to allow the gene pool to develop positively. The lack of wars and the curing of the devastating ailments of the early 21st century meant that something had to be done to contain the population of the world within the limits that could be sustained. It was a radical solution, but then radical solutions were commonplace as humanity dealt with the GRsΩHist.'

Nike was impressed. This woman knew a lot of stuff. Omo was impressed, but mainly by the way Angela's blouse was invitingly unbuttoned just one button too far.

Flora just wanted to know, 'Didn't people mind not having children?' She had vague memories of her own parents and she was sure her mother had cried when she came to The PROJECT△.

' Yes, people complained at first, but subsequently came to realise the importance, and benefit, to their own lives of this first major ULTIMATE® policy.' Angela neglected to point out that most people didn't even know it was an ULTIMATE® policy at that time. People still thought that their governments were in control. They soon learned.

'But now, in the second generation of the programme, people realise that ULTIMATE® has 'saved' the world, so it's not an issue of importance,' Angela continued.

'History, history,' Omo muttered.

'You're right,' Angela remarked. 'We don't have to worry about History now we have virtuality.'

'So why are you married?' Nike didn't feel totally at ease with Angela and that made him want to ask questions. Difficult questions. See how she performed under pressure.

'We were married before.' Pryce stepped in. He didn't want Nike to throw Angela off side. He didn't want to be left on his own with them for the next 48 hours or however long it would take to get things sorted. So he covered for her. It was what you did, wasn't it as a married man? Even if your wife was privately disappointing, you supported her in public.

'Yes. It was before.' Angela rolled her eyes, making it very clear to the kids that if she'd have had the option they wouldn't have got married. Pryce regretted having tried to bale her out. She was poison. He made an excuse and left the room.

Angela upped the ante. Decided to have some fun.

'Now,' she said in her slickest tone. 'Surely there must be other things you want to know. Things you've not asked – him?'

They took up the challenge. Angela was standing before them, sex on legs. What else would they ask?

'What about real sex?'

Flora and Nike were amazed when they heard this question come out of Omo's mouth. What had happened to him today? The Project Kids were not encouraged to think about such things. Of course they had access to the full range of virtual sex interfaces, but it didn't count as 'productive' work and therefore they didn't spend much time engaging with it. Virtual sex was considered something that only those outside the privileged world of The PROJECT△ needed to bother with. Like Habit∞. Project Kids didn't need either. They were special after all.

Angela preened. 'Let me tell you about sex,' she said. And she proceeded to explain how after the GRsΩHist, people got tired and scared and looked for the 'easy' way out. They were looking for a bit of fun, a bit of lightness, a new way of looking at the world. A new way to interact. Virtual existence merged seamlessly with 'real' life till you couldn't tell the difference. There were precedents. When television got boring, the population had moved onto YouTube and Facebook. They found virtual friends with whom they had more in common with than the people you mixed with in 'real' life. ULTIMATE® updated and adapted the virtual social networks and 'alternative world scenarios', integrating them with the porn sites and creating a new and acceptable virtual reality. Real life itself shifted under the watchful eye of ULTIMATE®. Sex undertook a similar shift. It didn't take people that long to believe, through personal experience, that Cybersex is better than no sex. Better than bad sex. Better than monogamous sex. If it's not harming anyone. There was no emotional come-back. No threat of disease and no danger of pregnancy. It wasn't that hard to get used to, once it got really good. The shift from 'safe' sex to virtual sex was seen by most people, if they were honest, as an improvement. After having lived through a couple of decades of the seemingly innocent obsession with the 'perfect' celebrity re-touched created identity, which made people generally dissatisfied with their partners and themselves but unable to do anything about it, ULTIMATE® sex made it all so much easier for real people to give up their messy, awkward, unsatisfying real experiences for ones which made them feel like perfect, celebrity gods.

'So you see,' Angela opined, 'what you call 'real' sex is more or less defunct for most people.'

She explained that ULTIMATE® had put a lot of effort into their virtual experience through the US™ and once people got used to good 3d graphics and avatars and the like... well, who could be bothered to sit in an overcrowded, overpriced pub with a bunch of folk you don't even know and with whose conversation you have no real interest in. When you could be home having virtual sex like a celebrity rock god. It was easy. And so successful that within the life of the 3ΔG project there was a lot of evidence from ULTIMATE® consumer feedback that the project should be extended for at least another 2 generations. With special privileges for people who avoided real sex altogether. As a test. And it turned out that people did not miss having children, or having children around, when they had the ULTIMATE® virtual sex life. And the ULTIMATE® sex life was rated as better than "real" sex by 98 percent of the population.

'And,' she completed as Pryce re-entered the room. 'For anyone who still isn't happy there's always Habit∞.'

Nike, Omo and Flora had all interacted with the data. None of them could see the point of families, marriage or children. But they'd never had this level of explanation. They were stunned.

Pryce watched Angela interact with the kids. They hung off her every word. What the hell had she got that he hadn't? How could she effortlessly deal with them when he found it like swimming through treacle on a daily basis. Her work didn't usually involve live interaction because she was involved in pure adaptive theory work. Yes, it was as boring as it sounds. It had its perks though and it certainly seemed that Angela managed to get what she wanted as a result of it. Yet now, as Pryce watched her interact with the kids, he thought he saw something of the Angela he'd known when they were both in their 20's. A side he'd not seen for a good ten years. She seemed freer with them, happy to talk, to answer questions and tell them things. Perhaps she would have been a good mother? Perhaps she should have had a job that involved personal interaction not one where all interaction was virtual. But it paid well and she was good at it. Omo said something, Pryce wasn't really paying attention to it, but he noticed that Angela laughed. He hadn't heard Angela laugh in he couldn't remember how long. It was attractive.

'What's it like being married?' Flora asked.

Angela wrinkled up her nose. 'That's a hard question to answer,' she said. 'It's an irrelevance to ULTIMATE® life really.'

Pryce wondered whether she was just very good at talking party line, or whether she really felt that way. He thought back to their wedding day in 2011 and to the vows they had made. Angela had not been sexually backward in the months leading up to their wedding and he had anticipated a honeymoon to remember. What he got was a wife who refused to leave the wedding party because she was having a good time, and then who sat up all night watching TV. It was the first of many times he'd felt used and cheated by her. He wondered if she'd felt marriage irrelevant all these years and if so, why had she married him? He'd asked himself this question often over the years and he never liked the answer he came up with.

'It's not really any different to the way you live here,' Angela continued. 'We rub along together and we share the things that it makes sense to share. But it's totally different from what marriage meant in history. Marriage is really a historical concept and we've never really got round to...'

'When we married,' Pryce interjected, 'you made a promise, to stay married for better or worse, until death.'

'Or until divorce,' Angela added.

'Divorce being as outmoded a concept as marriage. ULTIMATE® phased both out at the same time,' Pryce explained. He was sure he remembered some classic text which had stated similar, was it Hamlet? Those that are married should stay as they are, those who are not should not bother.. or something like that. This was effectively the ULTIMATE® policy.

However, it seemed that there was a limit even to Angela's diversionary properties and Nike was soon back on his old path, asking Angela (since he'd got no answer from Pryce and since it was a question more immediate to him than sex) about The Immortal Horses.

Angela didn't answer his question either. She did, he was sure, wink at him, however. And suggested maybe it was time to do something else.

'Why don't I take the boys to my office, to see the adaptive theory unit   and show them something of the advances in question theory?' she suggested to Pryce.

'Flora too, if you're interested.' Delivered in the kind of voice that told Flora she wasn't expected to be interested.'

'That's okay.' Flora said. 'I'd rather stay here with Pryce.'

'I don't know..' Pryce wavered. He was a bit uneasy about this, but didn't like to articulate his feelings. He was worried about Omo and Nike being out of his jurisdiction while the systems were malfunctioning.

As if she could read his mind, Angela pointed out they'd be as safe in her office as anywhere, because the US™ systems there were up and running, uncompromised, uninfected. It was only the look that she threw him as she said,

'Any other reservations?' that made Pryce determined to keep his second reservation to himself. He was worried about being left alone with Flora. He knew he shouldn't be but... and now he wondered if Angela had... no... how could she have an idea of his private thought? His 'guilty secret.' So he acquiesced.

'No, that's fine. You lot go and have a good time. We'll entertain ourselves here.'   And tried not to look too closely at Flora while he said it.

M.   DOWNSHIFTING MEMORIES

Meanwhile Helen was building up her Memory Bank for Nike. Despite her innate mistrust and disgust for the US™ technology and everything it stood for, she had to admit she was rather enjoying the process. As long as she didn't think that anyone other than Nick would get access to it. It was like telling him the story of his family. Something personal. It shouldn't matter to anyone else.

2005. The year they moved to Moray. Helen and Catriona were having what neither knew at the time would be their last walk together, on a wintery morning in the Galloway Forest Park. Catriona, now nineteen was studying at University in Edinburgh and had come home to help clear out her belongings before the big move north. Catriona hit Helen with the bombshell just as they'd stopped to marvel at the view looking down on Loch Trool.   A beautiful view on a cold shimmery morning, destroyed by a bombshell which, in retrospect, Helen should have been expecting.

'Mum. I'm not coming with you,' she said.

While Helen knew Catriona spent most of her time in Edinburgh, she still imagined that her daughter's real 'home' would be wherever the family was. Unable to process the information she replied, 'What colour would you like your new room to be? It's your choice. As long as it's not that awful sunshine yellow you picked when you were eight.'   She was startled by Catriona's response, although of course she should have expected it.

'I don't need a room. Of any colour. I'm staying in Edinburgh. For good.'

'Yes, but you'll want a room for the holidays. Somewhere to keep your stuff?'

'Mum. Don't you get it? I don't want to live in the country. I've moved out. I'm an adult now. Lauren and I are getting a flat together and we'll be there all the time.'

Helen didn't know how to respond to that. It seemed a bit inappropriate to feel that Lauren was a 'bad influence' on Catriona. After all, at nineteen, Catriona surely knew her own mind. If she was honest though, Helen couldn't help but feel uneasy about Lauren and it wasn't just the multiple piercings and red streaked hair. Helen could look beyond that. And when she did, she found something about Lauren that worried her. Helen wondered if she was just feeling jealous. Lauren was Catriona's best friend. Her choice. It's just that she was an urban girl through and through and Helen couldn't reconcile that with the daughter she thought she knew.   'Anyway,   you've   got Torquil. He's more use on a farm than I ever was,' Catriona dismissed the whole thing with the casual cruelty only a self-obsessed teenager, convinced she was an adult, could deliver, 'You'll tell dad for me?'

That really was the final straw. Helen couldn't bow to that. 'If you're old enough to move on, you're old enough to tell him yourself,' she retorted, somewhat shortly. And that was it. The last walk in the Galloway Forest Park was ruined for both of them. That mother/daughter bonding thing was history. Only sourness and recriminations remained as they trudged their way down the hill with the dogs, playfully unaware of the atmosphere, running circles round them.

Helen asked herself where it had all gone wrong? Catriona used to be her best wee pal, all the time she was growing up. Torquil was interested in tractors and machinery and noise and dirt but Catriona, like Helen, enjoyed the company of animals and the peace of the country lifestyle. Until Foot and Mouth. She reflected, not for the first time, on the trauma meted out by the Foot and Mouth epidemic of 2001. No one who lived through the experience came out the same. No one survived untouched by it. The senseless slaughter of thousands of healthy animals against a fear of spreading

182

disease. The rank smell of burning flesh lived in the nostrils and hung in the air for what seemed like weeks. It was overpowering and intolerable. It was infinite sadness. It made grown men cry, and more than that, it made them give up. It split up families and ruined livelihoods and generally depressed the countryside in a way nothing had done before. Helen and Randall had found it hard, but they were adults. Catriona was fifteen when her world changed.

Helen hadn't realised quite how much it had impacted on her daughter until now. It seemed that Catriona had felt her whole emotional life was being ripped away from her and she went numb. She turned away from the comfort of family and the country which no more represented peace but instead carnage. She went in search of other pleasures. And vowed to get away from the country as soon as possible. She moved out at sixteen and took Highers in sciences at the Glasgow Nautical College, from where she got into Heriot Watt to study Chemistry. She met Lauren who was studying Engineering, mainly, Helen unkindly thought, because it was something girls 'didn't' do. Helen had long since forgotten her own aspirations in that respect. She had been six after all. Life moved on. But Lauren seemed like the kind of girl who wanted to kick over the traces at every possible opportunity. A mothers interpretation is not always the most objective and Helen found Lauren a bad influence on a peaceful, naïve country girl like Catriona.

Catriona brought Lauren home to the Galloway farm a couple of times but Lauren didn't like it. She scoffed at the second rate nature of the bathroom, lack of a power shower, the mud around the yard, the smell of the beasts. And Catriona was fooled by it. Worse still, Torquil fell under her spell. But that was later.

Helen took a break from recording. She drank a cup of ULTIMATE® tea and wondered if it was meant to be Earl Grey or Darjeeling. You couldn't tell. Tea was just tea. Very few people drank it nowadays anyway. Perhaps precisely because it was more ULTIMATE® than tea. But it was hot and wet and filled a gap. It's just that for Helen it didn't fill enough of a gap. The gap that needed filling was her real past and it became more appealing the more she relived it for Nick. However hard she tried to stick to purpose, Helen was still worried by the notion of shared memories. She had come to realise that her own perspective might not be as objective as she'd always thought it was. Through this process of recall she was beginning to understand that memory is intensely personal and that sharing it is in some sense impossible. The memories which make up ones identity are the deeply buried ones which in some vindication of a strange quantum theory seem to become transformed when let out of one's head and heart and into the domain of another being.

In 1984 she'd felt excited as she left her job interview, hoping to see a man she didn't know. A man who would become her husband. But he wasn't there. How did he remember that event? She'd never asked him. She'd never asked him why he wasn't there. It had been enough for her that he found her again. But now she wondered what had happened that day. What was Randall's memory of the event? How would it differ from hers? It was trivial, but all the more important because she couldn't ask him. Her own memory was locked and there was no way of including Randall, the focus of the memory. He remained a projection of her memory. Was that all forty years of life together had achieved? She wanted to give Nick something he could hold onto for the future. Something more than memory. Some kind of truth. Otherwise ULTIMATE® had won. It occurred to her that ULTIMATE® had won anyway, but she refused to admit it. Even if she recorded her memories, even if ULTIMATE® owned the copyright, the meaning remained with her.

They moved to Moray in September 2005. Without Catriona. Torquil was sixteen and excited about the possibilities a new farm would bring. Randall was, if not excited, at least resigned to the difference that 'downshifting' would bring to their lives. They were all trying to stay positive. The major change was that instead of being tenant farmers of several hundred acres, they would now be owners of their land. A mere ten acres. All their savings had gone, but as Randall pointed out, this was their final move so it was worth it. The land in Moray was more of a smallholding than a farm and the aim was towards self-sufficiency. Randall had become disenchanted with the way agriculture was going, the way society as a whole was going and he wanted to be master of his own destiny as far as possible. He knew that things would only get worse, not better. And he was right.

The night before they left Galloway, with everything packed up and ready to go, they sat down round the fire one last time. Torquil was out with his pals playing pool at the local pub for the last time. Randall had no work to distract him and he picked up his guitar for the first time in years. There was still a dispute as to whether the guitar would make the trip north. Randall thought it a waste of space, Helen disagreed.

'It's part of who you are,' she said.

'It's part of who I was,' he replied, 'a long time ago. Times change. We change. I don't expect I can even play it any more.'

'Give it a try,' she entreated him, 'some of the old songs.'

He point blank refused to play any of the songs he'd written as Randall and the Reivers. She hadn't understood at the time, but now she realised that maybe he had personal memories he had not wanted to hold onto. After a few rusty chords, his fingers were soon back into their old rhythm and they sang a medley of country and folk classics together in front of the waning fire.

He paused for a break, obviously not enjoying the experience as much as Helen was.

'What will you miss most about Galloway?' she asked him.

'Uh... I don't know... what about you?'

'Nature. Things I just see. Being part of it.'

'Things like what?'

'Exploding thistles.'

'What?'

' You know. When the down just bursts from them, after the purple head forms.'

'When they set seed and make more work,' he replied unromantically.

'White daffodils.'

'They'll have white daffodils in Moray, I'm sure,' he replied.

'Cobwebs on the gate,' she added, determined to get some sort of response from him.

'Ah. Cobwebs. Of course.' He was laughing at her now.

'Oh stop it,' she said, realising he was taking the rise, 'you love it here too. Why are you acting like it's nothing? It was your dream first,' she added.

It hurt too much for Randall to say out loud how his dream had been brutally beaten by the reality they'd lived through in the last fifteen years. While Helen's memories of Galloway were of cobwebs on the gates and the soft down of 'exploding' thistles and the yearly excitement at the arrival of the white daffodils, Randall was bowed, but not totally broken by Chernobyl, and BSE and Foot and Mouth and being sold down the river by an increasing industrial approach to agricultural policy. He viewed Galloway as an example of betrayal. Of building everything up only to see it all knocked down because YOU DON'T OWN ANY OF IT.

'Ah, everywhere's the same,' he said.

'That's not true,' she added, 'if that was true we'd have

moved to Canada, or New Zealand, you know that. There are places where it's easier to make a living.'

'Make a living yes,' he replied, 'but we don't want to make a living do we. We want to live.'

'And that's my point,' she said. 'That's the dream. We know we're tied to this land. We both felt alien even in London. We have to stay in Scotland. And we'll own our own place now.'

'You sound like you're trying to convince me to move,' he said, 'I'm the one who's making you move from the place you love. Do you know how that makes me feel?'

'Don't be stupid. I told you then and I still mean it. I just want to be with you. It doesn't matter where.'

'As long as it's not Canada, or New Zealand or London or....' He was teasing her again. 'Go north old man,' he added in a mock-serious tone and picked up the guitar again.

Torquil entered the house to the strains of Dougie Maclean's 'Caledonia.' He'd never heard the song and he'd never seen his father play the guitar. They sat all three together by the fire, allowing themselves a moment of nostalgia. Making a shared memory before moving to a new life.

And Moray was no bad place to live. Helen got to keep pigs and goats for the first time, Galloway being a fiercely beef and sheep land. The soil was more fertile in Moray and this made the possibility of self-sufficiency more real, even if it meant a change in farming mindset for them all. Urban people like Lauren just saw farming as farming, but the difference between a primarily livestock based farm and a primarily arable production method was immense.

Randall used to joke that he was retired. He was used to being up at 4.30 every morning of the year. All through the winter of 2006 Helen and Randall enjoyed their first season of late mornings. They could still call 7am a late start. All around them, the Moray farmers who didn't have to answer the call of animals, only to plough and sow and harvest, showed Randall the possibility of taking life that little bit easier. They even had weekends.

The smallholding still provided plenty of work, however, and was still a harder life than the 'lazy ways' which was what Randall jokingly called largescale local arable farming. It would have been possible for Helen and Randall to become even more active and rooted in the community than they had been in Galloway. But they found that their time together became even more precious. They were working for themselves now and they resented any time spent away from this most precious of tasks. They shut themselves away, kept their heads down and lived for each other. And they loved it. They felt no need to be social beings, no need to take part in a life geared around social events and committees for the British Legion, civic pride and things which Randall scoffed at as part of the legacy of landed gentry than farming related activity. Things were fine as long as they lived in their own personal space. But inevitably, the wider world crept in. They found peace and learned acceptance in Moray but they also learned that the world is out there, and it won't let you be in peace. Not indefinitely.

In the autumn of 2008 Catriona made her first visit home. Randall was all for killing the fatted pig Helen had nurtured from a piglet. He had to make do with a lamb. He was excited about seeing his daughter again, having missed her during the three silent years while mother and daughter played out their mutual mistrust. Catriona had been too busy and Helen had been too proud. Randall had known better than to interfere but he had missed his daughter more than he had imagined.

'It's a new start,' he told Helen, 'we have to accept her as she is. Her life is her choice.'

Helen agreed to give it a go but when Lauren came too it felt like a challenge too far. Lauren despised the country. Catriona knew that. Why had she brought her?

'Maybe she feels she needs some support,' Randall

observed.

'Why? This is her home,' Helen began.

'No. It's our home. Not hers,' Randall pointed out.

The visit went much better than any of them expected. While Helen was worried by Catriona's pale, thin appearance, she didn't comment on it. She took it as a sign of urban living. She even made an effort with Lauren, resisting the urge to ask why she felt it necessary to festoon her face with ironmongery. Both girls showed interest in the pigs, Lauren even expressed an interest in the farm machinery and suggested some ways in which things could be made more efficient. Helen was forced to admit that Lauren's engineering skills had some practical benefits. But the person who was most affected by the visit was Torquil.

Torquil was about to turn twenty. He'd adjusted well to their new life, indeed he revelled in it, though Helen had been worried he wasn't 'mixing' enough. Between them, she Randall and Torquil had become if not self-sufficient, then perhaps too insular for their own good. It was okay for her and Randall, they had each other, but it didn't seem right for a young lad. As soon as he met Lauren, Torquil was smitten. There was more than machinery being discussed round the back of the hayshed, as Catriona found out when looking for the friend that her brother had hijacked. A lot can happen in a weekend when you're twenty.

At the end of the weekend, as they waved Lauren and Catriona off at the door, Torquil charged with driving them the ten miles to the nearest station, Randall reflected, 'Well that went better than expected, didn't it?'

Helen had to agree with him, though she still felt uneasy. 'Did you see the way she was making eyes at him?'

'Who?' Randall had been lost in the joy of having his daughter back, he'd seen nothing.

Lauren, with Torquil,' she replied.

'Oh woman. You need a television.'

'Why?'

'You're turning it into a soap opera,' he joked. 'They're just kids. Let them live their lives, eh?'

'He's a good looking boy,' she pointed out, ' a good catch....'

Randall kissed her. 'Don't judge everyone by your own standards,' he laughed. And that was the end of the matter.

Until a month later when Torquil announced he was going down to spend the weekend in Edinburgh with Catriona. Helen was reluctant.

'Your dad needs you here,' she said.

'Dad?' he asked.

'Don't be daft,' Randall replied. 'I'm sure you're due a weekend off. We can manage fine without you.'

'Why did you do that?' Helen asked when Torquil was packed off on the train.

'It's good for them to spend time together. And it might make Catriona more keen to come back up here. We're opening doors, or building bridges or whatever you want to call it,' he said.

'But Lauren...?'

'We can't live their lives for them,' Randall pointed out.

It was a statement he repeated the next spring when Torquil sat them both down to tell them his 'news.'

'Lauren's pregnant.'

'And?' Helen wasn't trying to make it harder for him, she just didn't want to hear what came next.

'And I'm the father.' There was a long pause. 'So we're getting married.'

'Congratulations,' Randall said, though Helen could tell he was as shocked as she was. 'I'll get us all a drink to wet the baby's head.'

Which gave him the excuse to leave the room and left Helen alone with her son, barely out of his teens, to deal with 'the situation.'

'You don't have to marry her,' she said, weakly.

He gave her a very hard stare. 'Mum. I want to marry her.'

'Yes, of course,' she backtracked, 'I was just....'

'Mum. You'd want me to do the right thing....' he continued.

She kept her question, 'the right thing for who?' firmly in her head. And they all drank to the uncertain future.

Despite Torquil's assertions, Helen was actually a bit surprised that a wedding followed. She hadn't seen Lauren as the marrying kind, too young, too flighty, a girl with too much living to do. But to Lauren a wedding was a great event. A party. The opportunity to gorge on consumer activity. Torquil went along with it because he wanted Lauren to be happy. He wanted to be a good husband and a good father and the learning curve was steep. Lauren was high maintenance. A pregnant Lauren was even more high maintenance. Torquil's world was changing rapidly in directions he'd never imagined possible. Randall joked that the marriage was less about losing a son and more about testing the limits of their self-sufficiency.

It seemed that Torquil and Lauren never had the conversation about what they would do, where they would live when married with a baby – a son as it turned out to be. Torquil just assumed that because he was a farmer they would live in Moray and Lauren just assumed that because LIFE was lived in the city, Torquil would adapt to her plans. It was not a marriage made in heaven by any stretch of the imagination. It was a car crash of massive proportions just waiting to happen. And happen it did.

Torquil Ellis Christie married Lauren Margaret Blair in July 2009. Their wedding seemed to be the last big party anyone ever had, before the country was plunged into recession. Nicholas Blair Christie was born in February 2010 in the middle of the coldest winter recorded in history. Fifty years to the day Helen was born. Better than a birthday cake. He was a snow baby as she had been. It gave them the strongest of bonds and Helen made a secret promise always to watch out for him, as long as he lived. A promise she had tried to keep.

Baby Nicholas was born in Moray because Torquil and Lauren were living with his doting grandparents, who were there at the event. It was not a happy situation. Lauren had stuck it out in Edinburgh until the December. Torquil had abandoned the farm to try and find work in the city, but had no qualifications and no skills and people were being laid off right left and centre. Even Woolworths went bust. At the time of course no one knew this was the start of the ULTIMATE® take-over of the world. Much was said about how the world had changed when Woolworths ceased to exist, but with hindsight, it was more cataclysmic than anyone at the time could ever have imagined. People's lives as individuals and also as a group, were changed for ever. Pryce was getting into ULTIMATE®. ULTIMATE® was getting into everything. And Torquil and Lauren retreated back to Moray. They came with the first fall of snow on December 18th. Randall and Helen's self-sufficiency would just have to learn to expand to feed another two mouths. It did so.

But Brand conscious Lauren would clearly never settle in rural Moray. Snow lingered until May that year and when it had finally gone, Lauren high-tailed it back to the city leaving Helen literally holding the baby. Lauren pointed out that someone had to earn money for her family and she was the only one capable of doing it. She left Torquil and Nick behind.

Helen found looking after a baby again a strange pleasure. She strapped him to her front while she worked on the vegetable patch, for every bit like a South American peasant woman. He grew up a real child of nature. But mothers have rights and Lauren, for whom everything was commodified, saw Torquil and especially Nick as her 'possessions' so Nick also became familiar with the train between Aberdeen and Edinburgh. Things went on like that for several years.

Helen wondered when it was that Lauren started with drugs. Had she been on them when she met Torquil? Or was it a response to a difficult situation. A way to escape a reality that was no longer what it had promised to be on the tin. Either way, drugs entered Helen and Randall's family like they did so many other families at the turn of the centuries. Insidiously, furiously and catastrophically. Helen didn't even know what drugs Lauren took. Lauren probably didn't know herself. But Helen was sure that it was Lauren who got Catriona hooked. Not the other way round. Helen rushed the memory into the Memory Bank because there was no easy way to relive it.

A spring morning 2016. A phone call. Torquil answered it. He was in for a cup of tea. A quick mid morning break from feeding the animals.

'No. NO.'

Helen rushed out of the kitchen as she heard her son give the kind of noise she hadn't heard since he was three and trapped his fingers in the tractor door. She found him pale faced and incomprehensible. She picked up the phone. The voice on the other end was calm, clinical, and Helen only picked up the vital words.

'Your daughter….. overdose… post mortem….. arrangements for the body.'

The family which stuck together through everything came unstuck that day. Each of them had a different grief.

Helen blamed Lauren. She'd known the girl was bad luck. Torquil blamed himself, he'd known Catriona was on drugs. He'd dabbled himself with the lifestyle his wife and his sister shared. Randall didn't have time for blame, but he shut his emotions away. Even when he was holding Helen's hand tight at the funeral, he was miles away emotionally. It was the first time she'd felt so far apart from him. Grief locks people away. Isolates them from each other. Grief, like memory, is intensely personal.

Catriona's death was the end for Torquil. The end of drugs. The end of Lauren. He saw his parents pain and he felt the responsibility for his own son more keenly. He and Nick retreated to the farm and locked themselves away. Randall buried himself even deeper in RIP, blaming society, not Lauren, for his daughter's death. Helen was just numb. For months. Until something worse happened. Which was always due because things were always going to get worse as ULTIMATE® tightened their invisible grip.

Helen closed her eyes for a moment to shut out the memories which were downloading in real time onto the US™ screen. It was too painful. She opened them with the feeling that she was not alone. She turned round, breathing deeply.

'Hello Nan.' Nike stood at the door.

That was unexpected.

'How much did you see?'

'Enough.'

'Well, it's your history. You wanted to know.'

There was a long silence. Helen finally broke it.

'Will you help me?'

'How, Nan?'

'Find out whether the RIP still exists.'

'Okay Nan. And do you want me to find out who sent you the cake?'

'Could you?'

'I think so. I've met… someone, who I think might be able to give me the answers.'

Helen was surprised, pleased and worried at the same time.

'Be careful, Nick'

He shrugged it off.

'Course I will, nan. There's nothing to be afraid of.'

If only he knew.

After Nick left, Helen returned to the Memory Bank because there was nothing else she could do. She was relieved that he had come in before she got to the crucial point. Although she knew he had to know it one day, she couldn't bear to be the one to tell him that his mother sold him to The PROJECT△ for Habit∞. She wanted to try and make sense of RIP past, and possibly present.

Randall had first become involved in 2011, but it wasn't till 2017 that he took a really active part. After the death of Catriona he shut down emotionally and physically. But when Lauren returned and left with Nick, he pulled himself out of his isolation. He couldn't live without feeling he had a choice in the matter. He had to do something to fight against a system which could do this to people. He told Helen it was about injustice but she thought it was more about trying to make amends. It was locking the stable door after the horse had bolted.

She had tried to talk him out of it. 'Can't we just stay us?... I don't care what's happening in the wider world,' she said as he prepared to go out for an RIP council meeting. She had lost all confidence in the outside world and wanted to keep what was important to her within sight at all times.

'It doesn't matter if you care or not. The changes will affect us either way,' he replied.

'Not if we don't let them. Not if we keep our heads down,' she begged.

'I have to get involved.'

That was it. He made his choice. The choice that changed all their lives. Or maybe that was unfair. Maybe ULTIMATE® was making the choices even then.

A sense of justice was something Helen thought she and Randall had shared. But looking back on it, perhaps they came at it from different angles.   It might be true, as her father had never tired in saying 'You can't fight city hall', but you could go down fighting. Randall's view had been that you couldn't just give in because you couldn't win. You did the right thing because it was the right thing to do after all, not because it was comfortable or because you would be praised for it.

In 2017 Torquil was devastated at the loss of his son. Randall was still reeling from the loss of his daughter and losing his grandson seemed to change something fundamental in him. They were men and they wanted to do something about it. The doctrine of acceptance seemed like weakness under conditions when men wanted to fight. So they fought. They didn't win. But they went down fighting. Their lives had had a value and a purpose. Looking at the magnolia walls, Helen felt not only that she'd let Randall down, but that she had let and was repeatedly letting both herself and Nick down. She remembered the words of a song….. *'pray for the dead and fight like hell for the living….'* and then remembered who had originally uttered the phrase, one Mother (Mary) Jones who was an activist at the beginning of the 20th century. She had died in 1930, exactly 100 years ago this year. Helen felt ashamed. Mother Jones had never given up fighting, for the mines, for children. She didn't let anything put her off. She was credited as saying 'I hope to live long enough to be the great-grandmother of all agitators.' And here was Helen, living like a dead woman in an ULTIMATE® Home. She had to resume the fight. If not for herself then for Nick. He was her only living relative, after all. She had to become an agitator.

'Enough is as good as a feast.' It was one of her mother's more prevalent and more annoying sayings. The first time Helen heard it was when they were planting an apple tree in 1965. It was a birthday present for her fifth birthday. She was overjoyed with the task of digging and ran inside to get water, covered in mud from head to foot.

'What are you doing?' her mother asked.

'Digging my tree,' Helen replied, overjoyed.

'However big is the hole?' her mother asked.

'As big as ever can be,' Helen replied.

'Well, just remember, enough is as good as a feast,' her mother said as she wiped the mud from Helen's face.

Helen hadn't understood the phrase then, and every time it was repeated throughout her childhood she'd failed to understand it. In her teenage years she used to laugh behind her mother's back at the ridiculousness of the construction. Once she even challenged it.

'It's such a stupid saying, mum. Enough is OBVIOUSLY not as good as a feast. A feast is much, much better.'

As she scattered her parents ashes round the apple tree they'd planted for her fifth birthday, by 2004 a large productive tree in a house with a sale board outside, Helen wished she'd had the chance to tell her mother that Randall had finally taught her to understand and appreciate that most favoured of sayings. It was not that the two things were the same, it lay in the concept of good.   A feast, by definition (ULTIMATE® or otherwise) required too much of something. Enough, was, well, enough. Sufficient. By definition, you needed no more. The sale of the house she had grown up in, and scattered her parents ashes in, helped pay for the move to Moray. She'd cried over not being able to move the tree.

'We can't move it.' Randall was practical. 'It's far too big. It would never survive….. and… it belongs here. With them.'

'How can I sell the house… with them here?' she asked, hoping Randall could make some sense out of a senseless situation.

'This is where they always wanted to be,' he replied, simply. 'And they're giving us the gift we need to be where we always wanted to be. That's enough. Surely?' He turned the key in the lock and didn't let her look back as they drove away for the last time.

Randall helped Helen realise that her parents had given her something more than money. Their house represented something more important than the careful, middle-class values which Helen had mostly despised. It represented acceptance.

Her parents had tried to teach her, but it was Randall who finally made Helen understand that enough was all you needed. You didn't need a feast, you didn't need to strive for perfection. The path to her own personal spiritual enlightenment lay in understanding that acceptance was the goal, not success. Success was a created capitalist concept which could never be achieved. Accepting life on its own terms, being happy with enough was deeply counter to the capitalist model, and therefore a revolutionary activity, albeit a peaceful and un-noticed one. Acceptance became the doctrine Randall and Helen lived by in Moray and was the value they had tried to instil in their children. Until ULTIMATE® changed the rules of the world. Then it was time to fight.

Helen had assumed it was a fight they had lost. She'd somehow assumed for the last ten years that RIP had been destroyed by all powerful ULTIMATE® machine like everything else she held dear.   But the birthday cake suggested otherwise. She felt a glimmer of hope. What would life be like if RIP did still exist? Could she dare to hope that Randall was still alive? No. That was a step too far. Her mind spun. If she or Nick could find out something…. Suddenly it occurred to her that rotting in an ULTIMATE® VCC home was a choice she shouldn't have made. Because Randall believed that even when you had no choice, you still had some choice. If nothing else you had a choice of how you faced your lack of choice. Attitude, not image, was everything to Randall. Helen was pulled up short with the horrible fear that she'd betrayed Randall and in doing so betrayed herself. Maybe after all it wasn't ULTIMATE® who had stolen her life, it was she who had laid it down, given up in the grief of losing the man who made her life complete.

N. TRADING PLACES

As Nike left Helen's to make his way back to Angela's office he had it in his mind that she, or her systems, might help him find out about RIP. Nike had great confidence in his own ability to use other people's knowledge, and if necessary knowledge bank interfaces, to his own advantage. And he had seen enough of the system Angela had access to, to know it kicked serious ass over Pryce's. Angela was much further up the ULTIMATE® food chain.

Angela was a puzzle. Nike had never met anyone like her before and so she interested him but it was what she represented that interested him more. Which was a bit frustrating because in the office Angela had seemed a lot more interested in Omo than in Nike. Nike found this unusual. In his previous admittedly limited social experience, when he and Omo were in a room together he was the 'interesting' one, the centre of attention, whereas Omo was the sidekick. He'd never questioned it before. He'd always just accepted it. But it wasn't like that with Angela.

It was Angela who had suggested that Nike leave them and go see his Nan. He'd jumped at the chance, not given it a second thought, but now that he was on his way back he kept wondering why it was that Angela had wanted to be on her own with Omo. He was sure he'd noticed something between them. And Omo had been acting really strangely ever since Angela had pitched up in The Project House. What Nike hadn't spotted was Angela suggesting to Omo that maybe he'd like some practical experience of 'real' sex. Nike had been too busy in the depths of Angela's highgrade US™ system, the likes of which he'd never seen before, to notice what was happening right behind him. Lucky Omo was so dark skinned or the blushes would have given it away.

Nike never heard Angela's offer, or Omo's response. All he knew was that suddenly, Angela suggested that he go and visit his Nan. It was less of a suggestion, more of an instruction. She promised him she'd tell him about The Immortal Horses at a later date, 'when I've got the up to date accurate data collated.' It felt like he was being palmed off but he'd bought it because he had to. But Nike was sure of one thing; Angela was the kind of person who only ever did anything with a reason. She would not act randomly, or on a whim. He'd seen in The Project House that she could run rings round Pryce (not that that was hard) and now he wondered if perhaps she'd run rings round him?

He shrugged. He'd get his own back. He was going to get an answer for his Nan. He wouldn't let Angela put him off. He'd get her data off her. He was so absorbed in the thought that he wasn't watching what was going on around him. And so he didn't see the man until he was right upon him, speaking to him.

'Hey. You want to know about The Immortal Horses?'

Nike looked up. The voice belonged to a man about his own age, slimmer but taller, sporting a sort of goatee beard and wearing a hooded top which covered most of his head. He couldn't help but look intimidating. Nike realised all too late that he'd been approached by what might be considered an 'ordinary' person. He didn't have a term of reference for dealing with such a person so he didn't know what to do. But he wasn't going to run. Or look scared. Or be scared.

'What?'

'I said, d'you want to know about The Immortal Horses?'

'Why?'

This was a high risk strategy, Nike knew. People didn't usually like you answering questions with questions but he didn't know what else to do. For the first time in his life that he could remember, he felt vulnerable. But also excited. Because of COURSE he wanted to know about The Immortal Horses.

'I'm not playing games here mate. You want to know or not?'

200

'Yeah. You going to tell me?' Nike sounded as cool as he dared.

'Come with me.'

It wasn't a command. It was only a statement. He could have walked away. He could have turned round, or pushed past the guy, or simply stopped the interaction. There was no gun, no knife, no threat, no coercion. Just an invitation. Come with me. It was enough. Nike went.

He entered the erstwhile Trading House, where The Immortal Horses had been tracking him from, trying to look unconcerned. He couldn't believe he'd never noticed the huge, glass fronted building before. In the extensive marble lobby he immediately began to attract attention from all the people who seemed to slip past in a blur as he tried to keep up with the brisk step of his contact. They went into a gleaming elevator and emerged some flights later. Nike was in sensory overload and didn't have time to take in the detail of their clothes and hair but he did notice that they were different. Very different. Except of course, since he was the odd one out, it was he who was different. It felt strange.

'Hey, it's a Project Kid,' some random guy spoke right to his face, as if he wasn't real.

Nike had never had the experience of standing out like a sore thumb. He was attracting all kinds of attention and it felt most uncomfortable. Of course he couldn't know that the main reason for the interest being displayed in him was that most of the people he was passing had been involved in the tracking process which had led him here. To them, he was the 'game' come to life. He was a living, breathing success. He was an object of pride and curiosity.

'Hey man, check him out.'

'Good job …'

Nike followed his contact in a daze through the building, trying to take it all in. They finally came to a halt at an office.

'Wait in there.'

And Nike was left. Waiting in there.

He took time to look round the room. Nike had never seen anything like it, although it would have been recognisable to any person in the pre-ULTIMATE® world as a company boardroom. It wasn't retro. It was antique. It was authentic in the true meaning of the world. It represented a haven of financial capitalism, re-appropriated by The Immortal Horses in a spectacularly bizarre example of the now obsolete doctrine of reduce, reuse, recycle. It was adapted to purpose. A large wooden table all but filled the room. Almost inevitably there was the ubiquitous US™ screen drowning one wall but it wasn't switched on. There were banks of smaller screens on the opposite wall. There was a two way mirror but Nike didn't know that. He wouldn't have known what a two way mirror was whichever side of it he stood. Observational techniques had gone on leaps and bounds since two way mirrors were the must-have boardroom tool.

After enough time to realise how unfamiliar his surroundings were, just enough to make him realise he was really there, the door opened and another man came in. This guy was older, more impressive. He carried himself with authority. He stretched out his hand – a long outmoded gesture, but Nike stuck his own out in response and felt the firm grip. The man looked him firmly in the eyes, but didn't introduce himself as an individual. Instead, he said,

'So here we are. We are the Immortal Horses. What did you want to know?'

That was such a big question Nike didn't know where to begin.

'Uh… who you are… why….?'

'Yes. I imagine it is overwhelming.'

A silence.

'We've been watching you.' The man was still watching Nike. Closely. Gauging his response. It made Nike nervous.

'Why?' His question just slipped out. He couldn't help

himself.

'That is a good question.' The man's stern face almost broke into a smile. Almost.

Nike found that strange. In his experience *Why?* was not a question he got praised for asking. Things here were different. Very different. In his dis-ease Nike rubbed his ßß™, a gesture which didn't go unnoticed.

'That's no good in here. We've disabled it.'

'What? How…?'

'Yes, they said you asked a lot of questions. They didn't say you just uttered question phrases without meaning.'

'Sorry.' Nike was well out of his depth.

The man relaxed slightly. 'Don't worry. You surely don't want the technical details, though I could provide them if you do. We've nothing to hide from you here. And anyway, we're the ones watching you now, not ULTIMATE®. We can control the input and output from it. And we've commandeered your login. You belong to us now. One way or the other.'

Was there an implicit threat? Nike realised he was in very, very deep water without any idea of how he'd got there or how, or even whether he'd get out.

'I'll tell you what I think you want to know. Based on our profiling of you. If that's not sufficient, just shout and I'll fill in the gaps. Okay?'

Nike nodded. He felt every question he'd ever wanted to ask float out of his head which became filled with what he now vaguely recognised as an emotion. Fear. It was not pleasant. And he couldn't shake it off.

'As usual with you Nick, (Nike noticed that the man called him Nick) you ask the wrong question to get the answer you desire. You think you want to know about The Immortal Horses, but really you want to know about yourself. You want to know about The PROJECT△. Don't you?'

'Yes.' Nike wasn't going to argue.

'Okay. I'll tell you about The PROJECT△, Nick. The things

they didn't tell you when you signed up. The things they've never told you.'

And he began. The man told Nike about the formation of The PROJECT△. On the big screen he showed Nike his own introduction into The PROJECT△. Nike found it both uncomfortable and strangely nostalgic to see himself as a seven year old boy, taken into The PROJECT△ by a woman he vaguely recollected was his mother. It was strange to be looking at himself all those years ago, and even stranger to be looking at his mother. He'd forgotten entirely what she looked like.

'She sold you. For Habit∞.' The man sounded hard. Almost brutal. But Nike realised that his mother was the target of the harshness, not himself. It did have a nasty ring after all, sold. Helen hadn't told him that. She should have. But he could understand why she didn't. He wondered how The Immortal Horses had these images. He wondered why they had them too but most of all for right now, he'd ask how.

'How do you have these images? They should be my memories. But I don't remember them. Well... not till I see them happening, and not like that. I don't remember it like that.'

The man replied, his tone somewhat lightened, 'ULTIMATE® never lets anything go, they archive everything, but they think they have a much more secure system than they know. We've been cross-referencing and storing your memories, the memories of your family, ever since that day.'

'Why?'

'Don't run ahead of yourself, Nick. You'll get your why. But you need context first or it won't mean anything,' the man continued to explain. 'In 2016 The PROJECT△ started taking kids aged between five and eight with the aim of turning them into ULTIMATE® future citizens. Their education was an ULTIMATE® education and they learned the skills they needed to survive in the ULTIMATE® world. And while they were learning, they were teaching ULTIMATE® how to hone its own skills. The power of *HYPE®* was developed into an art form. Call it auto-suggestion

204

or peer-group pressure, or marketing. Call it what you will, ULTIMATE® embraced all these concepts and manipulated the population mercilessly. These Project Kids were at the forefront of the creation of the UTheory∑™ without even knowing it. You know about UTheory∑™?'

Nike nodded. His knowledge was sketchy but...

The man continued. 'You were sold by your mother in 2017 and the first thing they did was to remove you from your memories. But they didn't wipe them they just archived them. You had so many new things to think about that you didn't even miss them after the first week. Young children are very, very malleable. And they had so much exciting, fun stuff to offer you. ULTIMATE®'s aim was to make the rest of the population just like you Project Kids. You were *HYPED®* and repackaged and used as the carrot for a generation of people who wanted something better for their children. The last generation who had children.   You know, that by 2020 getting into The PROJECT△ was better than getting into Eton. Or Oxford. And harder.'

Nike looked blank. He'd no idea what Eton or Oxford were of course. The man carried on regardless.

'They didn't have to pay people to put their kids in The PROJECT△ for long. Pretty soon, people were begging for it. Like all created scarce resources, a place on the ULTIMATE® PROJECT△ became the thing to aspire to. And the Project Kids were to be the leaders in utilising and shaping 'productive' work for an entire generation. The living embodiment of UTheory∑™. Did you know how important you are?'

Nike didn't feel important. He felt scared. He didn't know where this was going. The man seemed to read his thoughts.

'You can trust me Nick,' he said.

'Trust?' Nike echoed.

The man laughed. 'Of course trust isn't really an ULTIMATE® concept is it?'

Nike recognised the question as rhetorical, like the ones Helen was fond of asking.

'You can believe that I have your best interests at heart. However important you are to ULTIMATE®, believe me Nick, you are more important to me and to The Immortal Horses. To our cause.'

Yes, that was the point. Why was he here? What did they want with him? Nike struggled to form the questions.

'Look,' The man saw his confusion, 'It's all pretty overwhelming to you at the moment, I understand that. You've just discovered your world isn't what you thought it to be. You'll need time to assimilate the information. I just wanted to touch base with you. You should go back to The Project House now, and just keep your head down. You can come back here any time of course. Now you know the way. '

'But what about....?' Nike pointed at his ßß™.

'Don't worry,' the man replied, 'we can disable it at will. In fact we're working on how we can send false readings from archive through to your local server, but it might take a week or two to get that up and running. We've broken the back of the work. We've made contact with you and we've got the information we need now to finish the job.'

He didn't ask Nike if he was okay with that. It was implied. And Nike hadn't considered whether he had any choice in the matter. Choice wasn't something that he'd learned about in practical terms as a Project Kid. Choice meant ULTIMATE® coffee or ULTIMATE® coke; ULTIMATE® chocolate or ULTIMATE® chips. It wasn't a practical concept and it certainly wasn't a daily reality.

'What do you want with me?' Nike did manage to frame a sensible question as he was on his way out.

'Do you know what a Trojan Horse is? '
Nike shook his head.
'Or a cuckoo in the nest?'
'No.'

'Well, come back again and I'll explain them to you. But don't worry. Whatever we do, it'll be in your own best interest, long-term. And it might just save the world.'

And with that, Nike found himself ushered outside the Trading House, back on the street, where everything looked the same as it had an hour ago, and nothing was. He didn't go back to Angela's office. There was no point now. He went straight back to The Project House.

O. KEEP YOUR HEAD DOWN

Back in his room, with his US™ working again, Nike realised he should keep his head down. Make things look like they were normal. But nothing was as it had been before. Externally there was no change, but inside, Nike felt like he'd completely transformed. And he couldn't tell anyone about it. He didn't think he should tell his Nan, he couldn't talk to Omo and he knew he shouldn't breathe a word of this to Pryce. He was alone. Truly alone. In his case, knowledge was most definitely not power. He was beginning to experience loneliness for the first time.

He wasn't the only one with secrets now though. Omo had a secret. Angela had a secret. Put them both together and that WAS the secret. Yet another illicit liason that Pryce didn't know about. If he had, he might have wondered why it was that his wife was interested in having sex with any and every other man but not with him. Why were some women like that? Why hadn't ULTIMATE® done away with infidelity when they'd done away with everything else in the personal life? But Pryce was busy struggling with other questions. Pryce didn't even recognise the ball, so it's no surprise he couldn't keep his eye on it.

Right now, Pryce was under pressure from Graham to plug the gaps. He had to be extra vigilant. The system had been cleaned and checked and double checked and appeared to be safe again, but Graham was blaming Pryce for not pre-empting the problem and he was detailed to investigate Omo, Nike and Flora thoroughly in an attempt to work out how the breach in security had occurred. He had been left in no doubt that his career prospects were looking decidedly shaky if he made any more mistakes. And he had no idea how he was supposed to achieve the results Graham demanded from him. Even if he carried out 24 hour surveillance on the kids logs he wouldn't be able to work out what was going on. It was physically impossible for him to carry out real time data collection on three people. That was the point of having an automated system. To work effectively, the system had to be far too complex for a human to work. And he felt out of his depth.

Omo felt out of his depth too but for different reasons. He was still trying to make sense of what had happened between him and Angela once Nike had left the office. Not just how but why. He had no previous experience of real sex, precious little of virtual sex. Sex wasn't a taboo in the ULTIMATE® world at large, but in the world of The PROJECT⌂ things had evolved so that there were many other things to focus on. Consequently sex had never really featured. And certainly not sex with emotion. At least Omo thought what he'd experienced was emotion. He had no idea that Angela had seduced him simply because she could. He thought that she'd picked him because she liked him and that their love-making was 'the real deal.' Not that the phrase would mean anything to Omo. He had no conception of reality and nothing to compare the experience to. For the first time in his life he had questions and emotions and he wanted them answered. So like a good ULTIMATE® citizen he turned to the knowledge bank.

While Nike was doing everything he could to keep his head below the radar, Omo's amorous liason with Angela made him stick his neck out in a way that was bound to draw him to Pryce's attention. Maybe this was part of Angela's plan? But that was a thought Omo was incapable of having. Nike asked asinine questions about suitably meaningless topics, Omo started asking questions about love and sex, and Pryce was supposed to be following it all and making sense of things.

'What is love?' Omo asked the knowledge bank.

LOVE: Definition. In History, an intense feeling of deep affection or fondness for a person or thing. Generally associated with sexual passion and sexual relations.

Omo had experienced an intense feeling. It was a positive feeling so he assumed it was affection or fondness. He wasn't Nike. He wasn't going to waste credits getting definitions for 'affection' or 'fondness' 'sexual passion' or 'sexual relations'. He worked with what he had. His question was answered. He loved Angela. He was less bothered about what that meant than about what would happen as a result of the fact. Did Angela love him back? Of course she must. After all, they'd had what she called 'a shag'. He'd asked her what it meant. She'd had to spell it out to him. He'd felt such a fool. But then, quickly, he'd felt so good he wondered why he'd never known about this before. Why he'd never known that feeling could be so good. ULTIMATE® had never encouraged him to feel. If he was Nike he might have wondered why. But because he was Omo he just wanted to know what the feeling was, and when he could feel it again. And he realised this was a feeling quite unlike any virtual simile he could experience. ULTIMATE® sex focussed on physical sensation and that was enough for most people. What Omo had just experienced was physical sensation plus emotion. Omo could not believe anything could be better than the half hour he'd spent naked with Angela. Not even ULTIMATE® sex.

Words and definition provided no practical resolution to his newly found emotion. Knowing what it was didn't stop him thinking about it, or wanting to experience it again. So he embarked upon a dangerous path. Very out of character. He attempted to interface with Angela.

'Uh...'He was lost as he saw her face on the US™ screen, larger than life and even more attractive than he remembered.

'Omo. Hi. How're you?'

'Uh, fine.'

'What can I do for you?' Angela was a piece of work. She didn't bat an eyelid. Didn't seem concerned that everything they said was being logged and could be seen by Pryce if he only put in the effort to check the logs. Or maybe that was exactly why she did it.

'When can I see you again?'

She'd got him, hook, line and sinker. She knew it. One taste and he'd be back for more. She wasn't even flattered. She knew it would be this way. He wasn't the first, he wouldn't be the last. And she was completely in control. Which was just the way she liked it.

'Oh, I don't know, it might be difficult... can you think of a good alibi?'

'What's an alibi?' Omo had never heard of the word.

The US™ screen came to his rescue.

ALIBI: Definition. A claim, supported by evidence that when an alleged act took place, one was elsewhere.

This didn't really help Omo. He didn't know what an alleged act was.... Angela helped him out.

'We need to come up with an excuse.'

'Oh. Okay.'

'Why don't you think of one and then get back to me?'

And she was gone. Angela knew what she was doing. She was the last generation of women to grow up espousing the *'Treat them mean, keep them keen'* philosophy. ULTIMATE® had consigned such doctrines to the far reaches of the knowledge archive where no one was likely to find them. But Angela had slipped through the net. She had known the art of seduction long before she used it on Omo. She was already an expert when she'd met Pryce and she was only twenty years old then. Angela was more than a match for Pryce and Omo was a minnow to Pryce's trout. While Angela reeled Omo in, she was making her play for Pryce and Graham. Minnow, trout and shark. Three for the price of one. A job worth doing.

Omo came up with his excuse a few hours later. It wasn't a good one. He didn't have experience and he didn't dare ask Nike, who as far as Omo was concerned was the master of the good excuse. Alone, he did the best he could. Omo decided that his alibi would be that he had become interested in adaptive analytic theory after his visit to Angela's office and he'd like to know more. Why he didn't just ask the knowledge bank now it was back on line wasn't a question that suggested itself to him, though it was the first question Pryce asked when, later on, he looked at the logs. But Angela hadn't demanded a good alibi, just an alibi. And an alibi Omo gave her.

    'Hi. Me again. I wondered if you could come over and show me more of the analytical problems we worked on at your office'

    'You want me to come to your apartment?'

    'Yes. Is that possible?'

    'Should be. Will Nike be there too?'

    'Not in my room.'

    She pushed him. 'You want to be alone with me?'

    He felt his face heat up. His dark skin hid the blush, but Angela could sense his discomfort and played on it as though she could see into his mind through her US™ screen.

    'Yes,' he replied.

    She knew she had him right there. She could have toyed with him as long as she liked but Angela was equally happy just to get right down to it. Actually, although what she usually liked in sex was the control with its attendant power, Angela found that she'd been strangely attracted to Omo's innocence. She was used to using her considerable sexual prowess with the likes of Graham, men who could do things for her, help her up the ULTIMATE® ladder so to speak. Part of the challenge for her was to best men who were in essence themselves controllers. With Omo it was different. She was using him, of course, but he was just a pawn in her analytical game, and there was something naive and charming about him. And she found something sexually arousing about teaching him the practicalities and nuances of 'live' sex. It was a feeling she hadn't experienced since she first met Pryce, when they were both barely out of their teens. Ironic really.

'I'll be over in an hour,' she purred.

Omo didn't realise how long an hour could be. He found he couldn't sit at his screen and he wandered through to make a cup of ULTIMATE® coffee. There he found Nike. Avoiding 'productive' work as usual.

'Would you cover for me?' Nike asked, immediately.

'What d'you mean?'

'I want to go out,' Nike said.

Of course Omo should have asked where but he was thinking of his own alibi. Flora would stay in her room while Angela was there, none the wiser as long as they were quiet, but Nike could be guaranteed to intrude when least wanted. So this was a boon. Having Nike out of the way could only be a benefit and he'd offered Omo the perfect solution himself.

'Sure,' Omo felt that he might look like he'd given in a bit easily. So he added, 'say Hi to your Nan for me.'

Because, after all, where else could Nike be going?

Nike smiled. Omo didn't suspect a thing. But why would he?

'So if Pryce calls...' he began.

That pulled Omo up short. He hadn't thought about that. What if Pryce called when he and Angela were....?

'I know. Let's call him now. Get him out the picture for a couple of hours and then we can do what we like.' Omo was getting cunning. Like all lovers.

'Yeah. Good idea. Better still. Let's get Flora to call him.'

'Okay. How?' Omo still had a lot to learn.

'Leave it to me.' Nike reassured him. 'I'll sort it.'

And Omo, being Omo, didn't question any more than that. He really should have done. But it wasn't in his nature. ULTIMATE® had seen to that.

Several minutes later when Flora contacted Pryce, it was like a break in the clouds for him. And once again, he took his eye off the ball. It mean that just when he should have been able to see two potential problems (Nike going awol and Omo making love to Angela), Pryce had a more important task on his hand: dealing with Flora.

He determined that it was time to take the bull by the horns and set things straight with the girl. She had no good reason to call him. They both knew that. But he found he was flattered by the attention. It made it easy to convince himself that the problem in hand was to deal with an inappropriate teenage crush, the sort of thing that had to be nipped in the bud. He'd have to be smart and find ways to divert her. He didn't know enough about girls. He knew he should pass her over to a female social counsellor, but hey, why bother someone else on so trivial a matter. It would make him look even more incompetent. Surely he could sort it himself. He would talk it through with Flora and find something more 'productive' for her to spend her energies on.

So, while Pryce became convinced that Flora was his immediate concern, and obsessed over how to deal with her, he missed the fact that she wasn't his problem. THAT was his problem. Pryce was once more destined to miss the central point. His eye was firmly on the wrong ball. Again.

P. WHEN DID YOU LAST SEE YOUR FATHER?

Nike's trip out was not, as Omo thought, to see Helen. Instead he took the quick walk to the Trading House. Every step of the way he wrestled with the conflicting emotions of fear and excitement. Last time he'd been taken there. This time he was knocking on the door. He was making a choice. Acting independently. And acting against ULTIMATE® with every step and every thought.

Of course they had known Nike would be unable to resist coming back. No one could resist the pull of The Immortal Horses. It was like Habit∞. After being greeted at reception, this time Nike was ushered into a smaller room, an office which would have overlooked the street, had the blinds not been down. He hardly had time to wonder if he'd made a bad choice when the man he'd spoken with before entered the room.

'Glad you chose to come back. I hoped you would. Have you got more questions?'

Nike couldn't believe someone was actually encouraging him to ask questions. Whatever he didn't know about the Immortal Horses, he did know that they were quite unlike ULTIMATE®. No one was making him pay credits for questions. Ask, and he got. It was simple and yet....

'So Nick. What can I tell you?'

'It's Nike.' Nike decided he'd better correct the man. After all, Nike was his name.

'That's Nick to us.'

'It's just my Nan calls me Nick.'

'Because Nick is the name you had before ULTIMATE®. And we aren't part of ULTIMATE® here. Nick is your family name. We're family. So here, to us, you are Nick.'

'Okay.' He wasn't going to kick up a fuss about it. Nick, Nike, did it really matter?

'You can call me Troy.' The man volunteered, answering Nike's first unanswered question.

Nike took a deep breath. How far into his mind could this Troy read?

'I've got so many questions. I don't know where to start.'

'That's fair enough. This has all come on you as a surprise after all. And you're not properly trained in asking questions..'

Nike smiled at that one. Pryce would be livid. It was Pryce's job to see that he was trained in questioning, but he guessed that The Immortal Horses and ULTIMATE® had different views on what a good question really was.'

'Listen Nick. I'm going to tell you the History of ULTIMATE®. There are things you need to know. You need to understand the enemy before you can understand yourself. Okay?'

Nike nodded.

'Stop me at any point. Interject or ask for a more specific, detailed explanation. I want you to really know what's going on by the time we've finished here.'

That was a first. ULTIMATE® questioning never seemed to be about actually knowing anything. It was about fulfilling your 'productive' work quota. Questions were currency, not a means of gaining knowledge.

Troy began. 'Let's start with the HISTORY OF ULTIMATE®. We could call it the information transformation. Or the destruction of life as we knew it. Whatever. The title isn't important. We're looking for meaning not names. I know that you've asked questions about history before and I realise that you've got a basic picture of how things were IN HISTORY. What you don't know is the significance of that. Of how we moved from History to the ULTIMATE® present. You know, I think, about the GRsΩHist?'

'Yes,' Nike nodded, 'but it's never really interested me.'

'It should. It's your history after all. It's all of our histories,' Troy continued, 'okay, well you know that at the

218

beginning of the 21st century things were very different. Branding was a concept where people chose between alternative companies, alternative ideologies, but big business meant that convergence became the only viable financial state for a capitalist system under threat and huge scale take-over's and buy out's began. People didn't realise it at the time of course. They still believed in their brands as independent. Even when companies merged they didn't see the bigger picture. They didn't realise that with the global marketplace taking over, in fact their geographical set of choices regarding branding was getting ever smaller. Fewer and fewer companies, and fewer and fewer people had the real power. Branding was a smokescreen, but a comfortable, familiar state which people bought into. People don't like being challenged, especially when things are changing rapidly, as they were in the early twenty first century. They like to hold on to what is familiar, even if it isn't real. Follow me so far?'

Nike nodded. He couldn't see what this had to do with him, or his history, but he was hopeful Troy would come to a point some time soon. And he realised how much more enjoyable live conversation was compared with the US™ screen.

'At the beginning of the 21st century people got used to the idea that their Tesco clubcard held details of all their spending patterns and could be used for marketing purposes to target their shopping. That Amazon could suggest books to you based on your previous purchasing choices. Some people even found this distasteful. Some were cynical. Some predicted the death of civil liberty. But people are remarkably indiscreet, especially when faced with new technology which makes life more interesting or just more 'fun.' People didn't think too much about what was happening with the information they were exchanging about themselves on Facebook or Myspace or in Second Life. These were the brands which dominated everyday life between 2000 and 2010.'

'People didn't think about the giant databases in the

background, churning out algorithms for the purpose of understanding and then controlling the choice patterns of the entire world population. That's the stuff of conspiracy theories. People, even intelligent people, shrugged it off. Some of them even worked on the false belief that with so much information bombarding back and forth through cyberspace, they were actually safer, because who could actually 'look' at what any individual was doing. Who would be interested? They believed that the more information that was out there, the safer the individual would be. They comforted themselves in the belief that as long as the IRS was incompetent, how could or would any organisation actually get their act together to gather or use this information. They ignored the obvious signs that Amazon and Facebook were NOT the IRS. They saw Google as a 'cool place to work' staffed and run by people with a hippy/liberal view of business and this comforted them. They didn't look to the power behind the throne. As we came out of 'history' people stopped looking at historical trends. So historical 'truths' became unimportant and nothing could be learned from such statements.   It was easy for ULTIMATE® to do away with history. Contemporary studies became more important. History told us nothing in the face of an exponentially speeding up future.'

Nike wasn't really following now, but he didn't like to stop Troy in full flow. He had never seen a person speak so passionately, or with so much authority. And Troy seemed to know so much. Even Pryce had to refer back to the US™ screen all the time when he gave them study sessions. And here was Troy, speaking from his memory. Nike couldn't fail but be impressed.

'ULTIMATE® knew that he who controls the past controls the future. ULTIMATE® knew that knowledge is power. No one else cared any more. Everyone was too busy getting their kicks from the virtual world which offered them an escape from the real world which was, economically speaking, going

220

down the tubes. And by 2013 ULTIMATE® was there, a real alternative. At the time, no one even questioned how it came about, it was like it sprang, fully formed, from the minds of the economic gods. People thought it was to their benefit, so they accepted it, largely unquestioningly. Anything that made life better must be good. ULTIMATE® played on the shallow concerns of the individual. While all the time working to destroy individualism.'

'Of course during the transition time which we now refer to as The GRsΩHist, life changed radically. It was a time when people couldn't afford to eat out any more. Couldn't afford foreign holidays, lost their jobs, lost their cars... but it became easy to compensate for these losses. ULTIMATE® made it easy. For example: first they made food really expensive. Then they had numerous food scares, till people didn't feel safe eating anything. The combination of price and fear pretty quickly made eating out a less appealing concept. And you don't need to eat out when you can get cheap food delivered to your door by the ULTIMATE® delivery system. You just shop online and say what you want and they bring it to you, pre-packaged, precooked and tasting wonderful. You don't have to worry any more about free range chickens because all the food is genetically created, never mind genetically modified. And if you had concerns about this in the past, hey, ULTIMATE® have done a good job in convincing you that no animals were being harmed any more in your food production. That your 'meat' now tasted better than ever and it didn't harm animals, didn't ruin the economy and it actually protected you from cancer and heart disease and you would never become obese as long as you purchased from the ULTIMATE® range. And no one in the world is starving any more. Everyone has enough to eat. You've got to buy into that. ULTIMATE® are making the world a better place to be. I bet you've never even thought about it, have you?'

Nike shook his head. Then said, 'But I have tasted real

food,' He paused for effect. 'At my Nan's.'

'Yes?' Troy was giving nothing away.

'Yes. She had a birthday cake. A real one.' Nike wasn't sure if he should mention the RIP inscribed on it. He did realise he was in a new world with The Immortal Horses and he didn't want to get any deeper into trouble than he felt he already was. But he was curious, wondering if there was a link between The Immortal Horses and the RIP. However, he didn't feel he could ask Troy the question outright. He wanted to find out about RIP and he thought Troy might be the man to tell him, but he hoped maybe Troy would volunteer the requisite information. He did want to protect his Nan if possible. If Troy was interested in this information he certainly didn't express it.

'They did the same with transport,' Troy continued, 'first they made it really expensive. Then they piled on terrorist threats. Then they provided a virtual alternative. It's the same modus operandi, and the effect was the same. Whereas in 2000 people worried about personal transport and public transport and motorways and holidays and the cost of fuel and diminishing oil stocks and the like, by 2015 these things were more or less outmoded and by 2020 they were part of a History which people had already abandoned in favour of the ULTIMATE® alternative. And this was all planned. All part of ULTIMATE®'s social model. And The PROJECT△ is the core of it all.'

'Why is the PROJECT△...?' Nike couldn't help himself. 'I mean.. what is it for?'

'The big question should be: how did a bunch of kids surfing the net and living online change the world? The answer is simple. Because knowledge is power and information is a profitable commodity. ULTIMATE® took the idea of the 'information' age to its logical conclusion. At the turn of the 21st century they developed a means of analysing and eventually of controlling the population. 'Productive' work was the means to achieving this and The PROJECT△ was the place where they could really develop and perfect the concept,' Troy explained.

"Productive' work was born out of a combination of online elements which had become the forefront of the escapism from reality during the social transition period. It was Yahoo! Answers meets Amazon, meets chat-rooms, forums and social networking sites with a bit of online gaming and bingo thrown in. All developed by big business in order to increase their capital and dominance of the market. All used by individuals who the brands had convinced that these were must-have, lifestyle choices.' Troy sounded bitter now.

'The virtual life was easy to sell. And they sold to people who didn't even know the price they were paying. They sold these 'fun' possibilities for spending your life virtually once they'd made real life almost unbearable for everyone. The alternative to the virtual life was a life in debt, with the worry of constant repossession and unemployment and no pension to look forward to after a lifetime of hard, boring, unfulfilling work. It was the time when people's biggest dream was of a new conservatory, or a cruise and they realised they'd never afford their dreams and they'd still be in debt up to their eyeballs till the day they died. They realised that they'd never be able to retire till they were seventy and every day of life they'd have that sick feeling in their stomach that said *you're twenty grand overdrawn and counting*. And if you fell ill..... don't even think about it. Believe me Nick. I know about this. I saw it. First-hand. And it was all lies. All lies perpetrated by the capitalist companies for whom the ULTIMATE® model was the answer to all their prayers. It didn't need to be that way.'

Nike was a little bit frightened by Troy's tone but he was learning in a way the US™ never taught him. He felt like he was experiencing real life for the first time. It felt scary but good.

'But capitalism doesn't exist any more,' he said. 'It's part of History isn't it?'

Troy laughed. 'Nick. Thirty years ago you'd have been marching to MAKE POVERTY HISTORY. You'd have worn a white rubber wristband to show your allegiance. And a few left wing radicals subverted this in a postmodern/ironic statement, sporting a red rubber wristband stating MAKE CAPITALISM HISTORY. And no one believed it would happen and precious few wanted to make capitalism history. But then, the Capitalists didn't really want to make POVERTY history either. Poverty was something they thrived on. And yet today, you sit here telling me that CAPITALISM IS HISTORY, and you probably don't even know what POVERTY is. Am I right?'

Nike nodded. He felt stupid.

'I'm here to tell you Nick. Capitalism is alive and well. It's just ULTIMATE® capitalism now. Everything is subordinate to ULTIMATE®. Except us.'

Troy paused. 'But I'm digressing. By 2016 ULTIMATE® overtly launched as the ULTIMATE® BRAND and revealed that they had the whole world all signed and sealed as participants. And people didn't know, or didn't care. They couldn't see through the process and they didn't understand the implications. Yes, they might remember a time when Mars wasn't ULTIMATE® Mars, when Microsoft was Microsoft with Bill Gates at the head of operations. Before CEO's were all discredited and went underground. By the time ULTIMATE® BRAND LOYALTY became obvious, ULTIMATE® made sure that individuals no longer 'controlled' brands. It was a key selling point. Individuals no longer had to take responsibility or blame. And people had become so fed up of the 'fat cats' that they were happy when they disappeared from view. Loyalty to the Brand became the important thing, not loyalty to people.'

He continued, 'Anyway, people had got so used to all the big business buy-outs that they stopped questioning who actually OWNED anything. The power of the ULTIMATE® brand inspired unquestioning loyalty because it built itself on the accepted social fashions of the past while offering a new, improved version of the world. Whatever might have been considered a sacrifice was forgotten with the next ULTIMATE®

224

improvement, because ULTIMATE® were seen to be working tirelessly to make each person's lifestyle experience the best it could be. Individually tailored to your needs. At a tenth of the price of the old world. Which anyone in 2010 had to agree, was pretty second rate. By 2020 BRAND LOYALTY was born in the ULTIMATE® style. And the work of The PROJECT△ has been instrumental in bringing the world to an acceptance of the new ULTIMATE® model. Real choice had been eradicated, but no one noticed. And if they did, they'd probably consider it a small price to pay. ULTIMATE®'s greatest achievement was to make History HISTORY. Or to try.'

Nike's head was spinning. He knew that he'd just heard something really important, but it was all so contrary to his previous lived experience that he just didn't know how to compute the information. And he was struggling to see how any of this affected him, personally. Troy seemed to pre-empt his thought once more.

'You're wondering what all this has to do with you?'

Nike nodded. 'Yes, I mean it's interesting but it's the way life is and....'

'Did you want to ask me a question about your Nan's birthday cake?'

Nike was amazed. How could Troy read his innermost thoughts almost before he had them?

'Yes.'

'About the RIP?'

'Yes... .How do you...?' Nike was baffled.

'You need to understand Nick. There's all sorts of things I know. Important things. About your history. About your family. About your life outside The PROJECT△. RIP are not the important ones. The important ones are the 100 Men.' He laughed. 'See, you don't even know what questions to ask. You know nothing of ULTIMATE®....but how could you? That's the big question. Although for you there is a bigger one. A personal question which means nothing to anyone but you.' Now Troy was talking in riddles.

'Let me ask you a question Nick.'

'What?'

'When did you last see your father?'

Nike was trying to work out whether it was when he was six or seven and shut his eyes momentarily to concentrate. While they were shut Troy's voice invaded his thoughts.

'Use emotion Nick, not reason. Think outside the ULTIMATE® box.'

Nike opened his eyes, and found himself enfolded in an embrace from his father.

'Welcome home, son.' Nike could see the tears in Troy's eyes, blurred through the tears in his own.

Q. THE SEASONS OF A LIFE

Of all the things that ULTIMATE® had stolen from her Helen thought that, apart from freedom, the seasons might be the one she missed the most. Freedom could be reduced to a concept, even a relative concept, but the weather stuck with you. At least it did with Helen. And the lack of seasons was like living without the taste of real food. She couldn't believe she'd got used to both over the last ten years. It was wrong. Seasons didn't mean anything in the ULTIMATE® Home, or indeed anywhere, any more. And yet Helen clearly remembered when climate change was the pressing concern for humanity. ULTIMATE® had achieved its victory over climate change the same way as it had over everything else. It had simply caused it to cease to exist. People just didn't have to worry any more. They were hooked into a virtual world. If they wanted a tan they could get it without ever having to worry about the sun. And all the harmful rays were blocked out. But who even wanted a tan these days? Why would it matter? You lived more through avatars and virtuality than reality anyway it seemed, so what did it matter what you actually looked like. Who was going to see you?

Helen's favourite time of year had been what most people would consider winter, the months between October and February. The months, that in Scotland at least, may have been perishingly cold, but they also brought clean, clear air along with a sharpness and a brightness to the sky. Helen didn't mind being cold. She had always found her brain worked better in the cold, and her body preferred the option of putting on more clothes than the heat of summer where there was nothing you could do to restore a temperature imbalance. Everyone had always laughed at the layers she wore as standard between October and March.

'Mum,' Catriona used to say, 'You look like a tramp with

all those clothes on.'

'I'm warm,' Helen replied. 'Warmer than you with that skimpy little top on… it's December you know.'

'Thermals and two pairs of socks is the rule,' Randall laughed, 'October to March.'

'Don't forget your scarf,' Torquil chided his sister when she left for college.

'I won't need a scarf,' she replied, 'or thermals,' as she unpacked them from her case.

'It's Glasgow, not the Bahamas,' Helen had pointed out.

On this point Randall agreed with her, and took Catriona out to buy her a decent anorak.

'There's no such thing as bad weather,' he said, 'only inadequate clothing.'

Catriona took the coat. And the scarf. But she drew the line at the fingerless gloves her mother packed. That was too old lady. No way. She'd freeze her fingers to the bone rather than wear fingerless gloves.

Helen knew that dressed properly you could be warm enough to take advantage of the winter sunshine spreading over the blue, blue skies of Galloway, or Moray. It was a time when you felt more at one with nature than any other time of the year. And it was funny, because people who didn't like winter thought of it as a dead time. They had to put Christmas in the middle, a party to help you 'get through' the worst of it. Helen had never had much time for Christmas. Or for winter as death. Nature held death as part of a cycle, not as the end. Trees didn't die in the winter, they went to sleep and woke again in the spring. But even sleep wasn't the right description. Helen loved trees in the winter more than at any other time. She didn't need evergreens for comfort. She loved the bareness of the branches, showing you a vision that was lost, covered up during the summer months. Helen always felt that in the winter you saw things as they really are. Stripped back to reality. About as far away from the ULTIMATE® world as you could imagine.

That was a world without clarity, without simplicity, without reality; a world where everything was covered up by something else and nothing was simple or real. How could it be? Everything existed only to be a part in a great project, the ULTIMATE® scheme of things. The world how God might have arranged it, if God had existed and had little respect for people or humanity.

Helen sighed. You couldn't put the kind of feeling she had for seasons into a Memory Bank. They were a different kind of memory. Deep seated ones. Intensely private experiences of sight, sound and smell. A classic example of the fact that memories isolate. This experience of trying to lay them out for another person to share or make meaning from them had only shown her that it was an impossible task. Memories can't mean anything to anyone other than the person who experiences them. Even shared memories must be suspect because everyone experiences things in an individual way. No wonder ULTIMATE® wanted to control memory. It seemed to Helen that memory was the random element which UTheory$\sum$® sought to undermine. It was the bit which made humans human and what did ULTIMATE® care for humanity?

Helen had first questioned memories in the context of her mother's illness. She had 'died' of Alzheimer's a good three years before she died in person. Her dad had stuck by her all that time. It was a painful experience and he barely survived a year afterwards himself because of the toll it took.

Those years had been terrible for all of them, watching a woman become distanced, then confused then isolated before finally dying and giving them all a painful peace.

'Sing with her,' Helen's dad had entreated her, on one of their all too infrequent visits. 'She'll respond if you sing.'

But Helen was shocked by the fact that her mother only wanted to sing nursery rhymes and children's songs. Repeatedly. To excess.

'Come on mum,' she said, 'enough is as good as a feast,' when she'd endured *'I saw a mouse, where, there on the stair'* fifteen times. Her mother didn't recognise her own favourite catchphrase and Helen felt mean using her advantage. A memory that worked.

Her mum started to cry. Her dad picked up the song, *'a little mouse with clogs on, well I declare...'*

Even though he'd done this every day for a week. Non stop. Helen realised how much her dad loved her mum, even though her mum wasn't there any more, even though he was playing to a stranger who just wanted to sing stupid songs. She had a new found respect for him. But she felt sorry for him too.

'Dad.' Do you have to?

'It keeps her happy,' came his simple reply. And he winked at her. 'Can't fight city hall, eh?'

Helen wondered how her parents would have responded to the ULTIMATE® cure for Alzheimer's, which came too late to save them. Dementia was the next biggest social problem after climate change in 2012 and before long ULTIMATE® had found a cure. It was one of the factors that sent them mainstream. The 'cure' came in their creation of the US™ screen, backed up by its archives. An appropriate application of a technology that would take over the world. That would become the world. In this context it was known as ADAS® (Advanced Dementia Adaptive system) It worked. Quickly world consensus was to buy into the programme. They forgot the corollary – at any price and just signed on the dotted line. Problem solved. For now.

ADAS® worked like a dream. In more ways than one. People with dementia got upset because they couldn't remember things. ULTIMATE® took their memories at early diagnosis and stored them in an easily retrievable way, so that even if their memory span was less than five minutes, they could have streaming memories constantly either updating or circulating, to keep them happy.

The ends justified the means. Faced with a way to keep the aging population happy in their dementia, no one questioned the nature of the memories that were being pumped constantly through the US™ screens to the people formerly known as sufferers, now known as consumers of enhanced experience. No one wondered whether in fact ULTIMATE® cut corners, imported and imposed fictional or virtual memories on people who could no longer remember accurately their own personal reality. What would ULTIMATE® care about veracity? They were in the process of dismantling the whole concept of personal meaning and memory was just another tool they had to bend to their new systems need.

Helen firmly believed that memory was in some way tied deeply to personal identity. And now she was facing the fact that you could never transmit your memories accurately. You could never properly communicate your inner self with the external world. It was impossible. Fundamentally every man is an island. Even if the images stayed on the US™ screen for ever somewhere in ULTIMATE® archives; somehow what was real was locked inside her head, her soul, and on her passing, the memories would die with her. She was not afraid of dying, though she had experienced enough death to have a deep respect for it; but she did feel a terrible pang of sadness whenever she realised that on her death, her memories would be lost for ever.

Her mother's condition had served to convince her that one fundamentally existed only in one's own head. A created 'you' existed in the heads of everyone you knew, and in that sense you continued to live even after death. Personal identity was private and time limited. Social identity was eternal and largely outwith one's own control. And as such, to Helen, valueless.

The one challenge to Helen's theory was in the case of love. While both she and Randall despised social identity, in some profound way she felt they shared a personal identity.

Maybe this was what being soul mates meant? With Randall, she'd felt a kind of connection where at times she really believed that another human being had got inside her head and understood who she really was. And she'd felt that she really knew him too. The boundaries of personhood were smashed. Or so she'd felt. Now, without him, as she confront her 'shared' memories, she was left wondering if she had ever really known him, or if he, like everyone else, was to a great degree a projection of her own ideas and thoughts. Had she ever, for instance, really understood the importance of RIP to Randall?

'What's changed your mind?' she'd asked as he went out to join the group he'd always sworn away from. 'You've never been interested in politics.'

'I have to get involved,' he'd said. No more explanation. She had been left to make her own meaning. At the time she'd been jealous of the organisation that took him away from her. Now, looking back, she thought it the desperate act of a desperate man.

The Rural Interests Party had sprung out of groups as diverse as the Countryside Alliance, Farmers for Action and the Trade Justice Movement. Randall had always been cynical of the whole 'game' and he had learned through the agricultural disasters that preceded the economic collapse that society would sacrifice individuals without a care in order to keep capitalism working. Indeed his own family moving to Moray might have been seen as an acceptance of defeat. They had moved out of society back to a condition of self-sufficiency which turned its back on the concept of community. His mantra had been, 'We need to protect ourselves above all.'

Helen had agreed with him. 'You're right. I'm tired of trying to fit into a society which offers us nothing but debt.'

'It's not about money,' he said.

'I know. But... I feel, well, like the outside world doesn't want anything we have to offer,' she complained.

'It doesn't,' he responded, 'and you can't expect it to. We aren't part of the system so you can't expect the system to value us. We're on our own. It's the only way to be free.'

She'd questioned his definition of freedom.

'In our world, Helen,' he'd replied, 'the only freedom lies in freedom from control. And this freedom comes at a price.'

The price was isolation. She didn't mind that. He taught her not to care about the financial poverty.

'Think about it,' he'd said. 'If you don't believe in the moneyed system, how can you strive for money? If you're not willing to buy into it, or buy it, you don't have to worry that you can't afford it. It's not about money it's about freedom. About living a life.'

She agreed with him. You had to find a way to live as far as possible without money and stay as far below the parapet as possible. That was freedom. But it wasn't always possible. Not when they came looking for you.

They managed to live the dream for so long. So why had he gone with the RIP? She couldn't square the two things, even now. The nagging doubt remained that it had been a knee jerk reaction at the guilt Randall felt over the death of Catriona. But that didn't make sense. He'd first joined in 2011. He wanted to make a difference then. Had he seen the future? Was he trying to protect his children from the future? Had that taken priority over their present freedom? Perhaps Randall joining RIP had been an act of love to Catriona and Nick and Torquil, and not about her at all. It shocked her that she felt jealousy. She didn't want him to love them as much as he loved her. She wanted to have always been the first in his heart. He'd always been first in hers. He still was.

Helen wished she could go out for a walk in the woods and think clearly. She remembered that it was out on long lone walks with the dogs that she had done a lot of clear, calm thinking to a purpose and for the first time she realised that being cooped up in an ULTIMATE® Home might have taken more than a physical toll on her. Even that walk with Nick the other day had given her a sense of her brain coming back to life. She had walked, three times a day, every day for nearly thirty five years; and each walk while individual had become somehow one walk, which she could still remember clearly. Or maybe there were several walks, which changed with the season. The walk she remembered most clearly was the winter walk.

February. A clear, clean, crisp, bright day. Strong sun overhead. Crisp snow underfoot. The last of the snow, shimmering like diamonds and crunching like glass. Around it the ground, damp and with a browny tinge to the greenness, like it was exhausted from lying under snow and needed a few days to get over the hangover before it would grow its way into spring. The chill on the outside of your nostrils. The feeling of being enveloped by a purity filtered within the stillness. Breathing in the sharp cleanness while walking with mouth open, sucking it in till it filled your whole body. Helen didn't like ice-cream but she always imagined this feeling to be similar to that of the enjoyment of ice-cream, yet on a larger scale. Filling your whole body with clean, cold air was one of life's greatest pleasures.

And when she wanted a break from walking, she could sit up her tree. Even as a fifty year old woman, she would sit up the tree she would never describe as 'her' tree, but more accurately as the tree she 'belonged to'; a huge beech in a row of similar trees which looked out over the south west of the land they owned in Moray. Here, every day, she could look at a view that was comfortingly the same, giving her a sense of rootedness, but at the same time, every time you looked something was different, like a living version of the children's picture puzzle 'spot the difference'. It was in the hollow of this old tree that Helen had always wanted and imagined having her

234

ashes scattered so that somehow, after she was gone, she could be part of the tree's natural cycle. That would be life enough for her once her physical life was over. As she committed the memory to the Memory Bank, she wondered how she had forgotten that? How had she lived ten years without that memory being in the forefront of her mind? How had she lived without the view?

'Want to go to the beech?' she'd asked a three year old Nick.

'Bucket spade,' he'd said hopefully. He thought he knew what the beach was. He'd been there with his mum and dad last summer.

'No. This is Nan's beech,' she said, 'it's better.'

He ran along behind her and laughed and laughed when they arrived at the beech trees. He clapped his hands and constantly demanded to be taken to 'Nan's beech.' He learned to climb the tree after his Nan and perch precariously on her knee looking at the view. He learned how to name things. And he learned that you could make up your own, special names for things. Together they saw Randall ploughing in the winter.

'Grandad make patterns,' Nick said.

They saw the lambs and piglets in the spring.

'Babies dancing,' he called it.

They saw the crops grow in the summer and the harvest in the autumn.

'Chips and porridge fields,' he called them.

Going to the beech with Nan was a specific part of his life, with a meaning unlike that for other children, for whom the beach meant only the traditional sand and sea and salt and ice-creams. As she committed the memory to the US™ Memory Bank, Helen wondered if it would spark something in Nick's own memory. She wished so. She hoped so. She felt that it was something he'd been robbed of and she wanted to give it back to him. Even if it was her memory rather than his. It was a start.

Being at one with nature was being a part of the

seasons. This, for Helen, was one of life's most profound truths. One which no ULTIMATE® Memory Bank could store and no US™ screen steal from her. If only she could get back to the countryside and take Nick with her. She wondered what the countryside would be like now. ULTIMATE® had no need for it really. The population was more or less stabilised. People were used to living in smaller spaces, closer together and travelling less, so there were still vast tracts of land un-used. Helen imagined the unmanaged countryside may have reverted to a state more familiar in ancient history. Rural Scotland might be more beautiful and fruitful than it had been for generations. And here she was, stuck in a magnolia box, ruminating on what she'd lost. Why?

She had previously just accepted that her life was over, that things had changed, that there was no choice and no going back. But was this so? Could she make a life for herself back 'out there' outwith ULTIMATE®?   People must be doing it. The people who sent her the cake for example. They had sent a birthday cake and the promise to fulfil her wish; the possibility of an alternative way. It was a moment of clarity and she felt she must act.

Moments were more than memories. Moments were when life became as it did on those crisp winter walks, clear and bright and clean. When it became obvious what the right thing to do was. And the only path was to act on it. This was one of those moments. She didn't know how she would achieve it, and she knew she couldn't just walk out of the ULTIMATE® home that minute, which was what she felt like doing, but she knew that she WOULD walk out of there and she would find what was left of the RIP and if not resume her old life, begin a new one, not counting the cost.

For ten years she had been sucked into the lie that winter meant death. That she was at the final stage of her life, there was no spring, no newness to look forward to. But now she realised that she was in a state of February and she could move forward, rejuvenated, if only she would have faith and courage and make that move.

Helen had had such moments of clarity several times in her life before. The moments flashed from her mind. …. Standing on a platform at Tottenham Court Road tube Station with a head cold, on her way home from work, wondering what she would do if this was the last day of her life? And realising she would just go home and sleep…Sitting in Acton Park looking at the trees and realising that trees, not money made her happy….Seeing Randall for the first time and knowing he would be the most important person in the rest of her life….Sitting in a quarterly sales meeting realising that everyone else cared about the figures and she was just aching to go outdoors….Holding a dog with epilepsy in her arms during a seizure and realising their relationship had taught her more about caring and communication than any person ever had. The moments and the memories could mean nothing to anyone but her. But to her they were a fundamental part of her being.

She consolidated what she intended to be the last set of memories she committed to the US™ screen. She'd given ULTIMATE® enough of her life. She hoped she'd given Nick enough to lay a path for him. Now she just wanted to leave the ULTIMATE® Home. Like Lao Tzu, just disappear into the mountains for ever. She was sure now that it would happen, in time. She turned away, to make a cup of tea.

The US™ screen alerted Helen to an incoming message.

'Nan, It's Nick.' For the first time Nike didn't mind saying that name out loud. Standing next to Troy, he finally felt a sense of belonging, purpose, identity, family. He wanted to share this with Helen.

'Nick, how.. where are you? Is something wrong?' Something didn't seem right but Helen couldn't work out what it was.

'I'm with dad,' came the response.

237

'What?'

'My dad. Your son... he's here....'

The connection was lost.

'What happened?' Nike asked Troy.

'Sorry Nick,' Troy replied, 'she can't be allowed to see me. No one can see me. If ULTIMATE® could get a fix on me, they could find out more about The Immortal Horses than we want them to know. It would compromise us, it would compromise the RIP and....'

'Yes, what about the RIP? Do they still exist... Did you send the cake? Is my grandad alive?' The questions tumbled out of Nike and he knew he wouldn't get them all answered, not right away. He looked in Troy's face and he knew it. He had moved into a parallel world where information was precious and couldn't be obtained by 'productive' work or credits. It would only be given when earned through trust. But what did he have to do to gain that trust?

At her end, Helen was shocked and hopeful at the same time. Nick had found Torquil.   A son back from the dead proved to her that there could be life beyond ULTIMATE®. She wanted that life.

R. WHEN IS A QUESTION NOT A QUESTION?

Pryce was impressed when Nike contacted him via the US™ to ask for help.

'I'd really like you to explain something to me, Pryce.'

Fleetingly Pryce thought he'd started to get through to Nike. Could offer him a way forward….. and then, 'Do you need more credits?' he asked, suspicious. After all, this was Nike.

'No. It's question theory. I've been working on the US™, but I'm getting a bit lost in it. And I remembered you said you'd done work on Question Theory so, I thought maybe, ask the master.'

Pryce couldn't pretend he wasn't flattered, and blocked out the afternoon to spend with Nike. It would be time and credits well spent if he was finally making a breakthrough. And they both needed to impress right now. Ten minutes later, the enormity of the task ahead hit him as he sat beside an unusually eager Nike.

'What exactly do you want to know?' Pryce asked, not impressed by his own questioning power. Having run through what Nike had done so far, he saw nothing more than standard level interactions, not, he suspected what Nike was confused with.

'About questioning itself,' Nike ventured, 'about what makes a question a question and…'

'You've come to the right man,' Pryce reassured him, trying to reassure himself at the same time. 'But it's not easy. You'll have to concentrate.'

Nike threw him a look. 'Look Pryce, If you don't want to help me.'

'No. I just don't know where to begin. What exactly..'

'Well. I checked on some of your old work. About the proposition that both Logical and Psychological question theory are insufficient as paradigms. But I was getting lost about what comes after that.'

This really was game on. Nike was really engaging. Pryce felt good. Someone had actually, after all these years, accessed his best piece of work. In his worst moments of depression he had even thought the system hadn't kept it on archive. He'd never dared to use the credits to look. He smiled. 'The answer is Quantum Question Theory,' he said, giving it everything but the drum roll.

'And is that the pre-cursor to UTheory∑®?'

Back at the Trading House, Troy was rubbing his hands.

'Go, Nick.'

At the Project House, Pryce was also pleased. 'Yes. You could say that.'

'Well, can you explain it to me then?' Nike asked. 'It would take me months to get this via the US™ and I'm sure you can explain it better in half the time. I'm prepared to convert my 'productive' work schedule to this topic, but I really want to know NOW. Please help me.'

How could Pryce resist. 'Okay,' he replied, 'I'll adapt your work schedule 'on the fly'.'

'Can you do that?' Nike wondered if his wide-eyed innocence was coming on just a bit too strong but Pryce was oblivious and bought it.

'Sure.' And with a few commands it was done. He'd do the admin later. He knew there was a theoretical danger in what he'd just done but in practice what could go wrong? He had no idea of course that Troy was logging Nike through his barcode and that this subversion of the standard procedure allowed Troy and the techies at the Trading House to get a link into the system without anyone checking. They were all but cheering. Their boy was doing incredibly well.

'Does he have any idea what he's doing?' Griff asked Troy.

'Nick. Oh yes. He's a smart kid,' Troy replied.

Meanwhile Nike was listening, or pretending to listen to Pryce's explanation.

'At the quantum questioning level of theory one deals
with: Ill formed questions (IFQ)
            Well formed questions (WFQ)
             Null questions. (NQ)'
'Yes. I'm with you,' Nike nodded.

Pryce continued. Finally. Finally he'd got Nike interested in something serious. 'The status of the interrogator is vital. As is the domain of inquiry, the collection of observables, and the choice set.' He caught Nike's blank look. 'Okay, let's pull up some examples from the US™.' He asked for explanation and the screen gave forth.

'Does this question have an answer?' is an IFQ
But
'Does this question have an explication?' is a WFQ.
To which the answer is 'Yes'
And the explication is 'The statement is a WFQ that asks an IFQ,
a question about itself.'

'You see, we're dealing on the meta-level here.'
'Yes, I see,' asserted Nike, who didn't.

Pryce took a deep breath. So we might ask, 'What are the kind of questions?'

The US™ screen churned out the tired old answer:
What? and How? are functional questions
When?, Where? and Who? are Temporal/spatial questions
Why? is a metaphysical question.

'Yes, I know that,' Nike replied, 'but why separate them? They're all questions.'

Pryce got in before the screen. 'The question types are laid out in order of ascending unit value. Why? questions cost most credits because they are of least use to a system which knows all the answers. UTheory∑® prefers users to ask functional questions where ever possible. These questions yield the best kind of data to keep the system functioning at peak quality.'

He paused to let the credit drop. 'And that's why you're always running out of credits, Nike. Because you continue to ask the why question.'

'But aren't they the most interesting kind of questions?'

'Not to the system,' Pryce spotted Nike going off track. 'You have to stop thinking in an individualistic manner about these. It's not a question of choice. We are all cogs in a wheel.'

He couldn't believe he'd said that. Did he really believe that? What kind of a mentor was he? It was a hideous analogy. Even if it was true. Especially if it was true. ULTIMATE® must have had a million better ways of expressing that.

'Do you believe that?' Nike was right on him. 'That we have no choice?' It was a bit of a leap of faith, but Nike knew that he had to keep the interaction going as long as possible to give Troy and his men the best chance to completely analyse the system, so he just kept going. He'd deal with the consequences later.

'I'm not sure talking about choice is a good idea in this context.' Pryce gave party line. But wanted to engage. He felt he was losing Nike's interest. 'The algorithmic analysis of data structures from the first two sets of questions is actually both interesting and valuable.'

'I'll take your word for it,' Nike grimaced. 'Sounds dull to me.'

'That's because you're still not getting the deeper level of significance,' Pryce retorted. 'Are you sure you're interested in this?'

'I'm sure there's something interesting,' Nike observed, 'but, like all the good questions, I'm sure it's well buried.'

'Don't think of it in terms of individualistic choices,' Pryce ventured, 'when you reduce such questions to questions about the self you'll always end up in this sort of mess. Self isn't important to the ULTIMATE® world. Self is personal. Personal is meaningless. It's better to think in terms of systemic preferences. And always remember that the aim of Question Theory is to produce data which helps the ULTIMATE® system refine itself.' He didn't add that this effectively meant keeping the system one step ahead of the random elements of the system aka the population. That was beyond Nike's clearance level. He knew that.

'So what is the difference between a choice and a preference?' Nike asked, pretending to be interested. Neither word held any great meaning for him.

The US™ simply stated:

DEFINITION: Choice. The act or an instance of choosing. 10 CREDITS.
Pressed, it continued
DEFINITION: To choose. Select out of a greater number. Select between one or another.

Certainly there was no indication that a choice could be between things that were 'better' or 'worse' or that any emotional content could be involved. ULTIMATE® offered the definitions that reinforced its own system. Unsurprisingly.

'And preference?' Nike asked.

DEFINITION: Preference. The act or instance of preferring..

'This is getting stupid', Nike said, but went for the whole set anyway. After all, he wasn't wasting his own credits.

DEFINITION: To prefer. To choose. Or to promote.

'I am certainly not going to ask what it means by

promote,' Nike pointed out. 'I know when I'm going down a blind alley. This is what I hate about the US™. This is why I wanted you to tell me.'

Pryce understood Nike's frustration. He'd felt it often enough himself in his younger days, before he'd given in and learned to accept. Now, in his more depressive moods he felt that the ULTIMATE® definitions did in fact explain the role of choice in the ULTIMATE® world. The words had no meaning within the concept. He wondered how that had happened. He remembered a day when people had at least felt they had a real choices. Had they been wrong? Had choice never really existed except as a word in a lexicon. The lexicon had changed, the word had become redundant. The concept had always been so. Pryce remembered that Choice used to be linked to Freedom. Another personalised concept ULTIMATE® had done away with. He sensed he was losing Nike now and he wanted to get back in control. Offer something positive.

'I know it seems confusing,' he said. 'I can give you a systemic example if you like, so you can see that there is a meaning to things, just not always the personal meaning you think you want.'

'Okay.' Nike just needed Pryce to keep talking. He hadn't had a signal from Troy to say he could stop yet.

'Within UTheoryΣ®,' Pryce began, 'there is the understanding that by discovering specific user preference you can create/adapt preferences both for that specific user and more importantly for the general user. Preference is important on a systemic level. This is much more efficient and is known as the power of *HYPE®*.'

This was a concept Nike had heard but hadn't paid attention to previously.

DEFINITION: Hype. 1) Promoting with extravagant publicity. 2) Cheating, a trick.

'Of course you have to realise,' Pryce stated, 'that it's the promotion aspect we are dealing with.'

'So why did it mention a trick?'

Pryce sighed. He remembered that the subsidiary definition of cheating had also worried him once, but he had quickly learned that was something everyone had to get over if they were to stay working for ULTIMATE®.

'Sorry. You just have to accept that,' he answered. He knew it was no answer.

Hype had sold everything in the 20th century. By the millennium it was one of the most important and manipulated virtual commodities.

'You can't avoid it. It's one of the facts of ULTIMATE® life. The creation of *HYPE®* preference has made life easier for all. Systemically it made preference easier to predict and therefore to maintain. It's the world we live in.'

How weak was that? But it was an ULTIMATE® truth. By controlling preferences you could change belief systems and by changing belief systems you could change reality. It was simple.

'It's the beauty of the UTheory∑®,' he continued, 'and that's what all the question theory stuff really comes down to.'

Nike was not impressed. Of course he had been taught that the principle of UTheory∑® was the acceptance that theory changes as the system changes. A once ground-breaking concept was something he had never questioned, simply because it seemed to have no relevance to his life. It was just the way things were. He'd viewed the definitions when he was fourteen after all.

DEFINITION: UTheory∑® is essentially the theory of theories. It is Chaos theory meets Game Theory meets Semantic Theory….

And again at fifteen for a deeper understanding.

UTheory∑®is a theory of everything, non reductable to

the theory of everything in physics. It is a mutable theory. It works against primitive definitions of theory which state that: A theory is a system of ideas explaining something – especially based on general principles independent of the particular thing to be explained.

By seventeen he'd just accepted that not only did UTheory$\sum$® underpin the ULTIMATE® system, but that it *was* the ULTIMATE® theory. And he'd gone back to his gaming.

Now, at twenty, he was in a position where he had to address the question again. But only because he was working for Troy, trying to get answers for Troy, trying to get a link for Troy. It might bore him rigid, but it sounded like the kind of stuff that Troy would be interested in. So he feigned interest himself.

'So, what is the purpose of UTheory$\sum$®?' he asked.

Pryce was in his element now. Now he was really getting somewhere. Nike was asking intelligent questions for once. The kind of questions that had absorbed him as a young man. Was he witnessing a rites of passage here? Was he responsible for that rites of passage? Was he finally a father figure, explaining the facts of life to his son? Of course, it wasn't the sort of question that Nike should be asking but Pryce was so carried away in the moment he forgot that.

'The development of Chaos theory shows that even a fixed system cannot give a general result because every element in the system (never mind the elements outside the system) can alter it. This realisation of the importance to the system of the elements of the system and the randomness inherent was the start point of the development of UTheory$\sum$® in history. I was part of that history,' he couldn't help adding with a sense of pride.

'I thought we weren't meant to bother with history.' Nike threw back. That was Nike all over. Give with one hand, take with the other and all the while smiling as if he could never have thought to upset. Pryce choked. Nike's generation didn't have the concept of upsetting. It required too emotional a make-up. ULTIMATE had factored this out of Project Kids. He had to remember that and stop being so thin skinned.

'Yes. You're right,' he smiled back, 'I was just trying to give you a context that might make it more interesting.'

'Oh. Okay.' Nike smiled again.

Pryce continued. 'The relationship between actions and consequences used to be thought of as progressive, one way, linear. Now we know that it is at least symbiotic if not cyclical. Everyone is important to ULTIMATE® because within the ULTIMATE® system everyone is engaged in creating, refining and maintaining the theory itself. UTheory$\sum$®is not just the answer to our lives, UTheory$\sum$® IS our lives.'

And then Pryce got carried away. His own random element kicked in. He gave away information far beyond Nike's level of clearance. This was the danger of not using standard procedure. If he'd stuck to the prepared schedules and techniques this would not have happened. But it was out before he could help himself.

'UTheory$\sum$® brought about a shift from divisiveness to a holistic approach, that's an acceptance that everything is (or can be) related and therefore controlled. When you can control the random element you can control everything.' The moment it was out he realised his mistake. And of course it was the one moment Nike was paying attention.

He asked, 'what does controlling the random element mean?'

Pryce pulled back. He knew this was out of his depth. He'd better play safe. leave the answer to the knowledge bank which on cue gave the following definitions:

RANDOM: Definition, made without method or conscious choice.
ELEMENT: Definition, a component part
CONTROL: Definition, a means of regulation

'Why does UTheory∑® control the random element?' Nike asked. There was no way the knowledge bank would give him the answer to this one.

'Nike. That's back to the kind of why questions we've been trying to avoid,' Pryce sighed.

'Yes. But I want to know.' Nike wasn't giving up now. 'I thought you really wanted to help me understand. I thought you were my friend.'

That did it. Pryce couldn't resist that appeal now could he? He knew there would be ramifications. He knew if anyone was logging the interactions there would be a heavy price to pay, possibly even his job. But then, it was just possible that no one was logging real-time. And he could go and wipe the whole interaction. Against policy of course but..... he told himself it would be okay. He wanted to believe it.

'I will tell you, Nike. But realise that this is just between us. We should keep this kind of thing within established protocol. So...'

'Don't worry,' Nike stated, 'I won't tell if you don't.'

'Controlling the random element effectively means being one step ahead of it. UTheory∑® understands and accepts the random element as a necessary part of the system but unless it remains one step ahead of it, the random element could threaten to destroy the system.'

In a moment Nike realised the power of the information. The Immortal Horses were the random element. And now they were one step ahead of the system.

'Thanks Pryce.'

'I can trust you?' Pryce asked. It was a futile question to a generation who had no concept of trust.

'Of course you can.' Nike responded. He felt a sort of electric shock through his ßß™ and reckoned that was Troy's way of telling him he could stop now. He'd done his job.

Pryce headed back to wipe his files. He felt that he had done his job too. Not the job he was paid for by ULTIMATE® but his job as a mentor. Today, he felt Nike trusted him and that felt good. He felt proud. Was this what it felt like to be a father? If so, he was sorry he'd missed out. It gave him another reason to despise Angela.

Basking in their individual successes, neither Pryce nor Nike knew what lengths the ULTIMATE® system would go to in order to stay one step ahead of the random element. But they soon would. 'You can't fight city hall.'

S. A MATTER OF LIFE AND DEATH

However much Pryce felt that he'd finally made a breakthrough with Nike, he was mistaken. Nike no longer needed Pryce. He had found someone who would give him better answers. Answers more suited to his inquisitive nature. That morning he'd listened to Pryce's explanation of UTheory$\sum$® without asking too many awkward questions, just as Troy had instructed him. He understood that his job now was to gain information, not to cause trouble. On the surface he had settled down into his new 'productive' work schedule, but it was only because The Immortal Horses had given him a purpose. He was aware they were using all his information to build up their own database. They needed to create programmes to break into the system and they needed an open, linked terminal to achieve this. Nike's role was to keep the channels open and let The Immortal Horses do their work. It gave some meaning to his life.

Pryce thought Nike was genuinely interested in Question Theory. Nike asked the questions and listened to the explanations because the tutorial provided a good, robust set of algorithmic run time data. Or something like that. Nike's head just spun when Troy tried to explain the systemic workings. But he felt proud to be part of something. Something that was not The PROJECT△. Nike had given up thinking that ULTIMATE® had anything to offer. He'd stopped thinking that Pryce had anything to offer him, because he'd found a better tutor in Troy. Not just a father-figure, a real live father.

Nike sneaked out to the Trading House whenever he could, usually after a good long session doing his 'productive' work, when no one would be looking out for him. He had previously achieved such low targets that if he now put in a decent burst of work, he could go missing for a good couple of hours and no one looking casually at his output would notice. Pryce had too many other irons in the fire to check Nike in any more depth than by looking at his output log. Nike knew the cheat would only work for a while. But it didn't matter. It worked for now, and his father was sure to sort something better out soon. Even now, he understood that the geeks at the Trading House were working on a way of diverting his ßß™ signal so that he could be in two places at one time. It provided a real time application for Quantum Theory. Of course he was only in two places in theory. But that was good enough for ULTIMATE® systems. After all, virtuality was all to ULTIMATE®. The Immortal Horses exploited the systemic weakness. So, while virtually Nike was at The Project House more often than not he was actually at the Trading House. As long as no one thought to look in his room he was fine.

Meanwhile, in the hours they spent together at the Trading House, Troy explained about the importance of Meaning to Nike. Their father-son bonding was strange but powerful. Nike quickly learned to put his faith and trust in Troy. After all, Troy had the answers almost before Nike had the questions.

And if Troy's conversations were more like tutorials than intimate family chat, that went unnoticed by Nike who had, after all, forgotten what family was like.

'In the 20th century people fixated on the meaning of meaning,' Troy explained. 'In the 21st century ULTIMATE® have rendered meaning meaningless. While in History meaning was central to our human existence, and at one point it was considered that belief and meaning are interdependent, ULTIMATE® have achieved the goal of destroying both belief and meaning for the individual. And they've done it as a result of everyone in the system buying into it willingly. You've all been helping them every step of the way. Every bit of data collected, every question asked has helped them destroy your humanity.'

'But why would ULTIMATE® destroy people?' Nike felt it was a naïve question, but he really didn't understand. And he felt more comfortable asking Troy questions now.

'I didn't say they destroyed people as physical bodies, they need the physical bodies to keep the system afloat. They destroyed your humanity. Your being. Your individuality.'

'Why?' There was no point pretending he understood if he didn't.

Troy was patience personified. 'The evaluation of run time complexity became more important than the consideration of the emotional and social needs of the population. Models became more important than meaning. ULTIMATE® realised early on that personal meaning (purpose) has no value.'

'Doesn't it have value to the individual?' Nike interjected, keen to show himself a willing and thoughtful student and impress his father.

'Yes, but that is of no interest to ULTIMATE®. It becomes a tautology. Personal meaning only has meaning for the individual and the individual has no meaning in the system, therefore meaning has no value for the system and by logical extension...'

'The individual has no value for the system.' Nike filled in the gaps.

'Correct.' There was a pause. 'Yet somehow unacceptable, don't you think?'

Nike wasn't sure. He'd never really thought of his own meaning or his own value. He'd bought the line sold to him that Project Kids were valuable to ULTIMATE®...

'They always told us we were valuable because we were Project Kids,' he replied.

'But where is the focus of that value?' Troy asked.

Nike thought. Hard. 'Oh. Of course. The value is only to them.'

'It's a statistical, computational value,' Troy added. 'Nothing to do with you as an actual individual, a real person.

'Am I a real person?' Nike asked. He was baffled but beginning to enjoy this level of debate. In a world where metaphysical questions had become largely redundant, not least because of the credit charge placed on them over and above more 'useful' question types, Nike was robbed of the discovery that he would have made a good metaphysician. Like his old man.

In another time Troy might have been known by another name. Socrates perhaps. Or Fagin. Or the Imam of a radical sect. Or the charismatic leader of a religious cult. His identity was constant across history though his name changed. Troy had learned from his own father Randall, that name is the thief of identity. The Immortal Horses had also existed through history with a legion of different names. Like all such groups they were loyal and obedient only to their leader. Troy knew his History. And unlike ULTIMATE®, used history to his own purpose. ULTIMATE ® and Troy both appreciated the power of history, though they treated it differently. ULTIMATE® sold the story that History is bunk publicly but privately appreciated that it was powerful bunk and dangerous in the wrong hands. Troy used history as myth and narrative to explain present conditions. It was Capitalism versus Marxism. Evil versus Good. As Eric Blair had predicted ULTIMATE® buried the likes of George Orwell, yet Troy appreciated the truths held within his fiction, *'He who controls the past controls the future.'*

A casual observer from outside the system, if such a person could exist, might have opined that it was lucky ULTIMATE® didn't know of the danger in their midst. A cynic from outside the system might ask: But how could they not know? And if they knew about The Immortal Horses why didn't they do anything? Standing outside, commentating on the narrative might lead one to question whether it was possible the ULTIMATE® system had flaws. Couldn't do anything? Where, when and how had The Immortal Horses fallen through the gaps? What was the flaw in the system? How had ULTIMATE® not picked up on all the random elements? But everyone was firmly inside the narrative. Even Troy.

'Who makes meaning?' Nike asked, hopeful that Troy could come up with an answer. He'd never get enough ULTIMATE® credits to ask, never mind get an answer to this level of question.

'If we consider that belief and meaning are interdependent,' Troy began, 'and that personal meaning has no value to the system...'

'Yes, you've said that,' Nike couldn't help blurting out impatiently. A look from Troy told him to hang on in there. The difficult questions didn't always have easy answers.

'And generic meaning is constructed according to the benefits derived to the system, the profit motive if you like....'

Nike used his memory and came up with the rest, desperate to prove to Troy that he was smarter than he looked.

'The profit is for the shareholders.'

'Yes. Keep going,' Troy was determined to make Nick think for himself. 'What are shareholders?'

'They own the corporation.' Nike wasn't sure he knew what own or corporation really meant. He was about to find out.

'What is a corporation?' Troy challenged.

'ULTIMATE® defined it as an institution which can have a legal entity as a person but in fact is not one person. But I don't see the point,' Nike replied.

'Is ULTIMATE® an institution?'

Nike had never thought of that before.

'Uh.' He had always just accepted ULTIMATE® as a way of life. ULTIMATE® was everything, was behind everything, was everywhere.... It was the brand to which you gave your loyalty. Without thinking. It was the brand of choice because it was the only choice. Which of course meant there was no choice. But yes, now he thought about it, it wasn't just a system, behind the system was something that you might call an institution.. and if so.....'

'Does ULTIMATE® have shareholders?' Troy prompted.

'It could I suppose,' Nike answered.

'Or is it run by God?'

Nike nearly laughed out loud. God? Come on. That was such a wasted historical concept…. Then he realised, Troy was throwing a red herring at him.

'So behind ULTIMATE® are shareholders. People who are acting as one person through the legal entity of ULTIMATE®.' He didn't appreciate the significance of his response.

'Correct. Now why would they do that?'

Now Nike was stumped.

'You need another history lesson,' Troy observed. 'ULTIMATE® and its place in the history of power politics. Think about all the questions you've asked before. Make connections. Think.'

Nike couldn't make sense of it. He wanted to, but he was struggling. 'But History is meaningless,' he said.

'ULTIMATE® told you. Do you believe them?'

Nike had never realised you could challenge the system. Not in any meaningful way. He'd only done it to play games, pass the time, infuriate Pryce. Never for a real purpose. Troy had changed his fundamental perception. He liked it. It felt good. At least, as long as he was with Troy it felt good. It didn't feel so good when he was sitting alone in his room in The Project House. Then he felt small and vulnerable. Here he felt….

'The thing with the ULTIMATE® system,' Troy stated 'Is that you have to ask the right question to get the right answer.'

'How do you know what's the right question?' Nike asked.

'That's the point,' Troy replied. 'They've made sure you won't know what the right question is. Your role is just to ask questions to fill the databases and help the computational analysis. Not to derive meaning. For every question you ask, they get much, much more information than they ever let go.

That's why you have to be smart. And Nick. You are smart. Too smart for ULTIMATE®. That's why we want you to come here. Permanently. Do you want that?'

'Yes.. but.. how?' Nike couldn't imagine the possibility. ULTIMATE® was all he had known, all that he could remember. They'd made sure of that. Protecting their investment.

'I'm working on it,' Troy replied, matter of factly. 'But for now you're of much more use to us in the system. It won't be for ever. Just for now. Do you accept that?'

Nike nodded.

'Okay,' Troy said. 'Now, what I want you to do is to start asking awkward questions. It's dangerous, but we'll protect you. I want to test the system at its core and I need someone with a legitimate login to do that.'

'Okay.'

'Give me five minutes to get the technicians to set up your US™ logon from here, mirrored to your home terminal. Go back, and then start.'

'What questions?' asked Nike.

'What questions do you want to know?' asked Troy.

'Who runs ULTIMATE®?' Nike suggested.

'It's a good question. It's not one they're going to give you an answer to right away though. Use the question theory training you've been given and think of ways to pose it.'

Nike came up with a list of alternatives:

> Who runs ULTIMATE®?
> Who is behind ULTIMATE®?
> Who is in charge of ULTIMATE®?
> Who created ULTIMATE®?

Troy spoke up at last. 'Yes. You can go down this path. They'll try to divert you. Probably alarm bells will ring and your counsellor will come calling. But before he does, you've got to ask *the* right question. It's vitally important. We need to see if asking the right question will give the right answer.'

Nike went back to The Project House. He felt happy. He had a purpose. He knew he was a real person now. He existed. As an individual, not just a virtual pawn in the ULTIMATE® system. He felt free. He knew what he was about to do was dangerous. He didn't know how dangerous but he trusted Troy. He would do anything for Troy and Troy would make it all right. He was convinced of this and determined not to let Troy down.

He logged on. He started asking questions. 'Who runs ULTIMATE® ?'

The US™ screen responded: *Question does not compute.*
RUNS: Definition. There are multiple definitions EACH OF WHICH WILL COST YOU 10 CREDITS. Be more specific in your question for a clearer response.

Nike sighed. This was as they'd expected. Diversion. 'Who is behind ULTIMATE®?'

Question does not compute. BEHIND: Definition. The rear of, positional. ULTIMATE® is not a positional entity. Alternative Definition. Hidden by, does not make referential sense with regard to the question. Please redefine your question. THIS HAS COST YOU 20 CREDITS. To reduce your credit expenditure you should follow the accepted pattern of Question Theory as outlined to you in the training sessions.

Nike wondered if they were onto him. You didn't usually get this level of response from the knowledge bank. It just churned out the answer in the same unthinking way that it assumed you had asked it. He felt like he was playing at a much higher level now. He felt the danger but he wasn't going to give up now.

'Who is in charge of ULTIMATE®?'

IN CHARGE: Definition. Having command. Question makes no computational sense. Are you asking who commands ULTIMATE®?

This was going off script. Nike had to think fast. 'No, not commands. Who controls ULTIMATE®?'

Across the square, in Pryce's office, all hell had broken loose. Alarm bells were sounding in Graham's office. Lights were flashing on his monitor. Pryce's linked in US™ screen also highlighted this unauthorised activity coming from Nike's terminal. Graham called Pryce in immediately.

'What the hell is he doing?' Graham asked.

'I have no idea,' Pryce responded.

'Is this the result of your Question Theory sessions?' Graham asked, annoyed. 'Because if so, you need to seriously reconsider your teaching style.'

'It doesn't mean anything,' Pryce tried to calm the situation. 'It's just Nike. He's just bored and ….'

'It's dangerous. It's way over his level of access. You need to get over there fast and sort this out.'

Pryce didn't really see what all the fuss was about. Nike was always asking questions that didn't fit in with the patterns. What did it matter? He'd have moved onto something else tomorrow. And it would give them good data after all. Wasn't that what they wanted? Someone asking unusual questions. Someone actually testing the robustness of the system. But come to think of it, it was a good question. One he'd never thought about in years. Who *did* control ULTIMATE®? He didn't know.

In the Trading House, Nike's progress was being followed by Troy and his closest team with equal interest.

'Come on… keep going,' Troy muttered.

'He's running out of time,' Griff observed.
'He'll do it. I know he will.' Troy replied.

CONTROL: Definition. The power of command. Your question is self-referential from the previous question. ULTIMATE® controls ULTIMATE®. Redefine if dissatisfied with answer. THIS HAS COST YOU 30 CREDITS.

Nike kept on going, undeterred. 'Who created ULTIMATE®?'

CREATE: Definition. To bring into existence. This question refers to the History of ULTIMATE®. Before The GRsΩHist, ULTIMATE® did not exist. The existence of ULTIMATE® was brought about by the end of History and so the History of ULTIMATE® is a logically invalid subject. The general area of questioning regarding the workings of ULTIMATE® is too large for your remaining credits. Please earn more credits through 'productive' work or redefine and be more specific in your questioning. For example: You could ask questions on a temporal basis – describe the status of ULTIMATE® in 2020. Other subject areas include…..

Nike had stopped listening. He remembered Troy saying, 'You have to ask the right question to get the right answer.'
He took a deep breath and asked, 'Who ARE ULTIMATE®?' This time he got an unexpected answer.

'The 100 men.'

He went one step further. One step too far. 'Who are the 100 men?'

'Bingo!' Back at the Trading House, on the mirrored site, Troy was following the interaction and it was to his screen that the list started running…. They'd done it. They'd got the names of the 100 men behind ULTIMATE®. It was everything they'd wanted and more than they could have hoped for. Nike had come up trumps.

Pryce was in the rest room, preparing for his trip to the Project House and, as always, missed the vital moment. By the time he got to the Project House, Nike was no longer there. He was on his way to the Trading House. He hadn't stopped to see the list, it meant nothing to him. He knew he'd done his job and that was enough. He'd asked the right question. He knew he needed to get out of there and fast, to a place of safety. The Immortal Horses offered him the best chance of safety now.

But, being human, and therefore composed of random elements, he decided to go to the Trading House via his Nan's. He wanted to tell her about Troy. He didn't know when he'd be able to see her again, and he wanted her to know her son was alive. She must be wondering what was going on, since that last US™ interface where he'd been cut off. He owed it to her to bring her up to speed. He wanted to tell her who sent the cake.. He reckoned he'd have to keep his head down for a while soon, and visits to his Nan would be off limits. He wanted to reassure her. If Troy could save his son, he could surely save his mother too.

Despite an awareness of the danger of his situation, Nike left the Project House for the first time full of hope. At last he knew who he was. He had family once again. Life was looking up. He felt like he'd escaped from prison. He had escaped from ULTIMATE®. He'd bust the levels and got out of the game. He couldn't imagine the complexity of that statement and so it didn't worry him. He was happy. Troy would sort everything. He trusted Troy. He looked up and saw a pale sun, shining in the sky. Something he'd neither looked for nor seen in a long time. What he didn't see was the vehicle approaching him from behind. He didn't see it as it hit him and he saw nothing as he was thrown, doll-like over the bonnet, landing in a crumpled heap on the pavement. No light remained. Only blackness. Forever.

T. RECRIMINATIONS

'He wouldn't have felt a thing.' Pryce realised how ridiculous this comment would seem to the Project Kids for whom feelings were no longer a reality. But surely, this news would have some effect.

Project Kids, like most new millennium people, didn't have what Pryce would consider a real concept of death. They'd grown up with so much killing in their gaming, and with so much virtual living, that the reality never hit them. If someone was killed in a game, no problem, you just started over. If someone died in reality, they lived on through the US™ Memory Bank, the ULTIMATE® equivalent to the social networking sites which first gave people a kind of virtual immortality. In History, immortality had been for the few who had been painted, photographed, filmed or in other ways recorded. Social networking sites offered a more interactive experience. The US™ system was so ubiquitous that it blurred the boundaries even further. People spent so little time with other people interfacing in actuality, that death rarely touched them. But surely, Nike had lived with Omo and Flora for over five years. That must mean something. Pryce looked at them to gauge their response.

Omo was silent. When Pryce had come in, stony faced, instructing them to go into the common room, Omo had been convinced it was to challenge him regarding his affair with Angela. He was convinced he would be exposed. While his face remained calm, he was feeling an emotion, but the emotion wasn't sorrow, it was guilt. He wasn't used enough to emotions to be able to feel grief at the same time. It would take some time to sink in.

Flora was trying to compute the information. What did it mean?

'Will we get a new flatmate?' Was all she was able to ask. The girl who had cried watching the death of the last tiger, could not shed a tear over a real boy with whom she'd shared

263

her space for the last five years. Of course, she hadn't really shared her life, that was lived online and Nike was just someone who was 'around.' He would presumably be replaced. And with someone less annoying, hopefully.

Omo brought himself out of his stupor. 'What about his Nan?'

'What do you mean?' Pryce was confused by Omo's behaviour and this response didn't make any sense to him. Was this shock?

'Who's going to tell her. She'll be….' Omo couldn't find the word to describe how Helen would react. Devastated was not in his vocabulary.

'She…. Well, she loved him,' he managed. That was it. Love. Something Omo thought he was learning about. At that moment he realised the person who would know about love was Helen. He started to formulate a plan. It was uncharacteristic, but his experiences with Angela were changing him in all sorts of ways.

'We should tell her,' Omo continued.

Pryce was really out of his depth here. But if that was what it would take to get the Kids back on track, fine. Where could the harm be?

'Uh, Okay. I'll sort out transport for you to go there this afternoon if you like.'

'Sure.' Omo felt just another little bit guilty now that he realised his main reason for going to see Helen might not be to tell her about Nike's untimely death, but to find out what she knew about love. That he wanted to take from her, not to give.

Helen was unaware of the horror that was about to face her as she opened the door to the unexpected visitor. She was greeted by Omo and Flora, who looked, to put it mildly, uncomfortable.

'Nice to see you. Nick not with you?'

Omo and Flora looked at each other. They didn't know what to say. They hadn't thought this through. Hadn't thought how they would tell Helen and now here they were, unprepared.

'Uh…No..' Omo struggled for words.

'Can we come in?' Flora asked.

'Surely, surely,' Helen ushered them into the room, 'please, sit down,' she added.

They had to sit on the bed. There was nowhere else to sit. Only Helen's chair, facing the US™ screen from which she had risen to answer the door.

'It's about Nike.. Nick… that we've come,' Omo finally managed to get out. He had never believed it possible to experience this level of awkwardness.

'He's not in trouble is he?' Helen asked, not expecting what was coming next.

'He wouldn't have felt any pain,' Omo added, parroting Pryce's statement. What else could he do? He didn't know how you told someone that another person was dead. He certainly didn't know how to tell an old lady that her beloved grandson was dead. That was far beyond him.

'He's dead.' Flora asserted, quickly, so that there could be no confusion. Somehow she knew it was important that Helen got the information straight and quick.

Helen sank into her chair. The colour drained from her face, and Flora observed that she finally looked all of her seventy years for the first time. As they watched her, something changed. A light went out. She aged. A bit of her died. It wasn't the first time.

'How…?' she finally spoke. She needed to know.

'He wouldn't have felt any pain.' Omo repeated. He was glad Flora was with him, but surprised that she seemed to be showing more strength than he could find. Looking at Helen churned him up in a way he'd never experienced before and yet Flora, the girl who had cried at the death of some mangey tiger they'd never even met, seemed able to take charge and stay calm.

'He was run over.' Flora added the only detail she knew.

'How?'

'We don't know.'

'Where?' Helen needed more detail.

'I'm not sure. Somewhere between our house and here I think.'

'Why?' As if she needed to ask.

'I'm really sorry.' Flora rose from the bed and put her arms round Helen, 'we could get Pryce to come and see you if you like. He might know more.'

'No, it's all right.' Helen pulled herself together. She knew why, in broad terms, something bad might have happened to Nick. Something to shut him up. She knew ULTIMATE® was behind it and she didn't need an ULTIMATE® employee telling her lies.

'Was he on his way to see me?'

Flora and Omo looked at each other. They had no idea. But they somehow felt that Helen deserved some answers, so they gave her the one they thought most suitable.

'Yes,' they said, in unison.

Helen crumpled. It *was* her fault. If she hadn't got Nick trying to find out about RIP she was sure this wouldn't have happened. It was her fault. It must be. She needed to be alone.

'Should we get someone to be with you?' Flora broke the silence.

'No, No, I'll be fine,' Helen put on her stoical face again. 'I need some time on my own, that's all. Thank you for… for telling me.'

Omo and Flora got up. What else was there to do? Flora hugged Helen and Omo felt the right thing was to follow suit. As Flora headed for the door, he hung back a moment and before he even realised what he was doing he whispered,

'Can I come back and see you… alone? I need to talk to you.'

'Of course,' Helen whispered back to him and then let

him go. 'Whenever you like, Omo. Any friend of Nick's is always welcome here.'

And the door shut behind them, leaving Helen even more alone than she had felt twenty minutes before. She had promised to watch out for him. It had been a lifelong promise. And she'd failed. Helen struggled with a grief she thought she had left behind with the death of Randall. The mind plays tricks on you in these first stages of shock. She could not believe that Nick was dead. Even though the kids had told her, and they were obviously sincere, she found it impossible to believe that Nick, so full of life, was no longer there. It was a concept too hard to bear and her brain kicked in with the only alternative bearable. It wasn't true. She didn't know why ULTIMATE® would lie about it, but she was sure they were lying.

Another part of her brain had already moved into the post death grief state she had experienced too many times before. The contemplation of what death means. Knowing the person now lives only in your memory. Knowing you'll never see them again. You can't share meaning with them. Emptiness, loss. A reminder of your own isolation. That you'd give everything to just EXTERNALISE with them one more time. Reflection on your own mortality. The need to LIVE the rest of your life. How would she do that? What was left for her?

It brought her back to the desire to be rational even in her shock and grief. Logically, she worked out that either Nick was dead, in which case she could do nothing to help him, or he wasn't dead in which case she needed to find out what had happened to him and she wouldn't do that sitting in an ULTIMATE® Home. Either way, she needed to find out for herself where RIP were. Because either way, RIP must still exist. Either Nick had been killed by ULTIMATE® as his father and grandfather before him, for knowing too much, or asking too many questions; or he was alive, held somewhere for precisely the same reasons. It was the only sense she could make of this senseless situation. And if he was alive....

She had a flashback to her last interaction with Nick. That strange message from the US™ screen. When he'd said he was with his dad. Maybe he'd already been spirited away by ULTIMATE® at that point. She remembered the 1970's when people were 'disappeared' in Chile. She'd been approaching her teens and it was the first really shocking news she'd encountered. It had stayed with her. It was the hallmark of the totalitarian regime. And Helen wasn't taken in by the bright, light, brand loyalty of ULTIMATE®. She could see beneath it. Behind the brand was something far more frightening than corporate greed. It was a new totalitarianism. ULTIMATE® totalitarianism. The destruction of humanity.

She had to act and act soon. She had to find what was left of the RIP and try and reclaim some sort of personal truth out of this world of branded lies. Of course she realised that if she left the ULTIMATE® Home she would die too, probably within a couple of years, if not sooner. At this stage the thought did not bother her. It was subsumed beneath a feeling a lot like hope which told her she might LIVE for two more years. Actually live. A life of freedom outside the death that was ULTIMATE®. That's worth it. However short the timeframe. She'd been dead for the last ten years after all. It was time to be like a tree and experience spring once more. She longed to go back to the 'beech' and walk in the winter and grow vegetables in the summer and eat real food. All this had to be worth whatever price she would finally pay, however soon she had to pay it. Life under ULTIMATE® might seem to be comfortable and easy after a fashion, as long as you just went along with it but it wasn't REAL and a non-real life isn't worth living. It's no more life than a plastic flower. A dead tree has more life than a plastic flower.

How would she get away? She looked at the ßß™ barcode on her arm. It was a link to ULTIMATE® that she could not erase. Everyone had one now. Everyone was branded. She rubbed it. Not for the first time she thought about the tattoos of the Holocaust victims. ULTIMATE® may have done away with history for its citizens, but it had borrowed freely from whatever bits of history suited its purpose. Once upon a time tattoos had been for sailors and soldiers or primitive tribesmen. Then footballers and celebrities began to adorn themselves, calling it 'body art.' Fashion drifted down to the masses inevitably, till tattooing broached all social classes and ages. Then, as fashion and technology segued together, Brands started to enter the fray. Soon enough it had become the height of fashion to have a product or company brand on your arm, and soon enough the benefits turned into necessity. To be allowed to shop anywhere you HAD to have the appropriate brand. Your personal and financial details were contained on the logo on your skin and arms became like so many boy scouts shirtsleeves; the more you had the better a consumer you were. The more brand loyalty you had on your flesh the higher your status both socially and credit wise. Helen was glad that she'd never bought into this. It hadn't happened until they were far into self-sufficiency and it provided a good reason never to have to 'shop' in the mainstream. Only charity shops held out against the onslaught, until finally there were no more charity shops – because there was no longer seen as any need for charity. For a time a strange kind of black market style of shopping was undertaken in the old pound shops and charity shops and then out of the boots of cars, until all these things became consigned to history.

Catriona and Lauren, as good fashionistas, both had armfuls of brands. Of course behind all the brands was one brand. The one brand to whom loyalty was unavoidable in the end. ULTIMATE®. When Helen had been admitted to the ULTIMATE® Home, she had had to submit to having the ULTIMATE® Brand on embedded into her arm. At the time she'd felt like someone entering Auschwitz, but there was no choice. She'd felt numb and dead then anyway. But now… now she wanted to break free from ULTIMATE® once more. Now she felt there was no reason to stay and every reason to take a risk. But

ULTIMATE® wouldn't let her go that easily. The Brand would stay with her for life. That was ULTIMATE's® unique selling point. The clue was in the name.

Helen was not going to let the seal of ULTIMATE® on her arm stop her, however. If she couldn't get rid of the ßß™barcode brand which was not only tattooed onto her skin but contained a technologically advanced biological implant in her arm, she would try to get out of range. That must be possible. Or worth a try at least. The first thing would be to try and make contact with RIP. She did not have time to lose herself in grief for Nick. She needed to make a concrete, workable, escape plan.

U. WHO ARE THE 100 MEN?

The writing was on the wall for Pryce and he knew it. Even before the inevitable meeting with Graham, he knew it. And he'd had enough. He was tired of constantly running to keep up, only to find out that he was way behind the action. More and more he found himself yearning for a long gone past, for the dimly remembered world before ULTIMATE® had taken over everything, including his own life. He wondered where it had all gone wrong? Where did our priorities change from sex and holidays and family life to the easy life of virtuality, a life without responsibility or guilt or feeling of any kind?

Losing himself in his own Memory Bank, he spent his days re-living a past which seemed like the story of someone else's life. He wondered if other people felt like him. He couldn't stand the pointlessness of it all. He immersed himself in his Memory Bank, spending all the credits he'd amassed over a careful number of years, like an addict who'd been clean for so long he was convinced that first hit wouldn't affect him. Pryce saw his teenage self, obsessed with playing psychological thriller games online, pitting his wits against systems which always promised that if he was just smart enough he'd work out the answer, but which, like one armed bandits, made it impossible for you to win so that the game could squeeze every ounce of time and money from you before finally giving you the answer. From this perspective it all seemed so pointless. Yet he'd never stopped pursuing the quest – like Nike, he'd kept asking questions. He realised that was what they'd had in common. So when had he, Pryce, stopped asking questions? When had he started to find Nike's questions irritating rather than inspirational. When had he stopped seeing youth as optimistic hope for the future and instead seen it as a manifestation of a troublesome present? When had he changed and become what ULTIMATE® wanted?

Pryce felt like he'd betrayed himself. At some

unspecified point, he'd lost sight of what had once been important to him. People. Life. Meaning. And he wanted to get it back. He didn't want the death of Nike to mean nothing. By extension it would mean that his life was meaningless. And more than that, Pryce could not deal with the fact that Nike, annoying as he had been, could die and no one batted an eyelid. It was no more than a transfer of data and a set of interviews and assessments for a replacement. Had people really become so unimportant, so interchangeable? It seemed so.

But work wouldn't wait. He was still responsible for Omo and Flora, though he'd kept his distance from them. He'd told them to go and see Helen it was true, but that was really to shift them from asking him awkward questions. He hadn't even bothered to ask them how things had gone. At the time he didn't care. Now he realised he should have. But there was no time. In the moments when he wasn't stealing ULTIMATE®'s time to revisit his own past, he was undertaking the task Graham had set him of making a comprehensive report on the past month. At first he'd thought Graham wanted to make sense of Nike's death as well, but it pretty quickly transpired that Graham only wanted data to be able to close off the file. That's all Nike was. A file. A data set. To be archived. His life meant nothing. His death meant nothing.

Pryce tried to lose himself in his work, but in essence his interest was in trying to find answers – answers beyond the US™ system, in order to make sense of it. And the system didn't want to give up the answers. For the first time in his life, Pryce felt he was fighting against the system and it only served to show him how little in control of his own actions and mind he had become. He wanted to regain a personal perspective not mediated by Memory Banks and knowledge banks and UTheory$\sum$® and US™ screens. But he quickly found that even in order to challenge the system he needed its help. He couldn't gain any information any other way. His depression deepened as he realised that it was impossible to live in this ULTIMATE®

world without using and indeed relying on its resources. So, reluctantly, he logged into the analysis bank. It was a level deeper than the knowledge bank used by the Project Kids and not available to the population at large. It was reserved for employees of ULTIMATE® responsible for The PROJECT△. You had to be very carefully vetted for this information. But you still paid for it. Pryce was prepared to pay. It would be worth the cost and worth the risk.

'Who are The Immortal Horses?' he asked. It was the question Nike had been burning to have answered, and eventually had found out – to his cost.

'This is beyond your authorisation limit. Refer to your line manager.'

As expected, the system shut the door in his face. For once Pryce experienced the same level of annoyance that Nike had always exhibited at the US™ system and finally thought he had gained some understanding of the boy. Too late. Pryce reasoned that if the system didn't want to give him the information, it was information he needed to know. He was wondering what to do next, when the call he had been dreading, and expecting, came. Graham summoned him to a meeting.

For a thoroughly modern man, Graham still employed some shockingly traditional methods of exerting control over his subordinates. As Pryce lowered himself into the chair opposite Graham's overlarge desk, he noted, not for the first time, the pathetic tactic Graham employed of making sure his own chair was substantially higher, so that Pryce had to look up at his boss. Pryce had always privately ridiculed this tactic but today, for the first time, he really noticed how effective it was. It was clear to them both that Graham was in complete control of this situation. Pryce considered handing his resignation in then and there, it being the only thing he could think of to regain the initiative. But something stopped him.

'How are you?' Graham's comment disarmed Pryce.

'Fine.' If it was going to be a game of verbal chess, he'd play through the opening gambit.

'Good.' Graham affected a smile but it came out much more like a smug leer. Pryce wished he had the good old fashioned guts to hit Graham. But he didn't.

'How is your report shaping up?' Graham asked.

'Okay.' A taciturn Pryce was giving nothing away.

'When can I expect it?'

Pryce decided to employ one of Graham's own tactics. The long silence. And he thought it must have worked because Graham broke it.

'I know you've been under pressure..' he began.

This wasn't what Pryce wanted. This was putting him back on the spot. But Graham continued 'And I'm concerned about the amount of credits you've been using up on your Memory Bank. It's a sign of a troubled mind.'

Another long pause. Pryce was not giving in.

'I'm here to help,' Graham added. Like Pryce would believe that, 'is there is anything I can do?'

Pryce had had enough of this. He was a drowning man. He was going down for the third time. What did any of it matter now? He had nothing to lose.

'Do you mean it?' he asked. It was an opening move, not a cry for help.

'Of course,' Graham responded. He had his man where he wanted him now. 'If you have any unresolved questions, issues I can help with, just ask.'

He was not expecting what came next.

'Who killed Nike?'

There was just the briefest of pauses. Graham had not got to the position he held without being able to analyse situations on the hoof and regain the high ground.

'The Immortal Horses,' came the surprising reply.

Pryce didn't know whether his surprise lay in the response itself or in the fact that Graham had made it without batting an eyelid. But in for a penny…

'Why did The Immortal Horses kill Nike?'
The pace of the game was picking up.

'He had information which might prove dangerous to ULTIMATE®.' Graham responded without a blink. 'Is that all?'

'Uh…' Pryce couldn't think as fast as Graham.

'Because I really think that you need to get away from worrying about all this,' Graham continued, ' maybe…'

This was it. He was about to retrench Pryce, fire him, move him somewhere even worse… Pryce braced himself.

'..maybe you should have some time off?'

'No, it's okay,' Pryce responded through gritted teeth. ' I was really only asking because I felt the report would be incomplete without a resolution.'

Neither of them believed that, but what could Graham do?

'Still, maybe you should…'

'I'd rather work to a finish on this,' Pryce stated. 'With this information, I'm sure I can get the report to you completed by the end of the week. And after that…?'

'It depends on the quality of the report.' Graham sounded sharp. Maybe there was more to Pryce than he'd imagined. He hadn't thought he would put up this much of a fight. He'd need to think of another plan. Because Graham was determined to win in the end. And Pryce, like Nike, was just an impediment in his progress.

'Is that all?' Pryce asked, standing up and preparing to leave the room.

'Yes. That's all for now,' Graham replied.

Pryce started on his way out the door.

'Don't let me down,' was Graham's parting gesture to Pryce's back.

Pryce returned to his room fuming. He wasn't sure what

it was that annoyed him most. The dismissive way Graham had treated the matter of Nike's death, or the thought that he was being played like a cat played with a mouse. He knew his time was limited. He knew Graham would come up with something, but in the time he had left, he was determined to find out all that he could. He went back to Nike's logs with renewed vigour. There must be something…

He wondered whether what Graham had said was true. It seemed too convenient. It was the answer one would anticipate if one was dealing in conspiracy theories. But Pryce knew the obvious answer was rarely the right one. It had come too glibly off Graham's tongue. Like it had been rehearsed. He was sure it bore no relation to the truth. Though what chance did he have of finding a truth outside the system? One thing Pryce knew was that the death of Nike had not been an accident. The ULTIMATE® system had factored out accidents after all. Random actions were controlled within UTheory$\sum$®. Pryce scratched his head. He didn't know what to make of this. But he did know that Graham was rattled. That was enough to start with.

He needed to get his brain working. Pure thought. The kind of thought which ULTIMATE® had rendered unnecessary. He took a deep breath. Firstly, why would it matter to The Immortal Horses that Nike's information could hurt ULTIMATE®? Surely that was the aim of their organisation. They were the bogey man who frightened children. Not Project Kids of course, they were kept in a bubble away from the seamier sides of the ULTIMATE® world. But the ordinary population still needed something to fear and if they didn't have The Immortal Horses they would probably have feared ULTIMATE®.

Until now Pryce had never really been sure whether The Immortal Horses existed in actuality or were an ULTIMATE® virtual construction. If they were a construction the analysis system could logically give him the explanation that The Immortal Horses killed Nike because he threatened ULTIMATE®.

It was a good scapegoat. But there might be more to it than that. It might just be possible that The Immortal Horses really did exist. It might be possible that they had killed Nike, though what their reason could be eluded him. In the case that they didn't exist, it might equally be possible that ULTIMATE® killed Nike. How could he ever know?

Back to Nike's logs. It was clear, on close investigation, that Nike had both the motivation and the opportunity to contact The Immortal Horses. And that he had done so. A pattern began to emerge. Every time the logs drew a blank, Helen seemed to be involved, so Pryce reasoned that maybe Helen was a key to the mystery. But he couldn't just go in and ask her. He would have to come up with something smarter than that. And time was against him. He knew that once his report was on Graham's desk things would change. He quite expected all his access privileges to be withdrawn, even if it was just done with the excuse of moving him on to another counselling role. Nike and his stored information would be deep archived. So Pryce had to move swiftly. He went through Nike's logs with a fine toothcomb. He had to use all his old psychological skills to come up with intuitive possible alternatives. And, after several hours, he came up with a hypothesis worth testing.

What if Nike had been taken on by The Immortal Horses as an operative? What if he had been at the centre of the infection, the compromised system and The Immortal Horses had used him as a cuckoo in the nest?

He went back through the logs again, to test the plausibility of the thesis. He held focus and stuck with it to the end. Right to the very end. And then he discovered what Nike had found…… it was the last entry. It had happened as he'd been on his way to The Project House. It was the list of the 100 men.

The log entry showed simply that Nike had asked the question

'Who are the 100 men?'

And this list had been the response. There was no explanation, just a list of a hundred names. Pryce looked at the list carefully. And then again. He saw names that he hadn't seen, or thought about for many, many years. Names of people who used to be important before the GRsΩHist. Names of business men and world leaders and economists and scientists and financiers…. CEO's of every description rubbing alongside Nobel prize winners and the occasional sporting or creative professional. The human equivalent of the FTSE 100. The people who had banded together to change the world. To create what was laughingly referred to in 20th century conspiracy theory as THE NEW WORLD ORDER. The fictional bogey man in the days before The Immortal Horses took up that role.

Pryce hadn't believed in the New World Order any more than he had in The Immortal Horses. But somehow, looking at the list, it all fell into place. Things like the New World Order had been a smokescreen. But they hid something in plain sight. They hid the fact that there were people, important people, who were using globalisation to take control. These men were the ULTIMATE® shareholders. The power behind the system. The ones who were responsible for the way life had turned out. Throughout the history of the world people had lived with conspiracy theories and secret societies as explanations for the ailments of all. The men who had constructed ULTIMATE® had known that. They had been responsible for the economic collapse and they had rebuilt society, outwith and beyond history, to suit themselves. Between them they had decades of understanding how and why people acted and how and why societies worked and failed. And they had quite callously used all their combined knowledge to create the ULTIMATE® system.

They sat like 100 gods, controlling everyone and everything below them. They had built up the brands and they had built up Brand Loyalty. They had been the movers and shakers, the war mongers and the bringers of peace and as they destroyed history, they made history by signing a secret millennial pact, to privatise the world. It was the most daring, most complete act of corporate imperialism, beyond imagination. And it had worked. Of course it had. They had made people fear the future and then they had saved them. The whole world was built on a pack of lies. But nobody cared because ULTIMATE® used the power of the system to generate the hype that told people that their lives had improved immeasurably. They had achieved a bloodless revolution. They had achieved through capitalism what communism had never managed to achieve – total world domination of a compliant populace. They had drugged them and duped them and turned work into consumption and reality into virtuality and the end result had been slaves who believed they were free. People for whom fulfilment simply meant more and more consumption with less and less responsibility. People who were happy to be told what to do and to do what they were told.

Pryce finally understood why the list had been so valuable. Whoever knew these names, knew who they were up against. The security of the corporation was compromised when you could convert it to actual individuals. You might not be able to knock out ULTIMATE® wholesale, no one could destroy a system that huge and all-encompassing. But you might be able to destroy the individuals who were responsible for that system.

He wondered if Graham knew about this. Had that been the reason he was so keen to get the thing done and dusted? No, surely if Graham had known he wouldn't have left the information there for Pryce to find. It would have been easy enough for someone with Graham's level of authority to remove this last entry. So Pryce had the advantage for the first time. He knew something Graham didn't know. Something dangerous. Something Graham wouldn't want him to know.

And now Pryce knew he had a choice. A real choice for the first time in years. He could ignore this information, go back about his work and carry on within the system, taking whatever shit Graham dealt down upon him.   Or he could use the information, transmit it to the enemies of ULTIMATE® and play his own small part in dismantling a system which, though on the surface offered humanity everything it had ever wanted, did so at the price of their personal freedom and robbed them of their individual humanity.

When it came down to it, it was an easy choice. Pryce still knew what the right thing to do was, despite years of ULTIMATE® training. And he had no reason to uphold ULTIMATE® values, especially now he had a list in front of him of the men who were benefitting from his life as a bird in a gilded cage. He made a conscious decision to go in search of The Immortal Horses. He had found a meaning to his life. He would finish off what Nike had started. It might be the last thing he did, but he would do it, in memory of a boy who had dared to ask questions. He would bite the hand that fed.

V. DEFINE LOVE

Helen sat in front of the US™ wishing that she had a funeral to go to. Funerals were not part of the ULTIMATE® lifestyle. Death was not something to be commemorated or celebrated, because life must go on, and the death of one individual was no more than the extinction of a random possibility. A statistical variation. Helen tried to create her own commemoration by looking back through the Memory Banks she had so painstakingly created over the last months. She realised their intended purpose had been lost. They were no longer able to tell Nick the story of his family. Without him, there was no positive use for them at all. So she wanted to find a way to expunge them from the system. She didn't want ULTIMATE® to have access to her life, even virtually, once she'd 'left the building'. But she didn't know where to begin in a deconstruction process. She knew that her data would be stored somewhere on some ULTIMATE® archive and it irked her. More than that, she was worried it might provide ULTIMATE® with a way of finding her once she'd committed her escape. Although, she reasoned, they probably wouldn't bother. What interest was she to ULTIMATE® after all?

Helen had been trying a range of options to 'modify' her memories because she knew that 'delete memory' was not an option. Suddenly a message popped up on the US™ screen which surprised her.

ODYSSEUS CAN HELP YOU. ODYSSEUS CARES. GO TO RIP MEMORIES AND MODIFY

Helen didn't have a clue what this was about. She was suspicious of course. She had never stored memories to do with RIP as such although of course some of the memories she had stored must have touched upon that group. She tried to make sense of it. Who could Odysseus be? In history he had been the traveller but the name didn't ring any bells in Helen's personal memory. She was more concerned to realise that the US™ might be so sophisticated that it could index archived items by folders she had not herself created. But what could she do? If she couldn't delete memories, she couldn't delete references to RIP. She took a gamble.

'Go to RIP memory archive' and the US™ screen instantly obliged.

Helen found herself in a set of memories she was sure she hadn't created herself. She watched Randall at and RIP meeting in 2011, holding forth about the importance of standing up against the corporations who were threatening the civil liberties. Had she been there? The Memory Bank suggested it, but she couldn't remember it herself. While the US™ screen delivered the images from her perspective she was sure that she'd been at home with a teething Nick, and that Randall had come and told her about the meeting afterwards. Maybe she was wrong? Surely her memory wasn't that poor these days?

As she scrolled through more and more memories, she became more and more convinced however, that this was not her own Memory Bank. But it couldn't be Randall's could it, because he'd been killed 10 years ago? It was too sick to think that they might have extracted his memories out of him, like so much data, and compiled them into a Memory Bank against his will. But what else could this be. She decided to ask some questions.

'Memories unrecognised. Please confirm owner of memories,' she said.

Helen wasn't good at asking US™ screen style questions. It wasn't something Victims had ever been schooled in. Of course on entering the ULTIMATE® home they'd been given a basic tutorial in the workings of the US™ screen but it focussed on inputting rather than on questioning. Victims were not like Project Kids. They were the least useful members of society, at best held in magnolia cells, at worst guinea pigs for memory alteration schemes such as the ADAS®, the system which had, according to ULTIMATE®, transformed the lives of millions for the better but which Helen simply saw as cheating people of their own memories by substituting more acceptable ones which would keep them quiet. However, she hit pay dirt with this question. The benefit of not know how you should interact with the system meant that sometimes, just sometimes, you got the answers you wanted.

'This is the memory archive of Odysseus. You are linked to Odysseus' memory archive by cross referencing. If this is an error and you wish to modify, please engage with the following procedure or contact a technician. ULTIMATE® wants to ensure that your memories are correct at all times. Thank you for your attention.'

No. That was fine. Helen didn't want to modify things. She wanted to find out more about this person Odysseus and how it was that he had her memories in his bank. He was her link to RIP after all, and RIP was her best chance of getting out of the ULTIMATE® Home. She couldn't discount the possibility that Odysseus was an ULTIMATE® creation, there to trick her. But what did she have to lose any more? Living here, she was dead and if she failed to get out, she was dead. But if she could escape..... She jumped at the knock on the door.

'Come in' she said, tentatively.

It was Omo. Unexpected, but welcome. She'd half expected a burly 'technician' of the kind who were called in to deal with the 'difficult' clients of the home. Men more akin to her understanding of psychiatric wings where 'acceptable levels of restraint' was a stock in trade. However much ULTIMATE® tried to remove the past from people's memories, there were things in there which they could not erase. Not in people of Helen's age. Soon, in another couple of generations, it would all be lost or deep archived and the general populace, the true ULTIMATE® citizens, would have no memories that were not either virtually created or licensed by ULTIMATE®. This was the glorious end goal of the BRAND LOYALTY programme after all.

'Hi. Good to see you,' she smiled.

Omo looked awkward. He avoided her eye. He caught sight of the screen. He tried to avoid the name ODYSSEUS which was large on it. He didn't know where to look.

'Sorry. I didn't mean to disturb you...' he stuttered.

'No, it's fine I was just...' she waved at the screen. Hell, what had she to lose.. 'Do you know anything about Odysseus?' she asked, more in hope than expectation.

Omo returned a blank look. 'Sorry. No. Should I?'

'No, I just wondered if Nick had ever mentioned him?'

'No. He never... we... well... it would have been personal wouldn't it, and we didn't really talk about personal things.'

Of course not. She had embarrassed him. He might have shared a home with Nick for five years, but ULTIMATE® would not have encouraged the sort of friendship that meant sharing personal feelings or emotions. They might have talked about how to cheat on level 25 of a game, or the relative merits of one discussion forum over another, but why and how would they have been able to talk about family or..... or anything of value?

'Uh. I've actually got a question for you,' Omo blurted out. He felt his bravery slipping and he decided he'd best lay his cards on the table straight away. He didn't know much about Helen but he did figure she liked people to be clear and simple with her. She could only say no after all.

'Surely. What can I help you with?' It wasn't Nick, but it felt good to have someone there actually talking to her, actually interacting and asking for help.

'What is love?'

She laughed out loud. She couldn't help it. It was lucky Omo was so dark skinned or he might have visibly blushed. Helen had thought after the news about Nick that she would never laugh again, but here she was, already experiencing an unguarded moment. Vindicating the belief that the human spirit could not be crushed. She laughed because it was just so ridiculous. Here was this earnest product of The PROJECT△, the vanguard of the ULTIMATE® system, asking her about love.

'You want to know what love is?' She sought confirmation.

He hung his head, 'I've had a definition but....'

'Sorry. Sorry.' She wiped a tear from her eye. 'I'm not laughing at you Omo. It's just... just the way you came out with it.'

Omo failed to see the joke.

'Omo, dear, you ask the question as if there would be a simple answer. A simple definition, something the US™ system could give you if you only had enough credits. Whereas the question you are asking me, apart from being, I'm sure, not an authorised or acceptable ULTIMATE® question, is also one to which mankind from his earliest days has struggled to find an answer. And yet, you stand there in front of me, hoping that I'm going to give you the answer, just like that.'

'So you can't?' He was confused.

'You ask what love is. You are asking what love means. It'll get you into trouble Omo, because it's a question about personal meaning.'

'That's why I came to ask you,' Omo replied, 'I really need to know and....'

Helen didn't stop to wonder why Omo so badly needed to know what love meant, she just responded to his need to go beyond the limitations imposed by his ULTIMATE® education.

'All right. I hope you're not in a rush?'

Omo looked more perplexed. 'I've got an hour or so,' he replied. 'Pryce said I could come and see you. But I don't think he was too happy about it. I said you wanted to talk to me about Nike and he said it was okay but not to make it a regular occurrence.'

'I don't know that I'll be able to answer your question in an hour, or even in a lifetime,' Helen replied, 'but I'll do what I can.'

She beckoned him to sit on the bed and shifted her chair round by forty five degrees till she faced him.

'Love. What does it mean? Where do I start? What do you understand by the word already?'

Omo thought hard. 'The definition said it was an intense feeling of deep affection for a person or thing.'

'And do you think you have this feeling for someone?' Helen probed.

Omo couldn't bring himself to say the words but he nodded his head.

'Okay.' Helen knew that this was dangerous information. 'No wonder you didn't want to talk to Pryce about this.'

If only she knew, Omo thought. Better that she didn't. If only Omo knew that Helen wouldn't have been shocked at all. She came from an age after all, when love in all its guises visited itself on the wrong people in the wrong place at the wrong time, all the time. She could have given him chapter and verse on the nuances of lust and love and unrequited love and…. But fortunately his silence meant that she could just give him an overview. She was not counselling him on his own personal situation, merely explaining to him something which had once been all important to people and which ULTIMATE® had downgraded to a useless emotion, replaced by virtual sex and no more meaningful than shopping.

'If I tell you that throughout the history of mankind, probably more time has been spent on this question than any other, and more answers given than there are stars in the sky, you'll understand that your ULTIMATE® definition is quite useless. I don't think one can define Love, Omo and I think that it's probably a different answer for every person but I'll do my best to give you *my* explanation of love and see what use that is to you. Okay?'

He nodded his head again. And tried to stop thinking of Angela's naked body entwined round his own, as it had been less than twelve hours ago.

'Love is a guard against isolation. Love is never having to say you're sorry. Love is an urban myth. Love is a cliché. Love is a risk. Love is all that is worth living for and for which you lose everything. Love is all you need.' The phrases tumbled out. She was going to have to do better than this. She tried again.

'I think that love is a conscious decision one makes, though at the time, one is rarely aware that this is what one is doing. It is a decision in which you say to yourself – I'm going to give myself to this other person, I'm going to consider their needs before my own, I'm going to always give them the benefit of the doubt, the largest share, I'm going to try and be the best person I can be, just to make them happy and even if they never care for me, or love me back, I won't feel that I have wasted my time.'

'What do you mean give yourself?' Omo asked.

'I don't just mean physically, though of course that is important.' Helen felt like she was about to divert into a birds and bees conversation, which she hadn't done since Catriona was eleven, that would have been in 1997 and right now she wanted to stay on the path of love, not sex. But for a moment she wondered if it was sex, not love that Omo was asking about.

'Sex is not love you know,' she added, 'sex can be part of love but it isn't the same thing.'

Omo was confused but didn't like to say. He waited for further explanation. But couldn't stop thinking about Angela's naked body.....

'Love means giving something of your identity, something of who you are privately, inside; your soul, your essence... your very being... allowing another person access to that and striving to live up to the ideals of being worthy of another person giving you that access back.' Helen realised that

287

words like soul and even identity probably didn't mean that much to Omo, but she had no other terms of reference.

'Let me try and explain it better,' she continued. 'There are lots of different kinds of love. The way you love a child is completely different to the way you love a partner. The way you love a friend and the way you can love an animal are all variations on the basic theme. Which is that you have to step outside of your isolation and become bigger than one person. In some way by loving you externalise your identity. With a child, the love you have is protective and unconditional. Much like it can be with an animal. Although with a child it becomes more complex because the relationship changes over time as your child grows up and becomes an adult but your love seems stuck in a protective, unequal place and you have to re-negotiate. With an animal the love remains unconditional because the relationship never changes. With a friend your love changes as it stays the same. Perhaps with a friend you have to be more open to change, more accepting, because you have no 'rights' over their life or actions. But with a life partner, a husband or wife, for example, there is no room for half measures. You have to dedicate yourself every day to the duty of loving them, accepting them, giving to them, being for them what they need and putting them first. It's not easy. But the rewards are great. The price is high too. When you lose them you don't stop loving them. You just stop being with them and being able to show them your love. I loved my daughter and son but they both died before me. Something in me died with them, I suppose the something was the two-way love. But I still love them in my heart.' She paused, dealing with the pain.

'It's the same with Nick. There's a sense of loss in reality, but he's still there, somewhere. With Randall, my husband, it's the worst of all though. When I lost him I felt that the part of myself which made me whole was lost forever. The others were a part of me, but he was the whole of me. Our love meant that we almost ceased to exist as individuals. We existed together and our love was the part that created and sustained that existence. You might say love was the glue which stuck us together. For nearly forty years, I could only define myself in relation to him, I couldn't think of myself as a person alone. Then suddenly....' Helen broke off.... she couldn't help the tears.

Omo surprised himself. A month ago this expression of emotion would have been totally unacceptable to him and he'd have found a way to get out of the room instantly. Somehow now, he felt the need to stay.

'It's okay,' he reassured Helen. 'I.... I understand.' There was a pause while she tried to pull herself together.

'Well, I don't really understand,' he admitted, 'I mean I think I understand what you are telling me. But the feeling... I don't understand that.'

'You couldn't,' Helen replied. 'Not many people really experience that kind of love. It was a blessing. And a curse.'

'Anyway. There must be a reason you came here to ask me this question,' she continued, 'and here I am, blubbing over my own past. Come on. Tell me. Who do you think you love?'

Omo pulled up short. He hadn't expected this. But he found that he wanted to tell her. He wanted people to know. But he knew he couldn't.

'I don't want to say the name,' he said, 'I don't want to get her into trouble.'

'Fair enough,' Helen replied. 'Tell me about the feeling then.'

'Yes,' Omo nodded, 'It's the feeling. I've never felt... well... you know, they don't really encourage feelings and I've not been very good at them before. They aren't, you know, 'productive' usually, but now.... Well, I think about her all the time and I wonder what she's doing when she's not with me, and she's not with me most of the time and I don't know how she feels about me, but when we're together it's... well... it blows my mind, but then I can't understand how she can just leave me and go back to her life and leave me in my life and.... I suppose I want that thing you said about two people giving to each other, but I don't feel like she wants to give to me.'

'That's unrequited love,' Helen explained.

'Is it no good?'' Omo asked

'Well, it's not the best kind,' Helen added, 'It's the kind of love you have when you feel all the emotions but there's nothing you can do to externalise them. It's.. well let's just say it used to be pretty common. But it's also easily confused with infatuation. That's when you just can't stop thinking about someone but all the thoughts are really about your own perception of the other person.'

This was getting complicated. 'At your age, traditionally,' Helen confided, 'it would most likely have been infatuation. I think true love isn't possible till one has a decent grip on one's own identity. Until you know who you are, how can you either share or give of yourself in a meaningful way?' It wasn't a rhetorical question but Helen knew that Omo couldn't give an answer. This wasn't about answers, it was a voyage of discovery. A young man struggling, as so many had before him, to understand the inexplicable.

'How will I know the difference?'

'If it's infatuation it'll wear off. Sooner or later you'll look at her and she won't be the most beautiful woman in the world. The things she does which appeal to you so much now will seem crass and small. If it's unrequited love, you'll keep on feeling the same way, but it won't do you any good either way, because if she doesn't feel the same way as you, you're scuppered.'

'How will I know if she feels the same way?' Omo asked the sixty four dollar question.

'You have to ask her,' Helen said.

Omo was shocked. 'I couldn't do that.'

'Why not?'

'I... I just couldn't.'

'In which case,' Helen replied, 'I think your answer lies

in there. If you can't because you're frightened she might tell you she doesn't love you back, and yet you're not prepared to risk everything to find out, then you are not ready for love. It's hard, but you have to find out. Of course, sometimes, you just know, even without asking.'

She thought back to the first time she met Randall. Had she made a conscious decision to love him then? Very quickly it had seemed inevitable. The North London concert had certainly marked the clear moment she fell in love and being together had seemed the most obviously right thing in the world. The thing that would make sense of her life. Yet how had she known, back then, that he would love her back?

Was she asking Omo to do something which was impossible? Something she couldn't have done herself? Here she was, talking with the benefit of retrospect. Had she forgotten what it was like in that first stage?

'At some point,' she tried a softer approach, 'You will have to tell her how you feel and you'll have to find out what she feels. You have to do it straight out. There's no alternative. You have to take the risk. But only,' she added, 'when you're ready.'

Omo didn't think he'd ever be ready to do that. When he imagined the situation, all he could see was Angela laughing at him. He didn't take that to be a good sign.

'Have I been any help at all?' Helen asked.

'Uh... yes... I mean... I think....' Omo stuttered. He realised he was going to have to think more about this whole situation. And less about Angela's naked body.... Because he realised that this was all he had been thinking about. All the things that Helen had talked about were totally alien to him. He had just wanted to be with Angela, having real live sex, feeling good. It seemed that that wouldn't be enough.

Life had been so much easier before Angela. Before feelings. But could he go back to the way things were then, now that everything had changed?

W. QUESTIONS ANSWERED

'But why?' Omo asked.

His premonition was right. Angela just laughed. Laughed right in his face. It was not the sort of memory anyone would want to store in their Memory Bank. For the first time in his life Omo experienced real emotional pain.

He had not been able to resist. Helen's words stuck in his mind. *You have to find out.* He knew them to be wise words. He knew he had to act on them however much he wished he didn't. His timing might have been better, but probably it wouldn't have mattered when he'd said it.

'Why not,' Angela corrected him.

Omo felt tears welling up in his eyes. She was playing with him. And she was cruel. Surely this wasn't love.

'I love you,' was the one thing he knew he shouldn't say next, but the only thing he could bring himself to say.

'Don't be so silly.' Angela was stern, 'You'll spoil everything. Love doesn't exist and I don't know who's been giving you such ridiculous ideas.'

Omo tried to pull himself together. 'Do you feel nothing for me?' He asked, digging himself deeper into the humiliation that was bound to follow. Angela, after all, was a good ULTIMATE® citizen for whom feeling was anathema.

'Of course not, Omo. It's just a bit of fun.'

It didn't feel like fun now.

Omo should have left it at that and gone on his way. Learned something. That you don't mess with the Angel of guilt free intercourse. But he couldn't. His world had been rocked and he flailed around trying to save himself.

'How can you say that? How can it mean nothing to you...?'

She slapped him. Hard. 'You are being totally stupid.' Her tone was now harsh. 'You are just part of an experiment Omo. And you've failed it.'

'An experiment?' Would the shock and pain never stop?

'Yes. You're just like all the rest of them. However much ULTIMATE® tries to wean you all off guilt and emotion and power play, you all find ways of hanging on. It's sick.' She meant it. Angela had developed such a thick skin that none of her sexual exploits meant anything to her. She was totally dedicated to her research and her research showed her that men were fools. Even now when ULTIMATE® equality had supposedly been achieved, all it took was a live naked woman, prepared and able to fulfil their physical needs, and they lost all their sense of reason.

'Do you love Pryce?' Omo asked. She must be trying to let him down because it was wrong, because she already loved someone else.

'No. Love is a pointless emotion.'

'But you married him.'

'That was before,' she replied.

Omo realised that Angela had indeed lived in the world before ULTIMATE® existed, as Helen had, but there the similarities ceased. If Helen represented everything that was good about the world of History, Angela represented everything that was bad. And it seemed like the Angelas had inherited the ULTIMATE® world, leaving the Helens broken and beaten in the Victim Homes. The ULTIMATE® world suddenly didn't seem so bright to Omo. And when he looked at her again, neither did Angela. She looked hard, callous and mean. Completely the opposite of Helen. Okay there was forty years between the women, Angela was in her physical prime and knew it, but Helen was in a league of her own. Helen could inspire love. Angela had corrupted love. You couldn't love someone like Angela, Omo realised. ULTIMATE® had got rid of love and it was women like Angela who had done the work. She was a sham. She had sucked him in. But why?

'Why did you do this to me?' He asked, but now he was less interested in love and more interested in an explanation of

294

why she had chosen him as her victim.

'Because you were there, Omo.'

'So.. so it could have been anyone? It could have been Nike?'

She shrugged her shoulders. It didn't matter to her.

'Does Pryce know?' Omo asked. It was horrible but he was beginning to think the conspiracy might be wholesale. They might all be laughing at him.

That brought Angela up short. 'No. And don't you tell him.'

'Why not?' Omo started to feel that maybe he had a bit of leverage here. For the first time she looked less than in total control. 'If it doesn't mean anything and it doesn't matter, why not just tell him?'

'I should have known better,' she said, thinking out loud. Now she was in a messy position. Why couldn't the boy just have played along, had the sex, gone back to his gaming and left her with an anonymous case study and a few memories of her own to file away. It wasn't guilt that she felt, it was the annoyance of the fact that the situation was pulling out of her control. How could men be so stupid and then cause so much trouble?

'If you say anything about this, I'll report you to higher authorities and you will get evicted off The PROJECT△.' The harsh tone in her voice and the steely glint in her eye was enough to convince him that she wasn't joking.

Ironically, however, Omo felt a sense of relief. He didn't realise he had power over her for that moment; what he thought was that at least if Angela wasn't going to tell anyone about it, he wouldn't get into trouble. There had been enough trouble. He just wanted to go back to his old, easy life. He doubted whether that would be possible though. He didn't recognise the adage *Knowledge is power*, but he was beginning to realise that sometimes, once you knew something, you couldn't become ignorant again and the whole of life looked different to you. Angela had taken Omo through much more of a rites of passage than even she knew.

'I don't want to tell anyone,' he said, 'I just wanted to know what you were going to do about it.'

'I'm not going to do anything,' she lied. Of course she would. She wasn't going to leave Omo as a loose cannon. But he didn't need to know that.

'I don't love you anyway,' Omo stated baldly. 'It was just an infatuation. Thanks for nothing.' And he turned and left Angela, stunned.

Omo's words reverberated in Angela's head for rather too long. She might not believe in guilt but she was quite keen on revenge. Is revenge an emotion? Or is it the action of the emotionless? In Angela's case one might consider that revenge was close to its ULTIMATE® definition, available to all for just 10 credits.

REVENGE: Definition. Retaliation for an offence or injury.

Older dictionary definitions might have added an emotional content: *a vindictive feeling,* but for Angela it wasn't a question of feeling, it was a question of power. She had to win.

So while Omo returned to The Project House, no older, but a lot wiser; Angela turned her vicious mind to how she could exact the best revenge. Not just on Omo. She felt it was time to get them all, all the men whom she despised. Omo, Pryce and Graham. Three for the price of one. But perhaps that was when she got just too greedy.

She didn't play out all the possibilities and she committed that classic mistake of underestimating the opposition. She thought she knew Pryce well enough. Omo was no threat but she didn't know Graham quite as well as she thought. Whereas Omo and Pryce were easy, because fundamentally they were good, Graham was a man who had fully embraced all that ULTIMATE® stood for. Graham was not a man who was led by the nose of emotion. Angela had misjudged him if she thought their 'affair' was anything to do with emotion. Graham was playing Angela while she was playing him, and Graham was higher up the pecking order. Graham didn't get beaten.

Graham already knew what Angela had been up to. Like all good managers he had a lot of spare time while his assistants were doing all his work and he used this spare time to keep tabs on the people who interested him. Or who challenged him. He had Pryce and Angela on such a tight monitor that in pre ULTIMATE® years they would have been shouting about the violation on their human rights. But there were no more human rights. ULTIMATE® took care of that. ULTIMATE® gave you the lifestyle you thought you wanted and as long as you didn't actually question the system you'd never feel that you were being let down by it. The packaging was glossy. The presentation was slick. You were told that you had everything you needed and you believed it. Or you were virtualised.

Graham could sit in his office and know everything about Angela's sexual peccadillos. He could watch them like movies. He had access to a virtual two way US™ screen. For work purposes only of course. Though he used it mainly for pleasure. It was a company perk in the way that company cars used to be. Consequently, Graham knew just about everything about Pryce's depression and the marital arguments with Angela and a whole lot more besides. He made it his job to view weaknesses, manipulate them and then he used them to promote his own standing in the ULTIMATE® community. He was destined for great things. But Graham had a failing too. He spent too much time trying to make sure that he was on the up. Someone higher up than him was watching that of course, noting that his desire for individual success was at odds with ULTIMATE® goals.

UTheory∑® was big on the random element. And it

seemed that every member of the society still had a random element. In previous times it might have been considered a fatal flaw, or a personality trait, or indeed just the thing that made each person individual. But it was the random elements that the ULTIMATE® system was working to control and when any one random element got too dangerous, there was only one way out. However high up the system you went, there was always someone at a higher level, keeping tabs on everyone else.

Some days later Graham called Angela in to explain herself.

'What have you been up to? he sleazed and showed her a snippet from his vault. She was unchastened.

'It's guilt research,' she replied.

'I wasn't supposed to know about it?' his question was rhetorical but she side-stepped it.

'No, I knew you would. I wanted to get data off you regarding your responses to the situation,' she lied.

'You didn't clear your research project with me first,' he added, not taken in for a minute.

The ugly chess game continued.

'And Pryce? Does he know?'

'Why should he?' she replied. 'He's not a part of the study.'

'You NEVER make me a part of your research without clearing it with me first, get it?' he said, bored with the situation and desperate just to move things on.

'Okay,' she replied, cool to the last.

'So?' he said – and she took him up on the offer. They had sex. Graham planned to transfer her. Angela hoped he would. It was in the nature of these kind of transfers that they are promotions and that, after all, was what she'd been angling for all along. Angela was after all, the archetype of all women who ever slept their way to the top.

Pryce would have remained none the wiser. Except they all forgot the random element. Graham gave Pryce the job of setting Omo a work schedule that would keep him busy, very busy and free from emotion. The reason Graham gave was that he didn't want the death of Nike to impact on the others. They were to get a new PROJECT△ flatmate as soon as possible and other than that, things were to go on as before. But Omo wasn't to visit Helen again. They had to cut off all subversive links. And clearly, Helen was not good for anyone. Nor was he to see Angela again. Graham told Pryce that Angela had told him that Omo really didn't have what it took to understand adaptive theory at any advanced level, and it was wasting Angela's valuable time to be tutoring him. They had to get back on an even keel.

Pryce went to tell Omo. And then the shit hit the fan. Omo's random element came into play. He told Pryce everything. Well, mostly everything. Omo told him that Angela didn't love him (Pryce) and that she had been sleeping with him (Omo) and he didn't know why she'd done it, but it had upset him. He admitted that he had been experiencing emotional anxiety, which he knew was not necessary or condoned in the ULTIMATE® system, and he was sure that he'd probably broken some of the rules of his PROJECT△ contract. He was sorry. He hadn't meant any of it. He just wanted things to get back to normal and he didn't know who else to ask for help but Pryce.

Two months previously such a revelation would have rocked Pryce's world. But now, he took it with barely a thought. He should have known all along. Why wouldn't Omo be the latest in a long line of lovers, designed to demean and diminish him? Angela was a callous, calculating woman and Pryce knew that even by revisiting his Memory Banks he would never again see her in any other light. The woman he had fallen in love with had disappeared into the ULTIMATE® world; a natural for the new ways it promoted. Instead of focussing on Angela and what he had lost, Pryce determined to use the opportunity to recruit Omo to his own cause. It would be a small victory, but a victory none the less. With Nike gone, Omo was Pryce's only real chance of a link with The Immortal Horses. Through Omo he could get to Helen and Helen must know something. It wasn't much to go on, but it was a place to start.

X. UTHEORY∑® IN PRACTICE

The day after Graham gave him the clear instruction not to, Pryce took Omo to visit Helen. He didn't know what Graham's plan for him was, but he knew he was running out of time. And he wanted to meet with Helen. Omo didn't question why he and Pryce walked the fifteen minutes from the PROJECT△ House to the ULTIMATE® Home, along streets that had once been wide, leafy, middle-class aspirational, but now just looked tired, empty and a bit grimy. They passed the landmark buildings of the Scottish Parliament and the Commonwealth Pool, both long since no longer used for their original purposes, and had Pryce but known, they also passed the Trading House before stopping in the Park, outside the ULTIMATE® Home. Their walk was mostly in silence, neither of them knowing what to say.

'I might not be with you that much longer.' Pryce had initiated.

Omo had not known how to reply, and so had not replied.

'I think this will probably be your last visit to Nike's nan,' Pryce added, as they stood outside the lobby. 'I'll give you half an hour, then I'll come in. I'd like to meet her.'

It was true although Pryce had no idea what he would say when he did finally come face to face with Helen. That was one reason he gave Omo the half hour start. He needed time to prepare both himself and Helen for what was to come. Meanwhile, he sat in the park, trying to make sense of it all. Wondering how he would bring up the topic of The Immortal Horses with her.

As it happened, circumstances took over. Pryce might have been unaware how close to the hub of The Immortal Horses he was as he marched Omo past the Trading House, but Troy had Pryce and Omo under surveillance all the time. And as much as Pryce wanted to find out about The Immortal Horses,

Troy wanted to meet with Pryce. It was not so much a meeting of minds, nor even a meeting of opposites. It was more a meeting of random elements. A meeting of the true father with the surrogate father. One man with another.

A clandestine meeting in a park was of course standard practice for the outdated thriller genre of Pryce's youth, so perhaps he shouldn't have been surprised when a man wearing an outmoded trenchcoat approached him.

'Troy wants to see you,' the man said.

Pryce looked around. There was no one out in the park, as usual. He had no idea who 'Troy' was and of course he was suspicious, but he decided to take the risk.

'Follow me,' the man said.

Pryce followed. He was taken, as Nike before him, to the Trading House. It was reminiscent of his father's place of work and brought back memories of a world which, on reflection, hadn't been so bad after all. In the days before the GRsΩHist. Pryce's father had worked in an institution exactly like that which the Trading House had housed. But he had worked for a rival investment banking firm. They'd all gone under or become subsumed or, as Pryce now reasoned, consumed by ULTIMATE®. His father had taken early retirement and had lived out his days golfing until golfing gave way to virtual golfing and he died of a massive stroke, brought on Pryce had assumed, by lack of exercise. His mother had suggested it was because of a broken heart, because he couldn't get used to not spending his life out on the golf course.

Pryce's mother, like Helen, now lived in an ULTIMATE® Home but unlike Helen it was a privately paid for one. Pryce paid. Pryce always paid. Her place there was part of the perks of his job and he paused for a moment to consider what would happen to his mother if Graham got his way? His father hadn't had the opportunity to speak last words to Pryce, but Pryce knew those words would have been 'look after your mother.' He'd done his best, although he had to admit he hadn't seen the woman face to face in over five years. He interfaced with her once a month on the US™ though. And kept his family bank updated with lies about how happy he and Angela were, how busy they were, how successful they were, how great life was.

The familiarity from his own childhood, days spent in his father's office drawing pictures, meant that unlike Nike, Pryce recognised the board room into which the man took him for what it was and he noticed the two way mirrors. He smiled at the old-fashioned surveillance techniques. Still, somehow they seemed fairer than the all-encompassing ULTIMATE® alternatives. How life had changed. He didn't have to wait long before Troy entered and shook his hand.

'Do you now believe in The Immortal Horses?' Troy asked.

'What can you tell me about Nike?' Pryce rejoined, trying to keep his cool.

'I can thank you for doing a father's job,' Troy replied.

There was a moment's pause.

'Nick was my son,' Troy continued, 'So you see, we have something in common.'

'I've got something for you,' Pryce said, reaching in his coat for the list and handing it over. He had been carrying the list in his pocket since he'd printed it, and this seemed the appropriate place and time to offload it. He had no reason to doubt Troy's assertion. Only a sorrow that these were the circumstances under which they met.

'I'm sure Nike would have wanted you to have this. Do you know who killed him?'

Troy took the list, said nothing but signalled Pryce to follow him. They walked along a corridor into another room, reminiscent of a scene of crime room in a police detective series from the TV shows of his childhood. The walls were covered with pictures. A hundred of them. The faces of the hundred men.

'They killed him. They will kill us all. They have killed us all,' Troy stated. Then added, after a moment's pause, 'Welcome to the cause.' Troy knew he didn't have to worry about Pryce. He'd been watching him closely for a month after all. He knew more about Pryce's motivations than Pryce did himself. He knew how Pryce had been affected by Nike's death and how he was being affected by Graham's attitudes. He knew the fate that Graham had in store for Pryce. He knew everything. Troy knew Pryce's strengths and weaknesses. And how to play them. Pryce wasn't the first man who had stood before him ready to betray ULTIMATE®. And he wouldn't be the last. Despite a system which promised everything to its citizens, there would always be people who saw through the promise. Pryce had become one of these people. ULTIMATE® had made him that way.

'I'm glad we had the opportunity to meet,' Troy said. ' I think we can help each other.'

'How? Why?' Pryce asked. He was totally out of his depth.

'As to why, because you looked after my son. As to how.. do you know where your wife is right now?'

Pryce didn't have a chance to answer before Troy had flipped the large US™ screen (yes, Pryce was amazed to see that Troy used the US™ screen and could hack into it when and wherever he chose) and showed him the one thing he didn't already know. The one thing he'd suspected but hadn't dared to think about. The affair between Graham and Angela. Happening right there in front of them in real-time. It was the last time, but that made no difference to any of them.

'Is this Memory Bank?' Pryce asked, choking on the words. Was it possible it wasn't true?

'No, it's a live stream,' came Troy's inevitable reply.

There they were, Graham and Angela, naked and writhing in front of his very eyes. Pryce couldn't bear to look. But he couldn't bear not to look either. After the inevitable climax, which Pryce somehow found unbearably, unutterably difficult to watch sitting beside Troy, the substance of the event was that Angela was getting a promotion.

'You deserve it, after that performance,' Graham leered.

Pryce thought he saw just a touch of hatred in Angela's eyes, but maybe that was just the way she looked at everyone. Disdain, distance, insolence. Graham might just spectacularly have had Angela, over his own desk, but he didn't own her, that was certain.

In the age old way of shifting difficult personnel, Graham had got Angela 'promoted' to a research position out of his immediate department. From his point of view, the frisson was over. There were no regrets or recriminations. No words were wasted between them. Their relationship, after all, had been founded on self-interested pragmatism. They had almost perfected the ULTIMATE® affair. Almost, because they were both still motivated by an individualism that ULTIMATE® could not approve of. They both thought they'd won. They would move on without a backwards glance. The interaction was archived and stored. Used to refine UTheoryΣ® even further. With ULTIMATE® nothing was ever wasted.

'Why show me that?' Pryce turned to Troy.

'I understood you were a man who wanted to know the truth,' Troy replied. 'Here we deal in truth, no matter how unpleasant. And I thought you needed to know. To help you make decisions about your own future.'

'What future do I have? What choices can I make?' Pryce spat out the words.

'There's always a choice Pryce,' Troy replied. 'And if you want, we can help you.'

'How?' Pryce asked, knowing he'd say yes to anything Troy offered him now.

'You've seen what Graham has in store for Angela. Do you want to see what he has in store for you?' Troy asked. It wasn't a question.

Troy showed Pryce the fine detail of the plan Graham was even now constructing for Pryce's future. It made Pryce even more angry than watching that debauched liason between his wife and his boss. It was enough to ensure that Troy and Pryce cut a deal.

The plan Troy sold Pryce was the infiltration of the Project House. It would be effected by placing Griff in there as counsellor, alongside a 'new' Project Kid, who in fact had been groomed for the role over several years by the Immortal Horses. If, as Troy showed Pryce, he was about to be sidelined, he could have one last, lasting impact on The PROJECT△. The plan was well worked and ready to roll out. It just required Pryce to play his part. Troy was insistent that this should be Pryce's choice. So Pryce looked at all the documentation. The forgery was of such impressive quality he found himself forgetting it was all a fiction. He was sure Graham would buy it. The plan was elegant and simple. Having Griff and Bose in The Project House would give The Immortal Horses an unprecedented level of access to the US™ system, through which they could monitor and plan the undermining of the PROJECT△ spreading dissent and unrest over time amongst the generation destined to be ULTIMATE®'s most valuable citizens. And Pryce would have been instrumental in achieving this. He would also have the personal satisfaction of having duped Graham. And it would be Graham who would carry the responsibility if it was ever discovered. It was what they used to call a win win situation. Only Graham and ULTIMATE® wouldn't win. Pryce was satisfied. It seemed like a great revenge. A risk worth taking. The perfect murder. He agreed to the plan.

In return, Troy offered Pryce a place within The Immortal Horses. An alternative identity. A chance for a future outside the living death of ULTIMATE®. Pryce didn't need time to think about it. He agreed. But wanted to know how it could happen. It sounded a bit like the old-style witness protection schemes he'd read about as a boy. He'd never imagined such a thing to be possible even then. That a person could just take on a whole new identity. Troy had no such problems.

'You'll cease to exist, to ULTIMATE®,' Troy stated. 'You'll lose access to your Memory Bank. You'll become someone totally different. Everyone here has done it. Can you handle that?'

Now he thought about it, there didn't seem to be anything to lose, if Pryce was honest. He agreed wholeheartedly to Troy's plan. He would defect because only in losing his ULTIMATE® identity could he truly live.

'It's not without cost,' Troy stated. 'I lost my mother, my son.. everything that meant anything to me. Although ULTIMATE® was taking them all away from me anyway. But I did it because I believed there were things more important than my own life. I became a different person, but with the same aim. To overthrow ULTIMATE®. I've dedicated my life to doing that. Whatever the cost. But I can tell you about the man I used to be.'

Troy's face softened slightly as he went into his own memory – memory without the help of the US Memory Bank system.

'I used to be a farmer. My wife took that from me. And then ULTIMATE® took it from me. I used to be a father. My wife and ULTIMATE® took that from me. We are very much the same, you and me. I decided that I wouldn't let ULTIMATE® take my identity. My father used to say that name is the thief of identity. So I changed my name and my identity. Look.'

He rolled up his sleeve to show Pryce that he had no brand on his wrist.

'How?' Pryce marvelled.

'Torquil Christie had a brand,' Troy stated, matter of factly. Torquil Christie no longer exists except in the Memory Banks of my mother and the archives of ULTIMATE®. Troy doesn't exist at all. I can offer you the same choice. You can be who you want to be. With us. If you want to be.'

'Can you remove...?' Pryce looked at his own brand.

Troy laughed. 'Of course we can. I won't say it's painless, but it's a lot less painful than the alternative.'

'And Nike?' For one brief moment, Pryce wondered whether Troy had saved Nike. Whether the death had been an illusion and the boy was now living here, amongst The Immortal Horses.'

'Nick is dead,' Troy replied, crushing his hopes. 'Nothing can bring Nick back,' he added bitterly, 'and though I can see her whenever I want, I can't talk to my mother. You'll be the same. Can you handle that?'

Pryce flinched slightly at the realisation that he really didn't care if he never saw or spoke to his mother again. He had no one in the world who meant anything to him. If life was lived through social interactions, he was dead already. Troy was offering him a chance for a life, a meaning, a new start. He would take it. Of course he would take it. It was a way out of the ULTIMATE® depression. All he had to do was trust Troy and wait for the sign.

'There's one other thing you could do for me,' Troy said.

'What?' Pryce replied.

Troy flicked the US™ screen and showed Pryce how, oblivious to the plans going on round about him, Omo was sitting enjoying (if that's the right word) a cup of tea with Helen. She had been surprised to see him, but pleased. He'd explained that this would be the last time he could visit, because Pryce was being replaced and there were specific instructions for him NOT to visit Helen again. But he'd wanted to see her once again. If only to thank her for the wise words she'd given him about love.

'Did you ask her?' Helen asked.

'Yes. She laughed in my face,' he replied, surprised he could be that frank with Helen.

'Then it wasn't love,' Helen observed, sympathetically.

'No. It was infatuation,' he replied, matter of factly. 'I'm over it.'

'Never mind,' Helen said, 'You'll find love with someone, one day, I'm sure you will Omo.'

'I hope so,' he said. And he meant it.

Troy closed down the screen. It was too painful to watch.

'Tell my mother I love her,' he said to Pryce.

'I will,' Pryce replied.

The meeting with Helen was nothing like Pryce had envisaged it when ten minutes later he sat on her chair in her magnolia room.

'I wanted to come before,' he said, 'to say how sorry I was about Nike.'

'Nick,' she corrected him.

'Yes, of course, Nick,' he replied. He should give her that. It was her grandson after all. 'I'm sorry I couldn't save him from...' he wasn't sure quite what or who he might have saved Nike from. That was the core of the problem of course.

'It wasn't your fault,' Helen replied.

'Well, I suppose we should go.' Pryce stood up and motioned to Omo who uncharacteristically gave Helen a hug.

'Thank you and I really hope we meet again,' Omo said, Pryce noticed there were tears in his eyes. 'Nick was lucky to have a grandma like you. And he knew it.'

'As far as I'm concerned,' Helen replied, 'you're my grandson now, and if there's ever anything I can do...' she petered out, emotion getting the better or her.

As they left the room, Pryce remembered his promise to Troy, and gave Helen an embrace and a kiss. As he did so he whispered into her ear.

'Your son wanted me to tell you he loves you.'

'Torquil? Is he... alive...?' she could hardly get the words out.

'I can't say any more,' Pryce apologised.

'It's enough,' she replied. Though it wasn't. But it was a start.

As Pryce was leaving the room, she added, ' If you see him, tell him thanks for the cake.'

Pryce nodded towards the screen and said, 'I'm sure he knows.'

Outside the room, Omo was amazed at what he'd just heard and seen.

'What's happening?' he asked.

'I'm sorry, I can't tell you,' Pryce replied. 'But trust me, things can change. And for the better.'

They walked back to the Project House in silence.

A week later Graham thought he was being smart when he got Pryce to interview his own replacement. What he didn't know was that he had given Pryce just the leverage he needed to effect his own plan of betrayal. Pryce selected a very nice young man called Griff whose credentials were impeccable. And totally made up by The Immortal Horses. When Graham second interviewed Griff, he wondered for a moment where this paragon had been all this time, but he snatched at the opportunity to get such a guy on his team. Someone he could delegate to with complete confidence, leaving him free to fulfil his management role in as short a time as possible, thus allowing him maximum time to do whatever he wanted. Because however hard ULTIMATE® tried, it seems that work is always destined to be a four letter word and there is always going to be something more interesting to do.

Graham was immediately impressed by Griff's efficiency and convinced he'd killed two birds with one stone on discovering that Griff already had a young lad lined up to replace Nike. A lad who would be no trouble and indeed an asset to the team. His name was Bose and like the sound system he'd been named after, he represented sound quality.

Graham had no idea that Pryce and Troy had made a deal. How could he? How could he have imagined they could ever have met? It would have required more than a devotion to duty, more than a knowledge of UTheory$\sum$® and considerably more commitment to his job than Graham had ever possessed. Graham was much more interested in getting other people to do his job so that he could spend his time consuming sex either virtually or in real life. While the early 21st century provided people with opportunities to lose themselves in online pornography and virtual cybersex; ULTIMATE®'s development in this area had become more addictive than Habit∞ to Graham and in his elevated position he believed he could cheat the system in order to pursue his personal whims. The possibility that he was being observed the whole time never occurred to him. All the time the co-efficient ratio of his activities were actually being factored in like that of a lab rat. But then he probably wouldn't have minded had he known. Graham had gone beyond wondering if he had a valuable role in the system, all he cared about was his next fix.

Somewhere within the system a team of people and machines were analysing Graham's every move as data which they would feed into the system. The flexibility of UTheory$\sum$® was its strength after all. If ULTIMATE® couldn't get rid of the sex urge in humans, that didn't matter. As long as it was aware of the typology of the randomness and the situations in which it was bound to occur, the theory could control the set of randomness within acceptable margins. Graham was just another statistic after all. When the choice was made to live to consume rather than consume to live, a one way barrier was crossed from which there was no return. ULTIMATE® had changed producers into consumers and then they became producers of consumption. Graham was just as much a victim of ULTIMATE® as everyone else. More so perhaps, because he was completely unaware of his vulnerability.

Unlike Graham, Troy understood that people's

ULTIMATE® security was based solely on their ignorance of just who is watching them, who is logging their activity. And he also knew that for the system to survive someone has to be. Actions will always have consequences and those consequences, while unexpected and unpredictable to the actor, have been written by some god somewhere. Still, he believed that outside the system, with The Immortal Horses he had built a firewall so strong that for the moment at least, he was safe. He had sacrificed everything to achieve this. He had re-created his own life outside of the ULTIMATE® paradigm. He'd paid the price but he'd reaped the rewards as well. But the death of Nike made even Troy wonder how robust his own system really was.

A month later, Pryce's death caused no more stir than Nike's before him. Life goes on. Or not. Pryce was simply virtualised by the ULTIMATE® system, like many before him and doubtless many after him. Deaths like Pryce's were of little consequence. At best he had been a decoy duck. At worst he was just another statistic. A small man. A nobody. Valueless to the system. As far as ULTIMATE® was concerned, Pryce had served his purpose. ULTIMATE® knew that and so did The Immortal Horses. The only people who might have asked questions, Omo and Flora, were told he had been promoted. They accepted the change like all the changes they'd faced over the last few months. No more Nike, no more Helen, no more Pryce. Unusually, they had a short conversation about it
'I wish we could have said goodbye,' Flora said.
'Why?' Omo asked.
'I liked him,' Flora said, 'it might have made it easier.'
'I said goodbye to Helen,' Omo stated, 'it didn't make it any easier.'
'Just us now,' Flora summised, 'I suppose we'll get a new counsellor soon,' and they went back to their respective rooms to catch up on their 'productive' work.

Y. HOW A STORY ENDS

Some weeks later, Helen was asleep when the familiar voice woke her. But there was something strange about it.

'Helen, It's Odysseus. Wake up. I'm outside. Get your coat on and meet me at the door.'

She got up out of her bed and pulled on her clothes. It was the middle of the night and no one was about in the empty corridors of the ULTIMATE® home as she made her way to the front door. She stepped outside into a pale full moon, and blinked against the unexpected brightness.

She couldn't see anyone at first. Then she made out the shadow of a man standing beside a vehicle. It looked like a real car, not an ULTIMATE® transporter and as she walked towards it he waved, confirming she was doing the right thing. As she came closer she could see the car was a beaten up old Land Rover. The man had a cap pulled right down over his eyes and he was the last person she expected to see but as she came close to him it was unmistakable. She was looking straight into the eyes of Randall.

'Come on,' he urged. 'There's no time to lose.'

She got into the car without further ado, still stunned but with a strong desire to kiss him. As she sat next to him and he turned the key in the starter, she couldn't stop herself. It had been ten years after all and she had missed him like missing a part of herself. One kiss reminded her of everything she'd lost and she didn't even look back at the ULTIMATE® Home as they drove off. She was safe at last.

'Where are we going?' she asked, flashing back to her 40th birthday to Cairnholy and half expecting his reply to be *it's a surprise.*

Instead, he smiled at her and said simply, 'We're going home.'

She felt she should have questions. This was a situation she had never imagined, could not have dreamed of. She was

313

out of her depth. She was trying to process the unexpected and it took all her effort. The repetitive jolting and shaking of the car through the darkness of the night was all that she could handle at the moment. This was her reality. She gave herself up to the moment. She looked at Randall for as long as she could, but she found her eyes closing and her mind wandering. She was safe, she was warm, she was on a journey with the man she loved. Questions could wait. She was going home, that was enough for now.

Eyes shut, she could hear the rumbling of the tyres on the road as the Land Rover ate up the miles. She could swear she heard Randall singing but she didn't open her eyes, thinking that if she did, either he'd stop singing, or she'd find out that he wasn't really there at all.

She gave herself up to the music.

'life is but a dream.'

The song had changed. She must have been sleeping. She'd nodded off to a Randall and the Reivers classic and woken up to a children's song. It was Nick's favourite when he was three.

Helen and Nick sat on the big branch of the beech tree, singing and laughing, pulling back and forth against each other as they sang *'row row row your boat, gently down the stream, merrily, merrily, merrily, merrily, life is but a dream.'*

'Life is but a dream.' The unmistakable chant of the three year old as he giggled. 'A dream Nan, it's a dream.'

Helen opened her eyes. She felt odd, disconnected and the motion was making her slightly nauseous. She was relieved to see Randall at the wheel. He turned to her, 'Okay?' he asked.

'I was dreaming,' she replied.

'That's okay,' he said.

She felt comforted and closed her eyes again.

'Are we nearly there yet?' Catriona's voice rang in her ears. An eight year old Catriona on the long journey from Galloway to Dundee to visit Grandparents. Torquil was sleeping but Catriona was eager to get there. She wanted to tell Grandpa something 'secret.' The kids were pretty good in the car but by the time they hit the motorway and there was nothing to look at but miles and miles of tarmac and cars, the novelty wore off. There was only so much I-Spy you could play before the inevitable 'he's kicking me, she ate my sweetie, I need the toilet....' began to take precedence and the kids squabbled like so many puppies in a litter, each convinced that life was all about them.

'Settle down will you,' Helen said, then pulled herself back to the present.

'Sorry,' she spoke to Randall, ' I... I'm...'

'Disoriented?' he asked. 'Don't worry. It's natural. We'll be there soon. Just close your eyes. You don't have to do anything.' The calmness in his voice was reassuring and she felt her eyes closing again.

'I'm going to pick an apple from your tree, mummy.' Torquil had woken up. 'And make you a napple pie..... a napple pie....' he laughed.

'It's an apple pie, stupid,' Catriona butted in.

'No. I'm making A NAPPLE PIE,' he replied. 'Just for mummy and me, not for you.'

'That'll be lovely,' Helen said, 'I've been so lonely.' She was getting it all mixed up. The past, the future, the present. Life, memories, reality. Apple pie. Birthday cake.. the tastes all mixed up... the smell of coffee, real coffee.

'Wake up and smell the coffee... smell the coffee...' She couldn't place the voice. Was it her dad? Was it Torquil? Randall? Her eyes felt heavy and she had a taste of diesel in her mouth.

'Life is but a dream, life is but a dream.' Randall was whistling the tune and tapping on the steering wheel. 'You don't ever have to be lonely again,' he said.' I'm here now.'

'I... I'm so confused...' she said. 'I don't know where I am. I can't believe you're real.' She reached out and touched his hand, cupping hers over it, feeling the steering wheel judder. It felt real.

Touch. That first touch. When she'd first held his hand. A sensation like pulsing electricity all those years ago, relived. The touch that had redefined her life. Followed by a kiss.

'I love you, Helen,' he said. Don't fight it,' he added gently. 'Just go with it. This is life, Helen, you're free.'

She so wanted to open her eyes. When she eventually did so she could only make out Randall's dark image. They were off the motorway. They must be on the last dark winding road that led home. She was tired, so tired.

'It feels like dying,' she said.

He laughed. 'How could you possibly know what dying feels like?'

'It feels like this,' she said.

She woke up the next morning, enfolded in Randall's arms. He held her, as he had for the best part of forty years. All her senses told her she was home before she even opened her eyes.

'Good morning,' he smiled. 'How do you feel?'

She stretched. ' Fine. I feel.... Odd but fine.'

'Good.' He kissed her. And offered her breakfast in bed. But she wanted to sit at the kitchen table. She wanted to be in her house, feel it, touch it, smell it, all together and all at once. Like it used to be. Sitting at the kitchen table opposite Randall, it was all exactly as she remembered it. They ate toast with homemade jam and drank tea, real tea. It was too good to be true. But it was true.

'Why did you call yourself Odysseus?' she asked.

Randall laughed. 'Name is the thief of identity, remember. How else could I stay free and keep in touch with ULTIMATE®? We all have more than one identity, Helen, you know that. We are all the people we want to be in our heads and someone else when externalised. Nick became Nike, I became Odysseus; only you stayed the same. And perhaps even you could be known by a different name, in a different context, at some other time and in some other place.'

'And what about Torquil?' she remembered Nick's last message. If Randall was alive, which clearly he was, sitting here in front of her in a shirt that had not seen an iron recently, then he might know about Torquil too.

'He's re-invented himself,' Randall acknowledged. 'But you can't contact him.'

'Why?'

'Helen, there's plenty of time for that. Just accept it for now will you?

'Maybe one day?' she asked, not wanting Randall to burst her bubble. If Torquil was alive, surely one day.....? Alive. That was a question that needed an answer.

'How are you alive?' she asked Randall.

'Ah. That's a big question too,' he smiled. 'It's a long story. Let's save it for later eh? Start with the easy stuff shall we?'

'Has the RIP been going all this time?'

'Yes, in one form or another. It's not easy as you can imagine but some of us have managed to stay beneath the radar,' he pointed at the barcode on her arm, 'we'll have to deal with that.'

'Can you?'

'Yes,' he laughed, 'it's pretty easy really. Easier than branding a cow anyway.'

She shuddered, imagining that he was going to have to

inflict some pain on her, dig out the implant, something... but she gave her arm to him willingly anyway. She closed her eyes, waiting for the cut which never came. She opened them to see the pressure she'd felt was all that was going to happen. She had a silvery coloured plaster covering the barcoded brand. Surely that wouldn't work?

'It's incredible,' he said, 'there are so many simple ways to get round the system, if only you use some ingenuity.'

He explained that the chemicals in the plaster worked against the bio-laser which conducted the signal and that as long as she kept it covered she'd be out of range. That seemed impossible. To be out of range of the ULTIMATE® world.

'What about my Memory Banks?' She was beginning to believe she was free now, but she didn't want ULTIMATE® to have any of her, not even memories.

'I've had them modified and diverted into Omo's archive.'

'You what? How did you do that? You're a Luddite not a computer genius.'

He tapped his nose. 'You'd be surprised,' he answered. 'No of course I didn't do it myself. But I knew a man who could. And I thought it'd be important to move the memories, so that as far as anyone poking around is concerned you've just been virtualised. Who else but Omo would go looking for you anyway? I thought you'd want him to know. Having spent all that time putting them together, it seemed a shame to waste them. Don't worry. They're safe.'

'Have you been here for the last ten years?'

'Not all of them. I had to move around a lot for the first five years. Working out how to get out of the system wasn't that easy. Now of course it's easy, but we had to work it out from scratch. I've been here for the past five years though. The old place doesn't look that bad does it?'

Helen knew she should just feel happy that she was here, back home with the man she loved, but somehow something resembling anger was welling up inside her. She had to let it out. She and Randall had never had secrets. Never left things unsaid. However difficult, they had been in it together. Always.

'How could you leave me to rot there when you were here? How could you not let me know you were alive? How....' she burst into tears.

'Believe me, it was the safest option for you.'

'So why come and get me now?'

'The time was right. I've been working towards this since the day I left you Helen, honestly. It was as hard for me as for you. But I had to take the decision. And I don't regret it. I know it was the right thing to do.'

'We used to make decisions together,' she replied, aggrieved. Who was Randall to make decisions regarding her life and tell her she should be grateful for the pain she'd suffered. How could he know...

'I had to keep you safe. I was keeping an eye on you.'

'I didn't want to be safe. I wanted to be with you. Or I would have done, if I'd known there was a choice.' She paused, overcome with an emotion that felt horribly like betrayal. 'You should have let me know,' she said, weakly.

'I couldn't. Believe me,' he replied.

She wasn't sure she did believe him. For the first time in nearly fifty years, she questioned his integrity. It didn't feel good.

'Look. If you'd known I was alive there's no way you would have stayed there.'

'You're damned right,' she interrupted.

'And you couldn't have lived here on your own, knowing I was somewhere out there. I had to do all this, alone. Find a way for us to live a safe life. And I've done it now. It's time to be happy.'

'But we vowed to be together, forever. How could you do this to me?'

'I did it to us, Helen. But I did it for us too. I've missed you every single day. Every day I've asked myself if it was the right thing to do and every day I knew it was. You'll understand one day. It's a lot to take in. I hope that you'll forgive me.'

'I don't want to have to forgive you,' she replied, 'I want to still trust you.'

That was a body blow.

'Of course you can still trust me.'

That was when Helen realised something about the real world. It was distinctly different to the self-constructed Memory Bank of ULTIMATE®. Because here, in the real world, you had to negotiate with another person's view and another person's meaning. That was the joy and the pain of it, surely. ULTIMATE® had created a heaven of individual selfishness where each person thought they were the celebrity, the key player in the game, the protagonist of their own story. Underpinning this was the fact that no one was individual any more. People were just cogs in a very sophisticated wheel, all of which worked to the benefit of the ULTIMATE® system. Everyone had been wooed into the virtual world and given up their individuality while believing all the time that they were winning. They were the worst kind of slaves. They thought they were free. From Plato's cave to 1984, no fiction had come close to the complete domination of humanity that ULTIMATE® had visited on the real world. Helen shuddered. *You can't fight city hall.* Surely it wasn't possible to live outside this system? Surely something was wrong and they would be caught or…. These were the important issues she needed to discuss with Randall. She should leave the recriminations and the self-pity for later.

'Do you know what happened to Nick?' she asked. It was impossible to be in the same room with Randall and not talk to him. There was no time to be angry. There was so much to catch up on.

'Only in outline,' he replied, 'I can tell you it wasn't an accident.' He gave her time to compute this information before he added. 'but I can't tell you who killed him.'

'But why did they kill him?' Helen came from a time when there was a THEY to fear. Not the ULTIMATE® world where the marketing slogan *'there is no Us and Them only US™'*, had become a truth in a world of created truths.

'He knew too much.'

'Well if he knew too much, I'm sure I must have been next on the list then,' she added, 'Because I'm sure I knew more than him.'

'Not necessarily,' Randall replied. 'He didn't know what he knew. It doesn't matter anyway. We're safe now. As long as we stay out of the system, keep our heads down.'

'But what if they come looking for us?'

'They won't.'

'How can you be so sure?'

'Because we have nothing they want,' he replied. 'Their world is complete, Helen. We are nothing to them. No challenge, nothing. We don't even exist to them now. Our reality and their reality are completely different. They've virtualised us and we are free. I tried to explain it to Torquil, but he wouldn't understand. He wanted to fight against them. I just wanted to be free. For us both to be free.'

'Tell me about Torquil.' This time she was going to get an answer. It was time to know.

'He's reinvented himself, of course. He's dedicated his life to fighting the system. He's fighting for a freedom that can't exist because his freedom depends on the destruction of ULTIMATE® and Helen, you know that's never going to happen. But he's a young man. His perspective is different. We've had our lives. We've got what, two, five, ten years if we're really lucky. He, he's got another fifty to go and he sees walking away as giving in. He's still got a fire in his belly and a cause to fight for. Me, I just want us to be safe and free to live out the rest of our lives together without anything interfering with us. And I'm prepared to make whatever sacrifices that means. After all, we've made most of the sacrifices already haven't we?'

'But couldn't you have persuaded him to come home?'

Randall shook his head. 'No, Helen, I couldn't. And we must never, never see him or contact him again.'

'Why?'

'It was part of the deal I had to make, to get you here.' Randall said. A straight answer to a straight question. That was the man she knew. He could tell her things she didn't want to hear and he trusted that she would believe him and accept. It would take some doing, but with Randall beside her, Helen knew she could find the path back to acceptance again. She knew he was right. However much she yearned to see Torquil again, if the price she had to pay to be with Randall was that she lost her children and her grandchild, she'd pay it. It had been more or less paid in full anyway. And maybe one day.... But they had to think of themselves now. And the future, whatever that would be and however short it might be. They had a life to rebuild. To live. Together. Which was all she had ever wanted.

They went out for a walk, hand in hand, as they'd done in the old days.. yes, she really could look at them as the good old days. And she was living them again now. Her ability to live in the moment returned as if it had never been lost. The years in the ULTIMATE® Home were already slipping into memory as she drank in again the life that had been her complete reality for so long. She marvelled at the swiftness with which the brain would re-order itself, allowing past horrors to slip away into the subconscious, while you revelled in the reality of the present.

But there were still questions. She still wanted some answers. She had to make some sense of the narrative of her life. He picked up on her pensiveness.

'What is it?' he said, stopping.

'Why didn't you wait?' she asked.

'We've been through that,' he said, you have to believe me. I did what I thought was best.'

'No. I mean, when I went for the interview. You said

you'd wait. But you didn't.'

'I did wait. You didn't see me. You walked right past me,' he replied.

She didn't believe him. 'Why would you lie to me?'

'I'm not lying,' he said.

'Yes you are,' she said, 'I know it. What really happened?'

He took a deep breath, 'I did wait. Until... until I got a phone call...'

'You didn't have a mobile phone in those days,' she was not going to be fobbed off.

'I waited.'

'I don't believe you.'

'Okay. I'm not proud of it,' he said, 'I realised I was late for a meeting. I had the offer of a record deal. I waited as long as I could.'

'Did you get the deal?' she asked, trying not to sound too sour.

'No.'

'Oh.'

'And I came back for you. And waited more. I was only gone twenty minutes... I thought I'd easily.... I couldn't believe I would miss you. I wanted to.....' he was struggling. 'But in the end, you know, I came back.'

'And gave up music for me?'

'For us.'

'You didn't have to do that.'

'I did. I wanted to. I don't regret it for a minute.'

'Are you sure of that?'

'Yes. Dead certain,' he replied. 'Now, can we talk about something else?'

They kept walking. She had her answer. Everything fell into place. She wished she'd known. She wouldn't have wanted him to give everything up for her, even though she was more than happy and prepared to give everything up for him. Her everything had seemed so little and he'd had such promise. He'd made the real sacrifices. She'd never thought of it like that before. She loved him all the more.

'When did you first know you loved me?' she asked.

'When I realised I'd missed you that first day in London,' he replied. 'And I told myself if I found you again I'd never let you go again. And then I had to. Because I loved you. It's complicated.'

'And you were the man who said it was simple. That it was only we who complicate it,' she noted. 'That was the point of the story wasn't it? That life is simple and all we have to do is go with the simplicity to be happy?'

'Helen,' he replied, 'you know I've always believed we live in two places. In the moment and in the memory. But we are only truly free in one place and that is in the mind. The goal of ULTIMATE® is to take that freedom away from you but they can only succeed if you let them. Remember, reality is what you choose to believe and life is how you create it.'

'I have no life without you,' she replied. ' Our identity..it's.. fused… Do you know what I mean?'

'Just let go,' he said. 'I've always loved you. I always will love you. Nothing changes that. This is all that's real. Just us. Now. Here.' They were at the beech tree, gazing over the most familiar view in her life.

'It's enough isn't it?' he asked.

She smiled 'Yes. It's enough.' And let go.

Z. HOPE IS THE ULTIMATE CHOICE

At the Project House it was as if Nike and Helen and Pryce had never been. Omo had once again stopped asking questions. Both he and Flora seemed to have settled to the new regime under Griff and to have adapted to Bose's ways. All was right in the ULTIMATE® world. Except of course that it was all a fiction. The reality was that Griff and Bose were working hard to subvert the Project Kids through any and all means possible. And it seemed like they had achieved a level of success.

As Helen had predicted, Omo had found love at last. And so had Flora. Bose had played Pandarus to their Troilus and Cressida and Griff managed to keep the burgeoning relationship below the ULTIMATE® radar.   Together Bose and Griff introduced Flora and Omo to a whole new dimension in living. A life that was not being monitored by ULTIMATE®. A life beyond the screen. But it couldn't last indefinitely. They all knew that.

One evening, as Omo and Flora sat on the sofa in the common room watching some US™ stream, or not watching it because they were wrapped up in each other, their attention was drawn by the unexpected picture of Helen in front of them. Omo felt a slight tinge of guilt, realising he hadn't thought about Helen in a while. All his thoughts had been about Flora. Now, here she now was. But something was odd. She didn't seem to be in her ULTIMATE® room. They sat up straight and paid attention.

'Where is that?' Flora asked.

Helen was sitting, with a man Omo assumed must be Randall, drinking coffee and watching a beautiful sunset.

'Who is that?' Flora asked.

'It.. It must be Randall,' Omo replied, 'her husband.'

'But he was dead?'

'Shh,' Omo urged her. 'Just watch and we'll find out.'

Randall and Helen were relaxing in the part of the

garden they had constructed specifically for that purpose, the part which overlooked the sunset. Randall swung back and forth on his patio chair and they both drank in the beautiful full red sun as it made its way slowly over the distant hills. You could almost smell the coffee as they savoured it.

'I bet that isn't ULTIMATE® coffee,' Omo observed.

'They look so happy,' Flora noted.

'They *are* happy.' Omo pointed out. 'They're free.'

'Is this from your Memory Bank, Omo?' Flora asked.

Omo played around with the system to see where the picture had come from. He couldn't find the source. The US™ kept defaulting to LIVE STREAM.

'I can't believe it's a live stream,' he said…. 'because it means… it would mean…'

'That they're out there.' Flora spoke the words he was afraid to voice.

'I hope they are,' Omo replied.

They were distracted by the entrance of Bose.

'Hey, that's cool,' he said, looking at Helen and Randall. 'Is that your Nan and Grandad?'

'No' Omo replied… 'They're…' He was about to say Nike's, when Flora interrupted.

'Yes. Yes they are, in a way.'

'You're lucky, having folks alive outside of ULTIMATE®' Bose observed. 'My folks all died. If I had folks living on the outside, I'd go find them.'

'Really?' Omo was surprised.

'How would we do that?' Flora seemed to be taking this conversation seriously. She seemed to think that maybe there was a life out there.

'Easy. Griff can sort it for you. Want me to speak to him?'

True to Bose's word, it was as easy as that. Within half an hour the sun had barely set over the sunset garden and Griff had a plan sorted out.

'Wait outside for a man called Jason.'

'How will we know who he is?' Omo asked.

Griff laughed. 'Oh, you'll recognise him.'

'I've never heard of anyone called Jason,' Flora said, worried.

'Believe me, you'll recognise him,' Griff affirmed. 'Trust me. He'll take you there.'

'If we don't like it, can we come back?' Omo asked, ever cautious.

'Don't be stupid,' Bose said, 'You'll love it. It's freedom.'

It was like a whirlwind, but then everything had been turned upside down in the last few months and as long as Flora was with him, Omo felt he could try anything. He knew that he loved her and he wanted her to know that too. He wanted Helen to know. He wanted a new start, for both of them, in a world which would allow love, a world where maybe even they could start their own family, have a future....

'But you have to go now,' Griff added, ' and it means turning your back on The PROJECT△. Giving up the ULTIMATE® world. Are you prepared to do that?'

'What do you think?' Omo asked Flora.

'Nike would have jumped at the chance,' she said. A few months ago, Flora hadn't even seemed bothered when Nike died. Omo observed that she'd changed as much as him in as short a time. And he liked it. He loved it. There were so many things they didn't know about each other. So much to find out. And he wanted to do that. More than anything.

'And we owe it to Helen,' she added.

That was the clincher. She was right. If Helen had done it, why shouldn't they?

There wasn't time to think about it rationally. To weigh up pros and cons. This was the start of real life and the only thing to do was to dive right in, whatever the consequences. Take a risk. Omo was ready. He kissed Flora as he took her hand and led her out of The Project House.

'Let's go find Helen,' he said.

As they turned their back on it the US™ screen continued streaming. They had only just left the room when the picture changed, the sun set to black and then as the image re-emerged into light it showed a small, frail, grey haired woman sitting peacefully in her chair in a magnolia room, in front of her own US™ screen. Her eyes were closed as if sleeping. She looked happy. The face which had in youth turned a few heads had become a face which just might launch a thousand ships of dreams.

The ULTIMATE® world didn't matter to Helen any more. She was walking the familiar path up to the beech tree, surrounded by every dog who had ever owned her, with the sun shining on the soft snow and the familiar, comforting sound as the crystals crunched underfoot. The chill air filling her body like the taste of ice-cream and in her ears Randall's words – reality is what you choose to believe. She'd let go and it was enough. She was forever in February.

Oblivious to this version of reality, Omo and Flora stood outside The Project House, ready to embark upon their own journey. They stood waiting for a man who had once been known to them only by his surname, but who had finally understood that name is the thief of identity and had become Jason.

Appendix.

The story that Randall tells Helen which changes both their lives is the simplest of stories and the most powerful. It was told to me by a friend, now dead, who had been told it by a tribesman in Africa. It is a universal story, which, if understood, has the power to change lives. The story varies with the telling and below is 'my' version.

A FISHING LINE

A man was walking on a remote beach. He came across a girl cooking fish on an open fire. The fish smelt beautiful and he was overcome with desire to taste it. The girl, seeing his longing, offered him a bowl of the fish. It was moist and tender and quite unlike any fish he had ever tasted before, even though he had eaten at all the best restaurants and could afford all the most expensive dishes. When his bowl was empty he said to the girl, 'I have never tasted fish like that before.'

She smiled and said nothing.

From that moment on, the man could think of nothing else but tasting the fish again. The next day he woke with an intense hunger. It was less a hunger of the belly than a hunger of the spirit. His hunger was for the fish, cooked by the girl over an open fire. He walked down to the beach and in the distance he saw the girl fishing. He stood and watched as she cast and played the large sea-rod. His anticipation grew along with her struggle, as she reeled the fish in. He watched her deftly gut and fillet the fish and place it on the fire to cook. His nostrils were filled once more with the delicious aroma. His whole body craved to taste the fish again.

He sat beside the girl as the fish cooked. 'I would love to taste your fish again,' he said. 'What can I pay you for it?'

The girl smiled. ' I do not pay the sea,' she said and handed him a bowl of the freshly cooked fish.

Meal after meal the man came back to taste the wonderful fish, cooked over an open fire by the strangely beautiful girl who seemed to spend all her time fishing, cooking and tending her fire. No matter how many times he ate the fish, his hunger never abated and his thirst grew for understanding of the girl. He wanted to find a way to repay her, but he did not know how to.

One day as they ate their fish together he said, 'Your fish is so delicious I am sure it would fetch the highest price at the markets and would grace the tables of all the fashionable restaurants throughout the world. If you caught twenty or thirty a day instead of two or three....'

'Why would I want to catch twenty or thirty fish a day?' she asked.

'With the money that you made from catching the fish you could buy things to make your life easier,' he continued.

The girl looked at the man and smiled. 'Two or three fish a day,' she said, 'is all I need. You suggest I should spend all my days fishing. How would that make life easier?'

'Ah,' the man replied, 'but with the money you made you could employ other people to catch the fish for you. You wouldn't have to work. You could take it easy, enjoy life.'

'And how should I enjoy life?' she asked.

'Money buys freedom,' he said. 'You could go to the city, travel, do whatever you wanted.

She smiled. 'Eat fish at one of your expensive restaurants?'

The man felt that she was laughing at him. He was trying to help her and she did not seem to appreciate his advice. He looked at he, saddened. Then he noticed that her face had lost its smile and had become serious.

'So your advice is that I catch more fish, make money by selling the fish, with the money I make employ other people to do the fishing for me, leaving myself enough time to do whatever I want to with my life?'

330

'Exactly,' he replied. 'Finally, she had understood him.'

'But I do what I want now,' she said. 'I catch fish, I cook fish, I tend my fire. I can sit all day thinking, and all night looking at the stars. I do not have to bother with money or employees or profit, or whether I can afford to eat fish in a fancy restaurant. If I do all the things you say I will only end up where I already am. At best with more effort at worst less happy. What is the point of that?'

The man had no answer to her question. As he licked the rest of the fish from his fingers he realised that far from showing the girl a way that she could improve her life, she had perhaps shown him a way to improve his. He looked around the beach.

'Let me stay here with you,' he said. 'Teach me to catch fish so that I too can sit by the fire and live as you do.'

The girl held silence for a time.

'I catch fish, I cook fish and I eat fish,' she said. 'That is enough for me. But you crave fish, you dream of tasting fish, you want more and more and more. It is not the same. You would not be happy with this life.

As she spoke, the aftertaste of the fish turned sour in the man's mouth and he realised that she spoke the truth. As long as he stayed on the beach he would have an obsession, a craving which he could not fulfil. He would never be able to taste enough of the delicious fish and his life would become more and more miserable. He realised that the only thing for him to do was to leave the beach, leave the girl and never taste the fish again. He stood up, sad but somewhat wiser.

'Think of me when you eat fish in one of your fancy restaurants,' the girl said.

'I will never eat fish in a restaurant again,' he replied. 'But I will think of you all the same.'

The man left the beach and only when the fire was a speck in the distance did he turn round to allow himself a last look at the girl with the perfect life.

About the author.

Cally was born in 1963. She started writing aged 14 but abandoned her juvenilia aged 17, realising she had to have more life experience to be able to write anything of meaning. She subsequently got an MA (Hons) in Moral Philosophy and International Relations from St Andrews University, gained meaningless employment as a sales representative, took a postgraduate Acting course, turned professional (Dorothy in Gregory's Girl and Rita in Educating Rita) then, disillusioned by the waiting around involved in acting, retired aged 25 to pursue a career in writing and teaching. She has subsequently had a twenty year career writing for screen and stage with broadcast credits for BBC and Granada TV as well as a spell working as a script reader for Channel 4. She was Writer in Residence for DGAA from 2002-2004. She has had more than 10 plays staged. Brand Loyalty is her third novel.

Cally has also gained qualifications in social care and worked extensively with adults labelled with learning disabilities in the field of drama, co-facilitating ABC Drama Group from its inception in 2003. She is currently completing an MSc in Applied Psychology by distance learning and focuses her energies (when not writing) on her husband, dogs and vegetables with whom she lives in rural North East Scotland.

For more information about the author's other works
go to www.callyphillips.co.uk

Lightning Source UK Ltd.
Milton Keynes UK
21 September 2010

160140UK00001B/24/P